BEYOND ANTARES

MARKOV'S PRIZE

D1477777

BY

MARK BARBER

Beyond the Gates of Antares: Markov's Prize
Edited by Brandon Rospond
Cover by
Zmok Books an imprint of
Winged Hussar Publishing, LLC,
1525 Hulse Road, Unit 1,
Point Pleasant, NJ 08742

This edition published in 2018 Copyright ©Winged Hussar Publishing, LLC
Beyond the Gates of Antares is the property of Warlord Games and Rick
Priestley, produced under license by Winged Hussar Publishing, LLC

ISBN 978-1-9454302-9-9
Library of Congress Number 2018942069

Bibliographical references and index
1.Science Fiction 2. Space Opera 3. Action & Adventure

For more information on Winged Hussar Publishing, LLC, visit us at:
www.WingedHussarPublishing.com
Twitter: WingHusPubLLC
Facebook: Winged Hussar Publishing LLC

PROLOGUE

Merchant Vessel, White Nova
Docking Bay 369
New Gissel Station
Western Determinate

    A yellow light flickered on the inter-seat console, warning again that the igniter plugs for the number two engine required a periodic inspection. Lifting her head off her fists where she sat slumped in the second pilot's seat, Katya Rhona reached across and canceled the warning before sinking back into her chair. She looked out of the main viewscreen at the vast, empty, and quite frankly dull panorama of deep space that sprawled out in front of her father's angular cargo ship, ready for another haul and another potentially dangerous exchange at the far end. The battered, run down trading station was out of view behind her; her father had landed their corpulent cargo ship very deliberately on this orientation, in case they needed to 'hit the road quickly'. The only sound to break the silence was the hum of generators and the barely audible choking of the air conditioning; even the stale stench of recycled air had become normalized after such a long time confined to the ship.

    Katya momentarily considered whether to leave the ship's grimy cockpit and head back to the cramped accommodation area immediately aft, where her three-year-old brother Micha was still asleep. She shook her head – he would be better off left undisturbed, and she had schooling to think about. Taking a tatty hairband off her wrist, she tied her black hair back into a ponytail before swiveling her chair around to face the navigation console where she had left her datapad. The weariness induced by deep space travel did little to dull her enthusiasm and pride as she booted up the small tablet and initialized the education software package. She was already attempting assignments which were in the syllabus for thirteen year olds; she was three years ahead and still achieving top grades.

Briefly describe a nanosphere and the impact it has on your life.

Kayta closed her eyes; she considered the question, and how to structure her answer.

The nanosphere is how I am answering this question in this format, she thought, watching as her thoughts scrolled across the screen as text as soon as she had assembled the sentences in her mind. *It is made up of billions of tiny, robotic spores, so small the panhuman eye can't see them. We are all surrounded by a field of these nanobots, and they allow us to link up with machinery without having to touch it. We can communicate without seeing each other or even having to use a separate device. Planets and ships also have their own nanosphere, and as long as our nanosphere connects with the bigger one the planet or ship has, we can share thoughts and ideas and even jokes. Without it, we would have to operate everything with our hands instead of our minds. Doctors would have to see everybody in person to check them, teachers would have to see all of their students every day, leaders would not know what their people wanted and needed. Without nanospheres, we would live in the dark ages.*

Momentarily satisfied with her answer, Katya again canceled a miscellaneous warning light on the interseat console, reminding her to add another paragraph.

In the case of some situations where safety might be affected and a stray thought could be misinterpreted, old fashioned manual controls are used. Controls like this are used when operating vehicles or weapons.

She submitted her answer on her datapad and read through the next question.

Describe the threats to free will posed by the most advanced societies.

Katya reached across and grabbed her father's old military service jacket from the back of the first pilot's seat, wrapping it around her like a blanket and running her fingers over the rank insignia on the sleeve as she pondered the next answer.

Some societies have more complicated nanospheres than others and can use them like a disease to take over ships and planets. The IMTel used by the PanHuman Concord is a threat to those of us in free space. The IMTel can infect our nanospheres which would then infect us. It would control the way we think and the way we feel. We would no longer be free.

Light footsteps from the entrance to the cockpit caused Katya to turn in her seat. Micha wandered in from the accommodation area rubbing at his red eyes, his animal print blanket still draped over his narrow shoulders. He looked up at his sister and his face broke into a smile.

"Sister!" He blurted out as he waddled quickly over, his arms outstretched.

Katya returned the smile and picked him up to embrace him, sitting him on her lap and spinning their shared seat around by kicking at the floor with one foot.

"Faster!" Micha giggled.

Laughing with him, Katya span the chair around faster and faster, her still active mind wondering at how in a universe of nanospheres and predatory empires, a three-year-old boy could still be entertained more than anything else by a spinning chair.

"Kat!" Her father's voice crackled through the speaker on top of the cockpit's instrument cowling. "Fire up them engines, girl! We're in a hurry!"

Katya slowed her spinning and used her nanosphere connection to integrate with the communication system.

"What's happening, Pa?" She asked. "We're just…"

"Get those engines flashed up, now!" Her father yelled, his voice interrupted by what sounded to Katya like gunfire. "And get the dorsal turret online!"

"Go to your bed, Micha, quickly!" Katya urged as she put her brother's feet gently back on the floor. "Go back to bed!"

Spinning the chair back around, Katya flipped on the starter coils and was rewarded instantly with the familiar tick-ticking sound as they sparked and looked for a fuel source. Opening the fuel valves and switching on the pumps, she gently opened the throttles and let out a breath as both engines fired up to idle power instantly.

Her brother stared up at her in confusion.

"Go to your bed, Micha!" She urged, the severity of the situation dawning on her as she heard the dull *whump* of magnetically charged gunfire in the docking bay behind her.

The aft personnel door hissed as the outer airlock opened and the boarding ramp clunked down in place. Katya leapt up to her feet and rushed across to the cockpit doorway, looking down to the back of the ship to confirm it was her father. The familiar figure quickly shut and locked the airlock behind him before sprinting along the central corridor and barging past her to fling himself into the first pilot's seat.

"I said to power up the gun turret, Kat!" He grimaced as anger broke through his forced smile. "Now strap your brother in and plot me a route out of here."

"Where do you want..."

"Anywhere! Make it quick!"

Katya scooped Micha up and sat him down in his familiar seat at the engineer's station, strapping his five point harness into its quick release buckle before jumping into the second pilot's seat and repeating the process. The whole cockpit shook once, then twice, as a loud clang reverberated from the right side of the ship.

Katya's father powered the engines up and eased back on the control column, pointing the nose of the *White Nova* up toward the stars and away from whatever mess he had left behind in the docking bay. Katya was momentarily thrown back into her seat as the vessel accelerated harshly before it punched through the space station's shields and out of the effects of its artificial atmosphere. Her father banked around to the right and followed her plotted coordinates to bring them to the first safe and chartered jump gate she could find. Micha began to cheer and bounce up and down on his seat.

"You like that, little man?" Their father beamed, pulling his sweat soaked, purple bandana down from his forehead to dangle around his neck. "That was a close one, but we're still in one piece!"

"Doesn't look like there's anybody following us," Katya grimaced as she checked the external viewscreen projectors and the short ranged scanners. "Whoever that was, they weren't quick enough to get to a ship."

"Probably best, Kat," her father replied as he flashed her a cheeky smile. "Well, that was a hoot!"

She did not reciprocate.

"I'll get Micha settled down with some toys," she said quietly, unbuckling from her seat before recovering her brother and carrying him to the accommodation area.

When she returned several minutes later, her father had the ship on autopilot and was checking the inventory screen's report on the contents of the cargo hold. It took her a few moments to pluck up the courage to voice what was on her mind.

"He's three, Pa," Katya said quietly. "I'm ten. I shouldn't even know what guns sound like, let alone how to power them up."

"Won't happen again, Kat!" Her Pa winked. "That deal there just went bad. I got out of there with our money and half of the cargo. I didn't screw anybody over, I didn't do anything wrong, I swear. It was just one of the buyers was..."

"Pa, they shot at us." Katya found her tone a little more assertive but still not matching how she felt inside.

"I made a lot of money from that one," her father countered gently, "more than we've made before."

"What use is it if we're dead?"

"What do you want me to do? Hmm? It's just the three of us, Kat, and this is all I know how to do. It's all I've got. Who do you think this is for? You are a bright kid and I'm not saying that just because I'm biased, I mean you are really bright! You're passing lessons and exams which are meant for teenagers; you'll make something of yourself one day, but that schoolin' ain't cheap. This trip, this deal, I made enough for a year's higher education for both you and Micha, when he's old enough. Dammit, Kat, who do you think I'm doing all of this for? All of it!"

His roguish smile gone, her father sat down in the first pilot's chair and stared quietly out at the stars. Katya contemplated his words before walking quietly over to stand behind him and then tenderly wrapping her arms around him as their battered old cargo ship drifted slowly through the space of the Determinate.

***

The Grand Arena
Central Sports and Entertainment Station
Central Determinate

Another hammer blow struck Ryen Tahl in the jaw, sending him reeling backward and leaving a high-pitched whine in his ears as his vision swam in and out of focus. Still audible was the chanting, cheering, and roaring of over one hundred thousand spectators who were crammed into the arena grandstands surrounding the brightly lit fighting ring. His opponent, a gargantuan Algoryn who stood two full heads taller than Tahl, paced forward again with his teeth and fists clenched, his pale green skin dripping with sweat and blood. Clothed in the dark crimson trousers of an Algoryn Fighting Master, Vel Ye was the reigning champion of Determinate Fighter; the most popular and lethal martial arts tournament in all of Antarean space. And now, Tahl faced him here in the tournament final in his first year of full contact fighting.

Tahl caught a glimpse of himself on one of the enormous floating screens above the fighting ring, giving both the spectators and viewers in their homes across a thousand systems a ringside view of the action. Clothed only in white gi trousers and the black belt denoting his proficiency as a practitioner of kerempai, his shaven head and course stubble made him look older than his twenty years. Blinking blood out of his eyes, he brought his guard back up to protect his head and advanced forward to face the Algoryn man-mountain.

Leading with two rapid jabs and a cross punch to his adversary's face, he forced Vel Ye to raise his guard. Capitalizing on the response,

Tahl brought a deliberately slow side kick up and into the Algoryn's gut, feigning the main thrust of his attack to again shift his opponent's guard. The instant Vel Ye dropped his guard again, Tahl sprang into action, turning into a spinning hook kick to bring his heel smashing into the Algoryn's face. The blow made audible contact but only succeeded in knocking the huge fighter back half a pace. Tahl never saw the response but suddenly found himself lying face down in the center of the ring, struggling to raise himself up onto his elbows as a mixture of blood and saliva dripped from his open mouth and another wave of agonizing pain washed over the left side of his head.

The deep, bass pitch of a siren echoed throughout the cavernous sports auditorium, signalling the end of the round. Tahl forced himself up to his feet, staggered unsteadily over to his corner of the ring, and slumped down in the chair that had been hastily set up for him.

"Ryen?" Gavv, his ageing trainer leaned over and flashed a small light in his eyes. "Ryen? You hearing me okay?"

"...Stats..." Ryen slurred. "...What stats?"

"Get him sorted. Quickly." Another familiar voice from over his shoulder – Herres Warne, his manager, if that was the best word to describe his role.

"His vital signs are all stable enough," Gavv reported as Tahl's eyes began to focus again, "but he's got three fractured ribs, and a couple more blows to the head like this will need surgery to sort out. At best."

"Never mind that... you stupid, old bastard," Tahl gasped, "what do... the stats say?"

"You've got more strikes in than Vel Ye, but his are far cleaner and far harder. I can't see how the judges would side with you, Ryen. You're losing."

Warne swore viciously as he jumped into the ring and bent over; his wiry, bearded face now taking up most of Tahl's view. "This isn't good enough, boy! You haven't come this far to lose now! You get back out there and you kick this bastard's damn head off!"

"Don't pretend... this is about me getting the title." Tahl felt pain flaring up in his head and ribs as his breathing evened out. "This is all about you... and your damn money!"

A dismissive backhand slapped hard against Tahl's face, striking him exactly where one of Vel Ye's hammer blows had cut his eyelid open in the third round.

"Watch your mouth, boy!" Warne spat. "You remember who you work for and you remember that all the martial arts skills in the universe won't stop a shot in the back of your damn head!"

Tahl slowly raised himself back up to his feet and spat out another mouthful of blood. The huge screens at the top of the arena played slow motion replays of the previous eight rounds of the fight, showing highlights of the match as statistics scrolled across the bottom of the displays. Off to his left, Tahl could hear the rhythmic banging of several hundred spectators stamping their feet in time as the seconds counted down to the penultimate round.

Although only a little over average height for a panhuman, Tahl towered over Warne. His teeth gritted, Tahl leaned over to stare his manager in the eyes.

"The day will come... when you and I will have a proper talk," he seethed before barging his way past the little man and walking back toward the center of the ring, one arm guarding his damaged ribs.

Vel Ye was already out and waiting. The towering Algoryn shook his head in disgust as Tahl stood opposite him.

"How did you ever get this far in real fighting?" He grunted and narrowed his eyes as he cast a dismissive glance across the shorter fighter. "Go home to your play fighting, Concord."

Tahl remembered the sweeping green fields where he grew up, the simplicity of life when he was still connected to the IMTel, the positive energy and feeling of fighting in non-contact tournaments as a child within the PanHuman Concord. For a moment, he felt real sadness and regret before a boiling anger that seemed to define his very existence then surged back to the surface.

The siren sounded and a deafening cheer emanated from the crowd as the round began. Vel Ye moved confidently toward his smaller opponent. Tahl dropped his guard. No bouncing lightly on his feet, no preparation to dodge the killer blows from his hulking adversary. He stood still in place, one hand lightly up by the solar plexus; the other extended out in a low guard. He thought of the very basics, the essence of force and all that was required for that one, perfect strike. Timing, movement of the hips, concentration of every muscle to project the strike through and beyond the point of impact. He felt a calm which had been absent for a long time now.

Vel Ye lunged forward. Tahl stepped in to meet him, twisting into a basic reverse punch with clinical precision. He rapidly extended his arm and concentrated the clenching of every muscle to transmit all of his force and energy from his feet all the way up through his body and into the very point of his knuckles. Letting out a roar, he slammed his fist straight through the Algoryn's high guard and into his face, pushing through to keep that one perfect punch hurtling forward to an aiming point behind the back of his target's head.

With the audible crunching of breaking bone, Vel Ye's head snapped back before he crumpled backward to the floor. Tahl retreated back and resumed his guard, ready for his next strike. Vel Ye did not move. The roaring of the crowd intensified as statistical readouts scrolled across the screens above the ring. Vel Ye was dead before he had hit the floor. Tahl had won the title.

Markov's Prize   11

ONE

...Fifteen Years Later

Benin Province
Equatorial Region
Markov's Prize
Landing Day (L-Day)

Strike Trooper Lian Sessetti's visual display seamlessly patched into one of the external cameras of the C3T7 transporter drone he sat within, allowing him to look around in awe at the crystal clear waters and sun kissed waves which flew past either side of the company as they closed on their objective. Clear turquoise skies without even a hint of cloud allowed the system's twin suns to highlight seemingly every detail of the calm waters and the complex of islands which lay ahead of the force, made up of eight C3T7 transporters – known as 'Dukes' to the troopers, allegedly due to their visual similarity to the duke bird from Promoria – and their cargoes, escorted by a pair of C3M4 combat drones. He could have almost thanked the beautiful scenery that surrounded him for providing him with a momentary distraction from the fear of entering combat for the very first time.

As soon as that realization returned to his mind and the apprehension intensified, his visual display notified him that he was now receiving external aid from the unit's shard connection; a soothing wave of thoughts and signals were transmitted directly into his brain's amygdala and cerebral cortex.

"Stay focused, cupcakes!" Strike Leader Rall snapped. "Three hundred yan to the beachhead! I want a smooth egress and everybody ready for the advance on objective beta."

Sessetti winced – he knew the cupcake dig was aimed at him. Any administration of external aid would be automatically highlighted to the squad leader. As if in confirmation, Rall stared across the passenger hold to meet Sessetti's gaze. His helmet's face mask pushed back to the top of his head, Rall's dark brown skin and eyes stood out in stark contrast to the white and green of the armored plates that covered the rest of his body. The standard armor of a strike trooper was ergonomically designed for both ease of movement and to angle away the energy of incoming shots, although the torso region was far bulkier to house the power supply, ventilation, fluids and drugs, and processors.

The fear of the unknown ahead eased off a little and was replaced with a cold determination to get the job done. That was the beauty of the shard; the interlocking system of nanospheres that connected every trooper to their squad leader and, in turn, further up the chain of command. Rall's personality, strength, and experience filtered down through the shard to bolster the mental resolve of all of his soldiers. The connection was as real as a physical one.

Rall gave a momentary thumbs up to Sessetti before turning to look across at the remaining men and women of his squad. Eight of them formed Squad Wen; only Sessetti and his childhood friend, Bo Clythe, had never seen combat before. Sessetti looked to his right to where Clythe sat next to him, but his friend of nearly two decades looked just the same as the rest of the squad; a humanoid shape wrapped in white and green armor, his face plate was down and hiding any trace which might define him from any other trooper in the company.

"One hundred yan!" Rall warned.

The Duke rocked a little as an electronic hum sounded from somewhere to the left of the drone transporter. It took a second or two for Sessetti to realize that it was the shields flaring up. They were being shot at. For the first time in his life, somebody was trying to kill him. He tasted bile.

"Sticks and stones!" Rall grunted. "These people have barely made it into space so don't worry about their weapons! Ten seconds to egress!"

The transporter bucked and shunted a few more times before it hit the coastline, rolled up the beach, and turned sharply ninety degrees before coming to a standstill. The doors on the left side of the drone slid open and the passenger seat belts rapidly retracted into their housing. Rall sprang to his feet and dashed across to the open doorway.

"Out! Out! Get out!"

Hugging his plasma carbine into his gut, Sessetti jumped to his feet and followed the line of strike troopers out of the comparative safety of the drone, dropping from the open doorway to land on the sandy beach below. The C3T7 Duke was the third to make it up onto the beach and had turned to offer protection from enemy positions in the tree line ahead; Sessetti saw only the purple waters they had traversed across as he crouched down and awaited instructions from his strike leader. Cooling air flowed across his face from his battlesuit to counter the blazing rays of the orange suns as the troops disembarked. Ahead of them, the squad's spotter drone – a disc shaped machine a little larger than a panhuman torso – hovered at head height as it scanned for enemy forces.

Rall was the last out of the Duke, crouching down amid his squad as the next two transporter drones shot across the water and peeled away from each other to take their places along the beachhead. Puffs of sand leapt into the air in the open spaces between the stationary Duke transporters and ripples appeared in the otherwise calm waters behind them. Sessetti stared at the evidence of enemy fire in silence, hoping that the shard would administer another round of anything to calm his nerves. The shallow turret on top of the Duke span around to face up the beach before its plasma light support weapon opened fire, sending lines of superheated matter sweeping through the vivid trees at the far end of the beach.

"Squad Wen, advance to my marker!" Rall ordered as a waypoint appeared on Sessetti's combat array; a pale grey oval marker highlighting a seemingly arbitrary point where the beach met the trees of the dense, multicolored jungle ahead.

Gant, the squad's most seasoned trooper, hauled himself up to his feet and led the move up the beach, the hyperlight shields which cocooned his physical armor flashing purple a mere hand span from his torso as unseen enemy soldiers targeted him from amid the trees.

"Come on, buddy," Clythe urged as he ran past Sessetti, "let's go get stuck in."

The eight troopers struggled through the fine sand, their armored feet slipping as their shields flared with every impact from an accurate enemy shot. Above their heads, the plasma light supports of the transporter drones cut swathes through the blue-green foliage, sending branches and leaves twirling up through the air and snapping tree trunks in half. Off to the right, a C3M4 combat drone advanced toward the enemy position, its turret mounted plasma cannon firing shots so loud that Sessetti's earpieces struggled to filter out the deafening cacophony.

Jemmel, the squad's plasma lance gunner, dropped to one knee and raised her support weapon to her shoulder before firing a long burst into the trees.

"Keep moving!" Rall barked as he grabbed her by the exhaust unit on the back of her armor and dragged her to her feet. "Don't stop!"

Cycling through every visual channel at his disposal, Sessetti stared in confusion at the tree line up ahead where lines of enemy fire continued to stream down from.

"Where the hell are they?" Jemmel asked. "I can't see them! No visual, no thermal, nothing!"

Before anybody could answer, a high pitched whistle sounded

from the skies above, and then an earth shaking explosion detonated to the far left of the beachhead. A moment later, a second whistle followed, and the C3M4 combat drone on the left flank was torn apart in a colossal fireball.

"On the deck!" Rall yelled as he dived down to the sand.

Sessetti reacted to the command instantly, hurling himself to the ground as he frantically searched for better cover in his immediate surroundings. The ground shook with each explosion as projectiles continued to rain down from the bright turquoise skies above. A projectile landed close by, shaking Sessetti with enough force for him to bite his tongue and taste blood. Clumps of sand rained down on the squad, half burying them where they lay as enemy fire continued to sweep over their heads.

"Command! Squad Wen!" Sessetti heard Rall yelling into his communicator even through both of their helmets. "We're pinned in the open with indirect fire and rapid fire weapons in the trees at our objective! Request intentions!"

Sessetti looked over his shoulder at the waterline, just in time to see an enemy projectile slam into the sand next to one of the Duke transporter drones, the explosion lifting the huge vehicle up and onto its back. One of the transporters from the last wave drove up the beach but could not react to the flipped Duke in time. It plowed into the first vehicle and slid off its side, nosing over into the surf. Its doors slid open and its embarked strike squad all but fell out into the water, their squad leader grabbing troopers and manhandling them quickly out of the water.

"Off the beach!" Rall yelled. "Get in the trees!"

Struggling up to his feet, Sessetti followed Clythe as they continued to advance toward the colorful trees and foliage up ahead. Gant was at the front again, diving to the ground near the trees before hurling a plasma grenade into the dense foliage. A staccato crack sounded and clumps of earth and vegetation flew out from where his grenade had landed.

An unseen hand grabbed Sessetti by his back and flung him up into the air, his hyperlight shields flaring pale purple all around him as he was tossed across the beach like a discarded toy. All sounds were replaced by a shrill, even tone as he stared up at the bright sky, branches and leaves fluttering silently and seemingly in slow motion above him and landing all around him. His vision blurred, he looked carefully around in an attempt to locate his carbine. Staggering up to his elbows, his hearing and vision suddenly drew back into sharp focus as his battlesuit sent a shot of chemicals into his bloodstream to assist him.

"Casualty! Casualty!" Clythe was screaming from behind him,

his old friend lying in a smoking crater with steam rising from blackened holes in his armor. "Get a medi-drone over here!"

Fearing for his friend's safety, Sessetti staggered over and slid down into the darkened sand beside him. Next to Clythe lay the decapitated body of one of their squad. Sessetti stared in disbelief for a second before grabbing his shocked friend by the upper arm.

"He's dead, Bo! He's gone! We need to get into the trees!"

Struggling to drag Clythe to his feet, the two limped on toward the jungle. It was only as they were approaching the trees that Sessetti realized it was over. The bombardment had ended, the enemy fire had stopped. Up ahead, Rall and Gant crouched over a smoking gun and tripod. Rall looked up at the two troopers as they approached and shook his head.

"Sentry guns," he spat. "The bastards were never even here."

***

Operations Room
Concord Warship, Aurora II

Mandarin Owenne watched the warship's captain out of the corner of his eye. The tall, thin woman walked slowly from terminal to terminal, pausing by each individual crewmember who crouched over a holographic projection in front of them, monitoring a variety of ship's functions ranging from scanners and propulsion to weapons systems and long range communications. Owenne wondered why the Ops Room was so dark – probably some ludicrous naval tradition stemming back to the days when warships had portholes and light emissions would alert the enemy. He found 'ordinary people' awkward to deal with at the best of times, and Captain Uin was no exception.

Scratching one eyebrow with a long, pale finger, Owenne turned away from the two dozen naval personnel clustered in the center of the Ops Room and stared at the metal grate plates which formed the floor beneath his feet. The carrier Aurora II was the flagship of Task Force 1312, a Concord fleet of some thirty warships and minor war vessels, which was charged with establishing naval supremacy across twenty designated systems of Determinate Space near the Concord border. For the most part, this meant breaking off small groups of two or three warships to safeguard assaults on planets whose governments refused the Concord's invitation to join with them. The most recent of these was the assault of Markov's Prize, a relatively advanced planet in the adjoining Do System.

The mandarin looked up as Captain Uin approached him.

"Word from HQ, 44th Strike Formation, sir," the stern woman said impassively. "Our forces have a foothold on Markov's Prize. The landing has been a success with only light casualties."

"Yes, I know," Owenne continued to stare down, perplexed as to why a woman of Uin's seniority and experience would wait for verbal confirmation of that information, rather than just use a shard connection and find out herself.

Owenne knew precisely what was going on at Markov's Prize. He had monitored the landing, the assault, and was now monitoring the units establishing their perimeter. All of this was achieved via a simple transfer of information from shard to shard – trooper to leader, on to company command and then formation command. From there it was transmitted more conventionally to the Task Force, but then Owenne, as a NuHu, could utilize his vastly superior ability to manipulate nanites to grab that information straight from the warship's shard before even the communication technicians had dealt with it.

"Do you wish to initiate landings on Andenn?" The warship captain queried.

"No," Owenne replied simply.

Now was not the time to conduct two simultaneous planetary assaults across a four system spread of real estate. Owenne was one of three NuHu mandarins employed in Task Force 1312, and it was more logical to pool their collective experiences before making strategic decisions. In addition to that, a frigate in the Zolus System had detected something which concerned Owenne. Greatly.

***

Another series of staccato explosions sounded as engineering drones felled another row of bulbous, blue trees to make way for the new base. At the far end of the beach, the destroyed M4 combat drone was already being towed to a more suitable recovery site whilst repair drones set to work on the overturned T7 transporter; their efforts augmenting the slower, invisible repairs being carried out by the shell of nanobots which swarmed over the damaged drone. Semi-opaque kinetic barricades had been set up to form a perimeter to protect the soldiers and drones as the routine of setting up accommodation and messing areas, command and briefing facilities, and transmat pads was carried out with well-drilled efficiency.

His plasma carbine still held at the ready as his eyes scoured the northern horizon to his right, Rall walked over to where the six surviving members of his squad sat only a few paces from the water's edge. The midafternoon suns were high in the sky, and with his helmet removed, Rall felt the full force of the suns' rays on the back of his head. The closer of the two suns, Aen, blazed proudly in the clear sky whilst its twin, Boa, sat higher but many millions of yan further away, a more faded yellow next to Aen's burning orange. Sessetti and Clythe, the two new boys, stood up and dusted themselves down as soon as Rall approached.

"I've talked to the boss," Rall announced to his strike troopers. "That barrage that tore us to bits, it was an orbital artillery battery. And then there's the sentry guns they left here for us; no intelligence, just simple, automated weapons with a tracking system – cloaked, though. Turns out that the natives aren't quite as primitive as we were told. Their cloaking technology is better than we expected."

"Orbital artillery?" Gant exclaimed. "How the hell did they miss that? We're not talking about a hidden sniper here, we're talking about a massive floating platform in space with half a dozen guns as big as a house on it! Drop troopers or navy aerospace or some idiot who gets more credit than us should have taken that out days ago!"

Rall nodded but kept a stern stare locked onto Gant's dark eyes. Gant had five years combat experience under his belt and should have made strike leader already. A tall, swarthy man with curly hair, he had joined C3 straight from school, just as Rall had. Just as all the best troopers had before the war against the Isorians had intensified to the point of the C3 recruiting citizens for short stints of a few years. Citizens like Clythe and Sessetti.

"Navy aerospace took out the platform within minutes of it being detected," Rall replied. "Even them pretty flyboys can't kill the bad guys unless somebody tells them where to go."

"Wasn't quick enough to save Weste, though, was it, Lead?" Jemmel said, staring up at him from her crouched position in the center of the group.

Another experienced trooper, Jemmel's short stature and shaven head made her instantly distinctive from the other women of the company; her previous trade as a tattoo artist was evident in the line of stylized stars which were visible along one side of her neck.

Rall leaned forward to address the short woman. "He knew the risks, same as the rest of us. We lose people with every planet we assault. I don't like it, but there it is. We've established a perimeter, we've done the first part of our job. The operation is proceeding as planned."

"Lead?" Clythe cleared his throat.

Rall looked down at the freshly qualified trooper, his blue eyes unable to meet Rall's stare.

"What happens to Weste now? I mean, that explosion took his head off. Can he really be regen'd? Or is that it? Is he dead?"

"Don't know," Rall shrugged, "I've seen troopers come back from some pretty incredible stuff. If not, there's always a chance that his back-up consciousness can be successfully ported into a clone body. But whether or not we'll see him again? Don't know. C3 knows what is best. If the best is for Weste to rejoin us and the activation of his clone is successful, we'll see him in a couple of weeks. He won't remember you because the last time we all checked in for a consciousness save point was about six months ago; so if we get him back, his clone will only remember everything up to the save point. I've even known C3 to decide a guy's no longer fit for military service and so sends his clone back home with no memory of his war time."

"Or there's option three," Gant shrugged, "C3 decides that population control of the Concord takes priority and just leaves him dead. That seems to be happening a lot more these days. Seven out of our last ten dead, isn't it?"

"You stow that subversive crap!" Rall spat, his narrowed eyes darting from soldier to soldier in accusation. "If the system wants a guy to stay dead, then there's a good reason! Population control, c'mon! There's easier ways to do that then starting wars, so forget your conspiracy theory crap! We're part of something bigger here, and you guys aren't sitting around crying about how unfair life is, not while I'm calling the shots! Now dry your eyes and get it together because there's an entire jungle to the north which needs patrolling, and we'll be part of that, soon."

Shaking his head, Rall turned his back on his soldiers and walked back toward the command post. He had only taken a few paces when Sessetti and Clythe caught up with him.

"Lead? I just wanted to say sorry for..."

Rall had felt Clythe's disappointment and embarrassment through the shard already. Similar emotions were feeding back from Sessetti. He held a hand up to stop both of them from speaking as he continued to walk away from the rest of the squad.

"You were already topped out on shard mental assistance, which is pretty normal for a trooper's first time in combat," Rall explained, his tone almost soft, "but your suit was ripped to shreds by that explosion. That's what stopped your intravenous injection flow and that's what left you next to a mate with no head and no drugs to control how you felt. That's why you froze. Don't feel bad, Clythe, learn from it. Battlesuits get damaged and break down, now you know what happens and next time you'll do better. Just think about those poor sods we're facing who have to deal with this every day. No battlesuits, no shard mental assistance, no combat drugs, and if we kill these guys, they stay dead. Don't let Gant and Jemmel get you down, those guys just need a proper break and it's showing. You did alright."

"I didn't even fire my carbine, Lead," Sessetti exhaled. "I didn't do anything."

"You didn't run away, so you did better than me first time out,"

Rall said as he forced a smile. "Cheer up. It's sunny and we're not being shot at. Life ain't so bad."

"Lead?" Gant called from a few paces behind. "Senior's here."

Rall drew a breath before turning around again to stomp through the sand back over to his squad. Van Noor, the company senior strike leader and second-in-command after the boss, was crouched down amid Rall's troopers. Nobody had asked Van Noor how long he had been soldiering for, but it certainly preceded any member of the company. The veteran trooper's blonde hair was beginning to grow back through after a long period of shaving his head, but it was the wrinkles around his eyes which spoke volumes about his time served. Most of the temporary, citizen soldiers would only serve for three, perhaps four years before being released from military duty. Career soldiers, far rarer, would last longer; but in an era where dying of old age would happen after perhaps two hundred fifty years, all soldiers looked young. Those grey temples and handful of wrinkles put Van Noor at at least one hundred years old; and with his experience of soldiering, Rall wouldn't be surprised if most of his life had been in the military.

"Weste was a good guy," Van Noor nodded slowly as Rall, Clythe, and Sessetti approached, his tone soft. "We've just gotta hope that C3 wants him back with us and that his clone activation goes smoothly. I'm sorry you guys lost one today, it never gets easier."

"Thanks, Senior," Gant nodded slowly, his sentiments echoed by the other members of the squad.

"Any more news?" Rall asked as he approached.

"'Bout what?" Van Noor stood up.

"Why we're getting bombarded from orbital platforms by cavemen whose technology shouldn't be giving us problems."

"Intelligence is looking into it. As soon as I know, you'll know. In the meantime, we learn from this and we don't underestimate these guys. They're not cavemen, they're determined fighters defending their homes. They don't realize what we're bringing to them, they see us as a threat to their way of life rather than the future coming to embrace them. We've seen it before, and we've had surprises like this before. Don't let it throw you off your game. Anyhow, it's you I'm here to see, Feon. Let's go for a walk."

Feeling his brow furrow, Rall walked away from his squad to catch up with Van Noor. Ahead of them, engineer drones were digging underneath a shelf of rock, already making way for what would most likely be the accommodation area.

"You've been with these guys for a while," Van Noor began.

"They're good," Rall said. "Gant should have got that last slot as strike leader. The two new boys seem okay so far."

"I've recommended to the boss that it's time to rotate you round to a new squad. He agrees with me."

"Why?" Rall demanded, stopping in his tracks. "What's the problem? We're at the front, getting stuck in every time! I'm looking after them, our casualty rate is no higher than anybody else's! There's nothing I can do to stop an orbital..."

"It's not about that, Feon," Van Noor said softly, "it's about the effects of your personality on the squad shard, and through it, what's being projected onto every one of those guys and girls over there. You're what the boss calls a 'polarized character'. Most strike leaders can stay in place, but people like you, you achieve a hell of a lot in combat but your drive and grit can have real effects on your people."

Van Noor paused, his piercing eyes fixed on Rall's, as if waiting for a reaction. Rall met his gaze evenly but bit back a response.

"Listen to them!" Van Noor continued. "They're angry, pissed off, outspoken – they're like you. We need leaders like you front and center, but occasionally our people need a change or we lose variety in our ranks, and with it we lose flexibility."

"That's all just management buzz-word crap," Rall shook his head. "You're fobbing me off with psychology. If the boss agrees with this, why isn't he down here telling me himself?"

"Because it was my idea, and I said I'd talk to you," Van Noor's tone was a little less amiable. "If you're not up to acknowledging my authority as senior strike leader of this company, we can go see the boss right now."

Rall froze. The strike captain was an approachable and fair man, but he had seen what he was capable of. Worse, he had heard rumors, stories about the boss before he joined the military.

"That won't be necessary," Rall took a breath. "I'll tell my squad that I'll be moving on, and I'll be ready to follow your direction as soon as you have a new squad for me."

"Good man," Van Noor smiled, slamming an armored palm against Rall's shoulder. "It's not a criticism, just routine. I'll give you a shout as soon as we know who you're swapping with."

***

The din of construction continued to recede as the engineering drones moved further underground to work on the accommodation block. The gentle sound of the waves lapping against the smooth sand was accompanied by the cawing of large, almost skeletal thin sea birds with vibrant coats of red and green feathers. A gentle onshore breeze rustled the scattered, spikey patches of blue vegetation that sprouted up from amid the rocks which occasionally punctuated the long stretch of sand.

"How about 'call'," Clythe offered, "that should be easy enough to work in."

The two sat alone on their stretch of beach, looking out to sea as Sessetti prodded half-heartedly at the datapad that lay across his lap.

"I dunno, Bo," Sessetti winced. "I can see that end up a bit... contrived."

"What you guys up to?"

Sessetti looked up to see Ila Rae, another relatively new trooper from their squad, walk over to sit down next to them. Rae had been the squad's most junior trooper until he had arrived with Clythe. A young woman of average height with mousy brown hair, she had mainly kept herself to herself. Nonetheless, Sessetti was not entirely sure he wanted to pour out his heart and soul to a woman he barely knew, so he opened his mouth to come up with a convincing lie to respond to her question. Clythe blurted out a response before he could.

"We're writing song lyrics. We were in a band back home before we were called up. Today was a pretty big day, so I guess it's been kind of... thought provoking."

"A band?" Rae exclaimed as Sessetti sighed and shot a look at Clythe, "Wow! This must be quite a change of pace, being out here. You guys okay after this morning? I know the shard helps a lot, but seeing your first dead squadmate, there's only so much that can be repressed by those friendly brain waves they send to us. Before we go on leave, they'll wean us off the external assistance and the drugs and give us proper therapy, and we can talk it through then."

"Yeah, I'm feeling a bit better," Clythe nodded.

"I thought we'd lost you, too!" Rae blinked. "I'm glad you're okay."

"Thanks," Clythe shrugged uncomfortably, pausing for a moment before continuing. "So... what did you do before all this?"

"I was a junior fashion designer, believe it or not, which was something I really loved. Not much to say about it, really." Rae raised her brow and exhaled, as if disappointed in the lack of a response from her statement, before turning her head and nodding back in the direction of the base. "Anyway, here come the rest of the guys."

Sessetti looked over his shoulder as Gant, Jemmel, and Qan made their way over from where they had stopped to talk to the members of Squad Teal. As was standard away from combat, all three troopers had removed their helmets and replaced them with the black beret of the 44th Strike Formation.

"Hey, did you know these guys are in a band back home?" Rae announced as the three approached.

Sessetti bit his lip and looked angrily across at Clythe. The shorter man shrugged in confusion.

"What kind of music?" Jemmel asked as she flopped down on a

small rock next to them.

"We started off doing the same heavy strings stuff everybody does in their teens," Clythe answered, "but dance stuff was more popular, so we ditched the angst and went across to keys."

"Nevermind," Jemmel narrowed her eyes in disapproval, "you can always reverse that rather unwise decision with a bit more maturity."

"Oh, wind your neck in!" Gant snapped. "The dude is telling you about his art form, and you're just going looking to pick holes! We've all got different tastes and there's nothing laid down that says you're right and he's wrong."

"Alright!" Jemmel held both hands up. "It was a joke!"

"Well to me, some things are sacred," Gant said seriously, "and I don't joke about things back home."

"Have you heard the good news?" Qan remarked dryly. "We ain't getting catering out here. We're on food capsules for the foreseeable."

"Things could be worse," Rae pondered. "I mean, look at the view."

The six troopers sat in silence for a few moments as the suns continued their slow dip toward the horizon, painting the sky in horizontal bands of oranges and purples. The onshore breeze picked up just a little more.

"Who d'you think we're getting as our new strike leader?" Jemmel asked as she scratched the back of her shaven head. "Can't say I'm too bothered to see the back of Rall."

"Any chance we'll get Van Noor?" Sessetti asked. "He seems like a good guy to work for."

"No, doesn't work like that," Gant replied. "As senior strike leader, he always works in the command squad, with the boss. Rotating him back here with us would effectively be a demotion."

"I reckon it'll be Heide," Qan said, making an unsuccessful attempt to skim a flat stone across the glistening water. "He's a good egg."

"Any chance we'll get that hottie from Squad Jai?" Clythe asked excitedly. "She is literally the perfect woman."

"Good to see equality is still alive and well where you're from," Rae murmured under her breath.

"Rhona?" Jemmel spat. "The least experienced strike leader in the entire Concord? Yeah, good choice."

"He's right though," Qan mused as he failed to skim another stone, "she's the hottest woman ever."

Sessetti found himself glaring at Clythe, his old school friend, wondering how he had managed to lower himself to overtly blurting out sexist comments. It seemed to Sessetti to be one of many disadvantages of living life within the C3 military shard; some darker elements of panhuman nature were allowed, even encouraged to move to the fore. Comments such as these would have been stamped out before the brain had engaged the mouth back in the Concord civilian shard.

"It'll be Yavn from Squad Teal," Gant declared. "It's the most logical choice. Half of you have barely fired a shot – no offense guys – and Yavn's one of the most experienced strike leaders we've got."

"No such luck," Jemmel rolled her eyes before nodding at a point further up the beach. "Speak of the devil."

Sessetti turned to see Van Noor walking across to them with a second trooper accompanying him. The senior strike leader turned to face the shorter trooper and exchanged words for a few moments before giving her an encouraging shove to one shoulder and a thumbs up. The squad's new strike leader walked away from Van Noor and over to the six troopers on the beach. She stopped by the squad and flashed a lazy smile, her black hair falling over a tatty purple bandana tied around her forehead.

"You guys are with me now," Katya Rhona beamed. "Y'all make sure you get a good night's sleep. We've got first patrol tomorrow morning."

TWO

Benin Province
Equatorial Region
Markov's Prize

L-Day plus 2

Beams of early morning sunshine cut through the gaps in the thick, orange striped leaves above the stream which wound through the jungle. The trickle of water was accompanied by the persistent rattle of insects and occasionally punctuated by the now familiar shriek of a colorful bird. Up ahead, Gant stepped carefully out of the stream and up onto dusty earth, his body language speaking of a man focused and ready. Behind him was Jemmel, always recognizable even in full armor as the shortest trooper in the company, her plasma lance tucked into her shoulder. A large, lizard like creature with purple and gold scales and feeble wings suddenly shot across the ground in front of them. Jemmel tracked it with her plasma lance and watched it disappear back into the blue undergrowth.

Both troopers were highlighted by blue diamonds on Rhona's helmet array; the visual indication of their status as friendly forces was further reinforced by their armor appearing in its default white and green color scheme. In actual fact, to the naked eye, their armor was constantly changing appearance as it cycled through vivid blues, greens, and yellows to accompany its current surroundings, a function of the reactive color coating each battlesuit was covered with. A series of white arrows was also projected on the ground ahead, showing the recommended route for the squad's patrol from the perspective of their spotter drone, which hovered a little way off to the left, leading up to the squad's objective some two hundred yan ahead – Hill 512.

"Squad Wen, this is Command," Rhona heard a voice through the shard. She held up a clenched fist; every member of her squad immediately stopped in position and dropped to one knee, their weapons held ready.

"Go for Wen," Rhona replied.

A low, menacing hiss sounded from a tree to Rhona's right. She glanced across and shuddered as she saw a huge, legless serpent wrap itself around an insect the size of her head and devour it.

"Wen from Command," the strike captain's calm voice transmitted. "We have you at one-ninety yan south of Objective Delta. Send your sitrep."

"Command, Wen, my position tallies. All quiet, nothing to report," Rhona replied, her eyes scanning the surrounding trees for any sign of a threat.

"Wen, Command, copied, stay sharp."

Rhona switched her communication frequency to her squad.

"Just the boss after a sitrep, guys," she relayed. "Check your fluid levels and then let's push on."

Rhona mentally activated her battlesuit system readout and noted her power levels and vitals were reading green – all good. Nonetheless, she unclipped her helmet from the junction on the back of her neck and rolled it forward off her head, blinking as the unfiltered sunlight hit her eyes. The air seemed close and dense, yet somehow less claustrophobic without the constant and sometimes intrusive flow of data from her viewscreen. She tightened her father's bandana around her forehead and took a swig of real water from the canteen on her utility belt to augment her battlesuit's intravenous fluid flow.

Qan dropped to one knee beside her and brought his faceplate up to the top of his head so that he could talk to her face to face.

"You all good, Lead?"

"I'm just dandy," Rhona grinned. "Let's go walk up this hill."

She replaced her helmet and stood again, taking a second to absorb her artificial visual display as it replaced her genuine visual indications.

"Rae, go take point," she commanded, keen to give Gant a break and cycle her troops through the high-risk position at the head of the patrol.

"Got it, Lead," the slim woman answered, picking up her pace slightly to move to the front of the squad.

As soon as Rae moved past Gant, Rhona saw the woman trip and stumble on some unseen obstacle, and then her entire viewscreen blacked out for perhaps half a second. As soon as it had rebooted, a warning flashed across the upper left corner of her screen – 'EMP'.

"Get down!" Jemmel yelled.

Rhona dove to the ground as the jungle erupted into a barrage of noise. A fast paced chattering from an automatic weapon came from the higher ground ahead and to her right; Rhona saw the earth kicked up around Sessetti as his hyperlight shields flashed purple in an attempt to defend him against unseen projectiles before he was then knocked down to the ground.

"Hostile 1 identified!" The squad's spotter drone reported. "Hostile 2 identified!"

Two red diamonds appeared in an area of foliage up ahead as the drone transmitted the location of two enemy soldiers to the squad members' viewscreens. Rhona raised her carbine to her shoulder and opened fire, sending a stream of blue energy bolts tearing through the jungle ahead.

"Targets, directly ahead at my marker, open fire!" Gant shouted.

Two other plasma carbines and the single beam of a plasma lance joined Rhona's fire and blasted into the blue and yellow trees at the marker which Gant had just transmitted to all of the troopers' viewscreens, sending branches and leaves twirling in all directions as nature was scythed down by the destructive display of firepower.

"Enemy Squad, left ninety, fifteen yan!" the spotter drone called as a further eight red diamonds appeared on the display.

Muzzle flashes appeared from the left and Rhona felt a thud on her back. No pain, no damage reported on her display – her armor was holding. She took stock of the situation – an EMP grenade trap with two decoy enemy shooters up ahead, but the main enemy force was firing on them from a concealed position to their left. Even primitive weapons had a chance of taking them out unless she acted.

"Squad Wen, targets left at marker beta! Open fire!"

The squad followed her command and shifted their fire from the two soldiers ahead to the eight on the left by her newly uploaded marker, plasma fire again ripping down trees and foliage.

Rhona jumped to her feet and ran back along the route they had followed, distancing herself from the firefight quickly. She turned to the right and picked up her pace, weaving her way rapidly through the trees as she ran along a line parallel to the firefight off to her right, remembering her duty to report the situation up to command.

"Command, Squad Wen! Engaged with hostiles!"

"Wen, Command, do you require support?"

Rhona did not have time to reply.

She could see two of the enemy soldiers now as she advanced alone through the jungle to outflank them. Two men underneath camouflaged netting were crouched over a bipod mounted weapon, pouring down high volumes of fire into her squad. One of the red diamonds on her visual display faded away as plasma fire cut down one of the enemy soldiers.

"Squad Wen, friendly approaching from left of target, watch your fire!" Gant shouted across the shard.

Rhona swore – it was her job to keep her squad informed of

the plan and that was twice Gant had been forced to issue commands. Clambering up a shallow ravine, she reached a position above and behind the dug in enemy soldiers. She lobbed a plasma grenade down into the bipod weapon pit and then hugged her carbine into her shoulder before spraying rapid fire into the enemy position, her weapon bucking and rocking as it spewed out superheated packets of energy.

Her grenade detonated with a dull thud, lifting the enemy weapon operator up into the air and spinning him around as he was torn apart by the blast. Men were scythed down as they were caught in the crossfire of her own weapon and those of her squad. Jemmel's plasma lance sent another solid beam of blue energy up from the bottom of the ravine, hacking down a tree above the enemy firing position.

Two red diamonds were still visible through the smoke and debris as two survivors ran up the slope, desperately trying to escape from the deadly fire from the Concord strike troopers. Rhona changed her carbine's fire mode to single shot and held her breath, taking careful aim at the center of the diamond. She paused. Just two men, defending their homeland from invasion, now running away and presenting no threat. She did not fire.

"Squad Wen! Cease-fire! Cease-fire!" She ordered.

After a couple of seconds, the order registered and the firing stopped. Rhona remained knelt in place, peering over the nozzle of her smoking carbine as she waited for any indications of further hostile forces. She checked the vital signs of her squad through the shard. All in the green, no casualties.

"Lian, you okay?" Somebody asked.

"Shut up!" Rhona heard Jemmel bark. "They're still out there!"

"Eight hostiles eliminated, two escaping to the north," the drone reported.

Rhona eased her way back up to her feet and crept slowly down to the enemy ambush spot. Seven dead soldiers lay sprawled in their dugout; the ugly, cauterized burns of plasma wounds evident across their bodies. Rhona instinctively turned away and then felt a wave of calm wash over her from her shard connection, which immediately made her feel a little calmer. She approached the first dead man and grabbed his jungle green poncho, which was still invisible in her visual display. She removed her helmet and looked at the camouflaged garment with her own eyes, noting how much easier it now was to see.

"Squad Wen, Command, sitrep."

Rhona had forgotten her earlier transmission to the command squad.

"Command, Wen, we're good," she replied. "Hostiles engaged at my current position, one enemy squad forced back. We've sustained no casualties, but we've got hostiles defeated on the ground. We've got captured examples of personal cloaking devices."

There was a momentary pause before a reply came through.

"Wen, confirm you have encountered and defeated live enemy personnel?"

"Affirm."

"Wen, good job. Hold your position. Squad Teal are already on the way to reinforce your position. Secure any enemy technology you can find and await further instructions."

Rhona ran a metallic, gauntleted hand through her long, black hair as her squad emerged from the foliage to her right. Even with their helmets and faceplates in place, she recognized Gant and Jemmel at the front.

"You okay?" Gant asked.

"All cool," Rhona replied. "I saw Sessetti go down, is he good?"

"Yeah, I'm fine," Sessetti pushed his way through a thick, orange bush and into the clearing. "I got hit by whatever those first two were using, but it didn't go through, just knocked me over."

"We've been ordered to hold," Rhona said, "the boys from Teal should be here in a couple of minutes. Spread out and keep an eye out for a counterattack. I'm sending your positions now. Drone, get yourself to the high ground north."

Rhona quickly surveyed the surrounding terrain before assigning each of her squad members a position to form a cordon around the enemy dugout. The feedback via the squad shard gave her an instant feeling regarding each individual's mental state: relief from Sessetti, fear from Clythe and Rae, concentration from Qan, and anger and resentment from Gant and Jemmel.

"Jem, before you go, check those bodies and make sure they're definitely dead," Gant nodded to Jemmel, who instantly followed his instructions. "Lead, a word please."

Gant stomped back through the undergrowth to the south, away from the dugout and the route the enemy survivors had used to flee up to the high ground. Rhona obliged and followed him until they were some distance away from the squad, when Gant turned to face her and removed his helmet.

"We need to talk," he said coolly.

Sensing confrontation, Rhona planted her fists on her hips and tossed a lock of dark hair away from her eyes.

"So talk," she invited, meeting his glare.

"I shouldn't need to do your damn job for you as squad leader," Gant began without hesitation. "There's been a couple of times I've stepped in when..."

"You look here, boy," Rhona found herself adopting the same tone her father did whenever he would reprimand her as a child. "I know full well you were next in line for promotion, but I got it instead of you. So now you've got a problem with me. I didn't choose to join this army or to get promoted, and hell, while you and I are being so open, I don't give a damn for any of it. But we've got a job to do and now is not the time or place to argue over this. So you just fall into line, do as I say, and we'll talk when we're back at the basecamp. And if you try to override me just one more time, I'll make sure you wish you hadn't. You feel me, boy?"

Rhona did not give the startled trooper time to respond. Dragging her helmet back on, she walked back to the enemy dugout position.

***

The subterranean accommodation block gave Sessetti his first sensation of security since arriving on Markov's Prize. He lay on his bunk, staring at the artificial mountain scenery projected onto the wall of his alcove and thought over the past two days. Turning over onto his back, the bunk's suspensors kept him floating at waist height above the ground, his green issue blanket draped over his prone form. Now he was out of his armor, Sessetti felt the full force of the planet's gravity. It was not crippling, not as fatiguing as some planets he had visited in his childhood, but at even a few quantum more than the standard gravity on many planets and certainly all spaceships, it was enough to make him feel weary and lethargic. The eighteen standard hour day of Markov's Prize did not help. It would be that way at least until he became acclimatized. Until it became the norm.

The squad's accommodation arrangements were centered around a communal area, within which were some sofas, food and drink stowages, and an entertainment suite for projecting movies and games into a 3D holographic area near the southern wall. The engineering droids had dug eight alcoves into the walls surrounding the circular main room, giving each trooper an element of privacy; although in practice, the partition walls which cut off the alcoves completely were only activated for sleeping. Each alcove, as with the main chamber, could have a variety of images projected onto the walls, floor, and ceiling to give a more homely or relaxing ambience. Weste's alcove remained empty, a permanent reminder of the man they had already lost. Still no news had come back regarding whether or not his clone would be activated.

A single door led out of the squad accommodation area into a long, straight corridor connecting all of the squad accommodation hubs, but the stairs at each end of the corridor which led to the surface were only emergency exits. Each bed also doubled as a transmat pad and could be used to beam the occupant directly to a pre-designated pad on the surface, although as a defensive measure these transmat pads were only one-way. The squad's arms and armor were neatly stowed in each alcove; standards of dress were relaxed in accommodation areas and most troopers wore loose fitting trousers or shorts, and other non-military attire.

"Keep the noise down," Jemmel warned Clythe from her bunk.

The short woman had returned from the gym and lay suspended on her bunk in her gym gear, her muscular limbs seeming to jar with her elfin features.

"Your partition curtain is soundproof," Clythe called from where he sat on a sofa with a small keyboard he was writing a song with. "Use it."

Sessetti sat up and looked across at his friend. Even a minor outburst such as that was uncharacteristic. Nonetheless, there was no response from Jemmel. Aside from the sound of a simple major chord-based progression emanating from the keyboard, the room fell silent for a few moments, until Clythe spoke again.

"Where are Rhona and Gant? They've been gone a while."

"Difference of opinion regarding squad command," Qan remarked dryly from his alcove, where he sat watching a holographic projection of an action movie on his lap.

"I'd imagine it's progressed a bit further than that," Jemmel smirked. "They've been gone ages and you can practically see the tension building between those two."

"What do you mean by that?" Clythe sat bolt upright.

Any response was interrupted by a knock at the door.

"Yeah," Jemmel called out.

The door opened to admit Van Noor. The senior strike leader was still in his green and white battlesuit, his plasma carbine slung over one shoulder. The five strike troopers immediately stood up.

"As you were, chill out," Van Noor flashed a brief smile. "We're about to head back out, so I'm just doing the rounds and seeing how everybody is. Squad Wen all good?"

"Doing fine, Senior!" Rae answered enthusiastically from her alcove.

"Lian, Bo? How's the company's two newest heroes holding out?"

Sessetti exchanged a glance with Clythe before looking back into Van Noor's grey eyes.

"We're good, thanks, Senior. Interesting first two days on the job. We've both been shot now, so at least that's ticked off from the 'to do' list."

"That's the spirit!" Van Noor's face cracked into a wide grin. "I heard you were shot up by some local kinetic weapon. Gives you faith in the hyperlight armor, at least. These things are pretty solid. Hopefully your squad is taking good care of you and helping you out with anything you need. I'd hate to hear of any old school crap going on in my company, with self appointed combat veterans trying to talk down to the newer guys instead of helping them. Any of that going on, people might get to see the senior's evil side, hey, Jem?"

Jemmel nodded and looked down at her feet.

"Yes, Senior," she replied quietly.

"Good... good," a darker look in Van Noor's eyes did not marry up with his friendly smile.

"Senior?" Qan suddenly asked, stepping out from his alcove into the main communal area. "You got a sec?"

"Sure," Van Noor replied.

"I've been in this company for nearly a year now, and..."

"I know," Van Noor cut him off, "the party was supposed to be a surprise. I'm personally blowing up all of the balloons for you. Go on, what is it?"

The tall trooper winced for a second before continuing.

"Everything people say about the boss. How much of it is true? Was he really a circuit fighter who killed ten men with his bare hands?"

"Qan!" Jemmel exhaled a warning under her breath.

Sessetti looked across at the other members of his squad. Even as a newcomer, he had heard plenty of rumors and stories. Van Noor nodded slowly before checking over his shoulder.

"There's a lot of rumors floating around about your strike captain," he eventually said. "All you need to know is that he's the finest commander any of you are likely to work for in your time in C3. But no, he hasn't killed ten men with his bare hands. It was five. He fought three seasons in Determinate Fighter and won the title every time. That competition is full contact, so whilst fatalities are very uncommon, they're certainly not unheard of, but five dead in three seasons is pretty much a record. Sure - if a fighter gets killed, they ain't likely to stay dead long, what with full-freeze regen right there by the ringside. Still - can't be much fun waking up to find you're living in a tank for the next six months. The message from this one is not to piss the boss off. His evil side puts mine to shame."

"I'm not so sure I agree with that."

Sessetti looked to the doorway to see who had spoken from the shadows.

Strike Captain Ryen Tahl stepped into the room, also clad in his battlesuit.

"Company Commander!" Van Noor called, standing stiffly to attention.

The five strike troopers immediately snapped to attention. If Rhona, with her flawless beauty, fitted the stereotypical view of the beautiful fighting woman as seen on recruitment posters and highly sanitized action series, the ruggedly handsome, powerfully built Tahl looked more akin to the anti-hero of a dark thriller. His tired, blue eyes complemented his light brown, almost sandy colored hair that had grown out to the point of bordering on the maximum regulation length over the course of several successive campaigns, adding to the appearance of a man who was run down. Tahl walked slowly into the room, taking a few seconds before holding up a hand.

"Please, as you were."

Sessetti found himself shifting to the 'at ease' position, but certainly not relaxed.

"Well?" Tahl gave the slightest of smiles. "Boots fit alright? Mail getting through?"

Sesetti sniggered at the well-used catchphrase from a comedy series which was popular back home.

"All good, sir," Qan replied.

"Is Strike Leader Rhona around? I wanted to talk to her about something."

"No joy, sir," Jemmel offered. "We haven't seen much of her."

"Well, I figured I'd say a thank you for your efforts earlier today," Tahl said, "those recce cloaks you recovered from the enemy dugout have been passed on to Intel and have already been processed. I doubt you'll find any of them sneaking up on you for the remainder of this campaign. So good job, all of you."

"The troops were just telling me how they've at least been shot and blown up, so they're pretty much fully fledged strike troopers now, sir," Van Noor remarked.

"I dunno, sir," Clythe smiled, "I guess we need to kill something first."

"No, you don't," Tahl said seriously. "Remember why you're here, everyone. These people are centuries behind us in a hundred ways. Their average life expectancy is only one hundred years; ordinary people still have to work to pay for food, clothing, and shelter; all kinds of social prejudices are still openly tolerated. We're not here to kill them. Our strategic objective is to secure this island as a safe base of operations until we can disable the planet's defensive grid and allow the IMTel to take control. My personal objective is to keep this company as safe as possible in the process. So no, I'm not concerned about taking lives. What I care about is preserving them."

"Understood, sir," Clythe swallowed.

"Make sure you get plenty of rest whenever you can. We can't control pauses in operations, so make best use of them and keep yourselves fit and rested. Any questions for me?"

Tahl paused, his brow raised as his stern eyes fixed on each trooper in turn. Nobody spoke.

"I'll leave you to it," Tahl said as he turned to leave. "I hope you all have a good evening."

***

"Wait up!"

Van Noor ran through the dark, chilly corridor cut into the subterranean stone to catch up with his commanding officer. The younger man half turned to look at him as he caught up; Van Noor had known him long enough to know when he was less than fully content.

"I'm sorry, Ryen," Van Noor offered genuinely. "It's not my place to go talking about your personal life to the troops. Momentary lapse, bloody stupid, it won't happen again."

"I know, I know," Tahl nodded. "Just... see that it doesn't. We've all got a past, and I'm not proud of mine. I'd rather leave it in the past. It doesn't matter, let's just forget it and move on. We need to pick up where Squad Wen left off and scout out Hill 512 as a potential transmat station site. Now that we've hopefully put their stealth technology to bed, I'm confident that we can scout that route with just the four of us in the command squad, plus a couple of drones. What do you think?"

"Maybe worth taking a C3D1, just in case we need a bit more firepower," Van Noor offered. "If we're having a long night, it makes sense to lean a bit heavier on the drones rather than the troopers to save on tiring out our assets."

"They're noisy," Tahl thought aloud as he rounded a corner in the rocky corridor, "but we'll see them before they hear us." Tahl paused to consder the option for a few moments. "Okay, let's take one with us. Just in case."

THREE

Northern Hemisphere
Settlement Urban 218
City Center

L-Day plus 12

The deep rumble of a battery of x-howitzers from somewhere to the south announced an acknowledgement of Tahl's orders, only a few moments before a series of spectacular explosions lit up the northern horizon. Through the lower left quadrant of his visual display, Tahl saw the impact of the shells patched across from Squad Jai's spotter drone as a tall, grey apartment building crumbled at the foundations and collapsed in on itself to be replaced by a towering plume of dust and smoke. The dust blossomed up into the air, a little slower than normal due to the increased gravitational pull of the planet. The noticeable difference briefly reminded Tahl of the acid rain clouds of Prostock, the poisonous smog and half gravity of Vira 9, the thick viscous waters and deadly giant lizards of Maritanian. The list of planets assaulted and defended was near endless. At least now he needed only worry about his own company; the previous planetary assault at Prostock had seen Tahl temporarily promoted to Strike Commander of the entire Formation due to the mounting casualties.

"Beta Battery from Squad Jai," Rall transmitted across the shard, "correct fire, alter aim to updated marker."

"Beta Battery, acknowledged."

Content that Rall had the situation to the north under control, Tahl surveyed his immediate surroundings once more. Hunkered down behind the cover of a ceremonial stone fountain in the main town square of Settlement Urban 218, Tahl had positioned his four man command squad centrally a few dozen yan behind a defensive line made up of the strike troopers of his company. A pair of C3M4 combat drones assisted the left flank whilst a larger number of the much smaller C3D1 drones provided fire support to the right. The sprawling, grey city was now devoid of civilians. Many of its buildings had been destroyed by the pre-assault orbital bombardment and by artillery fire called in against the areas of resistance that had been encountered during the assault itself. The skies above were relatively clear, allowing rays of sunshine to light up the thick clouds of dust which hung over the entire city.

Tahl changed his view to survey the entire battlescape again, updating his awareness of the rapidly evolving situation with a fresh update from his squads' spotter drones. A platoon of six enemy armored vehicles – archaic looking things which moved across the ground on tracks – were attempting to outflank to the left whilst a concentration of enemy infantry was attempting a similar maneuver to the right. Meanwhile, Rall's Squad Jai held strong against a push against the center of the company's defensive line.

"Squad Teal from Command," Tahl addressed Strike Leader Yavn, "hostiles, six armored vehicles, moving to the northeast of your position. Engage with M4s."

"Command, Teal, copied," Yavn replied calmly. "M4 Alpha, move to my marker and engage hostile armor."

"M4 Alpha, acknowledged," came the deep, metallic response from the sentient combat drone as it led its fellow C3M4 against the manned enemy vehicles.

Tahl paused for a moment to consider his options. The main threat from enemy infantry so far had been when they managed to get in close – their firearms were like rain drops from far away, but up close they could and sometimes did penetrate the strike troopers' hyperlight shields, although the physical armor they wore was then normally sufficient to ward off the shots which made it through. Their armored vehicles were a different matter entirely; whilst the scientists of Markov's Prize had not yet progressed onto making magnetically accelerated weapons small enough to be handheld – let alone plasma weapons – they had at least managed to fit magnetic cannons to their vehicles, and these were a very real and very modern threat, capable enough even to destroy Concord battledrones.

Van Noor crawled over, keeping cover behind the shallow wall which ran around the fountain.

"Boss, we've got something moving in toward us. Spotter drone's picked up movement near marker echo," the senior strike leader informed him. "We've still got a gap somewhere in our line because these bastards keep on trickling through."

"Understood," Tahl nodded. "Probably just a probing move, but get some markers selected for Beta Battery in case it's anything substantial. In the meantime, we hold position. It looks as though the main counterattack is coming in against the left flank."

"Yeah, concur," Van Noor replied before turning to relay a series of orders to the troopers and drones which made up the remainder of the command squad.

***

The red diamonds projected onto Sessetti's viewscreen remained stationary as the enemy soldiers held position behind the cover of the semi-destroyed hospital to the north. Sessetti shifted in position in an attempt to relieve another bout of cramp entering his right leg. He remained prone in the cover of a collapsed residential building, his plasma carbine held at the ready and pointing across the playing fields to the north toward the hospital. At the far right of the company's defensive position, they had experienced sporadic resistance, but judging by the snippets of conversation relayed to him across the shard, things were far worse off to the east of the line.

"C'mon, little piggy," Jemmel murmured under her breath, "just poke your head up and take a look around..."

Sessetti looked to his right. Clythe lay next to him, plasma carbine at his shoulder; whilst a little higher on what remained of the first floor, Jemmel crouched over her plasma lance and urged the enemy soldiers to give her an opportunity to fire.

"Keep your eyes peeled," Gant reminded from his position to the left of the line. "Spotter drone's got movement to our right."

Sessetti could not help but wonder why these pearls of wisdom were issued from another trooper and not Rhona, their leader. The young woman crouched behind cover to his left, her helmet removed and her back to a wall between her and the enemy, her dark eyes fixed on a cloud up above.

"Two hours," Clythe whispered from next to him. "Two hours laying here and I had to pick a position with the corner of a brick pointing right between my balls..."

Qan sniggered.

"Stay focused, children!" Gant snapped.

"Hostiles, thirty plus, moving south of marker indigo," the squad's spotter drone suddenly announced.

Rhona sprang into action, dragging on her helmet and dashing over to the right hand side of the squad's line.

"D1 Alpha, Squad Wen, move to marker indigo," Rhona commanded, watching as a trio of disc shaped C3D1 light combat drones responded to her command and shot off at head height across the playing field toward the reported enemy position.

As soon as they were in the open, muzzle flashes danced along the windows and rooftops of the hospital building as a group of enemy soldiers opened fire.

"Enemy fire, marker alpha!" Jemmel shouted, not waiting for a command to return fire herself with her plasma lance.

"Squad Wen, marker alpha, open fire!" Rhona ordered, raising her own carbine to her shoulder and firing off an aimed shot.

Sessetti could only see the two dozen red diamonds on the far side of a playing field and the vague outline of the hospital building whose crisp lines were blended into a blur by the smoke and dust. He took aim, held his breath, and squeezed off a series of slow, deliberate shots at the enemy positions. After his third shot, one of the diamonds faded to nothing. Unless he had selected the same target as one of his comrades, he had just killed another panhuman. He lifted his head away from the weapon's sighting system and raised his helmet's faceplate, taking in a deep breath. He instantly felt the soothing embrace of the shard's external assistance wash over him and the numbness and nausea associated with the action dissipated.

He took aim again and resumed firing.

***

"There's a push on the right flank," Van Noor reported. "Looks like one group dug in at the hospital and another moving to flank."

"Yes, I see it," Tahl replied as he surveyed the battlefield, fighting the urge to pick up his carbine and sprint over toward the fighting. "They've moved the D1s in to fire; I'm content they have the line held."

A whizz like a loud insect suddenly shot through the air and Cane, one of the command squad troopers, span around where he crouched and fell to the ground screaming, clutching at his arm pit as blood spattered across his armored chestplate.

"Sniper!" Van Noor yelled.

The squad – even the drones – dropped to the ground. Tahl crawled across to his wounded trooper and grabbed him by one leg, yanking him from the position where he fell to the comparative safety of the cover behind the fountain. A projectile had struck him in the vulnerable arm joint of his battlesuit, easily penetrating the thinner armor and half severing his limb in the process. With analgesia already issued from his battlesuit, Cane's agonized screams had eased off to grunts and groans. Tahl grabbed at the medical pouch from his utility belt and took out the small cauterizing tool, quickly burning the wound shut to stem the flow of blood. He flipped his faceplate back so his wounded soldier could see his eyes.

"You're good, Dez," he smiled. "Just stay down and we'll get you proper care as soon as we can."

"Medi-drone, Command," Van Noor called. "Casualty, return to our position."

The medi-drone acknowledged through the shard as Tahl looked at his immediate surroundings. The enemy shot had come from the northwest, judging from how the impact had spun Cane around. Glancing up, Tahl saw only one colossal, towering building some two hundred yan in that direction.

"He's in there," Tahl declared, "tall, spired building at marker sierra."

"Got it, Boss," Van Noor acknowledged as he hugged his carbine in to his shoulder. "If you're happy, I'd recommend you stay here with Cane and keep the battle management going. Me and Kachi will go clear out the cathedral."

"That's not a good way to clear out a sniper, Senior," Tahl exhaled. "You know the standard drill."

Van Noor crawled back over, giving Cane an encouraging pat on the back as he passed, and then removed his faceplate to speak face to face with Tahl.

"That building's a thousand years old, Ryen," he urged, "it'd be a crying shame to do that to these people."

"I know, Bry, I know," Tahl murmured his response, as the medi-drone buzzed over from the west. "And it looks like a building of faith which makes this even more heartbreaking. But I'm not losing two of my soldiers to save an old building, especially when, for all we know, there's an entire squad in there waiting for you."

Tahl mentally activated his shard communicator and opened a channel to Beta Battery.

"Beta from Command," he spoke, "we've been engaged by a sniper at marker sierra. Fire for effect, over."

***

Squad Jai's position in the center of the line was amongst the rubble, debris, and carnage of the heaviest of the pre-assault bombardment. An industrial site had been flattened by the barrage into a sea of broken concrete and twisted metal. A sheet of broken grey covered ground that was once dozens of huge buildings and interconnecting roads.

Three waves of ten or fifteen enemy soldiers, their grey uniforms and black body armor well camouflaged against the debris, had attempted to cross the industrial ruins; but on each attempt, Rall's squad had beaten them back. However, the planet's military had managed to make their mark, and Rall already had one dead and one critically wounded.

"Enemy movement at marker ghia," their spotter drone reported. "Thirteen hostiles."

Rall checked his visual display and saw the familiar red diamonds picking their way through the rubble ahead, only moments away from a clear field of fire. The drone spoke again.

"Second enemy group, marker tare, ten hostiles."

"They've gotten around the side of us!" Pendel, his plasma lance gunner, seethed.

"They wanna get in close?" Rall growled, his brow twisted in fury. "They think that's where we're weak? Squad Jai, follow me!"

Leading his five remaining strike troopers through the treacherous rubble and thick, acrid smoke that poured from still burning fires all around, Rall closed with the second enemy group to the east. He dropped to one knee and held a hand up to signal for his squad to hold position as they drew closer to the enemy squad. The red diamonds crept closer until panhuman shapes could be seen crossing the ruins up ahead. Ten men, their primitive looking rifles held across their chests and their useless black helmets and body armor jackets standing out from their grey combat fatigues, moved into view.

"Squad Jai, rapid fire!"

On their leader's command, the six troopers opened fire with their carbines and lance set to automatic, painting the space between the two opposing groups with crisscrossing lines of boiling blue matter as their projectiles cut into the enemy group. With a bravery that impressed even Rall, the enemy soldiers screamed and charged at the Concord troopers.

"On me!" Rall screamed, sprinting forward to meet them.

His carbine tucked into his hip, he fired a long burst of scatter plasma fire which cut into the abdomen of the lead soldier, dropping him to the rubble. Two more men stepped over to meet Rall; he ducked low as one man attempted to tackle him around the neck and sprang back up on the other side, clubbing the second man around the face with his carbine and knocking him to the ground.

To his right, a tall enemy soldier tackled Pendel whilst a second planted a grenade on his torso which detonated on impact, tearing the Concord soldier in half at the waist and killing both of his attackers. With a cry of rage, Rall threw aside a bulky enemy soldier who lunged at his face with a bayonet before dropping back to the assailant he had knocked over with his initial attack, smashing his carbine butt into the soldier's panicked face again and again until he had split open the man's head.

He looked up for another target but found only dead bodies strewn across the rubble, some butchered savagely in the hand to hand combat, and others torn asunder by the enemy grenades. Three of his men lay dead amongst the enemy squad of ten.

"Enemy group, thirty yan north, closing!" The spotter drone reported with a tone of urgency which nearly humanized it.

"Get your act together, guys!" Rall growled at his three troopers. "They're coming in again! Chian, grab the lance!"

Rall was unafraid of hand to hand fighting, but even in the short moment's contemplation open to him, he had to admit that he was surprised by how many troopers he had lost in the last engagement. That was not the way ahead.

"Get in cover!" He barked at his troops. "We'll take them down with rapid fire on the way in!"

"Squad Jai, Command," Strike Captain Tahl's voice spoke through the shard, reminding Rall to check his position relative to the others on the company shard. "Hold position, you have friendlies moving to your east and west."

A sudden feeling of weariness washed over Rall as he saw blue diamonds on his display to his left and right. He was keen to return to the fight, but orders were orders, and he respected that. Patching in his squad's drone to the spotter drone of the command squad, he watched as Tahl and Van Noor caught the second enemy squad in a withering crossfire between their own weapons and a pair of C3D1 droids, cutting down the enemy in a hail of plasma before the battlefield fell silent once more.

***

Muttering a prayer under his breath, Tahl watched as the bodies of his eight dead soldiers were loaded into a C3T7 transport drone for ferrying to a transmat sight. Only two head wounds; that meant six of his dead men and women had a chance at least of full regen – having new body tissue grown for them. A fresh company of strike troopers had arrived in the early evening to take the line, and now his men and women were heading back to the south to rearm and reequip. Fires still burned in the city center and columns of black smoke punctuated the otherwise hazy yellow atmosphere.

His still smoking carbine held in one hand and his helmet in the other, Tahl dragged his weary legs away from the departing transport drone and headed back toward the fountain where he had left his command squad and where Cane's arm had already been healed by the command medi-drone. Squad Denne walked past him on the other side of the rubble-strewn street, their squad leader giving a respectful nod as they passed.

"Great job today, Denne," Tahl said seriously as he recalled their stoic defense on the left flank near the fortunately one-sided drone engagement. "Go get some rest."

"Piece of piss, Boss! Easy!" Strike Leader Vias forced a smile, although the looks on the faces of his troopers told a different story.

Tahl arrived back at the fountain where Cane and Kachi sat patiently with the squad's medi-drone and spotter drone, the height difference between the two men almost comical.

"Boss," the pale-faced Cane shot to his feet, the jagged hole from the sniper shot still visible in his armor, "sorry about before. Rookie mistake. I should have been taking better cover."

"A few of us learned not to underestimate these people today," Tahl said gently, "first and foremost, me. Let's all just do our best from it and move on. Where's the senior?"

"Went that way, sir," Kachi gestured to a narrow street to the right of the square. "Said he saw something. Nothing for us to worry about."

"Wait here," Tahl said, making every attempt to keep his tone neutral as he picked up his pace to follow Kachi's directions. As soon as he was out of view, Tahl sprinted down the street and around a corner to see Van Noor stood motionless a few yan away, facing a building with a small fire burning in its doorway.

"Bry?"

Van Noor looked across at him with red eyes. He turned back to face the building – a toy shop – before bringing up his plasma carbine, smashing the window and stepping inside the burning building. Tahl dashed to catch him up and saw his old comrade pick up a stuffed bear before wandering out into the street again.

"I saw this," Van Noor said quietly. "Couldn't let the poor little thing burn."

Tahl activated his mental link to the shard and checked Van Noor's emotional state. He paced over to the older man and grabbed his arm, flipping open the battlesuit's readout panel to physically check the fluid levels rather than rely on the shard feedback. Van Noor's emergency bottle of pskenthesis - a drug that could be used to calm the operator's nerves in extreme conditions when the shard's external assistance was not enough – was completely empty. Tahl closed his eyes and let out a breath.

"Why didn't you tell me?" Tahl laid a hand on his friend's shoulder.

Van Noor looked up at him as tears rolled down his cheeks.

"I just want them back," his voice croaked. "I want my wife. I want my children. I didn't do anything wrong! I just want them back."

Tahl placed one arm around the older man's shoulders and walked him away from the burning toy shop.

"I'm sorry, Bry" he said quietly, "I'm so sorry."

The old soldier burst into tears and sobbed hysterically as he clung to him.

***

The Wardroom
Concord Warship, Aurora II

The small planks of wood, each about the size of a panhuman fingernail, hovered steadily in the air above the half completed model of the archaic sailing ship. Mandarin Owenne stood by the long, rectangular viewport which stretched across the luxurious cabin – befitting of his rank – his hands clasped at the small of his back as he stared out into the nothingness of deep space and concentrated on the complexities of the model ship on the table behind him. Utilizing his own nanosphere, he had surrounded the model ship and all of the individual wooden decking panels with nanobots and now used his superior control over his shard to mentally move each panel, one by one, into its exact place on the model. As each little wooden piece was laid down, he mentally commanded the nanobots to break down the molecular bond of its edges and then reform it, gluing the pieces firmly in place.

Outside his cabin, the destroyer, *Inceptor*, held position some five thousand yan off the *Aurora II*'s port quarter, her long range scanners conducting sweeps of her assigned sector to provide early warning of any approaching threat. A pair of fighters swept rapidly and silently past the viewscreen, yawing to the left to depart from the carrier and take position in a loose circuit around the task force to join the other fighters already established on Combat Defense Patrol. Owenne gently laid down another plank in the very center of the deck of his model ship, careful to calculate the spacing correctly to a fraction of a milliyan, otherwise the positioning of the main mast would later cause him problems.

"One assumes you have called this meeting to discuss the recent discovery in the Zolus system?"

The voice in his head, as clear as if he was being physically spoken to by a visitor in his spacious cabin, came from Mandarin Narik onboard the cruiser *Dependable*.

"One assumes correctly," Owenne replied. "I'd say a Ghar battlefleet is cause enough to consider changing our plans, wouldn't you?"

"The chances of sustaining significant naval losses in a direct fleet engagement exceed ninety quantum," declared Mandarin Luffe from her cabin onboard the cruiser *Agility*.

"Yes, I know," Owenne replied as he began work on the awkward deck panels which ran along the curved edges of his model. "Perhaps you forgot that instantaneous data transfer from the IMTel is an ability open to all of us. Not just you."

"Perhaps my esteemed colleague suffered from a momentary yet understandable lapse in awareness due to your seemingly complete inability to conduct yourself in the manner one expects from a Concord Mandarin?" Narik countered coolly.

"Balls!" Owenne declared. "I'll conduct myself in any manner I see fit, thank you very much! Now, onto the more pressing matter. Ghar battlefleet. Initial reports have their fleet centerd around two large capital ships. Thoughts?"

"Let them make planetfall," Luffe said softly. "Whilst Task Force 1312 could undoubtedly defeat them, the losses to our warships would be highly undesirable. We should engage them in a lengthy engagement upon the ground rather than a swift and costly confrontation in space."

"So losing Concord troopers on the ground is desirable?" Owenne snapped, emphasizing the last word.

"You know precisely what she means, Mandarin Owenne," Narik said calmly. "Casualties are inevitable. Our business is that of risk assessment, management, and mitigation. The Ghar are more vulnerable when drawn into a lengthy conflict rather than a swift encounter on their terms."

Owenne laid down the last deck panel, allowing himself a slight smile as a reward for his patience not only with the delicate model sailing vessel, but also his two NuHu colleagues.

"And we are all agreed on the Ghar's target?" Luffe added. "I would place the likelihood of a planetary assault upon Markov's Prize at ninety-two quantum."

"Explain your calculations," Narik demanded, his tone still polite.

"Isn't it obvious?" Owenne sighed. "Those nasty little bastards are after the jump gate in the Sen System! It's how we got here, it's safe, it leads straight to densely populated systems teeming with the panhuman life they live to eradicate! And if this band of Ghar wishes to properly exploit the gate, long term, they will need a base of operations, and that base of operations will require slave labor! Slave labor just like we're currently engaged in fighting with on Markov's Prize!"

"Whilst your language does you no credit, Mandarin Owenne, I do agree entirely with your assessment," Luffe said.

"Agreed," Narik said after a barely detectable pause. "Then we are content to allow a Ghar landing on Markov's Prize so that we may enter into a war of attrition and defeat them whilst avoiding a costly fleet encounter."

"And what of civilian casualties?" Luffe asked.

"Tragic, but unavoidable" Owenne replied. "You need to grasp the bigger picture. What we're all thinking but none of us are saying is that if we go head to head with these frightful buggers in some set piece naval encounter, we might actually lose. If Task Force 1312 is beaten back from that jump gate in Sen, we're not looking at a couple of billion people on one planet. We're looking at several densely populated systems. We risk Markov's Prize so as to protect the gate. To stop the Ghar from getting access to a real prize. Besides, we're not really looking at the entire population of the planet, only those near the Ghar landing site and subsequent engagements."

"You seem very preoccupied with this particular planet, Mandarin Owenne," Narik's voice seemed almost challenging in its tone. "Perhaps there is something else about this planet which marks it out from the many others whose jump gate leads to a vulnerable population of billions?"

"You know full well what my thoughts are," Owenne retorted.

"You believe Markov's Prize is Embryo?" Luffe asked. "How many more planets will you scour before..."

"As many as it takes!" Owenne snapped, slamming a fist into the desk in front of him. "As many as it takes. I shall head to Markov's Prize myself. I have an old friend there, one of the company commanders in the 44th Strike Formation. It will be a fitting reunion."

"Caution, Mandarin Owenne," Narik warned, "the primary role of the mandarin is to provide strategic guidance, not tactical leadership on the battlefield."

"Rubbish!" Owenne declared boldly. "It does the proverbial soul no end of good to get stuck in with the fisticuffs from time to time! You stay here in your nice, warm space boat. I'm off to get my hands dirty."

***

Rhona left her helmet on the dusty desk at the door of the improvised Company HQ building as she entered. Night had fallen and the sound of discharging weapons sporadically crackled from the city to the north as Concord troops fought small skirmishes with the planet's defenders in the rubble. The HQ building was formerly a venue for social gathering and drinking. The rooms upstairs were used for accommodation whilst the main bar downstairs had been converted into a planning room, with holographic projections of the surrounding area painting pale blue images near the long wall at the back of the building.

"Take your time, Kat, no rush," exhaled Strike Leader Yavn of Squad Teal.

Yavn sat around a long, rectangular table with the other strike leaders of the company – Vias, Heide, Althern, and Rall. Tahl and Van Noor were nowhere to be seen.

"The Boss ain't here, so I guess I ain't late," Rhona replied as she pulled up a chair, span it around and mounted it like a saddle, leaning forward as she planted her armored forearms on the chair's back.

"We were told to be here two minutes ago," Rall scowled, "so no, you are late."

None of the other squad leaders interjected – the silence spoke volumes to Rhona.

"I was checking on the members of my squad," Rhona replied. "I guess that takes me a little longer than it does for you these days, Feon."

Rall jumped to his feet.

"And just what the hell is that supposed to mean?"

"You know damn well what it means, boy," Rhona leaned forward and rested her chin in her hands. "How many good guys died today because you led them into some dumb death or glory charge against a larger enemy force? Our job was to hold the line, not invade the north half of the city! We dig in, we stop them coming. If you'd stuck to your damn job, then those boys and girls would be getting their heads down to sleep right now, instead of being packed in frozen nitrogen."

Althern was next to stand up, pointing an accusing finger at Rhona as his face twisted in fury.

"Just who the f…"

"That will do."

A slow, commanding voice brought the room to a halt as Tahl descended the staircase from the first floor. Rhona joined the other strike leaders in standing to attention as the company commander approached.

"It's been a long day," Tahl said, his normally calm voice betraying some annoyance, "it's been a long week. Come to think of it, this is our fourth planetary assault in immediate succession – it's been a long year for all of us. Do not lose sight of the aim and start fighting amongst yourselves like children. I expect more from my leaders. Much more. Clear?"

A chorus of mumbled responses of 'sir' were issued in affirmation.

"Take a seat, all of you," Tahl said, his tone still far from relaxed. "I won't keep you long. The latest update is that the assault has broken the back of the planetary defense force. Our greatest threat remains the isolated units of enemy armored vehicles, of which we believe are still concentrated some 20k to the north of the city. Alpha Company will hold the line for the next two days whilst we remain here on standby to plug any gaps at the front. We're expecting reinforcements in the morning — ten troopers."

"Any old hands, Boss, or all straight out of training?" asked Vias.

"They're all new, so give them the time and effort they deserve."

"I hate to be the one to bring it up," Heide said slowly, "but has there been any more talk of leave? None of us are working to rule here, but our people are well overdue a break from ops. Our troopers are tired. We're all making mistakes that we shouldn't be making. It's not a question of..."

Tahl held his hand up to silence the blond haired squad leader.

"I know what you're saying, Walen," his familiar, softer tone returned. "Nobody is accusing our soldiers of shirking or looking for an easy ride. The rules are in place to ensure our people give optimal performance on operations, but right now the resources are not available to relieve us, and consequently those rules governing our time on continuous ops have been broken. I fully acknowledge what you are saying about errors and mistakes, but it's out of my hands. I'll call the company together first thing in the morning and apologize myself, but right now we're stuck here and need to be ready in case Alpha Company needs us at the front. One more thing from me — I've sent Senior Strike Leader Van Noor to liaise with the Intelligence Cell, he'll be away for a couple of days. In the meantime, Ci Yavn will be acting as Senior Strike Leader. It's only for a couple of days, but please support him until Bry is back with us. Any other questions?"

Nobody spoke.

"That's all," Tahl said, waiting until everybody had stood up before adding a few more words. "Feon, Katya, wait behind."

Rhona watched as Yavn, Vias, Heide, and Althern filed over to the door, recovered their helmets, and then departed into the night back to their squads. Tahl gestured for Rall to follow him to the far end of the bar, where the two immediately began an animated conversation. Rhona watched, assessing their body language until Rall stared directly over at her, a clear indication to her that she was very much the subject of his words.

She turned away, touching the bandana around her forehead and sparing a moment to think of her father and little brother. Life had thrown her a series of challenges, and she had very little idea how she had ended up as a soldier, a Concord soldier at that, and now holding a position of authority. She sometimes envied the relative safety of her previous life, even if it had felt far from safe at the time.

Rall stormed past her, staring daggers at her silently until he recovered his helmet and barged out into the night, slamming the wooden door behind him. Tahl walked over to her before pulling up a chair and sitting down, gesturing for her to do the same. Again, she swiveled the chair around to sit with her knees either side of the chair back, leaning forward over it.

"You doing okay?" The strike captain asked.

"Just dandy, Boss," Rhona replied, risking a wink.

Tahl's face lit up with a brief smile.

"You know that feedback you get through the shard which lets you know how all of your troopers are doing? That little indication of what they're feeling and how they're coping? I get that same feedback through the command shard from my strike leaders. I get that feedback from you. You've got a lot of anger welling up there."

"Me?" Rhona exclaimed. "What about that idiot you were just talking to who killed half his guys today? At least I'm..."

"Proving my point for me?" Tahl offered.

Rhona swore and looked away for a second before meeting his gaze again, her dark locks falling down over one eye.

"Yeah, I guess."

"We spoke about you learning karampei," Tahl said. "Maybe it would do you some good."

Rhona recalled the conversation. At the end of the Prostock Campaign – the last planet they had assaulted – she had shared a brief conversation with Tahl, and in an ill advised moment, she had decided to ask him to teach her the martial art he had once been famous for using in full contact competition fighting.

"Yeah... I guess that might help."

"Well," Tahl stood again, "if you change your mind, the offer is there. But, whilst I've got you here for a few moments, there's something I need to talk to you about... you know what? Never mind, we can talk about it some other time. Go get some rest, we may well be in the thick of it again before long."

"Got it, Boss," Rhona shrugged, grabbing her helmet before heading out into the hot night to find her squad and get some overdue sleep.

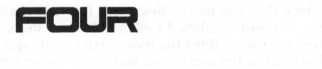

Firebase Alpha
Equatorial Region
Markov's Prize

L-Day plus 23

Rubbing his eyes and exhaling again, Sessetti planted his hands behind his head as he lay back on his bunk, staring up at where he had positioned the projection of his magazine on the ceiling of his alcove. It appeared to be the norm to leave alcoves open to the circular communal area; although even after two full days away from the frontline, Sessetti would still have appreciated some privacy. Firebase Alpha had grown exponentially since they had left for the last assault two weeks earlier; the site was now unrecognizable from the isolated beach they had attacked when Weste had been decapitated by an artillery shell.

Gant, Qan, and Clythe all sat on sofas in the communal area, attempting to kill each other on a holo-game which was projected into the center of the room between them. Rae sat on her bunk, reciting a letter to send back home; whilst Jemmel stretched out against her bunk in her own alcove, having just returned from a lengthy gym session. Ignoring the shouts of victory and despair which streamed from the trio of gamers in the communal area, Sessetti returned to his article on innovative musical compositions.

"Hey, Bo!" Rae called from her alcove. "I'm sending a letter to my brother. What kind of music is it that you play?"

"I dunno what you'd call it," Clythe replied as he stood up from the sofa, disconnecting from the game. "Lian? What do we play?"

"I don't like to give it a label," Sessetti shrugged.

"Don't be so pretentious!" Jemmel shook her head. "Just tell us what kind of music you play. Better still, play some and we'll decide."

"Now there's an idea," Qan grinned. "Come on, we've been a happy little family for a few weeks now. It's time we heard your tunes. Come on, put something on!"

"Promise we won't laugh!" Gant grinned.

"I don't," Jemmel gave a more sinister smile.

Clythe dashed enthusiastically across to his alcove and rummaged through his possessions to find his datapad.

"Leave it, Bo," Sessetti said, "these guys are just looking to take the piss."

"I'm not!" Rae exclaimed.

Clythe prodded a few buttons on his datapad, selecting a song which they had played live only a few times before leaving home to join the Concord Combined Command. 'Your Rose,' a song about Sessetti's first girlfriend, filled the room. Qan began tapping his feet and nodding his head as the percussion kicked in. Sessetti closed his eyes, inwardly cursing Clythe's naivety.

> *"The last time we met, you promised me forever,*
> *I never saw your face again, my pain still shows,*
> *You moved on from me so easily,*
> *You left me only with your rose…"*

Sessetti cringed at the lyrics he had penned, which seemed so deep and meaningful a year ago, but now sounded immature and contrived. It was made worse by hearing his own voice singing, something he never enjoyed. After a few minutes, the song ended.

"Well, that's ruined my entire day," Jemmel spat. "I really, really wanted you guys to be crap."

"Eh?" Clythe cocked his head to one side.

"This jackass," Jemmel nodded at Sessetti. "You can actually sing. You're wasted here. Sod off back home and get famous, you're upsetting me with your talent."

"What about me?" Clythe protested.

"He's the front man, you're an optional extra," Qan nodded sympathetically. "That's why he'll always get the first pick of the girls. And you, Jem – I resent your allegations of the rest of us being talentless. I can burp the entire alphabet."

"And I can fart it," Gant added seriously.

"To answer your original question," Sessetti turned back to Rae, "in a non pretentious manner, I'd describe our music as sonic visualization of emotional harmony."

Rae laughed.

"You tell jokes?" Jemmel raised her brow at Sessetti. "There's hope for you yet. I was thinking it'd be another year until we even had you speaking."

"He doesn't need to speak," Gant said. "You've got that covered for all of us, Jem."

"Somebody has to take charge of you guys," Jemmel shrugged, "especially since our illustrious leader isn't here. Again. Still, we've got her own, unique method of command to look forward to next time we're getting shot at."

To emphasize the point, Jemmel sucked in her stomach and pushed out her chest exaggeratedly, tilting her hips to one side and running one hand through imaginary locks of long hair.

"You boys better follow ma perfect ass into the fight," Jemmel gave a fair imitation of Rhona's distinctive accent, "because y'all got you here a born leader before yo very eyes! You hear?"

Gant erupted into laughter.

"What's your problem with Rhona?" Qan said seriously. "You two wanna spell it out, or shall I say it for you?"

"My problem is that she couldn't lead her own way out of a fix'n'tan cubicle, let alone lead a squad of strike troopers in a firefight," Gant narrowed his dark eyes.

"Is that why we haven't taken a single injury, let alone fatality, in this squad since she took over?" Qan folded his arms. "You're talking crap. Both of you. So here it is – Gant, you're jealous because she's got the job you think you deserve, and Jem, you're jealous because she's a lot better looking than you. That simple."

"If a guy is gonna judge me on what I look like, I don't really care about his opinion," Jemmel said.

"Qan, you've got some time served, but you haven't been doing this for as long as me and Jem," Gant said. "You haven't seen what happens when poor leadership takes hold of a squad. It's like a disease."

"I've been around long enough," Qan said. "I was there at Prostock and so were you. So was my buddy Varlton. He was in Rhona's squad when their Duke got hit by artillery and blown up. Three dead, one guy screaming with his legs blown off, and one serious casualty. Varlton loses the plot and panics. Rhona has already been blown out of the Duke by the explosion – she goes back in three times to recover her survivors, knowing the thing will blow up any second. She gets them all, gives a blood transfusion to the guy with no legs to stablize him, and then grabs Varl – her only combat capable guy – and runs back into the fight. So tell me, heroes, how would you have done that better?"

Gant sat down. Jemmel looked away.

"I... I'm fine with her," Rae admitted. "Don't you guys remember Rall? He lost half his squad last week. The guys say he was trying to get a medal. And us? We're all still here. I'm not complaining. I'm fine with her."

Sessetti sat up, considering his words carefully before speaking.

"She's trying her best. I have no idea what it takes to lead a squad, but I'm sure it's not easy. But I can't ask for anymore from her."

Jemmel nodded slowly.

"Okay, guys," she said, "okay. I'm sorry. I'm being a bitch. I'll... try to give her more of a chance."

Gant shook his head and remained silent. The silence lasted for several moments until Clythe spoke.

"And she's got massive boobs. You can even tell when she's in armor, and that's not easy to pull off. I'm told she's got a beautiful face, but to tell you the truth, I've never got that high."

Sessetti joined in with Qan as he laughed. Gant silently returned to his alcove whilst Rae stared at Clythe.

"Is there some way I can put in a complaint about you?" She said, her tone indicating to Sessetti that she was only half joking.

***

The C3T7 Duke shot smoothly across the purple waters as the midafternoon suns glinted and sparkled across the gentle waves, the foamy peaks breaking out in soothing shades of lilac. Van Noor leaned forward in his small seat, as far as his safety belt would allow, pressing his elbows down on his knees and idly tapping one clenched fist into an open palm. Returning to his company from several days with the formation intelligence cell, he had at least had some time to refresh; although the news he had learned whilst away was certainly disturbing. That was where the transport drone's other occupant came in.

Sat opposite from Van Noor was Mandarin Owenne. The New Humans, or NuHu, were the next stage in the evolution of the panhuman being. Tall, slender, hyper intelligent, and possessing a detached clarity of thought which very often led to the impression of callousness, the NuHus' connection with shards was so strong, that they could effortlessly control several dozen drones with but a mere thought, and even manipulate their own nanosphere to allow them to levitate.

Mandarin Owenne was not a typical NuHu. An individual who Van Noor had worked with in the past, Owenne was only a little over average height with thinning, off ginger hair which added only a little color in contrast to his pale skin. Whilst Owenne certainly possessed the intelligence one would expect from a NuHu, Van Noor had always found the man to be very different from the rest of his race.

News from Firebase Alpha was that the area was secure enough for barrack uniform to be worn instead of armor. This would no doubt be of some relief, as even with the most modern ergonomic design, battlesuits were fatiguing and also required careful maintenance which necessitated their removal and surrender to service drones. As a result, Van Noor wore the daily dress of a Concord trooper away from the frontlines – simple trousers and a shirt of olive green, with combat boots and his badges of rank on epaulettes on his shoulder. A black beret tucked into his left epaulette marked him out as a strike trooper. Owenne's dress was slightly more flamboyant, as was befitting his status of Mandarin – a long, double-breasted coat lined with white piping covered his green and white uniform.

The Duke began to slow as it approached the firebase. Van Noor briefly considered attempting conversation with the pale mandarin, but experience with Owenne dictated silence to be the better course of action. The transport drone turned onto the beach, came to a stop, and then gently sank down to come to rest on the sand before the doors slid open. Owenne's seat belt unbuckled and stowed itself without any physical interaction from his hands before he stood and clamped his hands behind his back, leaning forward and walking rapidly out of the drone with his pensive eyes staring down at the floor only a few paces ahead. Van Noor unbuckled and walked out into the sunshine, glad of the sweltering heat that still felt like a novelty after so many days of the sterile air conditioning of his battlesuit.

Firebase Alpha had changed. Lines of semi-opaque kinetic barricades, each standing head height, ran in a perimeter around the firebase, including off the beaches and out to sea. Whilst most of the base was built underground, there were still lines of shelters constructed out of locally acquired vegetation. Ranks of combat and transportation drones sat in neat rows along the tree line, where they were serviced and maintained by engineering drones and their own invisible nanospheres. A group of troopers had laid out a batterball court at one end of the beach and were noisily enjoying a game, whilst other smaller groups socialized along the beach or by the trees.

His hands still clasped behind his back, Owenne stomped purposefully up the beach and toward the wood and leaf huts. As with all NuHu, he could quite easily use his superior connection to his field of nanites to simply levitate instead of walking, but for some reason Owenne chose not to. Van Noor wondered briefly why he did not take the easier option of hovering from one place to the next; if it were any other mandarin, he would have guessed at it being out of manners, common courtesy to ensure that those who could not levitate did not feel patronized by the act. But not Owenne. From what little experience Van Noor had of the short, eccentric NuHu, Owenne had no such qualms.

Guessing at who Owenne was looking for, Van Noor followed him wordlessly, picking up his pace to keep up with the stone faced mandarin. Near the tree line, in the shelter of one of the huts, Rall was crouched over the tubular form of an x-launcher – a magnetically powered weapon used by strike trooper support units to lob explosive shells up into the skies to fall indirectly onto their foes. Tahl stood to one side and watched as Rall delivered refresher training on the weapon to his squad, including a few new faces who Van Noor had never seen. As they approached, Tahl looked across before his eyes opened wide, startled at the sight of the NuHu.

"Hello, Killer!" Owenne beamed, stopping a few paces short of the strike captain.

"Owenne," Tahl nodded a greeting, "it's been several years since I've heard that nickname. Hello, Bry, welcome back to the fold."

Van Noor moved forward to shake Tahl's hand warmly.

"Glad to be back, Boss," Van Noor said. "It's probably best the three of us go for a walk."

Tahl obliged, following Owenne and Van Noor along the tree line and away from Rall's squad.

"What brings you out here to a backwater little offensive like this?" Tahl turned to the mandarin as they walked.

"It might not be that backwater for long," the NuHu kept his eyes locked on the ground in front of him as he walked. "We may need to bolster this position. A Ghar battlefleet was detected in the Zolus system, and judging by what little data could be gathered, there is a chance it is heading this way."

Tahl's smile faded instantly.

"How likely is it they're heading to this planet, and what sort of size force would we be expecting to face?"

"The intelligence people think there's a better than even chance they're coming here," Van Noor added. "There's at least two capital ships, so we're looking at significant opposition if we are the target."

"Our entire assault is built around a single planetary assault force with mediocre support," Tahl exclaimed, folding his broad arms across his chest. "We can defeat a planetary defense force, but a Ghar battle group? Owenne, we'll be ripped to shreds! Half of my company has never even fought against a foe with modern equipment! What do they even want with this planet?"

"Don't panic, Killer!" Owenne flashed a sarcastic smile. "It's all under control! Reinforcements are already en route. I made sure of that. However, the state of this force and in particular this formation and, for that matter, this very company is of concern to me. Somebody hasn't been rotating their troops out of frontline assignments in accordance with C3 orders. Tut-tut indeed."

"I never knew you cared, Mandarin," Van Noor smiled.

"Do not confuse affectation with efficiency, Senior Strike Leader," Owenne waved a thin hand theatrically around his head as he spoke. "You standard panhumans can be somewhat... fragile. To operate at peak efficiency, one must acknowledge that adequate rest and relaxation is required. Gentlemen, you should not require me to lecture you on troop fatigue management."

Van Noor glanced across in an attempt to meet Tahl's gaze. The younger soldier stared impassively at the NuHu, his eyes narrowed.

"C3 has calculated every individual soldier's fatigue threshold," Owenne continued, a slight smile tugging at the corners of his thin lips. "If this threshold is exceeded, then a soldier enters the amber zone; reduced efficiency, but operations are tolerated in this zone in extremis. If this is left unchecked, a soldier enters the red zone. Massively reduced levels of arousal and efficiency, with poor judgment exercised on a daily basis. Not fit for combat. Gentlemen, seventy nine quantum of your men and women are running in the amber zone. Seventy nine quantum. Why has this been permitted to happen?"

Tahl looked across at Van Noor and held both of his palms out in defeat. Van Noor shrugged.

"I reported this up my chain of command," Tahl said. "We've been promised leave on several occasions. It has yet to materialize."

"So what, you just... carry on?" Owenne spat.

"Of course we carry on!" Tahl growled. "We've got a job to do! You expect these men and women to throw down their weapons and refuse to fight because they haven't had a good night out in a while? They're professional, they'll do the job to the best of their ability, to the bitter end! We haven't been given time off, so we carry on! It's what we do! We carry on!"

"Poor decision, Killer," Owenne remarked coolly, "but I would not expect any more from you. Because, old friend, your company has one soldier, in a position of authority I might add, who has been running red for over four months. Red! For four months! I think you know who this is."

Tahl let out a long sigh and turned away.

"I'm fine," he muttered.

"You think you are fine because you've lost the ability to assess yourself with any degree of accuracy," Owenne said, before turning to Van Noor. "And you, Senior, you should have been monitoring this. Your job as company second in command is to check above you in the chain as well as below. Just in case your strike captain were to do something ill advised such as, I don't know, activate a command override to mask his fatigue state from the paternal care of the C3."

Owenne turned to face Tahl, standing a little taller and straighter, but still not managing to bring his his eyes up to meet Tahl's.

"Strike Captain Tahl, effective immediately I am relieving you of command and sending you on leave. Two weeks, that's all. Best you go get it out of the way now, old chap. You never know when you might be needed. Go get some rest and then you can have your soldiers back."

"Two weeks?" Tahl exclaimed. "What the hell do you want me to do for two weeks?"

"I'd thoroughly recommend drinking alcoholic beverages until you can't stand up anymore," Owenne offered as he walked away along the beach. "Only custom I've trialed which makes absolutely perfect sense. See you in two weeks."

Tahl took his black beret from his head and ran his fingers through his brown hair. Van Noor watched the eccentric NuHu stomp off toward the accommodation block and shook his head.

"I'm sorry, Ryen," he offered. "I had no idea this was his plan when he said he was coming back with me."

"Never mind that," Tahl said after a brief pause. "How are you? I'm more concerned about how things were after I last saw you."

Van Noor folded his arms and bit his lip in contemplation. He, too, knew he was only days from being in the red with fatigue, even after a break from the frontlines, and it was seriously affecting his ability to deal with his problems back home. Not that it was his home anymore.

"I'm good, mate," Van Noor lied. "I just needed that little bit of time to straighten my head out."

"Don't lie to me, Bry," Tahl said seriously, "you owe it to yourself and the guys here who are depending on you. If you're not up to this, you need to flag it up."

"And do what?" Van Noor demanded, ignoring the irony of Tahl's advice given Owenne's accusations. "Go home to my wife and kids? Tell them that I never had the affair they say I did, because their real husband and father got his brains blown out by an Isorian sniper and now I'm here instead?"

"You're the same guy!" Tahl insisted. "Your memories up to a single point are real! And that affair happened after that point! It wasn't you!"

"It was in Becca's eyes," Van Noor sank down to sit on a felled tree trunk. "And even if it wasn't me, it still proves what I'm capable of."

"We're all capable of doing the wrong thing if we don't know any better," Tahl countered, "and now you know. You'd never do that. Not now."

Van Noor suppressed a yawn and looked up at the twin suns for a moment, taking a deep breath and pausing to listen to the waves cascading across the beach.

"You'd better get going," he said to Tahl, "you don't want another lecture from nano-man."

"We'll talk about this when I get back," Tahl said, replacing his beret.

"Have you told her yet?" Van Noor said.

Tahl looked down.

"Don't you think you'd better?"

Tahl nodded slowly. "I've tried a couple of times. I just haven't found the... I'll go do it now. See you in a couple of weeks."

***

With the fine sand between her toes and the system's two suns warming the side of her face, Rhona could have been on one of the idyllic family holidays she had read about as a child. With her boots and black beret in the sand next to her, she sat near the water's edge clad in her green trousers and shirt, a few qualification badges pinned above the left breast pocket and the red stripes of her rank on her epaulettes. Leaning forward against her knees, she looked down at the white datapad in her hands and thought through another letter to her brother.

"To be honest, Micha, I'm struggling. I don't like the military, I hate fighting, and I don't even get on with the people. Any of them. I'm watching decent guys and girls dying every few days – on both sides. Some of them I'm killing myself, and I hate it. I'm relying on shard assistance to stay sane and using up my battlesuit's emergency drugs faster than I should be just to keep depression at bay, and I miss home. I still miss Pa and it's been four years now. I'd do anything to just leave this all behind and come to hang out with you."

Of course, that would not do. Since she had lost her mother during her little brother's birth, she had always been the guardian and protector of Micha. That was her job as big sister. He did not need to hear the truth, it would only upset him and she wanted him to be happy, all the time. If she could not be happy, at least he could. And then there was that incident last time she visited him at college. He was only just talking to her again and any suggestion of another visit would be ill advised. She mentally deleted the entire message and started again, her thoughts appearing as words on the screen.

"Dear Micha,
How's the course going? I hope you're not studying too hard. I'm glad to hear you've got a good bunch of friends. Don't worry about that stupid girl you mentioned; by the time she realizes what she's missing, it'll be too late – you'll be with the right person. It's always the way, stupid girls go after the wrong guys until they grow up, and by then most of the good guys are taken. And trust me, Micha, you are one of the good guys.
Things are cool here, you should see this place! Sun, sea, and sand. We've got a batterball court, a gym, all sorts of stuff. It barely feels like a conflict. Don't worry about anything you see in the news, you know how people like to exaggerate. We're all fine here, only a few skirmishes now

and then, and I always seem to miss them!"

"Rhona?"

Rhona looked up and saw Tahl stood over her. She quickly scrambled to her feet and pulled her beret on, as regulations dictated. The brown haired man held one hand up.

"Don't worry about that," he said, but she continued and pulled her boots on regardless.

"What's up, sir?"

Tahl clasped his hands behind his back and looked down for a moment before meeting her gaze, but even then he looked away almost instantly.

"I need to talk to you. I've been meaning to talk to you about something for some time now."

Rhona folded her arms. She knew when a man was attracted to her. She had received this sort of attention for nearly ten years. The trick was not to be a bitch about it when the feelings were not reciprocated.

"I need to apologize," Tahl continued, "about your promotion. About the pressure I've put you under."

"Nah, it's cool," Rhona shrugged, "I've got this."

"You don't understand," Tahl winced. "When we need somebody promoting, C3 makes an assessment based on pure logic. A list of candidates for promotion is provided to the company commander, who then makes the decision. The decision has to be made by a panhuman as the whole point in us having our military shard is to give us that freedom of thought which civilians don't have. So we've got that tactical flexibility, and it's exactly the same with choosing who gets promoted – it's a panhuman choice. But it's very rare for a company commander not to pick the top name on the list, as the system doesn't really make mistakes."

"So... what?" Rhona asked in genuine confusion. "Where's this going?"

"The list had five names, in order of merit. You were fifth on the list."

"So why did you pick me over four better candidates?" Rhona asked.

Tahl opened his mouth to speak, but he looked away again and seemed to process a different line of though in his mind. The truth dawned before Tahl could manage to vocalize his thoughts. Rhona shook her head in genuine disappointment.

"I thought you were better than that, sir," she said, feeling a slight struggle to retain her calm composure. "You should be above using your rank and authority to try to score with good looking girls."

"It's not that!" Tahl closed his eyes in desperation. "I came here to apologize because I made a bad decision. I..."

"Well seeing that you and I had never even exchanged words before you promoted me, not once, I kinda draw the conclusion that you didn't promote me on my sparkling personality," Rhona said with deliberation as she planted both of her clenched fists on her hips.

"Yeah," Tahl admitted, "I promoted you because of the way you look. I'm sorry."

Rhona turned away and swore.

"Seriously? In this day and age? What were you expecting from me? You've put me in a position where my decisions affect whether people live or die. I'm the wrong person for the job, and for all I know, there's dead people who would be alive right now if you'd done your job properly and put the right guy in my shoes. What did you think you'd get out of this? That I'm the sort of woman who'd think 'yeah, cool! My commanding officer has promoted me so I might as well screw him!'? You've got a position of power and responsibility, and you abused it. You should be ashamed. Sir."

Tahl offered no resistance. Rhona unbuttoned her epaulettes and removed her rank slides, looking down at them pensively for a few moments before speaking again.

"I don't know where we go from here," Rhona said. "I'm not going to throw these at you like some petulant teenager. You've put me in this position, and now I have responsibilities to fulfill. You realize that this is grounds for a very serious complaint against you?"

"Yes, I do, and I wouldn't blame you. Or offer any defense."

"I'm not gonna do it," Rhona exhaled, "I'm not really the vengeful type and it wouldn't achieve anything. But if I'm honest, sir, I'd rather you kept your distance from me from now on."

Ignoring one final apology, Rhona slid her rank slides back on her shoulders and walked back toward the accommodation block.

***

As it always seemed, with her previous squad as well as the current one, the communal area of the accommodation rooms fell silent as Rhona entered. Gant, Qan, and Clythe sat playing holographically projected shooting games whilst Jemmel, Rae, and Sessetti lounged on their bunks in their respective cubicles. Rhona stopped just before her own cubicle and turned to face the others.

"We're going for a squad run," she declared. "Tomorrow morning, first thing. All of us together."

"Why?" Gant demanded, his back still facing her.

"Because every other squad is doing something every day to stay on top of core military skills, whilst we're doing nothing."

"Fair enough," Qan shrugged. "Sunrise suit you, Lead?"

Rhona paused suspiciously before answering.

"Yeah. Sunrise will do fine."

Rhona retreated to her cubicle and shut the sound proof partition behind her, throwing her beret on her bunk before using her mental connection to the shard to change the appearance of the room's walls, creating two false viewscreens which gave a simulated view of deep space. She sank down in one corner of the room, hugged one knee and stared out at the image of the stars which only an individual who had spent years in deep space could tell was false. She spent a few moments beginning to mentally process her exchange with Tahl before a light knock sounded against the partition.

"Yeah?"

The thin wall opened and Rae stepped through before closing it behind her again. Her battlesuit replaced with her olive green uniform, she appeared waif like and even vulnerable.

"You okay?" She asked, a little meekly.

"Yeah," Rhona replied, furrowing her brow to deliberately signal her confusion.

"I just...well... we don't see much of you. Just thought I'd say hello," Rae offered uncomfortably.

"Nah, I'm cool," Rhona said. "The thought is appreciated, though. Don't worry about me, I'm just happy in my own company."

"Yeah, me too," Rae said. "I guess we're a lot alike with that."

Rhona refrained from answering. In her opinion, she was nothing at all like Rae. They could both be very quiet women, but for very different reasons.

"Was life growing up outside the Concord very different?" Rae suddenly asked.

Rhona paused to contemplate the question. It seemed harmless enough. Rae perched at the end of Rhona's bunk.

"Yeah, it was different. A lot more dangerous, a lot more difficult, but in a lot of ways it was way more fun. Less sterile. It wasn't just this endless existence of comfort and fun that life in the Concord gives you, as a civilian at least. In the Determinate, life threw a lot more challenges."

"Well, life can be challenging in the Concord, too," Rae offered. "Before I joined C3, I had a fashion outlet with my brother. We designed clothes, evening wear mainly."

"Why?" Rhona asked. "There's no currency in the Concord, so why work for a living?"

"The number of people who wear your clothes still defines how successful your artistic pursuit is," Rae explained patiently. "So that's worthwhile. It gives a real feeling of accomplishment when you see your ideas being worn by a complete stranger, or your clothes getting a good review. But it's not easy. Lots of people want to do it, and even the drones which actually produce the clothes have enough knowledge to come up with designs of their own. It's hard to make a mark, creatively."

Rhona suppressed her initial thoughts.

"You got any pictures of your stuff?" She forced the conversation onward.

"Yeah," Rae sat down against the wall next to her and produced a small datapad from her pocket, using it to project a number of images in the center of the room which she proceeded to explain in some detail. Rhona feigned interest but could instantly see why the overly complex designs were not as popular as Rae would have liked. She still felt patronized by the other woman's belief that her life had been hard. She did not know hardship. Rhona waited for a pause in the conversation before changing subject.

"My mom died when I was seven," she said. "She died giving birth to my little brother. That could never have happened in the Concord. If I was raised as a Concord citizen, I'd still have my mom."

"I'm so sorry," Rae said sincerely. "I never knew, I didn't mean to…"

"I didn't mean to belittle your problems," Rhona lied, already feeling guilt for hijacking a perfectly innocent exchange with her burdens. "It doesn't matter now. I'm just sorry my brother could never know her. She was awesome, the best mom you could ever hope for."

"What does your dad do?" Rae asked.

"You ever see that old HV show, the one about the super cool smuggler who jets around the galaxy ripping off bad guys and screwing hot chicks in every episode?"

"Erm… Lone Rogue?"

"Yeah, that's it. My pa kinda thought he was the dude from that show. Even down to the bandana and flares. But pa was kinda dumb. He was a lovely guy and his heart was always in the right place, but he just wasn't half as smooth or half as clever as he thought he was. He made a lot of enemies out of a lot of dangerous people."

"I couldn't help but notice you used the past tense," Rae said quietly.

"Yeah," Rhona sighed, "we lost our pa, too. Pissed off one too many bad dudes. I had to take Micha and run. That's how I ended up in the Concord, I was on the run from the guys who killed my pa; but when I stop and think about it, there wasn't really any point as they didn't want anything from me and Micha. I don't know why I'm telling you all this."

"Sometimes it's good to get these things out, I guess?" Rae

offered. "I mean, I know we don't really know each other, but I think I'm maybe a better listener than any of those other guys through there."

"Yeah, maybe."

Rhona stopped talking. She already felt she had said enough. She hoped the silence would be obvious enough to encourage Rae to leave. Rae did not pick up on the hint.

"What did you do before you were a soldier?"

"I was a dancer," Rhona said, "in clubs. Both in the Determinate and for a year in the Concord."

"Like, ballroom?"

Rhona found herself laughing at that, genuinely. The few seconds of mirth were the best she had felt in weeks.

"No, not ballroom," she finally managed to smile at the red faced Rae. "I was a pole dancer and also did lap dancing."

"Why would you do that?" Rae blurted.

"Because... life outside the Concord ain't easy. It throws challenges at you. A couple of days after my eighteenth birthday, some crime lord and his boys come find me and explain how much money my pa owes them. They say they can either kill him or I can work off the debt. That's how I started dancing in bars. I did it for five years. Gave Micha another five years with his pa 'til even I couldn't keep them from killing him."

"I've got to stop asking you things," Rae sighed. "I'm so sorry. I'm so sorry your life has been so difficult."

"Hey, it wasn't all bad!" Rhona beamed. "Those five years were actually pretty cool at times. The girls in that bar were a real good bunch. We were as close as sisters. We all had a story behind how we got there and we all looked out for each other. And to tell you the truth, the pole dancing was kinda awesome. There's far worse ways to make a buck. After the first few weeks, I got into it. I was damn good at it."

"You think you'll go back to it after you're discharged from C3?" Rae asked.

"I dunno," Rhona yawned. "Look, I'm gonna go get some sleep. Thanks for the talk."

"That's alright," Rae stood up and backed off toward the partition. "Night, then."

Rhona waited until she had left before kicking off her boots and sinking down onto her bunk, switching off the lights with a quick thought command to leave her small room lit only by the stars. It took her a long time to fall asleep.

FIVE

"Formation Commander!" Van Noor bellowed as he snapped to attention at the doorway of the briefing auditorium.

The assembled strike troopers immediately stood, bringing their heels together as an absolute silence replaced the idle conversation which had echoed around the pale blue walls moments before. Strike Commander Orless, the formation's commanding officer, walked past him at the door, nodding a brief acknowledgement of the mark of respect for his rank. Tall, slim, with greying temples and hawkish features, Orless was a man of considerable combat experience. Two paces behind walked Mandarin Owenne, his pale features even more prominent in the stark auditorium lighting. The two senior officers stood at the front of the auditorium, where a stage and lectern were ready for the briefing.

"Take a seat," Orless instructed the assembled troopers.

The veteran commander cast his eyes around the assembled troopers. Three men on the back row briefly exchanged a joke as they sat; their smiles were instantly replaced by anxious expressions as Orless shot a withering state in their direction. Van Noor knew Tahl's reputation – the troopers knew he had killed men with his bare hands in the most dangerous fighting competition in the Antarean space. The ill-conceived logic, therefore, was that Tahl should be feared even by his own troopers. In actual fact, Van Noor found him to be quite the opposite – too warm, too caring, and often failing to produce results as a consequence. Orless was the exact opposite. Van Noor, even with his decades of experience, regularly found himself modeling his behavior and interactions on the cold-faced strike commander.

"I shall be quick, as I have to get around all six companies of the formation," Orless began. "First and foremost, congratulations on a job well done here on Markov's Prize. The government officially capitulated two hours ago. With most of the planet's defenses lowered, the majority of the population has now been integrated and are Concord citizens who you can depend on for support. However, several regions have refused to acknowledge the surrender signal and remain hostile. And whilst we've decoded most of their cloaking technology, they still have something in place which is preventing the IMTel from encompassing the entire planet. This is unfortunately not our main concern. Several days ago, one of our frigates detected a Ghar battlefleet in an adjoining system."

The pale, opaque image of the closest three planetary systems was projected at the front of the briefing room. It expanded to zoom in on the relevant area and highlight the position of the Ghar fleet as Orless continued.

"We have been tracking this fleet and it is now clear that it is heading for this system, and specifically this planet. For those of you who have not faced the Ghar before – and I'm aware that's most of you – this will be a very different way of waging war than you are used to. There is no need for undue concern – the Ghar form a relatively small empire and are of no great threat to the Concord. We will win, but my concern is doing so quickly, efficiently, and with minimal loss of life – both military and civilian. I'm confident that in Strike Captain Tahl's brief absence, your preparations are in the very best of hands with Senior Strike Leader Van Noor and Mandarin Owenne. I'll hand you over – if you are content, Mandarin?"

Owenne gave a slow and measured nod of the head to signal his approval for Orless to leave, before gesturing to the lectern. Van Noor took that as his cue and walked over to stand to one side of the briefing area.

"Ladies, gents," he began, "let's take a look at what we'll be facing."

Mentally activating the first animation in the intelligence brief, Van Noor glanced down at a holographic projection of a Ghar as it shimmered into life on the center of the wide podium at the front of the auditorium. The hairless creature stood a little over half the height of a panhuman, with orange-yellow tinted skin, and a hunched back. Large, red-rimmed, reptilian eyes dominated a face with a small, snout-like nose and a row of tiny, sharp teeth. The animated Ghar slowly moved its head, glancing around the room at the seated troopers. Van Noor expanded on the detail for the assembled soldiers.

"The Ghar is a panhuman morph, most likely genetically engineered by some civilization many thousands of years ago to act as an expendable soldier. Unfortunately, they've spent the last couple of millennia establishing their own empire, and it's now clear that the central aspect of their culture is an absolute hatred of anything alien to them, including us. The Ghar have no interest in cultural advancement, art, anything beyond waging war. He's chest high to us, and not as strong or as intelligent, but don't let the looks fool you. What's that movie, the fantasy one with the bad special effects and hot girls in very ineffectual armor?"

"*The Warlock* trilogy, Senior," a voice called out from the left of the auditorium.

"Yeah, that's it," Van Noor continued. "Anyway, these guys look like the bad guys from *Warlock*, but they couldn't be any more different. They have the ability to think tactically and they're relatively well led. Give them a weapon and they can shoot as straight as any Concord trooper."

Van Noor activated the next animation, and the Ghar was now clothed in a few scraps of lightweight armor and carried a long barreled automatic weapon.

"If you meet them in this form, your Ghar adversary is most likely to be equipped with a primitive assault rifle which uses a simple chemical reaction to propel solid projectiles at a relatively high rate of fire. This weapon, which the Ghar call a lugger, is very similar to the crude weapons used by most panhuman civilizations in the early days of firearms. But as I said, that's if you meet them in this form. This cheeky little fella you see here is an Outcast; that is, he is a disgraced Ghar who is sent into battle with just a lugger to act as cannon fodder for the main force and to draw your fire. He's probably not even done anything wrong himself – Ghar society is completely militaristic, and if a commanding officer is judged to have made a mistake, not only is he disgraced as an Outcast, but so is his entire unit."

"Squad Teal would be screwed then!" A voice shouted out cheerily from the back of the auditorium.

"Piss off!" Strike Leader Yavn grinned from the front row.

Van Noor suppressed a laugh and continued, knowing the high morale in the auditorium would be short lived.

"If one of you goes head to head with one of them, you're probably going to win," Van Noor said, "but then again you've got your battlesuit, which is sort of cheating, really. Your weapons and armor are at least twice as effective as theirs, and underneath that armor, you are twice the soldier he is. But that's the problem. You see, the Ghar are happy to cheat, too. They've got their own armor."

Van Noor activated the next animation. Audible intakes of breath, gasps, and exclamations were muttered. The Ghar Outcast was replaced with a suit of Ghar battle armor; a metal sphere atop three angular legs, with one clawed arm bolted onto one side and a large gun on the other. The broad, metallic war machine stood at nearly twice the height of an average panhuman. As if to emphasize the fear it was designed to cause, the head like sensor array on the front of the body turned to scan the audience whilst machinery inside the body clunked and whirred.

"This is what they use for armor. A single Ghar warrior is curled up inside the guts of this thing, plugged straight into the operating system by cables which attach directly to the spinal cord. The armored shell is made up of several layers of metal alloy and reinforced by a magnetic resonance shield. The gun is a multi-barreled plasma weapon, built around a central barrel capable of firing disruptor shells. This weapon's rate of fire is notably higher than a plasma carbine and has greater armor penetration capabilities. The entire suit and weapon is powered by a plasma reactor at the rear of the unit. It's all very low levels of technology, so the specialist measures we have for dealing with enemy technology simply won't work – this stuff just isn't modern enough for subverter matrixes or anything for scrambling circuits."

The room was completely silent. Van Noor could feel the fear filtering through the shard connection from troopers up to their squad leaders, and then up to him.

"How good is their armor, Senior?" Strike Leader Vias asked.

Owenne stood up from his seat on the front row and turned to face Vias.

"Post battle analysis carried out by the C3 Intelligence Shard indicates that accurate fire from a squad of five strike troopers will yield somewhere between a twenty five and thirty quantum chance of disabling a Ghar battlesuit."

"Five of us blasting away gives a less than even chance of disabling one of them?" Vias exclaimed. "Meanwhile, they're shooting back at us with a higher rate of fire and a greater chance of getting through our armor..."

"*Far* greater chance of getting through your armor," Owenne held up a corrective finger. "No no, you do not want to engage these bastards in a straight firefight under any circumstances."

"So what, we close with them and take them down in hand-to-hand combat?" Strike Leader Heide asked.

"Good gosh, no! You see that claw on the other arm? There's plenty of statistical data to suggest that this is almost as effective as the gun! No, one of these things will cut you in half with absolutely minimal effort! If a squad were to get lucky with five or six plasma grenades, you might take one down, but remember, these bastards tend to operate in groups of three to five," Owenne changed the animation on the podium so that three of the lumbering killing machines appeared next to each other, causing clear panic amongst the assembled troopers. "So you probably won't even be able to gang up on them. Nope, shooting or fisticuffs, these nasty fellows will take you down."

"So what the hell do we do, sir?" Heide demanded.

Owenne's features screwed up in confusion. Van Noor switched off the animations and stepped up to the center of the podium.

"The Ghar have weaknesses," he explained, "and plenty of them. Their reactors are crude and prone to failure. When they do fail, they can often go off with enough force to blow up the rest of their squad. Their suits are slow and clumsy; they really struggle in rough terrain. They're too large and bulky for any attempt at stealth, and their lack of flexibility makes it impossible for them to take cover whilst advancing. The gun, whilst powerful, doesn't have the effective range of our weapons. Don't worry, guys, these sods have got plenty of weaknesses for us to exploit. The main thing to take away from this brief is not to get caught in the open, and keep your distance. Don't engage them in a straight firefight, and above all, don't get anywhere near one of those damn claws. Also remember: these suits of theirs are horrifically over-engineered, way past their levels of technology. Their maintenance staff is barely able to keep these things ticking over; the longer a campaign lasts, the more they suffer from mechanical breakdowns and a lack of spares due to poor logistical planning. The longer a campaign goes, the more of those little runty Outcasts you'll see, and less of the battlesuits."

A few more murmurs echoed around the auditorium, the tone seeming a little more optimistic. Even the shard feedback was a little more uplifting. Owenne clamped his hands behind his back and began pacing along the front row of seats as he began to talk again.

"But remember, people, that's just the standard battlesuit. They've also got a variant specially equipped to be even more unstoppable in close assault, and a heavy weapon variant. Observe."

Another animation sequence began as Ghar assault and bomber suits faded into life on the podium. Van Noor felt spirits deflating around him as he pressed one palm against his forehead and took in a long breath.

***

A single room was one of the best perks of holding the rank of senior strike leader, in Van Noor's opinion. Sure, modern technology gave a soldier some real privacy and opportunity to rest and recuperate compared to the days of old, but even in that soundproof booth, one still knew that the rest of the squad was only on the other side of a thin wall. Van Noor sat back in the chair behind his thin, grey desk and looked at the picture frame propped up neatly to the left of his datapad.

The image showed Van Noor with his son, Jabe, sat on his shoulders as the family wandered around an animal park not far from their family home. Van Noor allowed himself a smile; they had such grand plans for Jabe's fourth birthday, but the little boy just wanted to do the same thing they often did – a family visit to that same park to feed the same animals. That image had been captured a year ago to the day, and only a few days before Van Noor's leave had expired and he had his consciousness uploaded to his clone before returning to the frontline.

And that was how it happened. The norm was to go to a mental coding facility, lie down on a bunk, and allow the medics to knock you out. You awoke seemingly only a few seconds later to be informed that your memories had been successfully stored. But not this time. Shortly after Jabe's fourth birthday, Van Noor awoke to find he was a clone. The original was dead, decapitated by a sniper some nine months after the memory upload. Nine months of complete unknown, during which he apparently had a ludicrous one night stand with an events manager on an entertainment ship, promptly confessed to his wife, and lost his entire family in one fell swoop. And here he was now, on his son's fifth birthday, preparing the company for all-out war against the most aggressive and merciless foe he had ever faced.

"Visitor – Strike Leader Feon Rall," the soft, feminine tone of the dormitory shard informed him.

"Admit," Van Noor answered, standing up and rubbing his eyes.

The door slid open and Rall walked smartly in, standing to attention before his desk.

"Good evening, Senior," he greeted.

"The formality is appreciated, Feon, but don't stand on ceremony. Pull up a chair."

The tall trooper sat down opposite Van Noor as he too returned to his chair. Rall looked up and frowned for a second.

"Are you alright, Senior?"

"Yeah, I'm good. Just a bit going on right now. Thanks for coming across, I'm speaking to all of the strike leaders individually just to make sure all is okay and there aren't any undue concerns to the change in operations we'll shortly be experiencing. Are your guys good, all things considered?"

Rall took in a long breath and then exhaled slowly, nodding.

"Yes, they're fine. It came as a bit of a shock that the Markov's Prize government just put their hands up and their weapons down. No last ditch defense of the capital, no climactic battle, nothing. I thought we were still in those early stages of flirting with each other and the proper battle hadn't begun yet."

"We hit them hard in the pre-invasion strikes," Van Noor explained. "Navy aerospace caught most of their armored vehicles and air power before they were ready. With no real support and suffering an attrition rate of ten losses for every one of ours, they were never going to last long. However, I've got my own thoughts. I reckon there's a fair chance our side bombarded them with images and data from previous Ghar invasions which may have convinced them that accepting us as conquerors is infinitely more pleasant than the Ghar."

"True," Rall agreed, "but if we had so much aerospace supremacy from the flyboys, why aren't we sending a carrier battlegroup into the Ghar invasion fleet to blow it up in deep space before it even gets here?"

"I think you already know the answer to that one," Van Noor smiled grimly. "The navy did the pre-invasion thing for us and then disappeared. Needed elsewhere, and it looked like this invasion was in the bag before we knew of the Ghar being just up the road. Sure, C3 could possibly bring the carrier battlegroup back, but think of the risk. It's far easier to replace a dead assault force than it is a carrier. I'm not saying we're expendable, just that we've got to be realistic. We're easier to replace if things go wrong."

"Yeah, yeah," Rall nodded. "We all know how the game works, gotta accept it for what it is. So what can I do to help, Senior?"

"You're one of only two strike leaders in the company who has firsthand experience of facing the Ghar. I'm going to be leaning on you and Althern quite heavily over the next few days. We need to work hard to keep our people alert, prepared, and confident."

"Confident, especially," Rall said. "I don't think the mandarin's little injections at your intelligence brief did anybody any favors. 'And remember people! Be prepared for a significant rise in your casualty rates! Up 'til now you've had it easy, now you'll really start to see some losses!' Wasn't very inspiring."

Van Noor laughed briefly at Rall's humorously accurate impersonation of Owenne.

"The thing about NuHu," Van Noor said, leaning back in his chair, "is that they are fully aware of what morale is and how important it is to us basic panhumans, but that doesn't mean they actually understand what morale is. The NuHu aren't really known for their... ability to relate to normal people. But the sad thing is, the guy's right. We're gonna take some hits and we need to be ready for that. But the thing that really has me thinking..."

"Visitor – Strike Leader Katya Rhona," the soft voice of the shard alerted both men.

Van Noor was glad of the interruption. It would not do for him to voice his concerns over Mandarin Owenne's motivations in front of his subordinates, no matter how much he trusted them. Something just did not add up. Markov's Prize was only of moderate strategic value – the loss of the jump gate and with it a path to billions of massacred and enslaved civilians would be tragic, but it would not change anything about the ongoing wars – yet the Mandarin was bringing in reinforcements from far and wide, soldiers and machines which could be employed elsewhere. Owenne wanted Markov's Prize, badly.

"We'll be ready, Senior," Rall said as he stood, "and you can count on me when the bombs start falling."

"That's all I ask," Van Noor smiled. "Send Rhona in, would you?"

Van Noor watched Rall leave his quarters, taking advantage of the short lull in between meetings to pick up his picture frame and select another image – one of him with both Jabe and Alora, his daughter. She would be seven and a half by now.

"Senior."

Van Noor looked up as Rhona walked casually in and halted in front of his desk, one hand clasped over the other in front of her as she flexed her knees slightly and looked at him expectantly.

"Grab a seat," he said, replacing the picture frame on the desk.

"Can I talk to you 'bout something?"

Van Noor looked up. Perhaps it was the frustration of being separated from his son on such a special day, but he found himself having to pause before responding, taking a second to control his rising anger.

"Well, it was me who called you here, but go on, what is it?"

"I spoke to Strike Captain Tahl before he left," Rhona said, "about my promotion."

"Right?"

"You knew about why I was promoted?" The black haired woman asked.

"You're questioning me about what, precisely, Strike Leader?" Van Noor snapped.

"No, no, nothing like that, Senior. I was just wondering if I needed to tell you the whole story or if you already knew. That's all."

"I knew," Van Noor leaned back and folded his arms.

"Well..." Rhona exhaled uncomfortably. "I expressed my disappointment. My discomfort over the whole thing. I told Strike Captain Tahl that I could submit an official complaint over..."

"You did *what*?" Van Noor demanded.

"No, no, I'm not doing anything," Rhona held her hands up in protest. "I'm just saying that I spoke to him about my right to complain..."

"Stand up," Van Noor ordered Rhona curtly.

"Senior?"

"Get on your damn feet, Trooper!" Van Noor yelled from the bottom of his lungs.

Her eyes wide in fear, Rhona leapt to her feet with enough force to knock her chair over, bringing herself smartly to attention.

"Who the hell do you think you are?" Van Noor hurtled around the desk to stand by her side, shoving his face aggressively into hers. "Sauntering into my damn office and casually dropping into conversation that you're threatening your commanding officer?"

"I..."

"Shut up! I'll let you know when you've got a speaking part!"

"Yes, Senior!" Rhona stammered.

"What's running red? Well? Answer me!" Van Noor boomed.

"A condition of physical and mental fatigue considered by C3 to be when a soldier is no longer able to be relied upon to carry out rational acts and reasonable decisions, Senior!" Rhona recited, her tone betraying her fear.

"Did the strike captain touch you?" Van Noor demanded.

"No, Senior!"

"Did he proposition you?"

"No, Senior!"

"Did he act in any way which could be considered inappropriate in the eyes of the C3 Code of Military Conduct?!" Van Noor screamed.

"No, Senior!" Rhona screwed her eyes up tightly as the interrogation continued.

"Your commanding officer was running red as a result of utter dedication to his duty! Over a year of frontline combat duties without a break of more than two days! You have no idea what that is like, no idea! None! And you dare to come strolling in here and judge that man? Who the hell do you think you are?! What does the C3 Code of Military Conduct say about errors and mistakes committed whilst running red?"

"Errors and mistakes are part of being panhuman!" Rhona recited. "Panhumans are far more susceptible to making errors whilst fatigued or stressed! Running amber or red is to be considered justifiable mitigation for minor transgressions and, in the case of major transgressions or offenses, will still be taken into account as potential defense in the event of..."

Van Noor held up a hand to silence her. He had to admit to himself that he was impressed with her ability to connect with the shard and instantaneously filter through reams of rules and regulations to recite policy whilst under pressure. He had never seen that done before by anybody other than a NuHu.

"I'm here to make sure this company is ready for war with one of the most dangerous forces mankind has ever faced," Van Noor seethed through gritted teeth. "Not to talk utter nonsense about the sort of crap I'd expect to see in a teen romance movie. The man made a mistake. One mistake. And he came to you to be open, honest, and apologize. If you ever talk disrespectfully about your commanding officer again, you won't have to fear the Ghar. The Ghar are nothing next to me when I'm angry. Understand, Trooper?"

"Yes, Senior!" Van Noor was finally rewarded for his shouting with the first signs of tears in her eyes.

"That's all. Get out."

***

"The trick," Gant explained as he ran the diagnostic scanner over one of his battlesuit arm plates, "is to hit the most obvious areas. The maintenance droids are bloody good, but they're programmed to really emphasize the difficult to see areas. The couple of times I've found a fault they've missed have been right in the center of a plate, not down in the joints."

Sessetti and Clythe sat either side of Gant on the floor of their communal area, their battlesuits spread out into component parts around them as they picked up part after part to double check the servicing had been carried out properly: not a mandatory check but something which Gant assured them was well worth taking the time to do.

"You think our suits will stop one of these Ghar bomb guns?" Clythe asked, a little fear evident in his tone.

"I think the senior hit the facts square in the face," Gant replied. "Don't go near 'em, don't get in the way of 'em. Stay well back and blast 'em."

The door to the communal area slid open and Rhona walked rapidly across to her cubicle, her face pale and her eyes red. Sessetti watched as she sank down to the floor next to her bunk and ran her fingers through her hair.

"You okay?" He called out.

She nodded without looking over.

Sessetti stood up and walked slowly over to her. "What's happening?"

"I haven't got time for this," Gant sighed, standing and walking toward the door. "I'll catch you punks later."

"It's nothing," Rhona whispered, "just had a chat with the senior, that's all."

Gant stopped dead in his tracks and then turned to face Rhona. "You just got Van Gnawed?"

Rhona nodded.

"Aw, hell," Gant's features softened as he walked into her cubicle and sank down next to her, putting an arm around her shoulders.

"I'm fine," Rhona managed slowly. "I'm not crying."

"Doesn't matter if you do," Gant said softly, "I've known plenty of guys reduced to tears by him. No shame in it."

Rhona stared rigidly ahead, tears welling in her eyes. Clythe looked awkwardly across at Sessetti. The doors slid open as Jemmel walked in, taking her beret off and tossing it with unerring accuracy across the communal area to land on her bunk before she threw both fists in the air in celebration.

"What's up with combat fashion accessory?" She asked as her eyes fell on Rhona. "You break a nail or something?"

"Van Noor," Gant winced up at her.

Jemmel's smile faded.

"Oh, hell. Nobody deserves that. Alright, Katya, let me get you a drink and you tell us all about it. You're with friends now, girl."

Rhona wiped her eyes and took a few deep breaths before composing herself enough to form a longer sentence.

"Should we forgive every mistake?" She finally managed. "Is it always okay to screw up?"

"Depends on why the mistake happened," Gant offered.

"And who made it," Jemmel handed Rhona a glass of water and sat on the edge of her bunk. "Some people are just pricks. What mistake did you make?"

"I... I don't think I did," Rhona said quietly. "I don't understand what just happened. We were talking and then I was stood to attention with him right in my face, screaming at me. I don't know what just happened."

"If I order you to die, you will damn well die - did he give you that line?" Jemmel asked.

Rhona shook her head.

"He can't have been that mad then. I've had that one. Twice."

"I knew a guy who made a mistake once," Gant started.

"It was you, wasn't it?" Jemmel asked.

"No, no. Let's call him... Grant."

"So it was you," Jemmel confirmed.

"So, Grant was on his final live fire exercise of training," Gant continued regardless. "His squad's Duke pulls up and the boys and girls all run out, bombs going off everywhere. In his haste to do a good job, Grant trips up and drops his plasma lance. The poor guy..."

"You," Jemmel interrupted.

"...the poor guy picks up his plasma lance but somehow ends up with it facing the wrong way. In his panic to turn it around, he hits the trigger with his thumb and manages to fire his plasma lance under his own arm and into the Duke behind him."

"How the hell did you fire a gun under your own arm?" Jemmel exclaimed.

"Fortunately, only superficial damage was done, but poor old Grant was now under the spotlight. Anyway, they made him re-do his entire final term of strike trooper advanced training. Now, that sounds like a punishment, but if you think about it, the chain of command has got to make sure this guy is fit for combat, because if he isn't ready, they've got to get him ready before it's for real. Where was I going with this? It's like the big book of C3 telling people off says."

"C3 Code of Military Conduct," Sessetti corrected him.

"Yeah, thanks Mandarin Lian," Gant snapped. "Anyway, point is that we all screw up. The conduct code book says we should be judged on a case by case basis. There's no right or wrong answer, but I think we should always try to look for the best in people. People aren't genuinely bad."

Jemmel wiped an imaginary tear from one eye.

"That was... beautiful," she whispered.

"Piss off. I'm trying to help here."

Rhona raised herself to her feet and nodded.

"It's alright. I'm alright. Thanks for the talk, guys, but I'm cool. Look, I'm gonna go get some fresh air. I'll catch you later. Thanks again, really," she said before leaving.

A few moments passed before Jemmel spoke.

"You did well there, 'Grant', you got your arm around her and everything. Good eye for exploiting the vulnerable woman."

"Shut up, Jem, she's not my type," Gant said as he wandered over to his cubicle and swung himself up to lie across his bunk. "Even a bastard like me is capable of trying to be a good guy once in a while."

#

Station RL503
Central Eastern Border
Concord Space

Another small group of Concord traders materialized on the transmat pads, their luggage fading into view next to them a moment later. Tahl watched as the four merchants in their brightly colored clothes gathered their belongings and then walked toward the terminal stores, talking excitedly as they walked. He sometimes envied their existence – moving from one world and one civilization to the next, seeing new things and meeting new people, but all without any threat of violence. Sat alone at a circular table in the window of one of the terminal bars, Tahl watched the comings and goings of civilian life as he waited for the next connection in his journey.

The cavernous space station was relatively quiet, which was to be expected in this area of Antarean space. Situated next to an Antarean Gate, the station sat on what was once a prime trade route. But now that the Concord had advanced eastward and taken over this region, there was no exchange of currency; and therefore very little trade resulted in the once thriving station now seeming vacuous and lifeless. Lines of what had once been shops were now simple restore points where travellers could take what they wanted, just so long as they were plugged into the Concord shard. Even the bar, which could happily have catered for a hundred patrons, now provided drinks for only Tahl and four small groups of traders.

Nearly halfway through his journey, Tahl was a little behind schedule and beginning to feel slightly concerned that he would be late returning to his unit. Given that his direction from Mandarin Owenne was to find a system just behind the frontline and relax, and he was now three days gate-jumping away, he knew he was setting himself up for trouble. He had at least taken the time to maximize on sleep, meditation, and practicing his kerempai forms. The opportunity to take several days away rarely presented itself, and he intended to put it to good use. The initial plan was to try to get all the way home and visit his mother, but after a day of travel, another idea had materialized and, as much as he wanted to do the right thing by his mother, there were other responsibilities he felt he had to address.

"Excuse me, sir?"

Tahl looked up.

Two young soldiers stood by his table, both wearing the crimson beret of the 3rd Drop Formation. An elite unit trained to use anti-gravity chutes for surgical strikes ahead of a main Concord assault force, the drop troopers were never short of volunteers to join their ranks, but few made the required grade.

"I couldn't help but notice your badge," the shorter of the two troopers pointed to the Anti-Grav Qualification Badge above the left breast pocket of Tahl's uniform. "Which unit were you with?"

Tahl smiled slightly as he saw the devil's head badge on the trooper's sleeve.

"3rd Drop Formation," Tahl replied. "Devil's Own."

Both men grinned broadly.

"You've got to come and have a drink with us, sir," the taller man said enthusiastically. "Once one of us, always one of us. We're just on a quick stop off on the way to the front. It would be great if you'd join us."

Tahl checked the time.

"Certainly," he replied, standing and grabbing his kit bag. "Very polite of you. Thank you."

The two drop troopers led Tahl down the station's main trading promenade toward another bar at an adjoining terminal.

"Where are you headed?" Tahl asked as they walked, threading their way through a growing number of traders and soldiers.

"Place called Markov's Prize," the short trooper said. "Ghar inbound, we're told."

"I've just come from there," Tahl replied. "At least the place is sunny."

"Who was in the formation when you were in?" The trooper asked. "There might be some familiar faces still with us."

"I doubt it," Tahl replied hopefully. "I left eight years ago."

"Eight years... Do you know Zhen Davi?"

Tahl felt a gnaw in his gut at the mention of the name.

"Yes, I knew Davi."

"He's our senior drop leader now, he's around here somewhere."

The trio turned a corner in the terminal to find another bar, crammed with some fifty drop troopers around tables seemingly fortified with their kit bags. Tahl's eyes immediately picked out Davi. The short man sat with three drop leaders, engaged in an animated conversation. Tahl winced as memories came flooding back. He regretted so much about that part of his life, so many mistakes and so many things he wished he could take back. Davi had been a quiet, earnest, and hardworking drop trooper. An easy target for a violent bully like Drop Trooper Tahl.

"Senior!" One of Tahl's escorting troopers hailed Davi as they drew near. "Look who I found!"

Davi looked up and his rounded features turned to stone. He muttered an apology to his comrades before slowly standing and walking out to meet Tahl.

"Hello, sir," he said coolly, "it's been a while."

"Don't worry about the 'sir'," Tahl risked a slight smile. "It's good to see you again, Zhen. It's been too long."

Davi folded his powerful arms.

"I'll stick with the correct marks of respect for your rank, sir, given the present company," he nodded to the drop troopers who flanked Tahl.

"Of course," Tahl said, "my apologies. Your guys say you're heading to Markov's Prize. We'll do far better with the formation looking out for us."

"It's what we do, if you remember," Davi said. "We look after our own."

"Could you give us a moment, please?" Tahl said to the two troopers who had found him.

Both men walked away quickly, leaving Davi and Tahl alone at the edge of the drop company.

"I owe you an apology, Zhen," Tahl said. "I was a terrible guy to work with back then and..."

"I wondered if this day would come around," Davi interrupted. "It's been nearly a decade and yet still there's things which remind me of you from time to time and leave me wondering why you went to such utterly extraordinary lengths to make me feel like a worthless piece of crap."

Tahl nodded, searching for some words which might put across the sincerity of his apology. He tried to look up to meet Davi's accusatory stare but failed and looked to one side.

"I was the worthless piece of crap, Zhen," he offered. "I was a screwed up kid who was angry with the entire universe and just looking to take it out on anybody and everybody. I don't have any excuses, only apologies for the way I treated you. I really mean that."

"If you've got time for apologies, she deserves them even more than I do," Davi pointed over Tahl's shoulder. "So go tell her. But you are right about one thing. It is you that's the worthless piece of crap. And I'm glad we met so I could tell you to your face."

Davi barged past Tahl to walk away. Tahl turned to look in the direction Davi had pointed, just at the same moment that Abbi Mosse turned to face him across the crowded bar. Tahl's jaw fell. Her uniform pressed immaculately and the toecaps of her boots polished to a mirrored finish, Mosse was the very picture of the professional soldier. Fiery red hair tied back in a ponytail complimented her attractive face as she leaned back against the bar, a bottle of beer in one hand. Tahl walked over to meet her, taking advantage of the few seconds to prepare his next wave of apologies. He was not surprised to see her rank badges as he drew closer: drop captain, boss of the company.

"Give us some room, guys," she commanded her nearby troopers curtly. "I've got an old friend to catch up with. Hello, Killer."

Tahl stopped a few paces from her. Mosse stepped forward and offered her hand. He took it, and she shook his firmly.

"Hello, Abbi."

Mosse smiled and another bottle of beer revolved up to the bar from the carousel underneath the counter as she mentally ordered it for him. She waited until her troopers were far enough away before handing it to him.

"It's good to see you again, Ryen," she smiled. "Eight years is a long time."

"I spoke to Zhen. And he's right. I should have contacted you sooner, Abbi. To say sorry."

"Cut that crap out, Trooper!" Mosse drawled. "We were both kids back then. We didn't know any better. It's all in the past, so don't let it get you down. I'm not holding onto anything from back then and neither should you."

"It's gracious of you to say," Tahl said, realizing that his hands were shaking.

"So how've you been?" Mosse leaned an elbow against the bar. "And what are you doing still slumming it in Strike? You never thought of coming back here on the pointy end?"

"I'm fine where I am," Tahl answered, looking down at the beer bottle. "I think I'm where I'm supposed to be. How about you? Things look to be going very well."

"I've been told I'm being looked at for command of my own formation at the end of the year, just got to get these boys and girls through a Ghar assault and out the other side in one piece, and then I should get my drop commander's epaulettes."

"It suits you well."

"I'm happy," Mosse said, "I've worked hard for it. But this is me, I'm married to C3 and that suits me just fine. We've both been there before, we've both done some time as commander of a formation."

"You know as well as I do that the real achievement is starting a campaign as a commander, not finishing it," Tahl said. "I've finished

two campaigns as a strike commander, and it's because everybody
above me was dead. But being selected for promotion on merit, rather
than because you're the only one left? That says a lot about you. You're
going places. You deserve it."

Mosse waved a hand dismissively at the compliment.

"How're things back home? Your dad talking to you again?"

Tahl shook his head.

"No, I seem to have a real talent for upsetting people. But you
harvest what you plant, right?"

"You've changed."

"What?" Tahl asked.

"You've changed," Mosse repeated. "When we broke up, I said
you could never change. I was wrong."

An unseen command filtered through the drop company shard
and the surrounding troopers stood and picked up their kit bags,
heading toward the transmat pad just outside the bar exit, which would
take them back to their ship. Mosse smiled in apology.

"That's us."

"It was good seeing you again," Tahl said. "I'm back at Markov's
Prize in a few days. Maybe we'll bump into each other."

"Yeah, maybe," Mosse finished her beer. "You take care, Ryen."

"You too."

Mosse slung her kit bag over her shoulder and walked two paces
away after her troopers before turning to face Tahl again. She walked
back and re-arranged a lock of hair at his fringe.

"You've grown your hair out a little bit," she said. "Looks good on
you."

Tahl watched her join the queue of soldiers who moved onto the
transmat pads to disappear in groups of four. Ignoring the growing
feeling of fatigue, he straightened his stance and sucked in a lungful of
air.

"Devil's Own!" Tahl yelled, and the bar fell silent as the drop
troopers all turned to face him. "Give 'Em Hell!" Tahl finished the
formation's traditional rallying cry.

The company of troopers roared a response, a few whistles
added to the bravado. Tahl continued to watch as the men and women
disappeared from view from the transmat. He wondered how many
would survive the carnage of a campaign facing the Ghar. Mosse waited
until she had ensured all of her troopers had successfully transported
back to the ship before she stood on the pad, dropping her kit bag down
next to her. She looked up at him and flashed a warm smile before she
faded from view.

***

Southern Hemisphere
Settlement Urban 127
Western Outskirts

L-Day plus 30

"They landed about five hours ago," Strike Captain Borras explained as he walked alongside Mandarin Owenne. "They came down in pods in the plains to the east of the city."

Owenne's pace did not slow as he walked briskly toward the Formation HQ building, which up until only a few days before had been a schoolhouse in the settlement's suburbs. The night sky was mostly clear, broken by thin strands of almost neon green gasses which were visible to the naked eye in the stratosphere only after sundown. The planet's rings were clearly visible, a diagonal line of faded grey which cut up across the sky as if it had been flicked over the panoramic view by an artist with one brush stroke. A gentle, warm breeze blew in from the equator, rustling the dry, blue foliage which grew up around the surrounding buildings. Van Noor walked a few paces behind the NuHu alongside Cane and Kachi, the other members of his company command unit. Borras, a shaven headed soldier of some eighty years of age, was the formation's most experienced strike captain; his company had arrived at Settlement Urban 127 only a day before Van Noor's but had already established a strong perimeter. An artillery battery made up of a trio of towering x-howitzers were dug in next to the Formation HQ; on the other side of the road, a repair depot had been set up where droids were busily at work on a pair of C3T7 transport drones.

Van Noor had already given orders to his squad leaders to set up a base of operations. There had not been time to bring in engineering drones to set up proper accommodation, so for now the troopers would have to make do with whatever empty buildings could be occupied. Such buildings were certainly not in short supply; after a warning to the civilian population, Settlement Urban 127 had been bombarded by naval gunfire in orbit in the opening rounds of the Concord invasion; and whilst the city center was a desolate wasteland of concrete and rubble, much of the surrounding areas still survived, intact but deserted.

"I see you have already deployed drones to scout the enemy positions," Owenne observed as they approached the HQ building. "I need to know what we're facing. Numbers, locations, I need intelligence. We need a ring of surveillance around their entire staging area."

Van Noor nodded to Cane and Kachi to remain outside as he followed Owenne and Borras into the HQ building. The ground floor had been stripped of all previous décor, and now a number of command consoles projected holographic images across a clear space in the center of the room, showing maps of local terrain, Concord force disposition, and lines of resupply and communication. The Formation HQ staff consisted of Strike Commander Orless and a handful of troopers and drones.

"Hello, sir," Orless greeted as Owenne walked over. "Glad to see you've arrived safely. Any updates on what's coming across to reinforce us?"

"12th Assault Force, including the 3rd Drop Formation," Owenne replied. "Beta Company is setting up alongside Alpha Company's accommodation areas. We'll get them sorted in the next hour and then out on patrols. The T7s are on the way to pick up Cian Company, who will be with us tomorrow night. The other three companies won't be far behind. In the meantime, I want every spotter drone in the formation out to the east and gathering data on the Ghar staging area."

"Understood. I propose we get strike troopers out in the eastern suburbs, so we've got a second line of warning in case of any advance elements of Ghar trying to probe our positions. Nothing too extensive, I don't want to fatigue our people with long night patrols which drones can cover. But I do advocate something as a second line behind unarmed spotter drones."

"Concur," Owenne said. "Senior Strike Leader Van Noor will assemble a roster of squads for patrols from Beta Company. I would suggest you get Alpha Company out there now to enact your plan."

Van Noor walked over to the holographic projection of the local area. Ghar forces were amassing only a few thousand yan to the east of the city, in a narrow ravine, giving them cover from artillery. If the Ghar were quick enough and had the inclination, they could be within weapons range before dawn.

***

Her teeth gritted, Rhona kept a steady pace as she jogged alone through the rubble strewn street, shattered buildings casting eerie shadows in the moonlight to either side of her. Her plasma carbine held across her midriff, she followed the waypoints on the viewscreen which acted as stepping stones to lead her back to her squad. Her situation report to Van Noor had gone as predicted. Even though she had followed her orders to the letter and set up a line of three observation posts behind the main detection line of drones, the senior strike leader still managed to find fault in every decision she had made and sent orders to her troopers to set up an entirely new line. The seemingly obligatory raised voice reprimand did, at least, feel far less soul destroying than the last one.

Rhona reached a familiar corner and looked to the east to where her first two trooper observation post was set up in the rubble of a burnt out residential block. A green light appeared in the corner of her viewscreen to indicate that the troopers had seen her and transmitted a message across the squad shard to inform her that she was cleared to approach them. Rhona jogged up to the building and then slowed her pace, mindful of the noises made by her armored feet so close to enemy positions. Picking her way through the rubble, she emerged through a jagged gap in an interior wall to find Gant and Sessetti propped up against the far wall of the building, their armor automatically having faded to a dusty grey to perfectly blend in with their surroundings.

"Y'aright?" Rhona greeted as she dropped to one knee next to Sessetti, peering out toward the Ghar positions to the east.

"We're good," Gant replied. "One of the drones picked up movement near marker ghia about twenty minutes ago, but we couldn't get visual. Could be a stray animal for all we know. We've logged it and sent it back to HQ as a possible sighting, but right now we're monitoring."

"Good job," Rhona said, patching into the spotter drone and utilizing the shard connection to send real time images of its surroundings straight to her viewscreen.

Nothing. Just yan after yan of desolated buildings.

"Okay, buddy," Gant turned back to Sessetti, "patch into the spotter near marker beta. Bring the thing up to about waist height, carefully now, and fire out a passive sensor sweep to see if you've got anything."

The young trooper followed Gant's instructions, using the shard connection to send an activation signal to the drone which was camouflaged in the rubble somewhere off to the east.

"Good, that's it. Take your time with moving these things, because whilst the drone's AI is pretty much sentient and capable of learning, remember that these things still process their decisions from a flow chart so they don't have your tactical flexibility. Just be careful about giving them too much independence because stealth and survival are not top of their priority list, data acquisition is."

Rhona listened to the seasoned soldier patiently tutoring Sessetti and again wondered why she was leading the squad instead of him.

"You guys seem cool here," she said, "I'm gonna go check on the others."

"We've got a good connection from here," Gant said. "Just get 'em on the shard. It's safer than wandering around out there on your own."

"Nah, I'd rather check on them face to face," Rhona said as she carefully crawled back to the other side of the room. "There shouldn't be anything this side of the surveillance line anyway."

"Some of their scouts could have got through," Gant warned. "Stay here with us and coordinate the op from here."

Rhona shook her head.

"I wanna make sure the others are okay. Keep on top of things, and if you get even a scent of anything wrong, you gimme a shout."

Back to the street intersection and another few minutes jog through the night, Rhona closed with the second observation point in the center of her line. Another green light through the shard to signal that it was safe to close with the post, and Rhona crawled through a narrow gasworks tunnel to where Jemmel and Rae lay half covered in rubble and debris at the edge of a bombarded power station.

"Kat's here!" Jemmel declared happily. "That's all the girls together! Yay!"

"Don't," Rae warned, "don't start singing that..."

"Tonight... is the night for love!
Tonight, me and my ladies are feelin' alright!
Feelin! Yeah, feeling al-right!"

Rhona blinked in confusion as Jemmel powerfully sung an instantly recognizable, fast paced electronica classic which had been popular several years before any of them had been born.

"She's been singing that damn song all night," Rae growled.

"I'm bored, I'm lying in a gas pipe in the middle of a bombed out city, and the only thing keeping me going is the thought that right here, right now, I'm on a night out on the town with ma ladies," Jemmel replied. *"Tonight... is the night for love!"*

"You guys detected any movement?" Rhona asked.

"Nothing," Jemmel replied, tapping the butt of her plasma lance impatiently. "We've got three drones set out in a standard surveillance pattern and we're rotating through passive sensor sweeps every five minutes. Nothing there. We haven't even picked up a stray badger."

"Badgers are rural animals," Rae said.

"Not all of them," Jemmel corrected, "could be a city badger."

"Look, I'm gonna go check on the other guys," Rhona said as she began crawling back down the pipe. "Stay sharp and call me if there's anything to report."

"Got it," Jemmel nodded before shoving her armored face next to Rae's head. *"Tonight... is the night for love!"*

Picking up her pace once she was clear of the power station, Rhona continued her run down to the south to the end of her squad's area of responsibility in the surveillance line. Van Noor had set up the third observation post in a transport hub, atop a burnt out public transport station. Rhona closed to within visual range and stopped. No green light. She looked up at the top of the station but could see nothing. She sent a request to approach the post through the shard. There was no reply.

Bringing her plasma carbine up and ready, Rhona dashed across the street to the bottom of the station. Her heart pounding, she looked up at a servicing ladder which seemed to be her best route up to the observation post. She quickly patched into the shard's short-range communication frequency.

"But the thing was," Qan managed to blurt out between bouts of laughter, "it wasn't even my sister! She was my cousin! Still really snaggy, though."

Rhona let out a frustrated breath and slung her carbine over her shoulder listening to Qan and Clythe's hysterical laughter as she climbed up the servicing ladder.

"What the hell are you two doing?" She demanded as she jumped down from the ladder and into their observation post.

The two troopers were sprawled out underneath the clear night sky, their carbines not even within reach.

"All under control," Qan said. "Three drones checking the perimeter. Nothing detected."

Rhona checked the observation post's setup through the shard.

"All under control?" You've got all three drones set to automatic with an alert signal to you if they have a confirmed sighting! I could have done that from back in our accommodation block! You're supposed to be coordinating this area of the line and anything might get through!"

"There's nothing out there!" Qan said. "We've been here for hours and we haven't found anything! The entire idea in spotter drones is so that they can do this nonsense and we don't have to! They don't get bored and tired!"

"Whatever's going down," Clythe added, "tonight ain't the night for a Ghar attack. They're not up for fighting right now."

"I hope you're right," Rhona said as she mentally reinitialized all three drones and transferred their supervision to Qan, "because I could have snuck right up on you two and taken your heads off, and I ain't a two man tall Ghar killing machine! Guys, pick up your weapons and get your eyes out! C'mon, do the job properly!"

Grumbling, both troopers recovered their carbines and took positions against the low wall, looking out toward the east. Rhona began climbing back down the ladder before a shout from Clythe stopped her.

"Hey! Kat!"

"This had better be good," Rhona warned.

"Something we were talking about before. Who'd win in a fight between fish and birds?"

"Which ones?" Rhona sighed.

"All of 'em," Qan replied as if the question was ludicrous.

"Birds," Rhona said after a few pensive moments before climbing back down the ladder and setting off for the first observation post.

***

A shrill tone inside his ear woke Van Noor from his slumber. Sitting up, he glanced around the darkened room in confusion, and in his half asleep state, he was numbly aware that he knew neither where he was nor what woke him up. In the space of only a few moments, he realized he was dressed in the form hugging body suit which formed the inner layer of his armor; the individual plates were on the floor next to him, ready to be quickly donned. He was in his quarters in the HQ building, a relatively comfortable bed made up of a blanket draped over a semi-opaque suspensor field that hovered only a few microyan above the floor. Cane and Kachi were waking up to either side of him, their sleeping arrangements were shared in one of the classrooms in the abandoned school building. Cane quickly set about attaching his hyperlight armor on over the top of his black body glove, a process quickly carried out through a series of mental commands to the individual armored plates.

Van Noor mentally canceled the wake up signal which had been transmitted to him across the formation command shard. He quickly dragged on and secured his armor before slinging his carbine over his shoulder and walking down toward the Operations Room, Cane and Kachi not far behind him. A pre-dawn glow allowed a little light in through the windows of both sides of the corridor as he walked, illuminating a wall full of colorful pictures which had clearly been enthusiastically painted by young children. Van Noor's suit alerted him to a shot of sedative being injected into his arm the instant he thought about his own son and daughter. He felt a little better.

"What's the alert, sir?" Van Noor called out to Owenne as soon as he saw the NuHu in the center of the ops room, regarding the local area map projection with interest.

The mandarin stood with his pale hands clasped behind his back, in between Strike Commander Orless and a trio of other soldiers of the HQ staff.

"The Ghar have begun testing our defenses," the mandarin replied. "A few probing attacks against our northern perimeter. Strike Captain Borras's company has reported several small scale pushes against their defenses."

"Shall I activate Beta Company, sir?" Van Noor asked.

"No. Not yet. They're only sending a few small bands of Outcasts to see how many guns we'll hit them with. I think it more tactically sound to allow them to believe our defenses are weaker than they are, and keep the advantage of an entire company in reserve to bolster any part of the line at a moment's notice. Have your squads assembled and ready to deploy, Senior Strike Leader."

Van Noor turned to leave, but a question forced its way to the front of his mind before he took a pace.

"Reinforcements, sir," he enquired, "any updates?"

"One assault force, as previously briefed," Owenne said. "Although we might be getting some help from the locals now that elements of their military are allied to our cause. In addition, the warship Steadfast has carried out a sensor sweep of this continent, and we believe we have located a lightly defended storage and maintenance facility behind their lines. A company of the 3rd Drop Formation will be carrying out an attack tonight. Make no mistake, Senior, we're on. This campaign is beginning in earnest right now. Get your people ready."

Van Noor scratched his chin thoughtfully. The information gleaned by the warship was certainly useful, but not worth risking an entire ship and its crew to locate a storage and maintenance facility. No, Owenne was looking for something else entirely.

SEVEN

Illarii
Eastern Panhuman Concord

The autumnal scents of moss and damp vegetation filled the air as Tahl materialized on the transmat pad. The planet's soft, green sky was broken up by a few thin layers of cloud which cast the surrounding, orange-brown forests into shadows. The transportation hub had several dozen transmat pads, allowing citizens from all over the region to instantly and effortlessly transport themselves to within walking distance of homes, entertainment hubs, and supply depots. Small groups of citizens would appear and disappear every few seconds as life carried on in this sleepy corner of the Concord. The main city was off to the north, but this scattered residential area out in the countryside had been Tahl's destination for several days now.

Picking up his kit bag and slinging it over his shoulder, Tahl began the walk down the winding country path which meandered between the forested hills to either side. Thanks to compression technology, his kit bag contained everything he could possibly need from bedding and sports clothing, to ceremonial uniform. He could have left it somewhere convenient, but he was a firm advocate of the age-old military saying: never get separated from your kit.

Up ahead, an old man of perhaps two hundred years of age leaned against a white wooden fence that ran around the perimeter of his land. A picturesque, three-story house sat on top of the shallow hill behind him. The white haired man looked up at Tahl and smiled.

"Morning, Strikes! How goes it?"

The fact that the old man had recognized Tahl's corps from his black beret hinted at the man having some past military experience, but Tahl dismissed the thought due to the use of the word 'Strikes' – a nickname which originated from a popular holovised drama series but actually had no use at all in the real military.

"Morning, sir," Tahl smiled. "Very well, thank you. Yourself?"

"Aye, good," the old man grinned. "Where you headed from? You been giving those Isorian bastards a good kicking?"

"Not this time around, I'm off east carrying out border security," Tahl said, mindful of both operational security and his duty as a soldier to withhold as much detail as possible about warfare from civilians. C3 had decreed it best to preserve normal citizens from the details of modern warfare.

"Well, good job nonetheless," the old man nodded, "I haven't seen you here before. You got family here?"

"Friends," Tahl replied.

"Who you visiting? I've been here all my life. I reckon I know pretty much everyone."

Tahl hesitated. It would not do her any good if her local community knew he was visiting, as rumors would probably spread, but being mysterious would probably arouse even more suspicion.

"Becca," he replied. "Becca Van Noor."

The man's smile faded.

"She lost her husband about a year ago. I guess you know that already."

"Yes, sir," Tahl said.

"Well, you treat her right. She's a good woman with two fine children."

"I'm just passing through to say hello, nothing more. I'm afraid I'm late already. Good day, sir."

Tahl continued the walk up across two more hills until he saw the house he had spent eight days travelling to find. He had visited it three times before, but never on his own. Ignoring a brief urge to abandon the whole idea and turn back, Tahl approached the garden's gate. Similar to the surrounding homes, the house was a wooden construct atop a small hill with several beautifully maintained floral gardens surrounding it. Two children were playing with toy spaceships amid the flowers. The smaller of the two, a boy of five years with blonde hair, stopped in his tracks and looked up at where Tahl waited at the gates.

"Mom! There's a soldier here!" He shouted.

Tahl offered a smile.

"Hello, Jabe," he said softly. "You remember me? I'm one of your dad's friends."

The girl ran inside, but Jabe walked slowly over, his head cocked to one side before a smile slowly spread across his face.

"Ryen!" He waved.

"Jabe! Get inside!" An angry shout was issued from behind him.

The little boy immediately turned and scuttled back up the garden path before dashing inside the house after his older sister. Tahl looked up and saw Becca storming back down the path toward him. Only a decade or so younger than her husband, Becca was a woman of relatively short stature whose pleasant features were framed by shoulder length, auburn hair. The woman came to a stop by the garden gate. With three decades of martial arts training to fall back on, Tahl saw the slap aimed at his face coming before she had even finished bringing her hand back to commence the strike.

Even with plenty of time in the last few days to sleep, Tahl still felt fatigued. The fatigue made him resent Rhona's allegations of misconduct, begrudge Owenne for sending him away from his company, and feel bitter toward Zhen Davi for confronting him so aggressively in the terminal. He knew the gentlemanly thing to do would be to allow Becca to vent her anger and allow the strike to hit his face, but he had run out of energy.

Tahl swept a clenched fist forward and out to block the strike, swatting away Becca's attempt to hit him. Her facial expression immediately changed from one of unbridled anger, to a more calm, serene, and accepting demeanor. Tahl had seen this sort of reaction before, from soldiers recovering from traumatic experiences. Becca was using a tranquil – a device to stay connected to the IMTel for artificial assistance with mental stabilization following a difficult ordeal. The IMTel had detected her anger and reacted with the only care it knew how to give, by immediately controlling her emotions and taking away the negativity. Such was the strength of the all-powerful man-machine interface which controlled all lives via the nanosphere shard connections.

"I am sorry, Ryen," Becca said, almost mechanically. "I should not have attempted to hit you. But I'm angry with you."

"What did I do wrong?" Tahl asked gently.

"It's what you didn't do. You knew Bry better than anybody. You should have stopped him."

"I had no idea," Tahl replied truthfully. "I knew he was tired, I knew he had a lot on his mind, and he was struggling with all of the people we'd both seen killed. A load of the guys went out one night when we were given a respite from the front. I stayed back. The next morning, he told me what happened with that... woman. As soon as he sobered up, he knew what he'd done and he regretted it. He contacted you within minutes."

The serenity behind her eyes faded again as the raw, powerful panhuman emotions fought to override the paternal care provided by the tranquil.

"You expect me to feel sympathy for that?" Becca demanded. "I'm back here, the mother of his children, and that's the respect he shows me? All of us? I assume you've come here to try to convince me to forgive him?"

"It's not even him," Tahl tried to explain. "The man who

committed that act is dead and gone now. The Bry Van Noor I now know has changed."

"It's the same man!" Becca seethed.

"Up to a point," Tahl persevered. "He backed up his memories, the same as the rest of us, and he... suffered significant trauma to the head. The whole process of getting somebody back up and running, it's not without its hazards. A person can lose huge parts of their memory or have their personality altered. The Bry I now know never betrayed you. It all happened after..."

"But he's still capable of it!" Becca snapped. "That bastard has shown me what he's capable of, and I don't want anything to do with him!"

Again, the angry woman took a deep breath and her brow unfurrowed as calm descended.

"Won't you come in, for a drink at least?" She managed a small smile. "You must have travelled a long way to get here."

"I did, and I've already missed a couple of connections, so I'll be late in returning to my unit," Tahl said. "But I had to get here. For Bry. Becca, he's learned from this. The man went into a chamber to upload his memories and then woke up to find that for him, a few moments had gone by, but for everybody else, nearly a year had passed. He remembers you, the children, and he loves you very much. He has no memory of the mistake which was made. All he knows is the fallout, and I can promise you that he would never, ever do that to you again."

The anger returned immediately.

"What guarantees can you give? If you knew him so well, you would have stopped this in the first place!"

"I couldn't see it coming, no!" Tahl retorted tersely. "I couldn't stop him! You say it as if we've all been lounging around, taking it easy, and enjoying life! You have no idea! Your husband was dead and gone, and we couldn't save him there and then because his entire head was gone! He was stood as close to me as you are now when that sniper hit him. I had to have fragments of his skull removed from my cheek. So no, I can't lecture you on much, but I can tell you that whilst you are here, pruning your damn garden, life is not so easy for us on the other side of the Concord borders!"

Tahl immediately regretted the outburst, knowing full well that it would be incredibly difficult raising two children alone, and that was something he could understand. Becca closed her eyes for several long moments. A gust of wind blew across the garden, bringing the delightful scents of the various exotic and colorful flowers.

"What do you want from me, Ryen?" She finally asked calmly. "It's been nearly a year and I still don't know what to do. I feel anger, I then have help from the shard, and I feel calm. But I never feel acceptance or forgiveness. I just... can't. I don't know what you want from me, but whatever it is, I can't give it."

"I know I can't convince you to change your mind about what happened," Tahl said quietly. "I'm not a father, I doubt I ever will be. I'm nobody to lecture on children or parenting. But Jabe and Alora... they need their father. My home planet acknowledges that the ideal family unit is two parents, that's science. Please, just let him contact his children. Please."

Becca buried her face in her hands, her shoulders trembling. She looked up, wiping a tear away before that same expression of calm descended upon her. She smiled warmly at Tahl as if she did not have a care in the world.

"Thank you for coming and talking to me," she said, her voice sounding void of emotion. "I will give it some thought. That is all I can promise. Don't tell him that I've agreed to anything, because I have not. I will think it through. That's all."

Tahl nodded and took a step back away from the gate. A thin mist of drizzle began to fall from the green-tinted clouds above.

"Take care, Becca," he said. "I'm so sorry this all happened. So very sorry."

He turned and walked away before she called his name. Again, emotion forced its way through the mask of indifference which the tranquil had provided her with.

"You're a good friend to him. To come all this way for five minutes. You're a good man, Ryen. Stay safe."

Tahl smiled and turned again to walk back to the transport hub and begin the long journey back to the frontlines. The weariness and loneliness, his constant companions, returned in force as he dragged his booted feet along the path, bringing him closer step by step to the guns of his enemies. The words of Davi and Mosse at the terminal echoed around his head, reminding him of those he had hurt in the past. Then, amid it all, Becca's words gave him some hope. 'You're a good man.' He realized just how few people had ever expressed those sentiments to him. Although his motive had always been to try to help his friend, this long journey for its five-minute conclusion was all worthwhile from a purely selfish view, just to hear those words from one person.

"Ryen?"

Tahl turned around again. Van Noor's daughter, Alora, stood behind him on the track. Tahl dropped to one knee to bring his eyes down to her level.

"Hello, Lora!" He smiled. "It's nice to see you again! You doing okay here?"

The girl transmitted a tiny fragment of data to him via the shard.

"Please give this to my daddy," she said before turning and

running back toward her home.

***

The rumble of artillery echoed from the west. The late afternoon suns continued to beat down along the dusty road that wound through the suburbs and the neat lines of gargot trees which separated the road from the abandoned residential buildings to either side. Three C3M4 combat drones powered their way slowly along the road at head height, heading from the Formation Repair Depot back toward Alpha Company's positions at the frontline. Beta Company had seen some isolated action against a few Ghar Outcast probes, but it always seemed to be Rall and his squad who ended up mowing down waves of the furious little creatures; Rhona and her squad were yet to fire a shot.

"Go on, what is it?" Rhona asked as she walked along the pavement, a kit bag full of compressed and recently serviced plasma carbines slung over one shoulder.

"What do you mean?" Rae asked as she struggled to keep pace with the taller woman and carry three x-launcher firing tubes.

"It's obvious that something's on your mind. You offer to keep me company on the walk to the repair depot, then say nothing all the way there."

A trio of troopers from Alpha Company walked past them on the pavement, two of the three soldiers flashing smiles to Rhona as they passed.

"You get that a lot?" Rae asked. "It must be nice."

"It was to both of us, not just me," Rhona said. "You can't blame 'em for it. Take guys away from home for months at a time, even two grimy women in dusty battle armor are gonna look hot."

"You always look hot, guys are always looking at you."

"You're changing the subject," Rhona said, slinging the kit bag over her other shoulder as they reached a small crossroad and headed south.

"Okay," Rae finally said, "I've been thinking about what we spoke about a few days ago, and I just don't get it. Why would you lower yourself to taking your clothes off in a bar full of strangers?"

Rhona threw the kit bag full of weapons down on the cracked pavement and turned to face the younger woman. Even with a couple of small suspensors fitted to the bag, it was heavy; and she removed her beret to run a hand through her sweat soaked hair before answering the challenge.

"Did I not make it clear that a crime lord was effectively holding a gun to my pa's head?"

"Yeah, you made that clear," Rae said slowly and carefully, "but if he owed money, why not just get another job and pay it back? There had to have been a hundred things which paid better than lap dancing and were more... moral."

"It's not about money, Ila," Rhona exhaled, "it's about power. Crime is about power. Crime is about being able to force the daughter of a guy who has pissed you off to do something she doesn't want to, and the guy would die if he ever knew his daughter was doing it. But that's life outside the Concord. People criticize the Concord way of doing things for being some draconian dictatorship where a faceless machine saps your free will. I'd rather lose some free will and live in a place where my mom survived childbirth and crime lords couldn't exist to take my pa away. I mean, I'm not saying it's perfect. I'd rather have the ability to feel emotional pain than have the big robot mind suddenly dampen my senses every time I think of something meaningful and real."

Rae nodded slowly as Rhona replaced her beret and slung her kit bag back over her shoulder.

"But lap dancing," Rae said, "I mean, how could you just get everything out and grind against some fat guy..."

"Jeez, Rae!" Rhona threw the kit bag down again and turned away from the punishing sun glare. "I'm here talking to you about politics and life, and you just wanna talk about lap dancing! You're like... I dunno, a guy! I'm not ashamed about what I did; it kept my pa alive for another five years. Like I told you, the pole dancing was cool. It was a high, being center of attention for something I worked hard at and was damn good at. The lap dancing? No, that was crap. I mean, real bad. I don't remember much of it because the only way I could do it was if I was so drunk I could barely walk straight. Some of the other girls were on stuff far worse than booze to go into those damn cubicles. Life outside the Concord doesn't necessarily consist of finding the right person, getting a huge house, and raising perfect kids with no other responsibilities to worry about. Life is very different out in the Determinate. Life out there can be... well, just be grateful for what you've got."

"Okay, okay," Rae held her hands up. "What do you mean about feeling pain? Why would you want that?"

Rhona dragged the bag up for a third time and began walking back to the company holding area as she talked.

"It's like a bath; if you're freezing cold and you put your foot in lukewarm water, it feels very different to when you're boiling hot and you get into that bath. It's all about perspective, and if you've never felt sadness and pain, you can't really feel and truly appreciate happiness. I don't want the IMTel getting in my head and turning off my pain. I want to feel it for myself."

A convoy of four Dukes rumbled past them on the road, their jets kicking up dust along the pavement and the noise of their engines putting a temporary stop to the conversation.

"Now that makes no sense at all," Rae said once the vehicles were clear. "Katya, growing up outside the Concord really messed you up. You want to feel pain and sadness?"

"It's one of the few good things about being a soldier and being on this less restrictive shard," Rhona replied. "I can get all of the external shard assistance and drugs stopping us from getting depressed when we watch our buddies get blown to bits, but back in the Concord proper? Hell, I don't want my humanity getting switched off by a machine."

"I'll be happy to go home, as and when the time comes," Rae pondered. "I know they say the system only picks somebody to be a soldier because it's either in the best interests of C3, or for the personal growth and development of the individual, but... I mean, it must be for me. I'm not exactly a natural born soldier. This has got to be for me. As and when I get released and go home, these experiences must be meant to help me somehow."

"Don't be so hard on yourself," Rhona said as the two finally arrived back at the company holding point. "You're good at this. Just as good as anybody else."

As soon as they arrived back, it was clear that something had changed. Seven Duke transport drones had come to a stop by the company supply dump and briefing area; the vehicles' markings were those of Alpha Company. A line of medical drones flew rapidly over.

Gant and Qan walked over to stand by Rhona and Rae as the battered vehicles sank slowly to the ground. Their cargo bay doors opened up in succession and wounded strike troopers were helped down by close by troopers from Beta Company.

"Let's give them a hand," Gant said.

The four jogged over to one of the drones. An uninjured strike trooper appeared at the door and called down to Rhona.

"Body boxes," he said wearily, "get some body boxes over."

Rhona and Qan ran back to the supply dump and quickly dragged one of the long rectangular boxes over to the Duke.

"Keep 'em coming," the trooper said at the doorway as he manhandled the body storage device into the vehicle. "Can one of you guys give me a hand in here?"   Rae jumped up into the doorway.

"Ila!" Rhona grabbed her by the wrist. "Go get more of the boxes, I've got this."

Rhona vaulted up into the cramped confines of the vehicle and looked inside. The floor was awash with blood. Five dead troopers were neatly lined up at the far end of the cargo hold. Two had been gunned down by accurate fire which had blasted through their torsos. Another had been shredded by a fragmentation weapon. The final two had been killed in close combat; one had been torn in half whilst the last pitiful corpses had been ripped limb from limb. Rhona's suit alerted her to a wave of shard external assistance being transmitted to her brain. She quickly set about helping the surviving soldier move the bodies of his dead squadmates. After each body was sealed in the box, the device's control unit was used to freeze the body solid for preservation, giving the unfortunate occupant a fighting chance of having their memories preserved for the long regen process, or transfer to their stored clone.

"Four of them," the soldier told her, "just four Ghar in their damn machines. We couldn't stop them, we couldn't do anything. We lost eighteen troopers in the last hour. We only took two of them down."

Rhona looked up at the exhausted soldier. She found no words of consolation. A message came through the company command shard.

"Squad Leaders, report to me immediately," Van Noor said. "The Ghar have broken through our lines. Tell your guys to get their gear together. Now."

***

The company's defensive line had been set up along the western edge of the city center. No camouflaged observation posts or passive drone sweeps – the positions were overt and dug in behind shimmering protective walls made up of lines of kinetic barricades. In the very center, crouched down within a c-shaped arrangement of barricades, Van Noor stared over the devastated remains of the city's central park, whose one peaceful sea of green was now dominated by chunks of masonry from the fallen buildings which had formed its perimeter.

Kachi knelt on one knee next to him, his carbine resting against a lip on the barricade. Cane lay prone a few paces away, lining up the sighting unit of his viewscreen with the corresponding receptor built into his carbine. Stood behind them, Owenne occasionally took a few purposeful paces up and down the line of defenses, one hand clasped at the small of his back whilst the other kept his IMTel stave – a functional tool as well as his badge of office - tucked firmly beneath one arm. Van Noor had worked with several NuHu mandarins throughout his career, and most exercised their right to individuality; he had seen flowing cloaks accompanied by IMTel staves which looked like a wizard's staff, whereas Owenne's predecessor was more reserved and subtle in her choice of attire. With a thick military style coat over his armor, an officer's cap drawn over his head, and holding his stave like a walking stick, Owenne reminded Van Noor of a stuffy character from some holo-vid of an ancient war. Only the five drones which hovered around in the mandarin's wake, under his direct control, gave him the appearance of a modern fighting man.

A text alert flashed across Van Noor's visor.

"Squad Jai have confirmed visual sighting of enemy units approaching from marker alpha," Van Noor reported to Owenne.

"I know," the mandarin replied coolly, his back to the enemy positions as he stared pensively out to the west.

"Squad Jai, Command, message copied," Van Noor transmitted a reply. "Support is available if required."

Two further lines of text scrolled across the screen: confirmed enemy sightings from Squads Teal and Denne. Van Noor focused on the battlespace picture provided by the combined inputs of the company's various spotter drones. Three squads were visual, all at the northern end of the north-south line of defense. It could be a feign – the Ghar certainly were not incapable of such a maneuver – but it could be the main thrust of an attack, in which case the defenders of the northern part of the line may need further support. Van Noor opened his mouth to present the options to Owenne but was cut off by an alert from Kachi.

"Our spotter drone's got something, Senior! Looks like Outcasts!"

Van Noor patched into the visual feed from the drone which was positioned to the northeast, in the corner of the city park. Two groups of small, hunched over humanoids scuttled rapidly across the park, ducking beneath felled trees and scrabbling over piles of rubble as they closed with the command squad. Each group consisted of perhaps ten Ghar, armed with primitive looking lugger guns.

"Sir!" Van Noor called across to Owenne. "We've got..."

"I'm well aware, Senior Strike Leader," Owenne raised one eyebrow slightly. "I've already taken precautionary measures. It is possible to issue orders to our units using the shard mentally, as it is intended, rather than crassly just bellowing them out."

As if in proof, a deep ripple of artillery fire sounded from the west, and a moment later, the park was torn asunder as explosive shells slammed down from above, blowing chunks of rubble and earth into the air in front of the advancing Ghar. The next volley corrected, accurately landing amid the scrabbling panhuman morphs and flinging them up into the sky, tearing them apart in mid-air with the concussive force of the blast and the deadly barrage of shrapnel.

"This is merely something to grab our attention," Owenne suddenly declared. "The main push is north of here. Battlesuits, a lot of them. I'm calling in our Planetary Defense allies."

Van Noor turned his attention away from the carnage ahead and looked back at the mandarin.

"What use are they?"

"They've got aerospace assets, sub-orbital craft. There's a concentration of six Ghar battlesuits to the southeast of marker beta.

Call in aerospace support, would you? Their callsign is Angel."

The mandarin closed his eyes in concentration as Van Noor returned to his own projection of the battlefield on his viewscreen, finding the marker and patching in to Squad Denne's spotter drone to see the fearsome image of half a dozen squat, three-legged war machines stumbling clumsily over a rubble strewn roadway toward a Concord barricade.

"Angel, Angel, this is Beta Command," Van Noor transmitted over the shard frequency which Owenne sent across to him. "Hostiles, strength six, transmitting marker, requesting support."

A deep, male voice replied immediately.

"Beta from Angel, target acquired, we're rolling."

As the boom of artillery finally stopped, the noise was instantly replaced by the banshee howl of aero engines. Two rapidly moving black dart-like shapes thundered in from the south, only a handful of yan above the horizon.

"They're coming in close!" Kachi said. "Why aren't they firing missiles from distance!"

"We sort of scrambled all of their vehicles' guidance systems when we invaded," Owenne shrugged. "It would appear they haven't had time to fix them yet. Still, good of them to come join the party."

Van Noor watched as the two crafts arced around and commenced their attack run. From the patched view from the spotter drone, he saw the Ghar battlesuits stop and swivel in place, their weaponry painting the sky with lines of green energy. The two crafts flew straight over the top of the Ghar. Van Noor never saw the munitions which had been dropped, but a second later, the Ghar disappeared from view as a long line of fire and thick, black smoke replaced the entire area where the enemy unit had been. He smiled as somebody whooped in victory over the shard.

His smile faded almost immediately. One after the other, five war machines emerged unscathed from the inferno behind them, leaving only a single suit incapacitated and burning.

"Angel Flight, back in," the lead pilot transmitted to his wingman. "Go for guns."

The two machines screamed in from the north, their mag guns chattering and kicking up the ground around the Ghar as thousands of projectiles tore through the sky. Again, the Ghar swiveled in place and opened fire with their multi-barreled energy weapons. A sheet of flame suddenly spat out of the rear of the second jet.

"Mayday! Mayday! May..." a panicked female voice yelled quickly as the swept wing, dart-like aircraft banked right and fell out of the sky, flaring its nose to impact roughly into the park ahead of Van Noor and his squad.

A wing tore off and spiraled through the air as the stricken machine flipped over, landing on its back as it ploughed a great trench through the mud. Again, it cartwheeled around and shed a multitude of parts before it finally came to a stop, a smoldering heap of twisted alloy at the far end of the city park.

"I've got an emergency signal," Cane called. "I think the pilot's still alive in there."

"I doubt it," Owenne sighed.

"Let's go get her," Van Noor stood up, mentally plotting his route across the park.

"Don't be ridiculous, man," Owenne spat. "You'll be cut to pieces before you get halfway there, and she's probably dead already."

"As soon as their government capitulated, they became Concord," Van Noor stared at Owenne. "That's a Concord combat pilot out there. I'm not leaving her to those bastards. If there's any chance she's alive, I'm gonna go get her. With or without your blessing."

Owenne waved a frail hand dismissively.

"Go on," he sighed, "go."

"Command Squad, on me," Van Noor ordered as he planted one hand on top of the barricade and vaulted over.

***

"Approaching range," Rhona announced as the frantic unit of twelve Ghar Outcasts sprinted through the ruined buildings, flowing forward like a liquid seeping through doorways and cracks in the walls as they closed on the defensive barricade.

Sessetti tapped his finger against the trigger of his carbine, lining up his sighting display with his weapon as the Ghar moved into the view of his own eyes. Content he had his targets sighted, he switched off the visual feed from the squad's spotter drone.

"Five yan from fire marker," Rhona's steady voice came across the shard.

"Stay cool, make your shots count," Gant said from his position to Sessetti's left, where the veteran trooper leaned against the barricade.

The dozen squat, spindly-limbed panhuman morphs flowed over the rough ground ahead, close enough now to hear their inhuman shrieks. Sessetti picked his target; a slightly bulkier individual with a metallic helmet, who waved his gun above his head like a banner.

"Squad Wen, targets front, open fire!" Rhona commanded.

Sessetti aimed at the Ghar's center of mass and squeezed the trigger. His first shot slammed into the Ghar's torso, just right of center, tearing off the creature's arm and sending it flailing to the ground. Either side of him, his squadmates sent streams of plasma fire tearing into the ranks of creatures. Jemmel's plasma lance fired one continuous, solid beam that cleaved through two of the Ghar in quick succession, vaporizing both.

"Got one!" Clythe reported gleefully from the far right of the barricade.

Their numbers thinning, still the rabble surged forth.

"Ghar battle squad, strength four, marker indigo," the spotter drone reported.

Sessetti glanced across to the left, toward the drone's reported sighting. The sight took his breath away. Four lumbering spheres clanked their way over a ridgeline in the rubble, the suns glinting off their thick, armored hulls.

"Visual," Sessetti said as he stared at the approaching fighting machines.

"Plasma lance, on the battlesuits," Rhona ordered. "Everybody else, drop those Outcasts."

Jemmel's plasma lance cut across the field of fire, sweeping along the ridgeline and through the approaching Ghar troopers. The normally lethal weapon impacted with the huge battlesuits, but succeeded only in causing one of the machines to reel back and stumble before moving forward again. Sessetti brought his carbine back to his shoulder and looked to the front again as the last four or five Ghar Outcasts continued to sprint toward the barrier.

"Squad Wen, rapid fire!" Rhona ordered.

Sessetti changed his carbine's fire mode and squeezed the trigger. The weapon jolted and leapt in his hands as pulses of energy spewed from its barrel. Blasts and hisses issued all along the line of the barricade as the troopers hosed the area in front of them with superheated fire, cutting down the last Ghar Outcasts.

From the ridgeline to the left, the Ghar troopers opened fire. A torrent of orange-red plasma fire swept across from the fighting machines, smashing against the barricade and tearing up the ground below and around it. Clouds of dust obscured vision in every direction, forcing Sessetti to change his visual display to thermal, giving him an unearthly perspective of the four armored titans than spat streams of fire in his direction.

"Targets at marker indigo!" Rhona shouted, the nervousness in her voice obvious even above the din of incoming fire. "Open fire!"

Sessetti fired a trio of aimed shots at one of the Ghar troopers. Two hit the machine square in the center but did nothing. The machines drew closer, tottering on their three squat legs as they waddled almost comically forward, their furious firepower never relenting. Blue bolts of energy continued to spew from the Concord lines, smashing against the Ghar suits' armored bulks, until one finally fell over on its side with a pair of holes punctured through its thick armor. The remaining two continued to advance.

"Orders from Command," Rhona said. "Position's overrun, we're falling back. Come on, guys, let's go."

Clythe and Gant were the first to move, reacting instantly to the command and running quickly toward the designated rally point to the east. Jemmel and Qan were next, turning to sprint toward the comparative safety of a single tall building which still stood only a stone's throw behind them.

"Lian, go!" Rhona shouted at Sessetti. "Get moving!"

Sessetti turned to run. Something punched him hard in the side of his abdomen, and for a second, he felt tremendous pain. His legs collapsed from beneath him and the sky fell forward on top of him, filling his view as the endless stitched lines of plasma continued to blast in every direction. He felt light headed and his vision swam in and out of focus. His battlesuit issued a medication report – severe trauma to the lower left torso, casualty, category four.

Category four. The medication must have been doing a good job, because Sessetti felt remarkably calm for a diagnostics readout which informed him he had less than thirty minutes to live, unless he received significant medical attention. Numbly aware that he was lying on his back, he looked to his left and saw his own outstretched hand, palm up on the ground. His smoking plasma carbine lay where he had dropped it moments before.

"I gotcha, pal," a friendly, feminine voice said as Sessetti was yanked up off the ground.

Pain broke through the barrier created by the medication as Sessetti was bounced up and down with each step, slung as he was over the shoulder of one of his squadmates. Peering under her arm, he could just about see the darkness of the building ahead as two strike troopers disappeared into the ruined ground floor. Only then did he recognize the voice of the trooper who had rescued him.

"Ila?" Sessetti whispered.

"Hang in there, Lian," Rae replied. "I'll get you out of this."

***

Seven of the survivors of Owenne's artillery bombardment had already reached the crashed sub-orbital craft by the time the three strike troopers arrived at the far end of the park. Three of the Ghar Outcasts had climbed up onto the cockpit and were frantically smashing the butts of their lugger guns into the canopy; one had succeeded in breaking a small hole in the viewscreen and had thrust a bony arm through, its clawed hand slashing and grabbing at the wounded pilot trapped inside.

Cane was the first to attack, tucking his carbine into his hip and firing a long burst of automatic fire into the closest Ghar. The little creature was blown back against the wrecked jet's fuselage, where it shivered and shook in a macabre dance as its guts were blown out against the wrecked craft behind it. A second creature let out a yell and hurled itself at Cane, activating a plasma grenade in one skinny hand as it did so. Kachi stepped up and swung his carbine at the creature's head, connecting with the jaw and lifting the panhuman morph up off its feet and tumbling through the air in a shower of its own broken teeth. The grenade exploded and the Ghar's limbs were scattered aside.

Van Noor ran past his two squadmates, shooting another of the creatures twice in the head as he closed range before pivoting on the spot and killing a second Ghar with a burst of fire to the chest. The three rage-filled creatures that clubbed at the cockpit still had not noticed the approaching troopers. Van Noor peeled one of the Ghar off the canopy and lifted it high up with both hands before bringing it crashing down on a jagged edge of wreckage to impale it through its guts. The agonized Ghar shrieked and writhed, still somehow finding the rage and hatred to attempt to claw at Van Noor in its death throes. By the time he turned back to the cockpit, Cane was kneeling over one Ghar and bashing its skull in with his carbine butt, whilst Kachi had the final Outcast grabbed with both hands, smashing its face into the nose of the jet repetitively.

Quickly searching for an emergency canopy jettison, Van Noor found a distinctive yellow and black striped handle and pulled it. The shattered canopy sprung open. A young woman sat in the pilot's seat, blood drenching one side of her terrified face and both of her broken legs. She held a pistol in one shaking hand. Van Noor slid his visor up to reveal himself as a friendly.

"Hold still," he said as he leaned into the cockpit, "we're getting you out of here."

Pale, her eyes struggling to focus, the woman watched him wordlessly.

"Gotta be quick, Senior," Kachi said, "we've got battlesuits closing in from both sides."

"Beta Company, this is Command," Owenne's voice transmitted across the company command shard to all squad leaders. "Our position is untenable. Withdraw to rally point alpha and await further instructions."

Van Noor unbuckled the pilot's seat harness and hauled her out of the smoking cockpit, wincing in sympathy as she cried out in pain. He lowered her over one shoulder and recovered his carbine with his free hand.

"The mandarin's called it, lads," he said to the other two troopers.

"Let's get out of here."

***

Main Docking Bay
Concord Warship, Ajax
High Orbit, Markov's Prize

The blast doors of the docking bay were open, giving an unprecedented view of the planet of Markov's Prize below. All that stopped the docking bay's occupants from being swept out into the void of space was a double layered kinetic barrier, shimmering faintly and adding a blue hue to the spectacular view. Markov's Prize was largely a shade which sat somewhere between purple and turquoise, the planet's warm waters making up some three quarters of its surface. Sandy yellow island chains were visible snaking in and around the larger blue and green landmasses. Cutting across the equator was Markov's Prize's planetary ring system, a grey line of dust and small rocks left behind from millennia before when a small moon had been knocked off its orbital trajectory by an asteroid.

The maintenance drones finished their preparation on the transmat launchers in the docking bay. The small machines hovered away to give room to the panhuman naval technicians who jogged forward to carry out their final visual safety checks. The fifty drop troopers of Alpha Company, 3rd Drop Formation watched the naval technicians carry out the work which would be the difference between a successful and fatal launch.

Drop Captain Abbi Mosse paced across to her troopers from the doors at the far end of the hangar. The captain of the Ajax had just issued her with a command update which changed the stakes for the task at hand. She opened a communication channel to the entire company.

"Alpha Company, we're five minutes to launch," she began. "Command update is that the Ghar have overrun Concord positions at Settlement Urban 127. The strike troopers down there have taken heavy losses and are retreating. They're our people, and they're taking a beating. We can take away some of that pressure, right now. You know our target – a major maintenance facility near the site of the main Ghar landing. Civilians are still in the city, so no bombardment – we're going in as a precision strike. We take this out, those battlesuits of theirs are going to start to fall to pieces around them. Remember, we're going to be facing unarmed technicians as well as the automated defenses. Don't let their lack of firepower fool you – they'll try to kill us with their bare hands, and they are definitely legitimate military targets. Eliminate every last one of them. We're Devil's Own. We give them hell."

A deep, booming shout erupted as one from all of her troopers, echoing around the cavernous docking bay. Drop Leaders took charge of their troopers as the company split into squads, forming up around the transmat launchers for the assault. Her heavy, armored feet clunking on the metal deck plates below, Mosse approached Squad Teal – her junior squad.

"You're last in," she briefed the six troopers. "Stay flexible, be ready to change your landing site depending on how things are going down there. You've got my most experienced Drop Leader to guide you, so you'll do fine. Devil's Own, boys. Give 'em hell."

Clapping an armored hand against the bulky shoulder plate of the group's squad leader, Mosse moved on to Squad Denne, her most experienced drop troopers. The six men and women turned to face her as she approached.

"You've got lead, Denne," Mosse nodded. "You get that roof cracked open and we'll be right behind you. The rest of the company is relying on you to get us into that installation. You've never let me down before, and I know you won't start now. Devil's Own, people, 3rd Drop Formation. You go screw them up."

The troopers of Squad Denne responded with staccato shouts before walking over to the transmat launchers, igniting their antigrav chute reactors as they walked. The six troopers took position on their pads, facing out of the gaping docking bay to look down on the world of Markov's Prize.

"Squad Denne, launching in five, four..."

Mosse mentally ordered the company shard to change from vocal alert to text across her viewscreen; she had always preferred visual displays to voices in her head.

Three, two, one.

Each transmat pad glowed dark red for a brief moment and issued a deep thrum as the trooper stood on top was propelled out of the warship, a mere speck in space within a second. The transmat beam would direct the troopers into low orbit and to P1 - the drop point - where they would then guide themselves in manually to P2 - the inversion point.

"Command Squad, light up," Mosse ordered as she stepped onto her pad alongside Zhen Davi and the other three troopers which made up her command team.

Mosse sent a mental signal to her suit's processor and fired up the small plasma reactor built into the back of the bulky armor. She felt her torso vibrate and tremor as the blue sphere of energy contained on her back rapidly wound up to operating speed, reaching self sufficient speed and reducing the charge from her battery to leave it ready for emergency power. She glanced behind her at the rest of the company, suppressing a smile as she saw some of the younger troopers had retained the old formation tradition of cramming their red berets on underneath their helmets, just visible through their raised face plates. Never be improperly dressed. Stretching her neck left and right, Mosse rolled her shoulders and gripped her carbine against her chest.

Command Squad, launching in five...

Mosse braced herself. Fifty-seven combat drops in twenty years service. Only two had gone wrong in the transmat beam. She did not intend to make this the third.

...two, one.

The warship seemed to be sucked away behind her in an instant. Shooting through space, so fast that even in the black void she could detect the motion, Mosse tilted her trajectory to achieve perfect heading, her neck craned back and her eyes staring ahead at her target, arms tucked in tightly to her sides, and her carbine magnetically locked to her right hand. She risked a glance to either side and was relieved to see her squad all tightly in formation with her.

Markov's Prize swam closer through space, the familiar optical illusion of an imminent collision with a colored ball in space soon replaced with visual definition of an actual planet as the squad approached the upper atmosphere.

"Squad Denne, P1," the drop leader of the squad ahead of them reported.

Her viewscreen glowed red as her suit began to heat up in the atmosphere, the temperature control unit regulating the change enough to prevent damage, but not enough to stop her feeling the burning. Sweat forming on her brow, Mosse saw bands of thin, wispy cirrus cloud swimming toward her as she plummeted toward the ground, all views of the blackness of space now gone behind her.

Six thousand yan to P1, the status report scrolled across her screen.

"Squad Jai, successful launch," the next report came through the company shard as up above her a third group of drop troopers were catapulted from the docking bay of the Ajax.

Four thousand yan to P1.

A layer of cloud momentarily obscured the view of the landing site below her, a flickering white crosshair on her viewscreen aimed seemingly randomly in the center of a continent near the equator. Her natural vision was now painted in a homogenous white, she saw only the projected path of the descent and the icons on her screen showing her target and the soldiers under her command.

"Squad Denne, inverting... in contact."

Her troopers were in contact with the enemy. Mosse fought the urge to increase her descent speed past normal parameters.

Two thousand yan to P1.

The command squad plunged out beneath the cloud and saw definition beneath them – the contours of hills, wooded areas, settlements. Beads of condensation left clear streaks on her visor as she descended. The flashing white crosshair on her screen which signified P1 swam up to meet her. Her suit fell out of the transmat beam from the docking bay in orbit above, and she was in free fall. Juddering vibrations and the steadily increasing hiss of air rushing past her helmet replaced the smooth transit of the beam.

"Command Squad, P1," she announced.

Years of training and experience kicked in without so much as a thought as mental commands to the small aerofoil fins on her back made minute adjustments to keep her suit in trim as she fell head first toward the ground. The decimated cityscape below rushed up toward her – acrid smoke from industrial areas blurred her vision; geometric roads cut unnatural angles through rectangular blocks of buildings. The next white crosshair designated the target building – a huge factory converted into a Ghar maintenance facility.

One thousand yan to P2.

Mosse looked to either side to check on the positioning of her squad.

"Close up, C2!" she barked to one of her troopers who was drifting away from the squad.

The target building was visual now; a broad rectangle made up of three separate production plants. She smiled grimly – gaping, jagged holes had been blown into all three roofs – Squad Denne had achieved the first objective. Mosse would be first in. P2 – the inversion point – rushed up.

"Command squad, P2!" She ordered, shifting her weight to flip through the air and point her feet at the ground: a difficult maneuver which two decades of experience had made second nature.

Mosse sliced through the air, falling into the building and looking down at the dozens of confused Ghar technicians who sprinted around the empty battlesuits which hung from thick chains below her. Mosse picked one of the small creatures, adjusted her flight path, and landed with one knee on the Ghar's back, crushing it into the concrete floor in a shower of blood. Remaining on one knee, she brought her carbine up and squeezed the trigger, firing a long burst of rapid fire into a group of four Ghar who rushed toward her, brandishing heavy wrench-like tools. She had cut down two of them by the time Davi landed with a thunk next to her, firing an explosive grenade from his carbine's underslung x-sling. The grenade slammed into an open Ghar battlesuit, plowing into the reactor and detonating it with a blinding flash of blue light.

The remainder of her squad landed, forming a circle with weapons pointing out in all directions in the center of the factory. No orders were necessary – all troopers remained in place and mercilessly gunned down the unarmed and unarmored Ghar mechanics as they frantically dashed for cover or scrabbled for weapons. An explosion sounded in the adjacent maintenance plant as Squad Denne dropped down from the roof and began a simultaneous attack. Mosse saw a Ghar scrambling into one of the deadly battlesuits on the far side of the factory.

"Cover!" She yelled, kicking herself away from the ground and using her suit to fly rapidly through the air at head height.

Plasma bolts laced the air around her as her squadmates sent waves of suppressing fire into the suits around her, felling more panic stricken technicians and trashing the open and vulnerable fighting machines. Mosse reached out toward the Ghar who was lowering himself into the seat of one of the machines. She wrapped an arm around his neck, tore him out of the seat, and positioned the screaming creature under one knee before allowing herself to fall out of the air, landing with her suit's full weight on the Ghar's skull and flattening it.

She span instinctively in place and saw another creature leaping off the top of a servicing platform at her, a wrench held high over its head. Mosse brought her carbine up and shot the Ghar square in the chest with a grenade. The creature exploded spectacularly, showering her with flesh and fluids. Momentarily blinded, Mosse sent a mental signal to her suit to raise her gore smeared visor up away from her eyes. Her squad had already moved up to support her, their fire destroying another trio of fighting machines which hung from chains from the alloy girders above.

"Squad Jai, contact!" She heard over the shard. "Defensive turrets online, trooper down!"

"Jai, Command, acknowledged," Mosse replied. "Fall back to the central maintenance building, marker alpha, we're clear here."

Mosse transmitted a safe path to Squad Jai as she checked the transmat pathway above her for her next inbound squad.

"Troopers, set charges!" She shouted to her command squad, dashing over to one of the empty Ghar suits which had been damaged by plasma fire, and attaching an explosive charge to make sure it would never operate again. Her squad moved rapidly across the cavernous room, setting explosive charges to battlesuits, supply crates, storage containers, anything which looked to be of use to the enemy.

Scrawny bodies of Ghar mechanics littered the floor; the sound of gunfire erupted from the factory buildings to either side of her. At the far end of the building, the main door creaked and rattled as it began to raise itself, allowing daylight to flood in. The door was barely open when a boxy, armored gun turret became visible as it swung around to line up on the drop troopers, before filling the inside of the building with streams of plasma fire. Mosse dived to the ground but saw one of her troopers react slower, a projectile catching him square in the chest and bursting out of his back.

"Squad Chyne!" She called to the next inbound squad. "Enemy gun turrets at marker beta, take them out!"

"Command, Chyne, copied."

Within seconds, five troopers fell out of the sky directly onto the turret, attaching explosive charges and then flying up out of view before the turret exploded spectacularly.

"Chyne, taking fire from Ghar reinforcements moving in from the south," Mosse heard the squad's drop leader call. "Looks like four, no, five battlesuits. We're taking heavy fire."

"Command, this is Jai!" A second frantic call came in. "I've got further Ghar units coming in from the north, three troopers down!"

Mosse made her decision instantly. Her squad alone had destroyed ten suits already – the war of attrition was in her favor. She did not want the Ghar to change the balance.

"Company from Command – Gemini!" Mosse transmitted the abort code.

She ran over to her downed trooper, clipping her carbine onto her back before dragging the cumbersome body of her downed man up into her arms. Davi and her other two troopers had already obeyed the command and had shot up through the roof to intercept the transmat beam which would take them back to the *Ajax*.

Mosse checked the vital signs of the trooper in her arms. Dead. At least if she got him back, there was a chance of getting him to regen.

With a clanking of heavy legs and a whirring of gears, a bulbous Ghar battlesuit appeared at the open doorway at the far end of the building, its sinister form silhouetted against the morning suns. Mosse knew better than to go head to head with the lumbering machine. Holding tightly to her dead trooper, she flew back up through the open roof and into the sky, wincing as enemy fire shot up around her as she fled. Below her, the charges detonated, sending plumes of thick, black smoke rising up from the factory buildings.

EIGHT

Firebase Alpha
Equatorial Region
Markov's Prize

L-Day plus 32

The door to the communal area of the squad's accommodation block slid open with a faintly audible hiss. Dragging her weary feet through the doorway, Rhona stumbled across the central hub to her own room, clipping her plasma carbine to its stowage on the wall, and dropping her battered helmet in the corner next to her bunk. Even though the subterranean accommodation block was designed with defense and practicality in mind, it somehow felt homely to her. Clythe's music posters up on the walls, Qan's pile of snacks, Jemmel's chin up bar – it all added personality.

Rhona hit the emergency jettison button on her battlesuit and breathed a sigh of relief as the bulky plates fell from her onto the floor, leaving her in the matte black body glove which formed the inner layer of the suit. She grabbed at the neckline and tore the self-sealing material open down to her abdomen before peeling it off her tired arms. The thought of removing it from her legs seemed like too much effort, so she settled for tying the arms around her waist. After three failed attempts at working with the thick material, she abandoned that idea, too, and sank down to sit on the edge of her bunk. She rested her face in her palms, feeling a sneeze rising as soon as she touched her bandana, and a layer of dust and sand fell from her hair. The planet's short day cycle was still playing hell with her body clock.

The door slid open and Jemmel walked in, following suit by hanging up her weapon and jettisoning her armored plates. The short, shaven-headed woman looked over with red-rimmed eyes.

"That look supposed to be sexy?" She sneered. "You look like crap, Rhona."

"Explain this," Rhona demanded, "we wear battle armor which

protects us to fight in space. In a vacuum. Our armor is completely sealed and air tight. So how, how the hell, have I got an entire desert inside my body glove?"

Gant was the next to wander through the door. He looked up at Rhona and forced a weary smile before poking his head back out into the corridor.

"Qan?" He shouted. "Come here, quick! Kat's in her bra!"

The sound of heavy, sprinting footsteps echoed from the corridor for the briefest of moments before coming to a stop.

"I can't," Qan called back. "I'm too knackered to run! Can you ask her nicely not to put anything else on? I'll be there as quick as I can."

Gant walked across to his room and collapsed onto his bunk, still clad in his dust-covered armor.

"That was a complete and utter waste of three days," he murmured.

"At least we all made it back," Rhona yawned. "I checked on Sessetti. He's recovering well. Clythe and Rae have gone off to see him."

"Can you put those things away before you kill somebody?" Jemmel suddenly snapped.

"It's a panhuman body, in underwear," Rhona sighed as she lay back on her bunk and set about tearing the body glove off her legs. "Get over it."

Qan appeared at the door and stared at Rhona with a huge grin.

"This is the best thing I've seen in about a year," he beamed, "but I kinda expected sexier underwear from the likes of you, Rhona."

"I'm kind of a traditional girl in that when I'm in combat with a bloodthirsty mob of genetically engineered killers, I like to be comfortable underneath and wear a massive suit of armor on top. But believe me, if the Concord Combined Command start offering the sort of armor which the women were wearing in that movie I caught you watching the other week, I'll be the first in line to volunteer to wear it. Although I'd imagine I wouldn't last long in a fight," Rhona added with a wink.

"You know, I bet you actually would, too," Jemmel said.

"What is your problem?" Rhona growled. "Yeah, I know I'm good looking. It doesn't define me. There's more to me, a lot more. I know that, I'm confident with that, and I don't give a damn what you think. So keep your opinions and comments to yourself. Just because you've given up on yourself doesn't give you the right to pass judgment on anybody else."

"Given up on myself?" Jemmel seethed, jumping to her feet. "What's that supposed to mean?"

"Aw man, I wasn't the prettiest girl at school so I'll shave my head, get tattoos, and spend my life yipping at anybody who opens their mouth," Rhona stared at the shorter woman. "Jeez, Jem, just grow your hair out, put some make up on, and act like a grown woman instead of an angry, fourteen year old boy."

"Woah! Woah! Woah!" Gant stood up, holding his hands out defensively. "C'mon, guys! We're all shattered from three days of running from killer midgets in battlesuits! This isn't us! Let's just stop, take a deep breath, and call it quits before this gets out of hand."

Rhona nodded and sank back down onto her bunk. She followed Gant's advice, inhaling a lungful of recycled air before breathing out slowly.

"I'm sorry Jem," she said, "that was a really nasty thing to say. I didn't mean that. You've got every right to live the way you wanna live and look the way you wanna look. Not my place to judge."

"It's cool, Rhona, don't sweat it," Jemmel sank down on one of the sofas in the communal area in the center of the block. "I'm just being a bitch. I could do it a lot less."

"Yeah," Qan nodded slowly, "yeah, we're all friends again. Now you two kiss each other and make up properly."

"Shut up and go... stick one of those movies on," Jemmel retorted.

The rooms fell silent for a few moments until Gant found the energy to carefully remove each of his suit's armored plates and then set about carefully cleaning them with a small equipment auto-servicer.

"How many casualties did the company take?" Qan suddenly asked.

"Twelve dead, same again wounded," Rhona replied, "nearly half of us. Post engagement report says we took out four Ghar battlesuits. Four."

She dreaded the thought of how it would all feel when the shard assistance being directed into her head had worn off. When the day came to face how many lives had been lost with clarity and no medication to fall back on.

"Yeah, but we gave those little unarmored bastards a good kicking," Gant offered, "we must have dropped a hundred of those."

"But they've got thousands more," Jemmel sighed.

"It's all the more reason to be thankful," Rhona said. "We've got two days here before we're back in the line. Two days of nobody trying to kill us. We can lie around here and worry, or we can go do something to pick ourselves up. C'mon, let's go get changed and get out of here. That mandarin says there's a safe area about two hours in a Duke from here and we're cleared to leave the firebase. It's some little coastal town which is on the right side of the lines and is now under our control. Let's just go find a bar and sit down by a beach with some drinks."

Gant and Jemmel exchanged looks.

"What?" Rhona asked.

"The population is mostly Concord now," Gant explained, "but there's still those who are IMTel incompatible. Not many, a real minority, but just a handful of people who's minds won't merge with our nanospheres, once there's one in place here. And they'll remember exactly what things were like before we got here. Just before you joined the company, Kat, a few of us went out to some city excursion when we had a couple days of second line respite. It was a planet called... W'Than Three. Anyway, one of the locals hadn't merged with the IMTel. Saw a bunch of strangers with military haircuts and put two and two together. He bombed the bar we were in, killed three of our guys."

"Sorry, Rhona," Jemmel said. "I'm not going through that again. If I've got two days off, I'm spending two days sleeping."

The room fell silent again. Rhona grabbed her datapad and set about constructing a letter to send to her brother.

***

Outskirts of the Nienne Desert
Equatorial Region
Markov's Prize

L-Day plus 34

The cramped interior of the C3T7 transporter drone seemed almost spacious with only three passengers inside. Tahl had often looked at the exterior of the vehicle and wondered how it was possible to cram ten troopers inside the angular hold which hung below the midpoint of the drone. If it was possible to apply compression technology to living matter without harming it, the T7 Duke was proof.

Tahl looked across at the other side of the passenger hold at the drone's other two occupants. Strike Leader Rall and Strike Trooper Sessetti had both been wounded in action whilst fighting the Ghar. Rall had taken a hit in exactly the way Tahl would have predicted – leading a head on assault against battlesuited Ghar. His squad of five soldiers had managed to destroy a single Ghar trooper with grenades. Sessetti, meanwhile, had been gunned down by a trooper whilst his squad held a defensive position. The medical reports described massive trauma to the lower torso – the young soldier had been nearly cut in half. Both men would be dead without modern medical care; the same care which allowed them to return to combat duties after being severely injured.

"Not quite what it looks like on *Infinity Rangers*?" Tahl offered a smile to Sessetti.

The young trooper blinked at him.

"I'm sorry, sir?"

"*Infinity Rangers*," Tahl repeated, "that holo-show that was popular a few years back Probably before your time. It's about soldiers from a fictitious force which looks surprisingly like C3, fighting bad guys across the galaxy. Their armor makes them look like drop troopers, but don't ever tell a drop trooper that! It's a sore subject. Anyhow, in the show, there's a whole lot of gunfire and explosions, but nobody ever dies and the bad guys aren't all that scary. Probably keeps the people back home from thinking the worst about what we're doing out here."

Sessetti smiled uncomfortably and nodded. Tahl could easily check Sessetti's emotions through his shard connection with the company, but he always found it to be something of an invasion of privacy unless it was in combat, where it was often necessary. Still, the spiritual side of Tahl's study of kerempai had led him down the path of interpreting non-verbal communication, and right now, Sessetti was where so many junior soldiers found themselves – uncomfortable with the rank gradient and therefore reticent to talk to higher ranking soldiers.

"Drop trooper," Rall nodded slowly, "now there's something I'd like to have a go at. Jumping down behind enemy lines, blowing stuff up. That sounds like the life."

"You only end up doing about one or two jumps per year," Tahl said. "It's a risky way to enter combat and it needs a pretty sterile environment if you're to avoid massive casualties. It's pretty exhilarating though, the actual jump along the transmat beam."

"You used to be a drop trooper, sir?" Sessetti asked hesitantly.

"Only for a couple of years, when I first joined up. I only logged five combat drops. The rest of it was pretty similar to what we do in the strike corps – a lot of time in the back of a T7."

The drone began to slow down as it neared its destination. Tahl patched in to the drone's cameras and looked out across the desert ahead. Fine, yellow sands stretched out in soft dunes, rippled by the light wind. Mixed in with the yellow in almost equal proportions were swirls of blue; the courser, darker sands uncovered by the winds and painting the entire landscape with a vivid and unique effect not dissimilar to marble. The horizon was broken with dull, orange hills made of jagged rocks with winding canyons and ravines snaking through. Up ahead was the construction site of Firebase Delta, the formation's next base of operations in the fight against the Ghar invaders. Engineering drones were already busily constructing a defensive perimeter made up of kinetic barriers, scanners, and automated gun turrets.

The drone slowed to a stop and eased down to touch the soft sand before the door slid open on the left hand side of the hold. Tahl stood up, holding out a hand to gesture for the other two troopers to go on ahead of him. Sessetti was first out – the six troopers of his squad stood waiting for him at the edge of the landing area. A few whoops and cheers were issued by his friends as he hopped down from the Duke before jogging over to meet them. Rall was next to jump down. Nobody stood waiting for him.

Tahl stepped down into the yellow and blue sand, the glaring suns causing him to wince and turn away as a single figure walked out to meet him. Dressed the same as all other troopers in the busy firebase construction area, Van Noor wore his battlesuit with his helmet replaced by his beret.

"Welcome back, sir!" Van Noor shouted over the din of the construction behind him, saluting smartly.

Tahl returned the salute and reached out to shake the senior strike leader's hand.

"Hello Bry," he smiled. "I've missed a lot. I've caught up on all that I could on the flight across."

"Mandarin Owenne says you're late," Van Noor said as the two walked away from the landing area, "but he's done a good job of keeping the company in one piece. We've taken a lot of hits, but Owenne ordered a fighting withdrawal as soon as it was obvious that we were outgunned. Intelligence says this is the area the Ghar are heading for, so here we are. Good fields of fire, at least, we can capitalize on our longer-range weaponry out here in the desert. No cover, though, until we get into those canyons. That concerns me. I'll take you to Formation HQ, the commander wants to get you up to speed on what you've missed."

Van Noor led Tahl toward a corridor which cut through rows of stacked packaging crates. Out of the corner of his eye, Tahl saw one of the soldiers from Sessetti's squad suddenly break away from their reunion and run across. He felt a gnawing discomfort in his gut as soon as he realized it was Rhona.

"Sir!" The young woman saluted smartly as she caught up with them. "Good morning, Senior."

"Not now," Van Noor said, "the strike captain has literally just arrived and we're heading to HQ for..."

"It's alright," Tahl gently interjected to stop Van Noor. "Give me a moment, Strike Leader, I'll be right with you."

Rhona saluted smartly again and walked out of earshot to wait in the shade of the stacked crates.

"She's changed," Tahl said pointedly as he turned back to Van Noor. "What have you said to her?"

"She told me she threatened you with regulatory action, Ryen," Van Noor said defensively, "so I put her back in her box. Firmly."

Tahl sighed and nodded slowly.

"I'll deal with that in a second. Look, Bry, I need to talk to you about something. I'm not sure where to start and I don't think you're going to like what you hear, but I've got to tell you."

Van Noor shot a confused look at Tahl, but he remained silent.

"Those two weeks Owenne gave me. I went to see your family." Van Noor's eyes widened in amazement. Tahl began speaking again quickly, eager to explain. "I only saw them for five minutes. You know how long it takes to get all the way back home. I know it's none of my business, but I had to try. I had to! I can't just sit idly by and do nothing whilst your world is falling apart, and you've done nothing wrong..."

"I did do something wrong!" Van Noor raised his voice, quickly checking over both shoulders to make sure nobody was within earshot. "Mate, this isn't your concern!"

"I know that, but I've made it my concern. Right or wrong, I've involved myself now. I'm sorry if this isn't what you wanted, but I had to try! I explained everything to Becca, everything I possibly could. I tried to tell her about how it all works, saved game points, the sniper..."

"Both she and I now know what I'm capable of, and so do you. I... appreciate what you tried to do, Ryen, but you shouldn't have gone." Van Noor turned away and placed his hands on his hips, wincing in the fierce sunlight for a few moments in silence before he spoke again. "Did she seem okay? Did she look alright?"

"She looked okay. Tired, but alright. But I disagree with you," Tahl said firmly, "on both counts. You're no longer capable of what... the other guy did because you've been educated now. You know the consequences. You'd never do it. And I'm glad I went, because whilst I didn't achieve much, she did listen a little. Just a little. And I knew I couldn't make things any worse."

"What do you mean, she listened?"

"As I was walking away," Tahl explained, "Alora ran after me. She gave me this to give to you."

Tahl took the carefully folded piece of paper which had accompanied him for light years of travel and handed it to Van Noor. The older man looked at it.

"What is it?"

"I don't know."

"You didn't look at it?"

"It's not for me. I was told to give it to you."

"You've brought it all this way and you didn't open it?"

Tahl shook his head.

Van Noor took it and carefully unfolded it. He immediately raised a fist to his chin as tears formed in his eyes. He wordlessly turned the paper to show Tahl. A beautiful, black and white picture of Van Noor holding hands with his two children as they walked along a beach had been drawn on the paper.

"You prick, you've made me cry in front of the guys," Van Noor smiled shakily, turning away.

"Your children still love you," Tahl offered, "it was worth making that trip if only to bring back proof of that for you."

Van Noor did not answer. After a few moments, he turned to face Tahl again, composed.

"Thanks," he said sincerely, "I mean that. Thank you. I just wish... well, I shouldn't be here missing my daughter grow up. Look at this! She can really draw! I should be back there, helping with... look, it doesn't matter. We need to get to HQ. You go talk to... her, and then catch me up. But you've done me a favor, mate, and I owe you. So let me at least speak my mind and give you some free advice. Steer well clear of Rhona. I do not get a good vibe from her. Beneath the pretty smile and the perfect teeth and the huge boobs, she's a nasty piece of work. Steer clear of her, mate. Don't let one pretty girl be your undoing."

Tahl opened his mouth to speak but realized he had nothing to say to Van Noor's accusations. The brawny senior soldier gave him a clap on the shoulder and walked away. Tahl turned to look at Rhona, who was busily checking her armor and rubbing away patches of dirt and grime. Tahl walked over to her.

"Sir," she looked up, "I'll be quick, I know you're busy. I just wanted to put everything to rest between us after our last talk. Senior Strike Leader Van Noor has spoken to me, and..."

"Drop the rank," Tahl said. "Just say what you want to say. I owe you that. This is nothing to do with our roles in the company, this is because of me treating you poorly. So just be open, say what you need to say, and then we can both move on."

"What was going through your mind when you picked me for promotion?" Rhona asked without hesitation.

Tahl paused and looked away, trying to remember his actions from months past. He looked back at her. She had cut her hair shorter, still long enough to reach halfway down her neck. Both styles suited her. He closed his eyes and shook his head. He doubted very much that he would have noticed such a relatively minor aesthetic change in any other woman under his command.

"It takes about two or three hours to select a new strike leader," Tahl began, "if you do it properly. Ideally you get a few people together and discuss the merits of the various candidates which have been presented by C3, then you make an informed decision. On the day I selected you for promotion, we were advancing across the Senai Plains on Valhr. I had to selected a new strike leader, submit a progress report for formation command, calculate our logistical requirements, prepare an intelligence brief, and write several letters of condolence to the next of kin of some of our casualties. Each of those jobs takes a couple of hours. I had twenty minutes before I was leading a reconnaissance patrol to scout enemy forward positions. I prioritized the letters of condolence and gave them the majority of the time I had. When it came to picking a new strike leader, I just looked at the list of names, picked you immediately without a second more thought, and moved on to my next job.

"Several days later, Senior Strike Leader Van Noor queried my decision. I had completely forgotten about it. It was only then that it struck me, and I told him the truth. 'I think I promoted her because I'm attracted to her.' It was too late by then, you had been sent away on the training course. He said I should tell you the truth, but I kept putting it off. Because I was too scared to confront you. It wasn't an intentional, premeditated, and malicious act on my part, it was a rushed, spur of the moment decision, made on the spot when I was trying to manage several very important tasks. I know that's no excuse, but it's the whole truth. That's the whole story. I'm really sorry, you deserve better."

Rhona bit her bottom lip pensively before replying.

"It's not as bad as it was in my head," she admitted. "I guess... well, I guess you had a lot going on, and we all make mistakes. Look, I'm over it. It's cool. I'm just... sorry I don't feel the same way. You're a great looking guy, I mean, really good looking, but you're just not my type. You're... a nice guy and that's all well and good for women who are one hundred and fifty and ready to settle down, but I'm twenty-five, I've got a century of little to no responsibility ahead of me and, well, given that I could get my head blown off any day and how much stuff I've got going on in my life right now, I'm not into nice guys. I'm not looking for a relationship at all. If anything, I'd probably end up shacking up with some bastard who'd treat me like crap for a few weeks before we both moved on anyway."

Tahl chuckled slightly at the irony of her words, describing exactly the man he was when he was twenty-five.

"Is there anything else you want to know?" He asked.

"No, I think that's it," Rhona took a step back. "Let's just forget the whole thing. I'm not gonna bring it up again, it's fine. I'll just do my job the best I can. I'm cool with it all, if you are."

"Yeah," Tahl nodded, "yeah, I'm cool. Thanks for your understanding, and I'm sorry I put you through this. But you're right, with what you said last time we spoke. Beyond what is absolutely necessary for us to operate together within a military context, I think it best we don't communicate with each other at all. You were very wise to say that, and I couldn't agree more."

Rhona's smile faded. She stood up a little straighter and nodded.

"Yes, sir," she said, "permission to carry on?"

"Granted, Strike Leader," Tahl replied, returning her salute before walking quickly toward Formation HQ.

***

Nienne Desert
One hundred and ten kiloyan northwest of Firebase Delta
Markov's Prize

Staring at every detail of the holographic image for what what seemed like the one thousandth time, Van Noor brought his daughter's picture across his array in an attempt to combat the effects of the dense sandstorm. That simple piece of data had given him a link to his children, a link which gave him real and perceptible strength. His battlesuit readout told him that he was burning less medication than before, even though it had only been a day.

A day of moving northwest to meet the advancing Ghar, digging in to hold a line which extended off to the left where Alpha Company stood ready, and the right where Cian Company held the flank. Beta Company was dead center, and Tahl had positioned his command squad just behind the middle of that defensive line.

"Bry? You good to go?" Tahl's voice echoed through his head via the command squad shard.

"Yeah, on my way."

Van Noor carefully folded up the piece of paper and secured it inside a pouch on his utility belt. The sandstorm was already beginning to thin and dissipate as he walked back to the remainder of the company. The seven C3T7 transporters which had brought them out were parked in a neat row, flanked by two very similar looking, but significantly upgunned, C3M4 combat drones. The company's fifty remaining strike troopers had separated into their seven strike squads and three x-launcher teams and waited for instructions. In and around them were the smaller drones – the vital, disc shaped C3D1 drones with their rapid firing plasma light support weapons, as well as the smaller spotter, medical, and shield drones.

Mandarin Owenne had decided to accompany Beta Company to set up the defenses and stood alone at the edge of the assembly, staring off to the northeast with his hands clasped behind his back and his IMTel stave tucked neatly under one arm. Tahl was walking over to him as Van Noor arrived.

"We can easily converse over the shard, chaps," Owenne said as the dust continued to clear and turquoise skies began to seep through the yellow. "It's what it was invented for."

"It's not a habit I wish to…"

Owenne held up a hand to stop Tahl's reply.

"I know, Ryen, I know, better to brief the men and women face to face. I accept your thoughts, I just don't understand them."

"If you're going to order young men and women to their deaths, you should at least have the common courtesy to look them dead in the eyes when you do so," Tahl said, removing his helmet and blinking in the fierce sunlight as the last sands of the dust storm carried on their way to the south.

"You've worked with panhumans long enough, Owenne," Van Noor pitched in, "you should understand us a little by now. Besides, you were the one who ordered our withdrawal last week. That order saved a lot of lives. Don't pretend there isn't a heart in there somewhere."

"Don't confuse tactical sense for sentimentality," the NuHu corrected with a grim smile. "Just because I don't want my assets dead doesn't mean I mourn their passing. I'm keeping soldiers alive because I need them, not because I like them. Leadership is not a popularity competition, gentlemen."

"I disagree," Tahl folded his arms, "leadership is the art of getting a body of men and women to do something you want them to do, but they don't want to do. You either do that via respect or fear. Popularity and respect do have some crossover. A popular leader is not a bad leader."

"And you, Killer?" Owenne looked at Tahl. "Are you a popular leader?"

"It's not my…"

"Yeah," Van Noor interrupted, "yeah, he is. Now we've got a significant force of angry little bastards in armored killing machines stomping our way over here, so shall we brief the boys and girls and go get stuck in?"

Owenne twisted at the torso, his hands still clasped at his back. He looked at the ground near Van Noor's feet, narrowed his eyes, and smiled again.

"You go and brief them, Ryen. You're far better with… people. Oh, and be sure to let them know how much artillery we've got this time. That should cheer the poor dears up a bit."

Van Noor bit back another response but then thought again. Why bother? The NuHu's control over the IMTel, nanospheres, shards, it was so acute that he could read thoughts. There was nothing to hide from the NuHu, which was one of the reasons why they were often feared by ordinary soldiers.

"I know," Owenne answered Van Noor's thoughts, "but I very rarely actually get into people's minds. It's not out of some outdated sense of chivalry and respect for boundaries like Killer here has. It's because you all bore the life out of me. Love, respect, hurt feelings, romance, art, politics, sex... blah, blah, blah. Now get the boys and girls in position. I want to inflict casualties on the bastards today."

Tahl tapped Van Noor on the shoulder and beckoned for him to follow.

"He's not that bad," Tahl smiled as the two walked back to the troops. "I'm sure he acts up just to get a reaction. I've seen him drunk, he likes building models in his spare time. And astronomy. Come on, let's double check all of our people are content with the plan."

"Squad Leaders," Van Noor transmitted across the company command shard, "to me."

The six squad leaders immediately broke away from their squads and formed a semi-circle around Tahl and Van Noor. Tahl dropped to one knee and gestured for the other soldiers to do the same. Used to their strike captain's preferences, the squad leaders all removed their helmets. Van Noor cast his eyes across the leaders. Vias, a man who had nailed that very thin line of combining being the company joker with a proficient soldier and respected leader. He would take the far left flank, backed up by the M4s. Yavn, experienced against the Isorians but clearly apprehensive in his first campaign against the Ghar. A good soldier with potential to excel, Van Noor had singled him out as needing support, as for the first time he appeared to be coming unstuck. Rall, his dark skin glistening with sweat, his angry eyes impatiently flicking off to the northeast where the enemy approached from. His squad would be dead center, where a man of his fearless nature would be best utilized. Rhona, her perfect hair stylishly arching down over the tatty bandana around her forehead, her dark eyes narrowed as if a seductive appearance was her top priority. Van Noor shook his head – she would never be a leader of fighting men and women. Heide – stoic, dependable, experienced. His squad had taken the most casualties and the two soldiers who had been sent across from Cian Company had both gone to him. Althern, the company's most experienced trooper after Van Noor and Tahl, the perfect man for commanding that exposed position on the right flank where a winding ravine connected their defensive line to that of Cian Company.

Tahl used a datapad to project a holographic representation of the surrounding terrain onto the ground in the middle of the assembled leaders.

"Last time we go through this. We've got dead center of the line, in between Alpha and Cian Companies. Echo Company has got our back, and we've got four batteries of artillery behind them so this time, if we see battlesuits, we've got a good chance to knock them down. Squad Denne has the left flank and joins us up with Alpha Company. Teal are next down the line. Vias, Yavn, you two will be close enough to each other to provide fire support, and you've got our two M4s as well as an x-launcher. Looking at the terrain, I'd predict you're the most likely to see a proper push from the Ghar; so if you do, hit them with everything you've got and we'll close around them from both sides. Rall – your Squad Jai has dead center. You'll be first on hand to support Denne and Teal if needed, but there's also a chance they'll hit you dead on, so take full advantage of the rocky terrain you've got to hand. Rhona, your Squad Wen is overlooking a steep ravine – I doubt the Ghar would tunnel themselves in, so you need to be ready to move fast – anywhere. You're my first choice to relocate and plug other areas of the line, so keep your Duke close by. Heide – similar story – be ready to move fast but also support Althern's Squad Xath on the right flank, as that's where the open ground is – good for our guns but also good for their limited mobility. Any questions?"

"Are we intending to slow them and make a fighting withdrawal, Boss?" Yavn asked.

"No," Tahl replied sternly, "we've got a pair of M4s on the left flank, artillery support behind us, and two units of D1 drones for rapid fire support. My intentions are to dig in and stop them right here. I'll make the call if we need to fall back, but you go into this fight with the mental expectation that we're going nowhere. The Ghar have had a good run so far. The moment they're in range of our weapons, that's going to end. Today. That's all from me – get to your positions and report in when you're set up and good to go."

***

Five hours had passed. The midafternoon suns were continuing their slow dip toward the horizon, the shadows cast along the ravines and rocks growing slightly longer with every few passing minutes. Sessetti looked across to where Clythe dragged an armored foot through the sand, scrapping away the top layer of yellow to reveal the courser blue beneath. As they watched, the sunrays burned the thinner grains of sand back to yellow within seconds, adding another layer of bicolored swirls along the ground.

Up ahead of them, the ravine wound left and right with jagged pillars of orange rock jutting out of the sand at irregular intervals. Behind them was open desert; yan after yan of undulating sand mounds, skeletal bushes, and dry blades of grass. The squad's C3T7 transport drone lay silently in the sand behind them, its plasma light support turret pointing ready at the ravine opening.

Sessetti looked at the other members of the squad. Gant and Jemmel stared patiently at the ravine opening, their weapons ready. Rhona crouched behind the line of troopers, her carbine resting across one knee. Clythe idly dragged his foot through the sand to create shapes and swirls in yellow and blue. Qan drummed his fingers impatiently along the top of his carbine. Rae was looking directly at Sessetti as his eyes reached her – she offered a friendly wave from her position at the end of the line.

"It's on," Rhona suddenly reported, "Cian company's got Outcasts attempting to flank them, all the way off on our right."

Sessetti listened in for the sound of gunfire but heard only the wind rustling dry vegetation and the scratchy call of some local lizard which miraculously managed to survive the heat. Then, a few seconds later, the rumble of artillery sounded from a battery many yan behind them.

"That'll show the bastards," Qan said.

Before he had even finished, the sound of plasma fire issued from somewhere off to the left, over on the other side of a broad plateau of sand.

"Squad Teal's engaged," Rhona said, "some sort of Ghar crawler."

Again the sound of artillery fire echoed from afar, and within moments, the whistling of shells cut through the hot air and impacted the ground somewhere off to the left, vibrating the very earth beneath their feet.

"Y'all get ready," Rhona warned, "we're either gonna get attacked real soon, or we're gonna be helping somebody else who is."

***

"Squad Denne, Command," Tahl transmitted to Vias, "there's a large concentration of Ghar closing in from marker delta – I'm relocating your M4s."

"Copied," Vias replied.

Tahl turned to face Van Noor, careful to remain hidden beneath the smooth lip of rock which jutted out of the sand which surrounded them.

"Bry, lay down some markers for the M4s – get them across to support Alpha Company as quick as you can. Looks like they're taking the worst of it so far."

"Got it," Van Noor replied, connecting with the shard utilized by the pair of C3M4 combat drones, and laying a safe path for them to transit along to support their neighboring company of strike troopers to the left.

"Squad Xath, Command," Tahl called. "Hostiles inbound from the northeast, get your people in cover, rain's coming down."

"Got it, Command," Althern's deep voice replied.

"Cian Battery, Beta Command," Tahl called one of the artillery batteries behind the frontline, "fire for effect at marker violet, corrective action will be issued by my senior strike leader."

"Cian Battery copied, marker received, firing in three."

Van Noor patched in to the overhead view of the battlefield which Tahl was using to direct his forces. Alpha Company to the left had a major push against them, centered around a tall, five-legged walker with a crew of three Ghar. At least twenty battlesuits were swarming forward around the Command Crawler, their weapons sending streams of plasma into the defensive positions of Alpha Company. In return, plasma fire spewed forth from the strike troopers' positions, accompanied by the carnage wreaked by the artillery which erupted in and around the advancing fighting machines. Van Noor's two M4 drones were quick to arrive on the scene, their opening salvo of plasma fire cutting down a Ghar battlesuit and sending the three legged machine sprawling into the dirt.

"Boss! Up ahead!" Kachi warned, firing his carbine from where he lay behind the natural cover of the rocks.

Van Noor looked in the direction of fire and saw five crude, mechanical flying machines of a similar size to a Concord spotter drone hovering at head height some ten yan away. The machines all had archaic looking surveillance devices hastily bolted on to a set of metal wings. Kachi's first shot impacted with one of the machines, blowing a neat hole through the center of its body and sending it buzzing down to impact with the ground. The other machines immediately buzzed back the way they had come from.

"Flitters," Van Noor identified the Ghar machines. "They know we're here now."

"They must have crept right past Squad Jai," Kachi said.

"Jai, Command," Tahl called. "Sitrep?"

"Six battlesuits! Taking heavy fire!" Rall replied. "I've got two casualties and we're pinned in place!"

"Teal, from Command," Tahl said calmly, "I'm sending you a marker to move to, to provide covering fire for Squad Jai. Artillery inbound in ten seconds. Squad Jai, wait for my orders to fall back to my position, how copied?"

"Jai copies!" Rall shouted. "Got one! We've dropped one of the bastards!"

"Jai, Command, good job," Tahl nodded. "Get your heads down, stay in cover, and wait for artillery support and covering fire from Squad Teal."

Van Noor checked the overhead view of the battlefield again and let out a curse. Another strong force of Ghar was moving toward Cian Company on the right flank.

NINE

"Got something," Gant declared as he sent an image feed from the spotter drone to the rest of the squad. "Look at this – just up around that corner ahead."

Sessetti looked at the image which was transmitted to his screen. Three Ghar battlesuits stood in the center of the ravine; one with its weapons pointing down at the ground and no light emissions from its reactor exhausts. The second machine's reactor blinked on and off whilst the lights from its sensor array flickered temperamentally. The last machine stood ahead of them, its weapons also pointing down the ravine.

"Looks like they're in trouble," Gant said. "We should go get them before they realize how close we are."

"Don't talk crap!" Jemmel snapped. "They know we're here, and they're just sat there waiting for us! Besides, we're supposed to be ready to reinforce the line, not go leaving our positions because we feel like it!"

Sessetti switched off the image feed from the spotter drone and looked at the ravine entrance ahead. It seemed taller, all of a sudden, more threatening. He considered voicing his opinion but decided against it.

"Our guys are taking a beating, and for whatever reason, there's three of these bastards sat there in the open, two with no power!" Gant urged. "We can get right on top of them and drop grenades in their reactors! Three of them, just waiting for it!"

"He's right," Clythe nodded. "C'mon, let's go finish them off before they call in help. No power. This will be easy."

The sound of battle to either side of the squad's defensive position seemed to intensify.

"No power?" Jemmel shook her head. "Simultaneously? Give your brains a chance, both of you! They don't just break down!"

"The intelligence brief said that if one reactor goes up, it can take out an entire squad of them!" Clythe said.

"That's an explosion, not a chained power failure, you idiot!" Jemmel scowled, a gauntleted finger pointing in accusation. "Look!

We've got our orders! We sit tight and shoot anything that gets close!"

"Grow a pair, Jem!" Gant snapped. "There's three of them and seven of us! They're sat there, just..."

"Shut up!" Rhona finally interjected. "All of you, shut up! I'm thinking, just give me a second!"

"We've got orders, Kat," Jemmel said calmly, "we're not supposed to just do our own thing!"

"We're selected and trained for our flexibility!" Gant exclaimed. "So let's be flexible! Let's go blow these sods up before it's too late! The mandarin said they'd start breaking down if we left it long enough."

Rhona nodded slowly.

"Gant, Rae – get up front. Jemmel, stick with me and be ready with the lance..."

"Seriously?" Jemmel yelled.

"Just do what I tell you!" Rhona shouted back. "C'mon! Let's go get them!"

"We telling Command?" Qan offered.

"Don't do that," Gant said, "they'll just tell us to wait here and it'll be too late."

Sessetti looked across to Clythe as the seven strike troopers rose to their feet. Whatever was going on in his friend's mind, it was hidden by the helmet's face mask. The squad moved silently and rapidly into the ravine, their armor changing to a darker orange-brown to fit in with the colors of the shaded rocks. Up ahead, Gant held up a clenched fist. The squad stopped in place. Sessetti checked the feed from the spotter drone again. He could see it up at the edge of the ravine, silently looking down at the Ghar below. Nothing had changed – one was powered down, one was struggling through some sort of reboot procedure, whilst the last stood guard over its vulnerable comrades.

"We hit the live one with everything we've got," Rhona ordered. "Gant – take Rae and Sessetti around the right, the rest of you follow me to the left. Wait for the guard suit to turn and check the other end of the ravine... Wait...Go!"

Sessetti followed Gant and Rae as the trio sprinted out of cover and ran into the open around the corner of the ravine. The lumbering suits were only a stone throw away, the live machine midway through a turn with its weapons pointed away. Halfway from the frantic dash to reach the enemy, the two apparently damaged Ghar effortlessly powered up. Sessetti felt bile rush into his throat. All three span around to face the approaching troopers and opened fire with the most intense barrage of destruction Sessetti had ever seen.

Bolts of plasma smashed through Gant, tearing off one of his legs at the knee and spinning him around in place as his armor was punctured by the projectiles. Two shots cleaved straight through Rae's torso; she tensed up and toppled over to the ground without a sound. The shard's communication frequency filled with panicked shouts, screams of pain, curses, and confusion.

Sessetti turned and ran. The cover of the ravine corner seemed to stay in place, refusing to draw closer no matter how fast he propelled his legs. A Concord trooper sprinted past him, plasma bolts chasing them down as they ran and flaring up their protective hyper-light shields. Sessetti had no memory of how or when he reached cover. He found himself collapsed on his knees, his carbine in the dust in front of him, panicked bodies crammed into cover all around him.

"Stay down!" Jemmel yelled. "Stay put!"

"Get back!" Clythe shouted. "We need to pull back before they catch us up!"

"There're Outcasts moving up the ravine behind us!" Qan exclaimed. "We're boxed in! Get the Duke here to get us out!"

"What about Rae?" Sessetti asked, picking up his carbine. "And Gant? We need to get them!"

"They're gone!" Jemmel risked a look back around the corner. "We need to fall back to the Duke, shoot our way through those Outcasts!"

"No!" Rhona shouted. "I'm gonna go get our guys! In five seconds, you give me all the cover you can!"

"Kat!" Jemmel grabbed Rhona forcefully by the forearm. "You go out there, you're dead! They're gone! We need to fall back!"

Sessetti opened his mouth to speak. He wanted to say that he would go with Rhona. He wanted to offer to go and get Rae. No words came.

"I'm not leaving them!" Rhona growled, throwing Jemmel's hand away. "I can get to those rocks and then drag them into cover! You ready?"

Jemmel grabbed Rhona by the neck.

"Don't!"

Rhona pushed Jemmel off with both hands and then turned to look up the ravine.

"Cover!" Rhona yelled, sprinting away and back toward the Ghar troopers.

Sessetti flung himself to the dusty ground around the corner of the ravine and brought his weapon up to bare before spraying the nearest Ghar with plasma bolts. Clythe dropped to one knee next to him, firing his own carbine at the same target. Rhona hurtled along the ravine, enemy fire blasting the rocks around her and kicking up clouds of dust. Jemmel's plasma lance impacted into the side of one of the Ghar war machines, pushing it forcefully back onto one bended leg but failing to damage it. By a miracle, Rhona dived to the ground and took cover behind a thick outcrop of orange rock. She was halfway.

"Keep firing!" Jemmel shouted. "Don't let up!"

Rhona hauled herself back to her feet and ran headlong for the two prone bodies who lay broken ahead of her. As if it were another trap, as if they had been toying with her, all three Ghar battlesuits turned their guns on Rhona and cut her down with accurate fire. Plasma bolts smashing through her hip and abdomen, Rhona crumpled to the ground. She let out an agonizing cry of pain which filled Sessetti's ears for a long moment before she fell deathly silent.

An unseen hand grabbed Sessetti and dragged him back into cover behind the ravine corner.

"Squad Wen, command override," Jemmel breathed. "Strike leader down. I have command."

***

"Command, Denne!" Vias shouted above the roar of gunfire. "I've got two dead and two cat four! We've taken out two Ghar troopers, but I've got another three pinning me down from marker omega!"

"Denne, hold position," Tahl urged. "You've got multiple units from Alpha Company moving in to provide support, seconds away. Is your position defendable?"

A few seconds of silence made Tahl fear the worst. He slid his facemask back and raised his armored fingers to touch his aching forehead. Finally, a response was issued.

"Command, Denne, friendlies visual, we're... we're good."

No sooner had Vias finished speaking when the next voice cut across the command shard frequency, accompanied by a flashing light on the holographic display of the battlefield which was projected in front of Tahl.

"Command, Xath," Althern called, "I've got three troopers down and we're falling back to... marker ghia."

Ignoring the hammering pain in his head, Tahl looked at the positions of all nearby units on the map.

"Xath from Command," he responded, "you've got hostiles approaching from the east; I'm re-routing three D1 drones to marker ghia to support you. Can you defend that position?"

"Xath," Althern said breathlessly, as the marker showing his position on the map moved rapidly toward their new marker, "affirmative."

Tahl looked up at Van Noor, Cane, and Kachi. Van Noor remained crouched next to him, providing a constant stream of corrective markers to the artillerymen who relentlessly bombarded the advancing Ghar. Cane looked across at Tahl.

"Do we need to move up, Boss?" Cane asked. "Time we go get

stuck in ourselves?"

Tahl's response was cut off by another communication across the shard.

"Command, Squad Wen!" Tahl recognised Strike Trooper Jemmel's voice. "We're pinned down at the ravine immediately north of marker indigo! Readouts showing... one dead, two cat four! Request immediate assistance!"

Tahl felt an immediate wave of nausea, replaced by calmness and clarity as his array warned him he was receiving external assistance to cope with what he had just heard. He reviewed Squad Wen's situation – cut off in a narrow ravine with three Ghar troopers to the north and some twenty Outcasts advancing from the south, the four surviving strike troopers did not have long. The Ghar troopers were too close to engage with artillery; but perhaps not the Outcasts.

"Cian Battery, Beta Command, engage targets at marker zion," Tahl ordered before sending a mental command to a pair of C3D1 drones which were attached to Squad Chyne, moving them toward the ravine from the east.

It still would not be enough.

"Command Squad, on me," Tahl ordered, hauling himself to his feet and sprinting off toward the ravine.

***

"They're nearly on top of us!" Qan yelled as he risked another shot, leaning around the corner of the ravine wall to fire another burst of plasma into the advancing three Ghar fighting machines. Jemmel yelled a stream of obscenities as she leaned over the top of the hole she had found in the rock face, firing another stream from her plasma lance toward the trio of immovable Ghar. Return fire from the enemy unit smashed against the rocks, chipping clunks of stone up which twirled into the air around the strike troopers amid a dense field of dust and sand.

Sessetti peered over the lip of the rock and looked at the three prone bodies of his squadmates which lay motionless where they had fallen, now behind the advancing Ghar. He attempted a suit readout from all three casualties, but at this range and with his control of the shard all but destroyed by his rising panic, he could only detect that one of his friends was already dead and a second would die within the next few minutes.

"Targets behind!" Clythe shouted, turning on the spot to fire a rapid burst back up the ravine. "Outcasts!"

Sessetti raised his carbine and fired an aimed shot at one of the small horde of hunched over creatures which scrabbled their way over the rocks toward them. His shot hit a Ghar Outcast in the center of the torso, flinging the creature's arms out to either side before it fell back, dead. The action felt futile to Sessetti. As he fired again and again, the realization crept to the fore of his mind that this was how he would die, surrounded in a dusty ravine on a planet he had never heard of, buried up to the waist in rock as psychotic panhuman-morphs in unstoppable battlesuits closed on him. He hoped that his clone would be activated, for his parents' sake.

With only the briefest of warnings in the form of a familiar, shrill shriek, the entire world to the south seemed to light up as artillery shells slammed down into the ravine entrance, shaking the earth and lifting clumps of blue sand and orange rock into the air. The next shells walked slowly forward, ripping into the advancing Outcasts and hurling them up into the air, slamming the creatures violently into the ravine walls and tearing them limb from limb.

Simultaneously, a pair of disc shaped C3D1 drones appeared at the edge of the ravine above and to the right of Sessetti, their plasma light support weapons firing rapid pulses of energy projectiles down into the flanks of the three battlesuits. The Ghar fighting machines stopped in place and twisted to bring their weapons to bear on the Concord drones, returning fire with even greater ferocity.

Amid the shouts, screams, explosions, and confusion of the battle, Sessetti saw three strike troopers suddenly appear on the opposite side of the ravine, firing down into the Ghar battlesuits. He watched incredulously as a fourth trooper climbed quickly down the ravine wall, threw his carbine aside and sprinted headlong out into the open toward the Ghar.

***

The first attack needed to be perfect. With fire streaming down from both sides of the ravine, Tahl had one chance to take an enemy down before he had lost the advantage of surprise. The three Ghar troopers drew closer with each step, their attention still dominated by the pair of D1 drones which fired down into them from the top of the ravine. Caught in a hail of fire, one of the Concord drones exploded spectacularly and showered the ravine with parts and debris. But it had given Tahl what he needed.

Running to engage the first battlesuit, Tahl stepped out into a long stance and brought one elbow forward, every muscle in his body concentrating on reinforcing the strength of the strike in the very tip of that elbow. Thirty years of martial arts training enhanced by the superhuman strength afforded to him by his battlesuit focused his elbow strike into the vulnerable side of one of the Ghar's knee joints.

The strike resounded with a loud clang, and the Ghar sank to one side as the knee buckled and bent. Tahl immediately followed up with a side kick to the exact same spot, letting out a shout as he again concentrated every ounce of strength at his disposal into that one point of impact. The knee joint gave way and parted as his armored foot slammed into its target, sending the lower half of the leg skidding across the sand as the Ghar fell pathetically down into the dirt. Van Noor, Cane, and Kachi were only a moment behind, diving forward onto the crippled Ghar war machine and packing plasma grenades into every joint and vent before running away as the Ghar suit exploded spectacularly.

Stepping up to face the remaining two Ghar, Tahl stood before the wreckage of his vanquished foe as the two machines turned to face him. He ran and rolled to the right, anticipating their rapid fire and staying one step ahead of the deadly projectiles as they tracked their weapons toward him. The same principles applied to fighting multiple panhuman foes as deadly battle machines: Tahl positioned himself to face one opponent so that the second was in a line and behind his comrade, isolated and unable to attack. Tahl let out another cry and leapt up, bringing a fist straight into the chin of the Ghar suit and sending its sensor head snapping back to look up at the sky. A shower of bolts and parts fell down to the earth as he landed.

Tahl quickly dropped to the left and rolled away from the machine's deadly claw as it darted forward and attempted to cut him in half at the waist. Tahl countered with a round kick to the knee, but he succeeded only in denting the armored metal of the fighting machine's leg. The claw came down again and Tahl met it head on with a high block which came sweeping up from his hip to above his head. The claw smashed through his block with ease, hammering him down and sending him sprawling into the sand, his forearm plate mangled and half torn from his arm.

Diving to the right, Tahl quickly repositioned himself to keep the two Ghar in a line and unable to attack him simultaneously. He ducked beneath another deadly attack from the machine's claw and then leapt up to stand on the Ghar suit's knee joint. Balancing precariously on the moving surface, Tahl swept his leg up into another round kick, which smashed straight into the machine's face and tore through the metal and shattering the sensor lenses. Seeing the opportunity, Tahl thrust his clenched fist into the jagged hole he had made and fired off a salvo of delayed fuse grenades from his wrist-mounted x-sling. He jumped down from the battered machine and stepped quickly away as the grenades detonated, sending a chain reaction of explosives ripping through the suit and leaving it smoking and burning where it fell in the sand.

The last Ghar turned to face Tahl, its sensor-head appearing to look almost frantically to the left and right as if seeking a way of escaping. Tahl stood his ground and brought his arms up to a guard position, his teeth gritted and a hatred of his foe that he had not felt in years surging back through his soul like an old, dark friend. Tahl rushed forward and avoided a claw attack, punching the elbow joint with enough force to send sparks rippling from severed cables and leaving the claw arm limp and useless at the Ghar's side.

He rolled straight from the strike into his next attacks, a front kick into the Ghar's head followed by a spinning kick into the side of the same target. Two powerful attacks to the head succeeded in nearly severing it; the Ghar suit staggered back, swaying on its three legs as smoke began wafting up from its neck joints. Van Noor, Kachi, and Cane appeared by Tahl's side as he advanced to send a volley of punches into the Ghar's leg, crippling the knee joint and seizing it up. The suit access panel sprang open and the terrified looking Ghar warrior inside frantically clawed at the cables which connected it to the machine as it desperately attempted to extricate itself from its metal coffin.

"Are we taking prisoners, Boss?" Van Noor asked.

"No," Tahl hissed through gritted teeth.

Van Noor and Cane ran up and pointed their carbines straight into the Ghar warrior, both of them firing extended bursts of three or four seconds which tore the little creature into pieces inside the suit's cockpit. Anger surging through him, Tahl turned his back on the three Ghar and folded his arms – the symbolic gesture of disrespect for a defeated adversary which was considered the height of disgraceful conduct in kerempai. It still seemed fitting to Tahl.

"Crack open that first suit as well," he ordered his men, "make sure its dead."

The thump of artillery to both the north and south continued. Orders and reports streamed across the shard command network. Tahl removed his helmet and looked down at the ground, drops of sweat immediately falling from his face and mixing in the sand at his feet. He checked Squad Wen's shard for vital signs on his three casualties. Two were dead, one had a few minutes left.

"Get a medi-drone up here and stabilize that trooper, now," he ordered Van Noor before turning to face the survivors of the squad.

Jemmel, Qan, Sessetti, and Clythe stared at him in silence. He did not need to check their emotions through the shard; he could see it in the way they stood and regarded him. They were more terrified of him than the enemy.

"You four," he stared at them, "get your act together and follow me. I'm only just warming up with these bastards."

***

The numbness and confusion was more uncomfortable than the pain and nausea as Rhona slowly opened her eyes. She lay on her back in a darkened room, with some source of light only visible as a blur to her right. She tried to sit up but felt an iron grip along the left hand side of her body which prevented her from moving. Blinking the sleep out of her eyes, she turned her head to the right.

A long viewscreen showed her a panoramic view of the stars. Somewhere off across the eternal blanket of space, a green planet punctuated the blackness, but with her vision still blurred, she had no idea which system she was in. Rhona lifted her left hand, surprised at the effort it required, and ran it tentatively down the left hand side of her body. An alloy glove cocooned her from left knee up to her armpit, with various cables, pipes, and tubes feeding into it from a machine to the left of her bed. Only then did she remember looking up at the colossal Ghar who stood over the broken bodies of her friends, their guns pointed down at her as she desperately tried to reach Gant and Rae.

Rhona closed her eyes again. There was no Squad Wen, the eternal presence of that shard and the familiar feeling of those she shared it with was gone, amputated from her mind. A few deep breaths, no doubt kick started by whatever drugs were being forced into her by the machine she shared the room with, gave some relief from the panic rising within her. She opened her eyes again and made out a doorway perhaps half a yan from the foot of her bed. She concentrated on the features of the door and tried to focus her vision as mentally she reached out for a shard – any shard – that she must be connected with to find some other source of life.

Ward 2, Recovery, Patients' Communal.

Rhona was already connected. She breathed a sigh of relief as she felt the presence of other Concord soldiers in her mind, a familiar comfort akin to the knowledge of friends to either side in times of adversity. One presence leapt out at her, one she knew well.

"Gant?"

The reply through the shard was instantaneous, the familiar voice in her head as clear as if he shared the room with her.

"Kat? You're up? You okay? How d'you feel?"

"What happened? How did I get here? Where are we?"

"We got hit pretty bad, buddy. You've been out for days now."

The doors at the foot of the bed opened and a medi-drone hovered into the room at waist height, moving up to stop near Rhona's shoulder. The small droid had two arms dangling down from a bulbous central core – one arm was fitted with manipulators similar to a small claw for physical surgery whilst the other had a bio-scanner.

"Good morning, Katya," the droid said gently. "Are you

comfortable with me calling you that?"

Rhona looked up wearily at the drone and nodded mutely. If anything, she was more uncomfortable by the amount of time and effort which went into programming medical drones with a bedside manner; whilst most drones were sentient and capable of conversation, it was only really the medical ones which attempted to mimic panhuman nuances in an attempt to put their patients at ease. It did exactly the opposite with Rhona.

"You'll be up and running soon," the drone said with a positive tone, "you'll make a full recovery. You've been in a coma for twelve days now. We had to do that to allow your brain to recover."

"My brain?" Rhona slurred. "I got shot... in the side. I remember... I took hits in the..."

"There's no easy way to tell you," the drone said, "but remember, you will make a full recovery, there's nothing to worry..."

"Tell me what?" Rhona demanded.

"You died," the drone replied. "By the time medical aid could get to you, you were technically already dead. Your heart had stopped for over seven minutes."

Rhona felt panic rising up from her gut again.

"I'm dead?" She stammered. "So I'm a clone? So I'm not real? The real me is dead and I'm just a clone?"

"I died! Gant, I died! I'm not me, this isn't me!"

"It's alright," the drone said soothingly, "you are not a clone. We were able to save your original body. You need to try to relax and calm yourself. We were able to repair all of the damage to your brain. You will make a full recovery, but you need to give it time."

"Impossible, you must have the wrong end of the stick," Gant replied. "Don't believe what's outside the window. We're still on Markov's Prize."

"Where am I?" Rhona raised one hand to her head, trying to process the overflow of information.

"Settlement Urban 21, locally the city is called New Wryland. The hospital here has been substantially modified since the planet joined the Concord. You have the most modern medical facilities available to take care of you."

"What can you see out of your window, Kat?" Gant asked. "They have a prod around inside your head and they project some soothing scene on the window to try to relax you. Don't worry, we're okay. It's snowing where I am, and I'm only three rooms down from you. Don't worry, we're okay."

Rhona looked at the viewscreen to her right again. With her vision clearing, she could now make out the falsities in the imitation of the view of the stars. Out of nowhere, a thought hit her with a panic overriding anything the medications could do for her.

"Where's Ila?"

There was a silence before Gant replied. The drone continued to talk to her, but the words fell on deaf ears.

"She didn't make it, Katya. We lost her."

The machine next to Rhona began to bleep some sort of alert.

"Katya, try to calm down, I know this is a lot to..."

She remembered walking next to Rae in the sun, sweating from carrying the squad's carbines back from the servicing depot. The talk they had about emotions, feelings, what was real and what the IMTel took away. She remembered Rae's inability to comprehend why Rhona would ever want to feel pain and sadness. Rhona had ordered the attack in the ravine. She had ordered Rae to her death. She owed Rae that sadness.

Reaching up with her right hand, Rhona grabbed a firm hold of the tubes which fed into her left forearm and wrenched them out of her veins. A more urgent tone emitted from the machine. The medi-drone rushed over to Rhona's side. As if a filter had suddenly been removed, the impact of Rae's death hit Rhona full on. She was gone, her life stamped out at the age of twenty-two. Rhona remembered the T7 explosion at Prostock, when her entire squad was torn apart during the assault on some last bastion of planetary defense, of running back into the burning vehicle again and again as she tried to drag out the bloody bodies of her troopers. She remembered her father's death, of the last desperate look the tired man gave her as he shouted for her to take her brother and run as the enforcers surrounded him. She remembered how many lives she had taken since joining C3, how many men and women she had gunned down whose only crime was defending their home, their way of life, from invasion. But above all, she remembered Ila Rae.

Rhona curled her legs up as far as the medical constraints would allow her, turning to one side and crying hysterically as Gant's voice echoed in her head and the medi-drone desperately tried to re-attach the medication tubes into her arm.

***

Crystal Sea
Two kiloyan west of Firebase Alpha
Equatorial Region
Markov's Prize

L-Day plus 51

The convoy of C3T7 transport drones cruised smoothly across the clear, purple tinted waters on the final approaches to the base carved out of the jungle at Firebase Alpha. Mandarin Owenne sat bolt upright in his narrow chair in the lead Duke, his eyes closed in concentration. Even after the battlefield repairs had been carried out the previous day on the drone, the magno-fan in the left wing continued to intermittently screech and squeal with each revolution of the suspensor generator. Owenne connected himself to the vehicle's shard and ran a quick diagnostic check. Power output was at eighty quantum, so certainly sufficient to reach the proper maintenance facilities at Firebase Alpha.

Owenne glanced at the other occupants of the vehicle. Tahl sat opposite him, his one remaining eye closed either in concentration or due to weariness. He had lost his other eye in hand-to-hand combat with a Ghar assault trooper three days before. It was a minor setback – the medical facilities at Firebase Alpha had already grown a new eyeball for him based on the data held in his medical records, and it was only a minor operation of perhaps an hour or two to have it fitted.

Van Noor had approached Owenne and requested that he recommend Tahl for a medal for his valor in the previous seventeen days of continuous combat. His only justification was that Tahl had personally destroyed eleven Ghar battlesuits in hand-to-hand combat. Whilst this was impressive, Owenne had been forced to remind Van Noor that medals were awarded based on individuals overcoming seemingly insurmountable odds and exceeding C3 expectations of them. Given Tahl's background as a martial artist of universal renown and undefeated cage fighter champion, the odds were heavily in Tahl's favor every time he closed to within striking distance of a Ghar. Of course Owenne would not recommend him for a medal; by Tahl's own standards, he had only achieved a touch above mediocrity.

As if guessing what Owenne was thinking about, Van Noor grimaced at him from the other side of the cramped passenger hold. Owenne flashed what he hoped was a sarcastic smile in return. Van Noor looked away. The only other occupant of the vehicle was Cane. The fourth trooper of the command squad, Kachi, had been gunned down by a Ghar bomber seven days ago.

"Mandarin Owenne," Mandarin Luffe's soft voice intruded his thoughts, "you are back within communications range. I have been waiting to converse with you."

"Go on," Owenne replied.

"I am analyzing the data of the previous seventeen days of confrontation now. I am pleased to see that your force stopped the Ghar dead in its tracks. We needed a victory."

"I would describe it as a stalemate," Owenne countered. "The 12th Assault Force has taken up the line and the Ghar are still there. But these men and women need rest. They were shattered when I got here, and the last seventeen days haven't made it any better. They've suffered forty quantum casualties, and half of that is permanent."

"Then get them rested, as our strategic situation is not improving. A second Ghar force has landed in the Banaab System. Our resources are stretched."

"Aren't they always?"

"There is more, Mandarin Owenne. Whilst you have been, how did you put it, 'getting your hands dirty', a shuttle landed on the far side of Markov's Prize at these coordinates. I have traced the ship's progress over the past few days. It has come from Freeborn space. I believe the ship originates from House Selestov."

Owenne frowned, holding up a hand to silence whatever nonsense Van Noor was trying to tell him.

"Why are Freeborn mercenaries landing on Markov's Prize?"

"Why indeed, Mandarin Owenne."

"The question was rhetorical, Luffe, although I see only a few likely answers and none of them are good news. Leave it with me. I'll find out what's going on."

"You fear they too believe this planet is Embryo?" Luffe queried.

"I fear nothing, Luffe. But it... concerns me."

The drone jolted softly as it landed within a simple circle on the ground at Firebase Alpha's transportation section.

"Oh, we're here," Owenne remarked, mentally unfastening his seat harness.

"That's exactly what I told you, sir, a few seconds ago," Van Noor grumbled.

"I was busy."

"I thought NuHu were renowned for their mental capacity?" Van Noor shrugged.

"You're more than welcome to go head to head with me in any intellectual comparison you care to imagine, you hulking primitive," Owenne smiled smugly. "Now be a good fellow and open the door for me. I'm more important than you are, remember?"

The doors slid open and even Owenne found himself surprised by the sight which awaited him. Perhaps fifty soldiers, their green uniforms immaculately pressed, stood in three ranks facing the Dukes as they landed. A loud command was bellowed out by a woman who stood in front of them, and they all stood smartly to attention. Their crimson berets marked them out as elite drop troopers. Perplexed by the odd display of military ceremony, Owenne stepped down from the drone and pulled his battered peaked cap onto his head as another T7 landed further down the line.

The female drop captain marched smartly out to Owenne, a highly polished ceremonial saber held steadily in her right hand. The last Duke landed and another battered and disheveled squad of strike troopers filed out to behold the rows of shiny buttons and polished boots which stood in wait for them. As the last drone's engines wound down to silence, the female drop captain came smartly to attention in front of Owenne and saluted smartly. He returned the salute, connecting to the drop company shard to find out who she was. Drop Captain Abbi Mosse, a rising star in the drop corps, recently singled out for potential promotion to drop commander and decorated many times for bravery and leadership.

"Drop Captain Mosse, Alpha Company, 3rd Drop Formation," the red haired woman announced. "We heard about the 44th's defense of the line in the Nienne Desert. We wanted to show our respect and welcome you back."

"Err... Tahl?" Owenne shuffled uncomfortably. "Sort this one out, will you?"

Tahl limped over to Mosse, pulling his black beret over the bandages wrapped around his head and missing eye. He brought a hand up to salute her.

"Hello, Abbi."

"Welcome back, Ryen. I'm glad you're okay. Your boys and girls have made quite a name for themselves over the last few days."

Owenne noticed the use of first names and quickly looked over Mosse's service record. One reprimand, many years before. Inappropriate romantic relationship with a trooper under her command. Drop Trooper Tahl. Interesting, Owenne mused. He changed his mind almost immediately. It was not remotely interesting to him.

"This is for the 44th Strike Formation," Mosse said, carefully handing over the gleaming ceremonial sword. "Hang it up in Formation HQ or something. We've spent the last few days carrying out strikes on Ghar supply bases behind their lines. Their defense was a lot weaker than we anticipated. C3 says it's because they've moved so much to the frontlines due to the casualties they've taken. We were supposed to be supporting you, but it turns out that your lot have been supporting us."

"Thank you," Tahl said as he accepted the sword, "and thank you for the gesture. This is a lot of effort, especially on ops."

"This?" Mosse smiled. "My drop troopers always have their dress uniforms immaculate and their toe caps gleaming. This was only five minutes work."

Tahl laughed and nodded.

"Thank you."

Mosse saluted and turned to her right before marching back to her soldiers. The assembled drop troopers gave a series of loud cheers to the returning strike troopers.

TEN

Emerald Wing – Assigned to C3 Medical Corps
New Wryland Hospital
Markov's Prize

Outside the window, life seemed to go on regardless of the fact that a Ghar invasion force was locked in bloody battle with C3 forces on the other side of the planet. Pedestrians walked the sun-drenched pavements, lined by trees clinically cut into smooth shapes like blue sculptures. Scenic fountains gently babbled away in the center of every road intersection. Concord drones carefully set about changing the roles of buildings that were no longer required now that the planet was part of the Concord; anything related to the outmoded need for money and finance would be removed from society.

Changing the controls on her chair, Rhona allowed the suspensors to power down and bring her back to a seated height which was just above the floor. She was clad in the same garb as every other patient in the recovery suite – simple white trousers and a plain, white t-shirt with a square, open neck not dissimilar to the dress uniforms she had seen on naval personnel. Perhaps twenty other patients shared the recovery room with her, all of them from the 44th Strike Formation, but only half a dozen of them were men she knew from Beta Company. The open plan room had comfortable sofas, immersive movie suites, holographic games; plenty to keep the mind occupied whilst bodies healed naturally, now that modern medicine had played its part.

The doors at the far end of the room opened to admit Gant, who limped in with a protective suspensor field gently glowing around his new leg. He flashed a smile to Rhona and slowly made his way over.

"What you up to?" He asked as he stopped to lean against the white wall next to her.

"Sending a letter to my brother. More lies, more stuff to stop him worrying."

"I've got three older sisters," Gant nodded, "about twenty years between each of us. My oldest sister's grandson has just joined up, apparently. He got the call a month or so back and is training to join the navy."

"Beats living in a trench, I guess," Rhona leaned back in her chair. "How's the leg doing?"

"It's weird," Gant blinked, "I can feel my toes, but I can't feel anything in between them and the knee. I can't complain, at least I'm back to having the same number of legs I had at the start of the month. So that's progress."

The doors at the end of the recovery room opened again, and Rhona was surprised to see Tahl and Van Noor enter. Both men wore their green barrack uniforms, their shirt sleeves rolled up neatly out of tradition rather than as a method of combating the heat – the uniforms were able to regulate their temperature automatically. Tahl moved straight over to sit down next to Leonis, a trooper from Squad Xath who had been nearly torn in half by a Ghar assault trooper. Van Noor looked across and saw Gant and Rhona, and he immediately walked over to them, his features stony.

"Get me up," Rhona said, "if I'm taking another Van Gnawing, then I'll do it on my feet, not in that damn chair."

"Don't be stupid," Gant replied, "you're hurt, stay in the chair."

Pain flared up the left hand side of Rhona's body as she forced herself to her feet.

"Help me!" She urged Gant.

The tall soldier slipped an arm around her waist, a pained cry suppressed by his gritted teeth. Rhona put an arm around his neck to support herself, leaning on her right leg to take the pressure off her injuries.

"Fate's a funny thing, isn't it?" Van Noor greeted with a dangerous smile as he walked over. "Three of Squad Wen get cut down, and two make a miraculous recovery. Not the one who deserved it. Not the one who followed an idiotic plan with courage and loyalty. She's dead now. But you two? You're okay. You're all good."

Rhona took her arm from around Gant's shoulders and supported herself on her own two feet.

"Anything to say for yourselves?" The burly senior trooper asked.

"No, Senior," Gant shook his head, looking down at the faded blue carpet at his feet.

Rhona saw Tahl engaged in a lively conversation with Leonis. Both men were laughing.

"I expected better from you, Gant. 'Don't talk to command - they'll just tell us to wait here'. That's pretty much what you said according to the recordings, isn't it? Perhaps now you can be clearer as to why you're still not wearing a red stripe even after all of your pals from training have been promoted. Strike Trooper Rae deserved better," Van Noor continued, "better support from her peers. Better leadership from you, Rhona. Better..."

"You think I don't know that?" Rhona spat. "You think I don't know I let her down? I'll carry that with me for the next two hundred years, or the next two weeks until the Ghar kill me! You come in here looking to turn that tragedy into an excuse to lay into me? That's where you wanna go with this?"

"Katya..." Gant urged.

"No, no," Van Noor folded his powerful arms and leaned back, "go on, Rhona. Say what you've got to say."

Rhona stumbled momentarily on her injured side. She pushed Gant's offer to assist her away and drew herself up to her full height and faced Van Noor.

"I had conflicting advice from my two most experienced soldiers. One told me to do one thing, the other told me to do the opposite. I had to make a decision right there, right then. I made the wrong decision. But I did make a decision. I made the decision to close with the enemy and I did it leading from the front! If it was Feon Rall, you'd be here telling him that he made a good go of it, and it's a shame it didn't work out. Casualties are a part of the game, can't account for luck, all the normal lies. But it's not Rall, it's me. It's not somebody whose face fits in around here, it's mine. So say what y'gotta say, Senior. Go for it. But it'll be in one ear and out the other because where I come from, respect is mutual, and whatever you think of me, I guarantee I'm thinking something pretty similar about you."

"Strike Trooper Gant, go get yourself a drink," Van Noor said without taking his eyes off Rhona's.

Gant limped away without a word. Van Noor leaned in until he was well within Rhona's personal space. She did not yield one iota.

"Of course I've got no respect for you," the veteran soldier began, "why would I? You're hopeless at what you do, you bring nothing positive to this company, and you shun any attempts to bring you on as a soldier. You order a perfectly capable young woman to her death and what's your response? 'I made a bad decision'. Is that all she meant to you, you callous, arrogant bitch? She's dead because of you, and you need to take ownership of that. So yeah, I don't like you. But it's a long queue I'm joining. Nobody likes you. The strike leaders in this company are a fraternity, a family, and you repetitively raise your middle finger to all of them because you think you're better. You won't learn from their years of experience, because you think you already know it. You don't stop to wonder why everybody else gets along and nobody likes you, whereas anybody with a shred of humility would stop and take a good, long look at themselves. Whereas you get your own troopers killed through you own incompetence, you think it appropriate to judge and threaten your own company commander because of your opinions regarding his conduct. I've spent nearly forty years as a soldier, and I consider it an absolute privilege to serve alongside every other man and woman in this formation. All of them except you. Because you are nothing better than a dumb, stuck-up, Freeborn ex-stripper playing dress up as a soldier. So if you want to get theatrical and offer to hand in your rank badges, please do so, because I will happily call your bluff and tear them up right in front of your smug face. Now, have I made it perfectly clear how everybody here feels about you, or do you want me to expand on any of the points I've covered?"

Rhona turned away for a moment and then faced him again.

"Sorry, what? D'you say something to me?" She grinned. "Like I said, in one ear – out the other. Senior."

Van Noor uttered a word which Rhona would never have used to describe even her most hated enemies, and then stormed off out of the recovery suite. Once he was gone, Rhona checked nobody was looking her way, and then she turned her back on the room, struggling to control her breathing and fighting back tears from the impact of his words.

"I'm sorry, Ila," she whispered as she wiped at her eyes, "I'm so sorry..."

Her wristband bleeped to let her know she had used up all of her medication. Taking a deep breath, Rhona looked down at her chair.

"To hell with it," she muttered to herself, limping slowly and painfully past the suspensor chair and over to the duty medical drone in the corner to top up her medication.

She limped over to the long window at the far side of the room and looked down as the world carried on below her in the early afternoon suns. Again, tears welled up as she thought of Ila Rae.

"You okay?" Gant asked as he hobbled over.

"Yeah... yeah I'm cool."

"Don't let him get you down," Gant offered. "It's just like you said. You made a bad decision. It's not all your fault."

Rhona's eyes flashed up at Gant. She opened her mouth to speak but thought of Van Noor's words and decided against it.

"Just gimme some space, dude," she turned away. "I want some time to think."

Gant stumbled away and took a seat on one of the vivid, orange sofas in the center of the room. Rhona watched as Tahl moved on to the next trooper and shook his hand warmly before engaging in conversation. She turned away. The thought of composing a message to Rae's parents or the brother she spoke so fondly of entered her mind. Three times over the course of the next hour she set about starting a recording, but every time the guilt and uncertainty made her stop and erase the message. After perhaps half an hour, Tahl moved on to Gant and sat down next to him on the sofa. Within minutes, the two were laughing. Rhona realized that Tahl had spent ten or fifteen minutes with all of the Beta Company casualties in the room, except for her. She would be next. For some reason it made her feel sick.

She turned to look at her own reflection in the glass next to her and frantically set about adjusting her hair to make sure it looked perfect. She had upset him enough and had clearly made a lot of enemies – ensuring she looked smart and professional seemed to be a good idea. After a few more minutes, Tahl stood, shook Gant's hand, and walked over to Rhona. She folded her arms and brought one foot back to rest on the wall behind her, making sure she looked casual. Tahl stopped in front of her.

"Glad you're okay, Strike Leader," he smiled, "stay tough."

With that, he turned away, pulled his beret on, and walked out of the room. Ignoring the pain which flared up along her midriff, Rhona quickly limped after him and shot through the door into the empty, sterile corridor outside the recovery suite.

"Hey," she shouted after him, "sir!"

Tahl stopped and half turned to face her.

"You spent, like, a quarter of an hour talking to everybody else. Why won't you talk to me?" She asked, aware how hurt her tone of voice must have sounded.

Tahl closed his eyes and exhaled.

"Because you'll carry on assuming I'm somebody I'm not," he said quietly. "You'll think I'm trying to get something from you which I'm not."

"I won't," Rhona answered immediately. "Look, sir, I just said I wanted to be treated the same as everybody else. That's all. This isn't treating me the same, this is just excluding me."

Tahl opened his eyes and turned to face her, wearily dragging his beret off again. He gestured back to the recovery suite. Rhona turned and limped back inside, the pain in her abdomen causing her to hiss every time her left foot touched the floor. Tahl followed her to the corner of the room by the window and sat opposite her as she slunk down into one of the orange sofas, away from the conversation which buzzed around the rest of the room. Tahl leaned forward and rested his folded arms on his knees.

"So what do you want to talk about?" He asked softly.

"I dunno," Rhona said, mimicking his posture, "the senior's already come over and had a talk with me about some things."

"I know, he's already submitted a complaint against you for insubordination."

"Already?"

"Yes. Look, you leave that with me. I'll talk to him and calm him down. This won't go anywhere. But he's already told me what you've said to him this afternoon. I don't agree with the way he has gone about this, but I need to be honest with you. If it comes down to any sort of complaint between you and Bry Van Noor, I've got his back. Unless there's a very good reason not to. Loyalty is everything. So don't push this further, I'll deal with it and put a stop to it."

"Why does everybody see me as some whinny bitch who just wants to play the system and cause trouble?" Rhona exclaimed. "It's not me! I'm trying my best, sir. It's not me."

She looked up and saw genuine sympathy and care in Tahl's features.

"Look, it's cool," she smiled dismissively. "I can take care of myself, I always have. So... what were you talking to the other guys about? Sure seemed to make them laugh."

"Ah, this and that," Tahl shrugged. "I can talk about things other than company level attacks and carbines, believe it or not."

"Right," Rhona nodded, turning her eyes away. She hesitantly looked back at him. "So... can I ask you something?" Rhona ventured.

"Depends."

"How did it all happen?" Rhona asked. "My pa used to watch your fights. You were famous. How did you go from that to, well... this?"

"It's probably more of a story as to how I ended up competition fighting in the Determinate," Tahl shrugged.

"Well, go on, I'm listening," Rhona leaned forward.

Tahl looked away, one foot tapping as he drummed the fingertips of one hand against the knuckles of the other. After a long pause, he began to talk again.

"My father was a famous martial artist where I grew up. It was a foregone conclusion that I'd study kerempai as soon as I was old enough, when I was five. I took to it very well and my father was a great teacher. By the time I was nine, I was winning all sorts of competitions, medals, trophies. I was noticed by Master Janshea. She is the most experienced and proficient martial artist alive. Anywhere. She saw potential in me, and my entire family moved planets just so that I could study under her. She was nearly three hundred years old when I began studying, so to say she had a lot to give would be an understatement.

"With this natural ability I'm told I've got and the best teacher alive, I studied all day, every day. When I was sixteen, I could enter adult competitions. I was winning everything I was entered for. Then, when I was twenty, the master entered me into a competition on the eastern fringes of the Concord, as it was then. Unfortunately for me, my reputation had spread past the Concord's borders. A twenty year old martial arts prodigy with an unbeaten record in competition fighting was too good an opportunity to miss – a guy called Warne arranged for the ship I was on to be attacked by pirates. They killed most people onboard and took me off to the Determinate."

Tahl leaned back and folded his arms, forcing an unconfortable smile. "That's how I started full contact competition fighting."

"But you would have been wrenched out of the IMTel!" Rhona exclaimed. "You know how it works – for a Concord citizen to be moved onto the reduced support of the military shard takes a couple of months of Behavioral Activation
Training! To be... just completely severed! That would..."

"Give me behavioral problems?" Tahl offered. "Anger management concerns? Mental health issues? Just made me a better fighter in the cage, in their eyes."

Rhona looked into his eyes. He understood. He did not know yet, but he understood her. He understood loss, betrayal, being used by the grand circus that was organized crime in the Determinate; he knew about all of it. She reached out to hold his hand but thought better of it. Tahl sprang to his feet.

"Don't feel sorry for me," he said quietly, "I don't want that."

"You told anybody else about all of this?" Rhona asked.

"In the last four or five years? Just Bry. And you."

"Why d'you tell me?" Rhona asked, struggling painfully up to her feet.

Again, Tahl closed his eyes and exhaled.

"You know why, Katya," he said before turning away and leaving the recovery suite.

***

Firebase Alpha
Equatorial Region
Markov's Prize

L-Day plus 53

Rain plummeted from the green-grey clouds above, turning the sands into an ankle deep sludge which cascaded down to the turbulent purple waves of the beach. Sessetti wished, for once, that he had his hyperlight armor on rather than the thin, green material of his barrack uniform. Even with the rain shield projected just above his head providing an invisible energy plate to protect him from direct rainfall, the wind still blew enough around the sides to soak his entire uniform. The news he had received from Strike Leader Althern had come as something of a surprise – now that replacement troopers had arrived, Squad Wen would be reforming and he was to return to it. After the disastrous charge against the Ghar in the ravine in the Nienne Desert, the four surviving members of the squad had been split up and sent to act as temporary replacements with other squads, hence Sessetti's role in Squad Xath under Althern. He had not seen Jemmel, Qan, or Clythe in days, except for fleeting glances across crowded briefing tents and during guard changeovers.

Sessetti dragged his boots through the sludge, his shoulders hunched up as the rain cascaded down from the darkening skies above. One thing which crossed his mind regarding the decision to reform Squad Wen which had not been mentioned was the loss of Squad Chyne. Heide and all seven of his troopers had been killed in one engagement when they were caught out by a rapid counterattack and torn apart by a squad of Ghar assault troopers. The help arrived too late for Heide and his soldiers, but the four Ghar assault suits had been swiftly dealt with – Sessetti had arrived in time to see one of the Ghar hacked down by plasma fire, another torn asunder by a C3M4, and the final two Ghar broken apart by Strike Captain Tahl. Sessetti had watched in amazement as his company commander had ripped the two lumbering battlesuits apart with thunderous strikes from his elbows, feet, and hands. He had lost an eyeball in the process, but that had been repaired already.

Breathing a sigh of relief, Sessetti stepped onto the dull, red transmat pad outside the firebase's accommodation block and was beamed inside, away from the wind and rain. He stepped off the pad into the grey, concrete corridor and began the familiar walk to the old accommodation rooms. After a few corners, he arrived at the door to the squad's communal hub and stepped inside. Jemmel and Qan were already there, unpacking their possessions back into the storage boxes in their respective rooms.

"Hey, Georgi Hax!" Jemmel smiled as she saw him, a reference to a famous singer from their parents' generation. "You're back!"

"All in one piece!" Qan stepped over to shake his hand warmly. "Looks like that's half the band back together!"

Sessetti nodded, his smile fading when he saw Rae's empty bunk. He had not known Weste for very long, but every time he walked past the spot where Weste had been killed, it always pained him a little. The pain inside from losing Rae was on another scale entirely. He knew who he blamed for the decision to attack the Ghar in the open, but that did little to mask the guilt he felt for failing to find the courage to follow Rhona and try to drag Rae to safety. The post battle analysis had said she was dead before she even hit the ground, but he did not know that at the time. If she had have been alive, he would have failed her. He would have failed the soldier who had the courage to drag him to safety when he needed it.

"You okay?" Qan asked.

Sessetti looked up. Before he could answer, Rhona, Gant, and Clythe arrived together and walked into the communal area, dumping their kit bags in the center of the room in front of the sofas.

"Hello, guys!" Qan grinned broadly. "The lil' family is back together!"

"Not all of us," Jemmel snapped, folding her arms. "We've got another bunk empty."

Rhona nodded slowly and stepped out into the center of the room.

"Look, I'm sorry," she began, her hands outstretched passively, "I made a dumb call. I shouldn't have done that."

"Not you! I don't expect much from you, you don't know your arse from your elbow! But you!" Jemmel hissed as she pointed a finger at Gant. "You made the dumb call! You went all Feon Rall on us and convinced us to run into the most obvious trap I've seen in four years of soldiering! You are the one who should have known better, you prick!"

"Me?" Gant exclaimed. "I didn't give anybody any orders! I gave my opinion, that's all. Rhona made the call, not me. I'm not in charge."

"Yeah, she made the call," Jemmel yelled, "based on your expert opinion! She did her job, which was to listen to the advice of her most experienced guys and make a decision! I don't have a problem with that, I've got a problem with you! And now you don't even have the balls to man up and face the responsibility of your actions, you weasel!"

Sessetti lunged forward and grabbed Jemmel by her arms as soon as he saw her stomp toward Gant with her fists clenched. Qan jumped to his feet and stood in between Jemmel and Gant, his arms outstretched to hold them apart. Rhona sank down on her bunk, her face in her hands.

"Leave it!" Clythe growled at Jemmel. "Gant saw an opportunity and he voiced his opinion! It's easy for you to stand on your pedestal now you've got the benefit of hindsight! Now you know you were right! You didn't know at the time! None of us knew!"

"Who the hell said you had a speaking part?" Jemmel demanded, yanking her arms free from Sessetti's grip with a surprising strength. "Some wet behind the ears little moron like you doesn't get to express an opinion!"

That was enough for Sessetti. Everybody else had spoken. His anger rising, he was on his feet almost before he had formulated his sentence.

"Just stop!" he snapped, stepping into the center of the altercation. "We've been shot at, blown up, and have gunned down and killed just the same as you! We're not new anymore, we're in this. We get a speaking part. And here's mine. You and Gant both expressed your opinions to

Kat. You both gave her options. But you, Bo! You came wading in with some crappy, gung ho attitude and you tipped the balance! That's what I remember! You, Bo! Not them!"

"Me?" Clythe's eyes widened in surprise. "I did nothing! I..."

"Just stop," Rhona commanded, jumping to her feet and pacing toward them, "all of you. Squad Chyne is dead, all of them. Squad Teal has lost five guys since we got here. Squad Jai has lost six, including replacements. We've lost one and it's tearing us apart? Rae deserved better, she didn't deserve to die like that, but she's one casualty in something bigger. We need to close ranks, look after each other, and move forward; not look for blame. Y'all want blame? You want a bad guy in this? That's me. I'm in charge, the responsibility rests with me, I made the call. I got Rae killed. You wanted to hear it? There it is. I got her killed, and I'll carry that with me forever. So you guys need to stop bitchin' at each other and get your act together, because we're gonna be heading back to the front real soon, and we're doing it together. You wanna hate someone? Hate me, I don't give a crap. I hate myself enough for the way things went down, so you might as well jump in on that party. But you guys need to quit kicking each other because it won't make us work well as a team, and more importantly, it won't bring Rae back."

Pushing her way past the others, Rhona walked out of the room and headed back to the transmat pads. After a few moments of awkward silence, Sessetti followed Jemmel's lead and began quietly unpacking his kit.

***

After finally conceding defeat, Sessetti opened his eyes and sat up in his bunk. The cushion of warm air escaped from beneath his duvet and the artificial coolness of the air conditioning in his room hit him. He checked the time: still a good couple of hours until the rest of the world would wake up. Sessetti clambered out of bed and smeared a handful of shaving foam across his jaw, waiting for a few seconds until it had dissolved his stubble before wiping it off again. He pulled on his uniform and opened the door from his tiny room into the communal area. The other doors were all shut except for Jemmel, who lay on her bunk with her hands behind her head, staring up at the ceiling.

"You're up early," she remarked without looking at him.

"Bit weird, being back in this room," Sessetti admitted.

"Fair enough. Go for a run or something, it might take your mind off things. The weather's cleared up again."

"Yeah," Sessetti shrugged, "I'll go for a walk, I guess. Catch you later."

Sessetti walked down the cold corridors to the transmat pads, pulled on his black beret, and then beamed up to the transmat station just outside the subterranean accommodation block. The first fiery orange sun was just peering over the horizon, painting the world in pale, pastel shades and casting long shadows across the soft sand. Sessetti had never noticed before that the colors of the world were quite different when only one sun was above the horizon. Alone on the long stretch of beach between the jungle and the purple sea, Sessetti risked thrusting his hands into his trouser pockets as he kicked his way through the sand, content that no strike leaders would be on hand to reprimand him for an unmilitary bearing.

A gentle breeze brought the scent of the sea to Sessetti's nostrils as he walked. Thoughts of his parents and sister, his life back home, and his music forced their way to the fore. Music seemed ridiculous, now that he had taken life and seen it wither and die beside him. The stretch of beach was more beautiful than the lush pastures and steppes back home, but that beauty was tarnished beyond repair by what he had done, been forced to do, over the past few weeks. He momentarily considered penning some song lyrics, but it seemed pointless now. Almost childish.

Up ahead of him on the beach, a lone figure stood motionless in the sand, a long silhouette cast to his left. The figure stepped left into an uncomfortable looking, long stance and held position as steady as a rock before turning and bringing a kick up to the face of an imaginary opponent with clinical precision. Sessetti watched as the man linked a series of powerful strikes and kicks into a regimented pattern in the sand before coming to a halt, back on the same spot he had started. Sessetti walked closer and was not surprised to discover the man was his company commander.

Tahl dropped down to his knees, his back upright and his eyes closed as he faced the ocean. Clad in loose trousers of white, a faded black belt around his waist, and a form fitting white t-shirt, his physique reminded Sessetti of images from biology classes which depicted a body whose perfection was only possible through surgery or decades of training.

"Morning," Tahl greeted, his eyes still closed.

Sessetti immediately yanked his hands out of his pockets.

"Good morning, sir!" He said clearly, bringing his heels together to stand to attention.

"Don't worry about that," Tahl opened his eyes and stood, turning to face him. "You're up early."

"Not getting much sleep, sir," Sessetti admitted, "some of the other guys talk about the gravity or the hours in the day. I don't mind that. But I still don't sleep."

Tahl nodded.

"Might as well get outside and see something of this place, I guess. If the Ghar had to keep us locked in combat on one planet, at least they did it here. I'd rather be stuck on this beach than getting covered in that acid rain we had on Prostock."

Sessetti gave what he hoped was a polite smile and nodded. Tahl stepped closer and folded his broad arms, looking him dead in the eyes as if assessing him.

"Things not so good in Squad Wen, then?"

"We're good, sir," Sessetti said, "nothing we can't sort out between us."

"You're in good company, Lian. You've got a good strike leader and two of the most experienced troopers in the company. I've got no concerns over any of you. You're a good squad."

Sessetti mumbled his gratitude and looked out to sea for a second before turning back.

"How do you do it, sir?" He asked suddenly. "We've all watched the footage from the spotter drones showing the Ghar suits you've taken down. How do you take out a machine twice our size with just your hands and feet?"

Tahl raised a fist to his chin and paused before answering.

"Practice. And luck," he finally responded, "the C3 Unarmed Combat Program you learned at the academy is a one size fits all, simple technique to give you the skills you need to kill an adversary in hand to hand combat. Kerempai is very different. It's the difference between a martial art and a fighting style. You've learned a fighting style and you can now fight. Martial arts are only partially about physicality; just as much if not more is about the mind. It's all about being the best person you can be, body and soul. A fighting style is about tearing a guy apart."

"So if martial arts are better, why don't they teach us one at the academy?" Sessetti asked.

"I didn't say they're better," Tahl replied calmly, "just different. A fighting style is quicker to learn. If you've got somebody who needs to learn skills fast – like an academy recruit – kerepai is no good. It takes too long, years until it suddenly clicks and falls into place. You need something simple and accessible, and that's where the C3 UCP excels. It's a very good fighting system."

"But not as good as kerempai, sir?"

"Given enough time, no," Tahl said, "but that's just my opinion, not fact. I'm biased."

Sessetti nodded. He found himself only mildly interested about the differences in fighting techniques and the physical aspect. The spiritual side, the mastery of the mind, that fascinated him.

"Would kerempai teach me to be calmer, sir? If I learned any, would I panic less in combat? Would I deal with how bad it feels afterward any better?"

"Yeah," Tahl nodded, "yeah, you would."

"How do I learn?" Sessetti asked.

"I'll teach you," Tahl replied.

Sessetti let out a breath. It was not the answer he expected.

"When... when do I start, sir?"

"Now," Tahl shrugged, taking two steps back away from him. "Drop to your knees, the left first and then the right. Place your hands flat on the ground in front of you, thumbs outstretched, to form a triangle. Left first then right. Bring your forehead down to your hands to bow."

Sessetti followed the instructions, kneeling and bowing to Tahl as the older man returned the gesture and bowed back to him.

"Kerempai is governed by twenty principles," Tahl explained, "the first of which is that keremai always begins and ends with respect. You will respect me as your teacher. In return, I will always respect you as a willing student. That's why we always start and finish by kneeling and bowing to each other. This might not be for you, Lian, you might find it boring and give up. But if you don't, if you stick this out, this might just make a few little changes in your life for the better."

ELEVEN

17th Assault Force Force HQ
New Wryland
Markov's Prize

L-Day plus 54

The city hall building was, in Owenne's opinion, the perfect place for a C3 Headquarters. Now that the Concord had taken over, there was no need for politicians and bureaucrats, so the building was obsolete. The structure would be a waste if not employed in a fitting role, and acting as one of the Assault Force HQs was just such a role. He floated absentmindedly along the broad corridor on the second floor, his booted feet skimming the thick, crimson carpet. Paintings hung on the wood paneled walls to either side of him; depictions of famous historical events from the city and even the very square outside the building where apparently a famous coup was staged a few centuries before. Owenne normally found himself abhorring a lack of technology, but the archaic building with its cavernous hallways, marble pillars, sculptures, and intricate wooden furniture was somehow pleasing to him.

Owenne floated swiftly into the building's main conference room, another traditionally designed area with vast, wooden tables whose smooth surfaces were illuminated by sunlight which poured in through a long line of tall windows that ran along the front of the entire building. Some fifty military officers were assembled in the spacious room, grouped together in pairs, trios, circles of six, all of the little social habits which panhumans adopted and still confused Owenne. At the top of the tree were two commander-in-chiefs – Hawess and Deitte – who commanded the 12th and 17th Assault Forces respectively. Each assault force was made up of three formations, led by a strike commander. Each of those strike commanders had six companies, led by a strike captain. So whilst on the battlefield the strike captain was king, here in the upper echelons of planning and management, the captain was merely another pawn, a low ranking officer whose job was to implement strategy, not to devise it. The participants were dressed in a bewildering array of colourful uniforms upon which almost all wore merit ribbons, campaign badges, and bright citizenship pins.

Today's selection from the utterly bewildering array of attires open to Concord military personnel was the Number 3 Uniform; smart trousers and a shirt and tie, with a single breasted jacket, all in pale green. Medal ribbons and qualification badges were arranged neatly over the left breast pocket. Owenne's eyes were drawn to Drop Captain Mosse, something of a local celebrity due to her rather aggressive antics behind Ghar lines with various surprise attacks. To add to the confusion, the military insisted on keeping alive with their different uniforms for different occasions, thus Mosse wore a thin skirt instead of trousers. Owenne found it completely unfathomable that different regulations existed for men and women regarding haircuts, let alone a woman's right to wear a skirt if she chose. In Owenne's mind, it should just be short back and sides and trousers all round. And one uniform. Cut down on the ceremony, the confusion, and the unnecessary logistical burden.

"Shall we get started?" Commander-in-Chief Hawess raised his voice from his position at the head of one of the long tables. Hawess was a man with a reputation for brutal efficiency; although at nearly two centuries of age, his physique was not what it had been in his youth.

A mandarin could easily take command of a company, or even a formation, if needed. But not a force. The regulations did not allow that. This was perhaps why commander-in-chiefs were happy to start command briefs without consulting Owenne first. It irked him.

The assembled soldiers seated themselves around the table as a holographic projection of Markov's Prize illuminated in the center of the room. Intelligence Commander Zann, the 17th Assault Force's tall, thin intelligence officer, stood to begin the brief.

"Sirs, ladies and gentlemen. As of this morning, the main Ghar advance in the Nienne Desert has been halted by the 44th Strike Formation. However, the Ghar frontline is spreading to both the north and south, which threatens to outflank us or, even worse, push past our defensive positions and threaten the civilian populace."

As Zann spoke, lines animated along the ghostly globe in the center of the room, showing exactly where the fighting had been taking place.

"The 12th Assault Force is currently holding the line until the 17th is in a position to be able to return to the front. Naval Intelligence has detected two further Ghar fleets moving toward this system; one of which they believe is intended to reinforce Ghar forces here on Markov's Prize, whilst the second is most likely heading for the Banaab System. In short, we've halted the advance, but it won't take much for a Ghar advance to find gaps in the line to break through."

"And our reinforcements?" Strike Commander Van Wellen, the commanding officer of the 48th Strike Formation, asked.

"Nothing can be spared at the moment, Thom," Commander-in-Chief Diette replied. "We hold with what we've got. That was why it was imperative to get the force back away from the frontline to recover, because it looks like we're in this for the long haul. We've still got a trickle of replacements coming in straight from the academies, but no actual units on route to us. We dig in with what we've got."

"There's more," Owenne cleared his throat, standing up and pacing slowly around the edge of the table with his hands clasped behind his back. "For those of you who don't know already, the cruiser *Agility* detected a shuttle landing on the far side of the planet two days ago. It appears the shuttle is from the Freeborn House Selestov, a rather large and aggressive house with a track record of selling their mercenary services to anybody wishing to oppose the Concord. It would appear at this point that their most likely reason for visiting the planet is to sell their services to the local rebels who are still holding out against Concord care."

The assembled leaders certainly did not need to know why he had given orders to the *Agility* to scan the planet's surface. If Embryo was indeed what the locals now called Markov's Prize, as all the evidence suggested, then Owenne's decade long search would be over.

"The 'local rebels' refer to themselves by the planet self-defense force's original name: the Markov Alliance Army," Zann continued. "This appears to be a rather political statement by their leader, Marshall Grynne, who is claiming that the Markov's Prize government who surrendered to us were nothing more than collaborators and traitors. The MAA can muster perhaps a division of soldiers – not a significant threat in its own right - but if they enter battle with weapons and armor supplied by House Selestov, we could have a real problem. That would be aside from the fact we're already locked in combat with the Ghar. The sooner we can locate and disable the remaining nanosphere shielding on this planet, the better."

"That's worst case," Commander-in-Chief Hawess rested his hands over his somewhat corpulent belly as he sat back in his chair. "I can't imagine the locals are particularly happy with the Ghar, either, so I'd imagine they'll be just as happy if not more so to attack them. Remember, they may see us as invaders, but it's the Ghar who have been massacring the civilian population, not us."

"Probably best we assume the worst case," Commander-in-Chief Diette tapped his chin pensively. "If I was in Grynne's shoes, I'd probably be looking at attacking both invading forces. We may well find ourselves locked in a three-way war with the Ghar and an alliance between the local military and Freeborn mercenaries. You said you had some int on the Ghar leader, JJ?"

"Yes, sir, a little," Zann replied. "Intercepted communications have revealed that the Ghar assault is led by High Commander Drej."

The image of Markov's Prize in the center of the room was replaced by the snarling, scarred face of the Ghar commander in question. Owenne had heard of him before but quickly read everything C3 had on the creature to refresh his memory.

"12-38-19 Drej is a clone, like any other Ghar, but his batch was genetically modified to provide an improved stock of military leaders and strategists. Two of a later, improved batch - Karg and Fartok - you will all no doubt have heard of. Drej is less well known in the Concord but no less dangerous."

"Karg," Owenne interrupted, closing his eyes for a moment to think, "he was that odious little creature that led the Ghar on the Xilos campaign. Now if memory serves, and I believe it does, that batch of genetic reprobates had some rather interesting diversions. Karg, for example, is rather well known for his love of drink, fine foods, and collecting beautiful women from his enemies to be his slaves. Not very Ghar-like at all. Perhaps this Drej has some weaknesses of his own that we can exploit."

"If he's anything like his old friend Karg, perhaps we can entice him with women of our own, eh, Drop Captain Mosse?" A grey haired officer from force intelligence remarked.

Mosse looked up at the man from where she sat at the far end of the table.

"Don't know about that," she replied coolly, "I'm sure you scrub up okay, but there's only so much we can do with a girl like you. Some old saying about polish and turds leaps to mind. But pop around later, me and the boys can try to doll you up a bit."

A ripple of sniggers echoed around the conference room.

"Well, now that idea has been put in its rightful place, let's have a think about a more effective military strategy," Commander-in-Chief Diette failed to suppress his glee at Mosse's comments. "We need a robust, long term plan. Now, the Ghar have stalled and right now the frontlines are relatively quiet. We believe they're expecting reinforcements, but we also need to take full advantage of this lull in the action to get our people ready. The 12th Assault Force has the frontline covered at the moment and is holding this line you see on the map here across the Veneen Basin, nicely flanked by mountainous terrain which is completely impassible in a Ghar battlesuit. The 12th is fresh and at good strength. My 17th Assault Force is not as well placed. I'd like to keep them back for a while, get them rested, and get this trickle of academy replacements settled in and ready to fight for when things heat up again."

"Agreed," Hawess nodded, "my force can hold the front whilst we get your boys and girls sorted. My only concern is over what will happen if the MAA decide to join the party, and how easy it will be for them to get modern weapons and equipment seeing as our naval presence in the area is so limited. We'll need a plan for that. Shouldn't be too much of a problem, I hear one of you boys took out ten Ghar troopers single handed."

"Eleven, old boy," Diette beamed. "Anything to add at this point, Ryen?"

"No, not from me, sir," Tahl said quietly from his place next to Mosse.

"Well, that's the 17th for you," Diette continued proudly, "most of my soldiers can take out ten or eleven Ghar single handed. Let's hope the 12th can keep up."

"Yes, yes, very good," Hawess raised one eyebrow and held up a hand to stop the excited chatter from around the table. "The MAA, and plans to stop them. Bring the map up again, let's take a look."

Owenne's eyes searched the surface of the holographic projection of the planet. If he wanted to hide a research facility away from prying eyes, he wondered where he would have put it.

***

"Company! Stand at...ease!" Van Noor bellowed to the assembled strike troopers.

Rhona, along with the other three dozen assembled troopers, lifted her left knee to waist height and brought it down to the ground with a crash about a shoulder width apart from her right foot, simultaneously bringing her fists from their position against her thighs to overlap her palms at the small of her back. Beta Company had been assembled outside of the accommodation block at Firebase Alpha, where Van Noor had then lined them up in three ranks at attention in the late afternoon sunshine.

The senior strike leader took a step back as Mandarin Owenne turned to face the assembled soldiers, his thin form hidden beneath his thick coat and peaked cap despite the blistering heat.

"Chaps," the mandarin began, his tone uneasy, "I'll get the reprimand out of the way first. Forthwith, the practice of 'Ghar Scutter Racing' is to stop. Captured enemy vehicles are not there for your amusement, and the enemy is certainly not above booby trapping their own vehicles. So pack it in. Onto happier news, you've been at it here for over fifty days now. Longer, seeing as most of you came here straight from Prostock. I'm giving you three days leave. Don't confuse this for a sign of weakness or sentimentality on my part. It's simple man management. If I want you at peak efficiency, then I need to rest you. There are two hotels with rooms booked for you in New Wryland city center. Transport leaves here in two hours. Go and drink, exchange bodily fluids with the locals, whatever you want. Just stay out of trouble and be back here at 0800 three days from now. That's all. Dismiss them, Senior."

"Company! Attention!" Van Noor yelled. "Turning to right in threes, dismissed!"

Rhona's eyes met Gant's as the assembled company quickly split into squads in the excited buzz of conversation. She flashed him a broad grin and a wink, unable to suppress the excitement of the idea of drinking herself into oblivion and finding a dance floor.

"Two hours!" Qan beamed as he jogged over. "Two hours to get all prettied up and then hit the clubs! Can you believe that? Three days in a hotel in a city on the other side of the planet from the fighting?"

"This'll be awesome!" Clythe planted his hands on Qan's shoulders and jumped up in the air. "I can ditch this uniform for three days, sleep every day, and get annihilated every night!"

"I've already taken the liberty of checking the club scene in New Wryland," Jemmel said as she wandered over to join them, a datapad in her hand. "There's a place called 'Voltz' which seems to have the best reviews and ratings. I'll pass that around to the rest of the company. You coming, Kat?"

"Hell yeah!" Rhona nodded. "I need to teach you boys how to dance properly!"

The positive atmosphere which surrounded the banter and jokes as the squad walked back to the accommodation block came as an immediate relief to Rhona. The tension and arguments of the past day seemed to finally be eroding. Three days out of uniform would be perfect, for everybody. Rhona headed straight to her room and shut the partition behind her. She put on some loud music and quickly discarded her barrack uniform before washing, wrapping a towel around herself, and then unpacking her arsenal of cosmetic goods from her kitbag, filling the top of her bunk with rows of options as they were decompressed after being removed from their storage. She was halfway through adding thin streaks of dark blue to her hair, after combing it back out to a little past shoulder length, when she heard a knock on the partition.

"Yeah?" She shouted, turning the music down.

The partition slid open and Jemmel walked in, shutting the door behind her. She was still dressed in her barrack uniform. The short woman looked Rhona up and down, frowning.

"Jeez, Kat, you look like you were drawn by a hormonal fourteen year old boy."

"Yeah, yeah, I know, I'm awesome. C'mon, Jem, get changed."

"That's why I'm here," Jemmel replied, her tone betraying an unease which Rhona had never detected from her before.

"What's the problem?"

"Help me look half-decent, would you?" Jemmel asked. "I know I'm not going to look like, well, you, but give me a fighting chance of looking okay. Without making it look like I've tried too hard. In fact, without making it look like I've tried at all."

Rhona nodded as she finished her last blue streak and then turned to face the shorter woman.

"Girl, you came to the right place. Playin' dress up is my thing. Now I know this is gonna get you all pissed off, but the first thing we're doing is sorting your hair out. Or the lack of."

"Don't make me look like a sodding princess," Jemmel tutted.

Rhona grabbed her hair brush and quickly cycled through the many options on the display screen, selecting a hair growth pattern that would suit Jemmel's aggressive look.

"Just trust me, would you? You're the veteran soldier, you know guns and killing and all that stuff. But now we're talking about looking hot on a dance floor. You're in my world now."

***

"How does my ass look in these?" Qan said, emerging from his room in an uncomfortably tight looking pair of metallic silver leggings, "I mean, shiny is cool, but I don't know if this is too much."

"No, you look good," Clythe nodded, his tone serious. "Stick a floral shirt with that and the girls know you mean business. You're not there to mess around wearing that."

"It's not about the clothes," Gant called from his room, "women aren't that shallow. It's about your hair. You guys would do better spending an hour on your hair. Like me."

Sessetti glanced out of the corner of his eye and saw Clythe emerge into the communal area, wearing similarly skin tight trousers made of thin, shiny thermally reactive material which changed colors and patterns with each step he took.

"Remember these?" He grinned broadly, nodding proudly, "Huh? Retro, right? Girls love retro! They'll look at me in this and say 'there's a guy with a sense of humor. And a great ass.' It's the whole package. Just need a shirt to go with it."

"Open top blouse," Qan replied, "something loose and shiny. Show off the pecks. C'mon, guy, transport's leaving in less than an hour!"

Sessetti finished tying his belt and walked out into the communal area, prepared for the abuse which would follow.

"What's that?" Qan laughed. "We've going out to destroy some local girls, not to beat up an end of level bad guy."

"Yeah, seriously," Clythe added, "you look like something out of a bad sheng-fu movie."

"It's a kerempai gi," Sessetti explained, "I'm off for a lesson."

"Now?" Gant called from his room, "you ain't got time, bro. Get changed quickly."

"I'd already arranged the lesson before we knew we had tonight off," Sessetti said, "I'm not cancelling now. I'll catch you guys up later."

The partition to Rhona's room opened and Jemmel walked out. Her hair grown out to just past her ears, her feminine look effortlessly combined with a tomboyish appeal took Sessetti by surprise. She was dressed in black leggings and a crop top displaying her toned arms and abdomen to finish the look.

"Don't look so surprised, guys," she folded her arms, "I can look like a real girl, from time to time. Now, take a good look and let me enjoy being center of attention for two seconds until that bitch comes out and takes the spotlight for the rest of the night."

As if on cue, Rhona walked casually out of her room. Wearing a miniscule dress of metallic black with matching knee boots, she had somehow managed to surpass her normal levels of beauty and transcend to a level Sessetti had never seen before. The room fell silent until Qan finally spoke.

"How drunk do I have to get you to nail you? I can't believe I just said that out loud."

"You can't say that, you prick!" Jemmel said in disgust.

"Don't sweat it," Rhona shrugged. "I know y'all thinking it, I can feel it through the shard. Besides, you don't go out looking like this unless that's what you want guys to think. Lian, what's with the fancy dress? C'mon, boy, get ready."

"He's not coming with us," Clythe said, "he's going for a kerempai lesson."

Rhona's jaw dropped.

"Say what now?"

"I'm taking lessons from Strike Captain Tahl," Sessetti explained, "I'll catch you guys up later."

"You're doing what?" Rhona demanded, planting her clenched fists on her hips.

"Ease off him, Kat," Jemmel said. "What's the big deal? If I knew the boss was giving lessons then I'd probably go. Pretty cool opportunity to roll around the floor with him in all manner of chokes and locks."

"And what the hell is that supposed to mean?" Rhona demanded.

"I mean he's hot!" Jemmel said. "Or are you pretending you

didn't notice? It's not just these guys who get to drool and say sexist stuff! What's your problem?"

"My problem is that that's our company commander you're talking about!" Rhona snapped. "And you should show him some damn respect! And you, Sessetti, you shouldn't be... taking up his time with kids' beginner lessons! That guy was the Determinate champion!"

"We know, Kat," Qan said, "we watched him kick three Ghar machines to death whilst you were lying in a desert, bleeding out."

Before Rhona could respond again, a knock rapped against the communal area door. Clythe walked across and opened the door to admit Van Noor. The senior strike leader walked in, still wearing his barrack uniform.

"Evening gents, ladies," the broad man smiled. "You ready to go?"

"Pretty much, Senior," Qan answered. "You not coming?"

"I've got a ton of reports to write, on you bastards, mainly. No, maybe tomorrow night. But... I'm here with good news and bad news for you. Let's do the good news first. Fire up your HV set, you guys have just had a message sent through from the home systems."

Sessetti activated the holovision set, mindful of the time and how it was only a few minutes until Tahl was expecting him. Van Noor transmitted an access code across to him from the command shard, which Sessetti fed in to the HV box. Instantly a holographic projection of a familiar woman appeared in their midst.

"Hey, guys," Rae smiled, "if you're seeing this message then I'm dead, so I just wanted to say something to all of you. Nah, I'm just kidding. I'm back home now, I'm all okay, they managed to get me all regen'd up."

Smiles lit up the faces of every member of Squad Wen. Clythe let out a cheer which was immediately silenced by Gant as he leant in closer to listen to the recording.

"The system decided I've done my time, so I'm afraid I'm not coming back. I'm back home with my parents and my brother. I'm missing you guys already and missing the fun we had, and how exciting every day was to be with you all."

The last phrase Rae said resulted in confused and concerned glances being exchanged between the troopers.

"I don't really remember much about the end," Rae continued, "I guess you guys got me out of trouble, so thanks for taking care of me. I've been telling everybody back here about all of the fun times and how amazing it was to travel everywhere and see so many planets and civilizations, and how great an experience it was. I sometimes try to remember the fighting... and... I can't... I remember all the great times we had!"

162 of Beyond the Gates of Antares

Sessetti watched with a mixture of happiness and relief to see Rae alive, but sympathy as her eyes would glaze over or change focus as her emotions were restrained every time any negative connotation of military life threatened to enter her mind. C3 had that all under control. Best to only send positive messages to the civilian shards back home.

"Well look, you guys'll be busy and I don't want to keep you. I'll try my best to keep in touch, and I've sent you all my home address with this message. Please do come and visit me if you ever get the chance. I know this was only a tiny part of my life, but I'll always remember it and always be thankful that I had my little second family for a little while. You guys take care! And make sure you visit!"

The message faded away. Clythe whooped excitedly, looking around at the other soldiers before his smile faded into confusion.

"What? That's great news, right? She's okay!"

"Sorry, Senior," Jemmel turned to Van Noor, "did you say that was the good news or the bad news?"

"Your mate's alive and well," Van Noor said, "that should be good news. To anybody. She's survived this and C3 has let her go home. For whatever reason, they decided that the brief bit of time she had with us was enough to positively affect her life and now she's done. She's one of the winners."

"But half of her brain is fragged," Gant countered, "she can only remember a small quantum of what we went through."

"Yeah, and I envy her that!" Van Noor snapped. "She gets to go home with only some flower tinted version of what actually happened. And you guys are all moping around like that's a bad thing! What would you prefer? Go home like the good old days with a host of severe mental health problems from combat and end up killing yourself? C3 is looking after us. You should appreciate it."

"I agree," Sessetti admitted as he processed his thoughts. "Ila is safe and she only remembers the good times. That's the best news I've heard for a long time."

"Right!" Clythe agreed. "She's fine! C'mon, let's go hit the city and celebrate!"

"And the bad news?" Jemmel turned back to Van Noor again.

Van Noor beckoned to Rhona.

"Come with me. We need to talk."

***

Rhona followed Van Noor into the corridor outside the squad's accommodation block. The senior strike leader wasted no time in casting a disapproving look over her.

"You're going out? Dressed like that?"

"Aw, shucks, daddy, you think I'm showing too much leg?" Rhona rolled her eyes. "This is my spare time, I'm off the clock, I'll dress how I want to."

"There is no off the clock!" Van Noor countered. "You're a junior leader in the Concord Combined Command, and as the company second-in-command, I expect you to display some standards! Might not matter anyway. You know the drill – when a firebase is on reduced manning, somebody needs to stay back to monitor security of the perimeter. So we need an individual to stay here tonight."

"That's a bad joke, right?" Rhona exclaimed. "What about Alpha Company? They live here too."

"They've already volunteered one guy. The regs say it requires two, so we're providing a second trooper."

"What about you?" Rhona folded her arms. "You just said you're staying here tonight."

"I don't need to explain myself to you, Strike Leader," Van Noor leaned closer, "and I've already told you that I'm spending my leave catching up on crappy paperwork that somebody at your rank doesn't need to worry about. That doesn't lend itself to checking the drones and walking the perimeter wire, does it? Now, I can't tell you to volunteer for this; that would be bullying. What I can tell you is that, thanks to the message from the former Strike Trooper Rae, your squad is the only squad in the company that hasn't lost a single guy. That's why I've selected Squad Wen to provide a security detail for tonight. You're in charge, so you pick somebody. I'm sure you'll make the right decision."

"Well, it's me, isn't it?" Rhona growled. "I'm not gonna go in there and tell one of those guys their leave is canceled. I'll do it."

"Good," Van Noor smiled aggressively, "you can make the odd right decision. Now wash that blue crap out of your hair, put a uniform on, and present yourself to HQ in fifteen minutes looking like a Concord soldier rather than a Freeborn slut who earns a living on her back. Go on, get to it."

Rhona heard her fists clenching by her sides as she watched Van Noor walk away to the transmat pads.

TWELVE

Voltz Nightclub
New Wryland
Markov's Prize

Sessetti stood motionless in the cubicle as the scanner beam quickly swept over him from head to toe. The interior of the booth glowed green, the signal that he was not carrying any weapons or narcotics. Sessetti wondered if such stringent measures were still really necessary now that the Concord had taken over and the overseeing man-machine interface would intervene automatically if any hostile intentions were sensed. Intervention would be automatic for the overwhelming majority of citizens who were fully compatible with an IMTel shard, at least.

Vacating the security booth to allow the next man in the queue to step in front of the scanner, Sessetti walked quickly over to the transmat pad which would transport him up to the club's main floor. He checked himself over in the mirrored walls as he walked; he was dressed relatively conservatively in black trousers and a dark blue collared shirt, but he wore his cuffs undone and the shirt unbuttoned halfway as was the current fashion. He had refused Clythe's polite offer to provide matching eye make-up; as outdated and bland as it might seem to others, Sessetti had never found himself drawn to men's cosmetic enhancements. It always seemed a bit feminine to him. Van Noor had seen him as he dashed for the last transport, stopping him to cast a judgmental eye over his appearance. The simple assessment had been positive: "Good, son. Good."

The familiar consent form was transmitted to him from the club's shard as he walked – questions revolving around if he welcomed advances from strangers, whether he was looking for long term romance or something more casual and less meaningful, his gender preferences, the same form which he had filled out countless times at many clubs back home with the same red, amber, and green answer coding. Nothing had changed – he filled in the same answers as he always did in the few seconds it took to walk over to the transmat pads. It occurred to him briefly that the whole endeavor was relatively pointless – the system knew everybody's preferences – but the illusion of choice for Concord citizens was a positive thing in itself, no doubt. It just took the reduced intervention of a military shard for him to be able to see and think that. The consent form, the transmat pads, all recently installed touches which marked out the planet, and its entire culture as well, on the way to being completely integrated within the IMTel.

Sessetti stepped onto the newly installed transmat pad and watched as the entrance hall faded away and was replaced by the spectacular interior of the nightclub. A cavernous main hall, perhaps five floors high, was dominated by a huge dancefloor. The floor itself was illuminated with dazzling lights and holographic projections of spectacular, swirling shapes, their edges softened by the knee-high field of sweetly scented smoke which rolled in from the floor edges. Colored spotlights cast beams of light down from the ceiling way above in the darkness, and four curved podiums snaked in from the corners of the hall, each with a beautiful woman dancing around a pole. Curved stairways led up to four other floors, each with seating areas looking down on the main dancefloor. Perhaps a thousand people occupied the club, maybe two hundred of which were crammed onto the dancefloor, moving in time to the booming music which issued from all corners of the building with outstanding clarity.

Patching back into his squad shard, Sessetti located his squadmates – Jemmel, Qan, Gant, and Clythe were all sat around a table on the third floor, overlooking the dance floor. Sessetti carefully pushed his way through the crowds and up the stairs, politely declining an invitation to dance which was sent across the club shard into his mind from a girl in the center of the dancefloor. Not what Sessetti was looking for, but the invitation was appreciated nonetheless.

Qan waved enthusiastically from the table as he approached – the near deafening music faded to an altogether more sociable level as soon as the club's shard detected he was attempting to engage in conversation.

"You took your time!" Gant grinned, thrusting a glass of beer into his hands as he approached the table. "Has the boss turned you into some ass kicking sheng-fu master?"

Jemmel tapped the table and the center opened, elegantly elevating a carousel of drinks and smoking options. She selected a thick cigar and passed it over to Sessetti.

"Try one of these," she ordered, "it's local. It's good."

Sessetti snapped the end off the cigar and felt it instantly warm as the chemicals inside reacted with the air to ignite. He inhaled a lungful of the wood scented herbs and then took a swig from his beer. Life was pretty good.

"It's pretty cool, you getting turned into a Ghar annihilating machine!" Qan offered.

"Let's not give the boss too much credit," Jemmel argued, "he should be spending more time making the hard decisions and calling the tough shots, and less time charging around the battlefield getting stuck in. That's our job, not his."

"You've got a problem with the way he runs the show?" Gant laughed.

"He's soft," Jemmel said evenly, "a company commander's job is to use his assets to defeat the enemy, not wrap his boys and girls up in cotton wool."

"What a crock of nonsense," Gant stepped in to cut off Sessetti's equally passionate defense. "I've worked for strike captains before who adopt that mentality. We get the job done just fine the way it is. I want somebody above me who has my back, not somebody who'll throw me away to impress his bosses."

"Yeah, well, that's the difference between you and me," Jemmel shrugged, "I'm able to see the bigger picture."

"Hang on, hang on!" Clythe suddenly sat up enthusiastically. "I've got another message! It's my second invitation to dance! It's... another man."

"It's the way you dress," Gant grinned, "and by the way, Lian, whatever you do – don't offer any of the local girls a drink. I've looked it up now, but apparently it's considered an insult around here. Something to do with the implications of forcing intoxicating substances onto others. However, I've found that here – the same as every bloody planet I've ever been to – the men are expected to chase the women."

"It's social customs," Jemmel countered as she blew purple-tinted smoke rings from her cigar, "same as it's always been. Guys are expected to initiate the courtship rituals. Men need to do the chasing. It's not right, but there it is."

"So that's what we're fighting for?" Clythe grunted. "To be treated differently based on gender in a club?"

"Oh, dry your eyes and don't even bother playing the gender card," Jemmel drawled. "It's exactly the same back in the real Concord as it is out here. It's just that you're only noticing it now."

"So you've been propositioned?" Qan asked.

"Three so far," Jemmel replied, "two to dance, one for a meeting in a booth. None of them have rocked my world, however."

"So if you don't like the way these clubs work, why'd you pick this place?" Clythe demanded. "You chose this place and dragged the entire company here."

"I had a plan," Jemmel replied, "a cunning scheme. But now Kat has been Van Gnawed again, and we've left her behind, my plan ain't gonna work."

"He does seem to have it in for her," Sessetti offered, deciding against the cigar and stubbing it out before selecting a berry scented hose and nozzle from the carosel and taking a drag.

"He wants to screw her," Gant shrugged, "can you blame him?"

"Maybe, just maybe," Jemmel smiled sarcastically, "d'you reckon we can go one evening without all talking about how amazing Rhona looks?"

The table fell silent for a brief moment, the lyrics of a familiar dance song lifting in volume automatically to fill the lull in conversation.

"You look great, Jem," Sessetti offered. "I'm not trying to be weird or anything. But in front of the other guys, I just wanted to let you know that I think you look really great tonight."

Jemmel looked across at him but did not reply.

"He's right!" Gant smiled, throwing an arm around Jemmel's shoulders and forcing her into a rough embrace. "Keep your hair longer like that, dude, it suits you better. Don't worry, you still look badass."

"I'll keep it like this if you shave yours off," Jemmel countered, tousling Gant's curly locks.

Gant laughed.

"Gimme a few days and you've got a deal. I just want to look this good for all of our leave so I can nail everything with a pulse which will let me near it."

***

The lilac tint to the clear night sky seemed unique to Rhona as she stared up at the stars. Years of travelling space with her father – admittedly the same parts, over and over – had given her more exposure to the wondrous variations so many different planets had to offer, but nothing was like the night sky of Markov's Prize. The cut of the planet's rings across the sky, the soft glow over the horizon, the gentle shapes of the gasses in the upper atmosphere, it all added together to present a picture of unique beauty.

Rhona shook her head as she pictured a Ghar scout creeping up behind her to slit her throat.

"Concentrate, you dumb bitch," she cursed herself, carrying on her walk along Firebase Alpha's perimeter fence and looking out into the jungles beyond.   The trooper from Alpha Company she was sharing the duty with seemed okay enough, but she did welcome the opportunity to carry out the hourly check of the perimeter drones to visually ascertain that all was well. The cold plasma carbine felt strange in her bare hands; guard duty in a secure location called only for a trooper to wear an eye piece to connect to the base shard and give enhanced visual options in addition to barrack uniform and a weapon.

The perimeter was securely patrolled by the tireless force of little spotter drones and their larger, armed, C3D1 cousins. Although the likelihood was extremely remote, it was not completely unknown for a drone to suffer a system failure, and for that failure to escape the notice of the security shard. That was why a periodic, physical check by a trooper was written into the guard routines. And as hugely disappointed as Rhona was to be missing a night out, if she was stuck here on guard duty, then she would carry out a damn good job of it.

The security shard alerted her to a figure approaching from the southwest, identified as another Concord trooper. Rhona turned to face the trooper, wondering why the guy from Alpha Company would leave his post to talk to her when communication through the shard would have been easier. After a few moments, she saw the trooper and walked out to meet him. As she drew closer, she recognized that it was not her guard comrade, but her company commander.

Rhona stood smartly to attention before bringing her right foot out and smacking into the heel of her left, tilting her carbine forward for inspection. Tahl returned the formalities of her presenting of arms with a salute.

"Anything to report, Strike Leader?"

"No, sir. Perimeter secure; no unservicabilities in drones or surveillance devices, sir."

"Good. Hand over your weapon."

Rhona swung the weapon around to lie horizontally before presenting it to Tahl.

"Sir! Weapon is fully charged, loaded but not made ready. Ionic compression pack is checked and correctly functioning."

Tahl took the carbine, gave it a visual check, and then slung it over his shoulder.

"Right. I've got the guard duty. Off you go, go catch up with your friends."

"Say what now?" Rhona exclaimed.

"I'll take it from here. Some of the guys from Delta Company have a late transport on. If you run, you'll have time to get changed and go. Come on, hand over the eye piece, too. You shall go to the ball, my pretty," Tahl winced immediately and exhaled before continuing. "I didn't mean anything offensive by that. It's just a famous line in a children's story where I'm from. I didn't mean..."

"It's okay, Boss," Rhona suppressed a smile, "that story is famous where I'm from, too. But I can't go. The company commander shouldn't be pulling guard duty. Plus the senior strike leader specifically told me to..."

"You leave the senior to me," Tahl interrupted softly. "Besides, it does me good to remind myself of duties like this once in a while. Go on, go take your leave."

"Right," Rhona hurriedly unclipped her eyepiece and handed it to Tahl.

"The senior strike leader has spoken to me about some of your recent conversations," Tahl warned. "You need to have a think about the way you're addressing him. I appreciate you two don't see eye to eye, but he is the most experienced trooper in this company, and he does outrank you. I want you to have a good think about the way you conduct yourself around him in future, okay?"

"Yeah, absolutely," Rhona nodded, checking the time and mentally planning her outfit and hair. "I'll make sure I get my act together and give him the proper marks of respect in future. What time did you say the transport leaves, sir?"

"About twenty-five minutes," Tahl replied.

"Cool," Rhona turned on her heel and started sprinting back toward the accommodation block.

She stopped after a few seconds and turned back to Tahl.

"Tonight's gonna be awesome!" She beamed excitedly.

Tahl gave a curt nod and turned to patrol the perimeter fence.

***

Finishing mid-pack, Sessetti slammed his empty glass down in the center of the table and watched as Qan and Clythe struggled with the fiery liquid. The world swam a little, the club shard warned him about his alcohol intake and offered remedial medication; he ignored the advice. Gant let out a cheer as Clythe finally finished before hitting the table to bring the drinks carousel back up so he could start pouring again.

"Right," Gant said as he finished. "I've had an offer from a girl who appears to meet my lofty standards, so I'm outta here. I'll catch you losers in an hour or so."

"By an hour, you mean five minutes, right?" Jemmel smiled sarcastically.

Gant shrugged and staggered off toward the stairwell leading down to the packed dance floor. Qan reached across to the carousel, unwound a pipe and nozzle, and began smoking a sweet, flowery smelling gas.

"We staying up here all night or are we heading down?" He asked.

Before Sessetti could state his opinion, Clythe smacked him on the shoulder and pointed down to the dance floor. The most attractive woman he had ever laid eyes on danced her way across the floor, bouncing from man to man as she lithely displaced a sequence of salacious moves. Wearing a tiny dress of metallic black which left little to the imagination, the dark haired woman attracted the attention of every man and woman near her as she navigated her way toward the stairs.

"That's Kat!" Qan suddenly blurted out. "How the hell did she get here?"

Rhona made her way to the stairs and then walked up and across to their table.

"Better late then never!" She grinned, tossing her perfectly sculpted hair cockily over her shoulder.

"I thought you had guard duty?" Clythe asked.

"One of the other guys took it for me," Rhona replied.

"That's a pretty crappy way to spend the night," Qan offered. "I hope you thanked him properly."

Rhona paused.

"No. Come to think of it, no, I didn't. I didn't say thank you at all."

"I'm sick of you," Jemmel greeted as she passed a beer over to Rhona. "I was quite enjoying my night until you turned up to snatch any shred of limelight from anybody else."

"This is that jealousy thing again, huh?" Rhona smiled, her voice a little slurred. "Is this because in the five minutes I've been here, I've already had fifty-two propositions sent my way?"

"Fifty-two?" Clythe exclaimed. "I've had three all night!"

"Fifty-three now," Rhona corrected, downing her beer and reaching for another.

"Are you already pissed?" Jemmel asked.

"Yeah, kinda – fifty-four – the guys in Delta Company who gave me a lift across had loads of beer – fifty-five – so I've been drinking for quite a while – fifty-six. Jemmel, I'm sending all of these requests to you now so you know I'm not making this up."

"Already drunk," Jemmel nodded, leaning back with a suspicious smile, "interesting."

"Only kinda – fifty-seven," Rhona slurred, "I can handle my drink. I've had a lot of practice. Fifty-eight – oh, she's hot! I haven't gone down that route for a few years. But… I'm a little out of practice, I've drunk a lot, it hasn't mixed well. And now if you'll excuse me, I think I'm going to be sick."

Sessetti grabbed an antidote pill and glass of water from the carousel and pushed them quickly across to Rhona. She took the pill and exhaled as her eyes sharpened back into focus a little.

"C'mon guys, let's all go hit the dance floor."

The rest of the night passed in a whirl of drinking, smoking, and dancing for Sessetti. His main recollections later on would be standing on the dance floor with Clythe, Qan, Gant, Rhona, and Jemmel, their arms all around each others' shoulders to form a circle as they sang at the top of their lungs, passing drinks, and smoking sticks around as they did so. It was a moment he would never forget.

***

Tahl groaned as he opened his eyes. The last three times he had awoken were due to the temperature in his room – fluctuating seemingly at random between too hot and too cold – but this time it was something different. He sat up in his bunk and checked the time. One hour since he last sat up; two hours until his alarm would wake him. Then he heard the banging at his door again and remembered that was what had woken him up. Even half asleep, he was confused at why the visitor would not use the shard to announce themselves or what would cause a visit at such an unsociable hour. Tahl, who had fallen asleep in just his white gi trousers, pulled a black t-shirt on and wandered over to the door. There must have been a fight at a nightclub. He could think of no other reason why he was being woken, if not to diffuse some situation his troopers had caused with the local authorities.

Tahl's eyes widened in surprise as he opened the door. Dressed in tall boots and a dress which just about adhered to Concord decency laws, Rhona leaned seductively against his doorframe. The smell of intoxicating perfume and alcohol vied with each other for control of the air.

"Hey, Boss," Rhona fixed her unfocused eyes on his and traced a finger along his chest. "I realized that I forgot to say thank you for taking my guard duty. And... I know you're really into me so I came up with a real good idea to show my appreciation."

Rhona stepped toward him, tripped up over the doorframe, and collapsed giggling to the floor before tottering back to her feet.

"Pretend that never happened!" She laughed. "Honestly, I'm really good at this! Just shut the door again and we'll start over... right, where was I?"

She leant against him and slipped an arm clumsily around the back of his neck. Tahl had not been counting, but he realized then that it had been over six years since any intimacy with a woman. Six years, and he had never laid eyes on anybody who looked like Rhona, even in those dark days of competition fighting and celebrity status. But she was drunk and not in control of herself. But it had been six years. The decision was easy and he made it instantly.

"Get inside, before somebody sees you," Tahl said, pulling her into his room and shutting the door behind her.

"That's more like it, sir," Rhona slurred, "I may be a terrible soldier but I absolutely guarantee you, I'm incredible in the sack. Seriously, just gimme a minute…"

Tahl left Rhona fumbling for the fastener on the side of her dress as he found his medical kit and recovered the unit's multi-tool. He returned to Rhona, selected a detoxification program, and stabbed a small needle into her shoulder. Rhona's eyes immediately sharpened into focus and her skin turned to an ashen grey as hours of natural processes were accelerated and her hangover kicked in instantly.

"Ahh! Why would you do that?!" Rhona yelped, collapsing down to sit on the edge of his bed and sink her face into her hands.

Tahl quickly cycled through the other options on the medical multi tool and combined various painkillers with other mild sedatives, anti-nausea medication, and hydrators. Again, he administered a shot of chemicals into her shoulder. He watched as the natural color flowed back to her skin and the realization of her situation flooded to the fore of her fully functioning mind. She shot to her feet.

"Sir, I am so sorry," she said desperately.

"Sit down, Katya," Tahl said quietly, sinking to one knee opposite her as she did so to bring their eyes level. "Are you okay now?"

"I…can I have something soft to drink, please, sir?" She asked politely. "Anything to take the taste away."

Tahl poured her a drink of strong flavored juice from local fruits, watching with a mixture of amusement and sympathy as Rhona desperately pulled the hem of her dress down and the neckline up, her narrowed eyes and clenched teeth showing the mental self-flagellation that was wracking her mind. She took the drink and the scent of alcohol very quickly dissipated.

"I'm so sorry," she repeated, "I know I'm in a hell of a lot of trouble. I know this is really inappropriate, this is insubordinate, it's… I'll accept any punishment. I'm so sorry."

"Don't worry about it," Tahl stood up and opened the door for her. "Come on, go get some sleep. It doesn't matter."

"What?" Rhona asked as she stood. "You're not going to carry out disciplinary action?"

"For what?" Tahl shrugged. "Getting drunk with your friends and doing something stupid? We've all been there. To tell you the truth, I'm just impressed you found a way back to the firebase at this time. Go get some sleep in your block and then catch a lift back to town to catch up with your friends when you're rested."

Rhona walked to the door and then stopped to face him.

"Why do I never get in trouble with you?" She asked softly. "Why do you always protect me?"

"It's not you, I'd do the same for anybody in my company," Tahl replied honestly. "I'm here to look after my people, not tear them to pieces for having a good night out. Now go on, as soon as you walk out of here, I promise I'll forget this ever happened. I'll never even mention it again. Go on. Good night."

Rhona nodded and walked away. After only a couple of paces, she turned around and rushed back to wrap her arms around his neck and kiss him fervently. Tahl reached up to push her away, but the last of his willpower in resisting her was spent. After several long moments, she broke away but rested her forehead against his, her eyes still closed.

"That was a mistake," she whispered, "a really dumb mistake. And I know it's going to make things really awkward between us."

She took a step back and looked up at him with a wry smile.

"But I'm really glad I did it," she added before turning and walking away.

"W... wait!" Tahl called after her. "You said I wasn't your type."

"Yes, sir, yes I did," Rhona smiled over her shoulder, "and it was a huge lie. G'night, Boss."

***

Nausea reared its ugly but now familiar head as Sessetti woke up in his hotel room for the second morning, sunlight fighting against the automatic filters of his windows. He felt blindly on the table next to him for his medical tool, mentally thanking his past self from the night before for leaving it within reach, before selecting a program to rid him of his hangover.

That was that. Leave was pretty much over, back to the frontline to relieve the guys from the other assault force. Back to fighting Ghar. Sessetti felt the nausea returning again. He jumped as a body moved beneath the sheets. Looking down, he realized that he was not alone. Frantically piecing the previous night together, he tried to recall any girls he had met in the various bars he had visited with Clythe, Qan, Gant, Rhona, and...

Jemmel poked her head up from beneath the sheets and looked up at him.

"Aw... crap," she whispered hoarsely.

Sessetti leaned back and closed his eyes, groaning uncomfortably.

THIRTEEN

Firebase Alpha
Equatorial Region
Markov's Prize

L-Day plus 58

Sharp blades of grass pushed up through the fine sand of the small, rocky outcrop which overhung the beach. The gentle lap of the waves was accompanied by the tuneful songs of a dozen exotic bird types in the blue trees behind them as Squad Wen lounged in the early morning sun. Each of the troopers wore their hyperlight armor and berets; their weapons and equipment were already stowed in one of the half dozen Dukes which lay silently in a row down on the beach, awaiting the call for activation which could come at any moment. The other squads of Beta Company were similarly scattered around the staging area as the last few minutes before deployment to the frontline ticked quickly away.

Sessetti gazed out to sea, the gentle onshore breeze rustling the grass around him where he sat. Off to his right, Gant, Qan, and Clythe were enthusiastically engaged in conversation about their various sexual conquests over the past three days leave – from the odd snippet which Sessetti overheard, it appeared that Gant was winning. Jemmel paced restlessly along the tree line a few yan behind the rest of the group. Rhona was also alone, lying on the sand in the sun with her hands behind her head, chewing a blade of grass and smiling as she gazed up at the blue sky.

The last two days had been awkward for Sessetti, to put it mildly. It at least would have made some sense to him if Jemmel had treated him differently, been standoffish, or uncomfortable around him; anything except for the cool and casual dismissal of anything happening between them on that second night of leave. He had tried to speak to her, waited for the right opportunity, but whether by design or coincidence, she was never alone. Perhaps this was the best chance he would get to talk to her. He looked across at her. She instantly looked back and shook her head curtly.

"You not joining in with all the macho crap?" Jemmel turned to look down at Rhona. "I thought all of this talk about notching up sexual prey would be your thing."

"Didn't notch up anything over the past few days," Rhona smiled, "not one."

"Perhaps you should have tried harder," Qan offered. "Pity can get you a long way. Clythe'll tell you all about it."

"Never said I didn't try," Rhona shrugged, "just got turned down is all."

"You seem strangely happy about it," Gant said suspiciously. "Sounds like there's a story."

"Go on," Jemmel crouched down next to Rhona, "tell your best buddies all about it."

"Well," Rhona sat up and faced them with an enthusiastic smile, "you know the night I had to stay back on guard duty? You'll never believe what happened. I was guarding the Ghar prisoners and I got talking to one of them. Turned out he was a really nice guy. The more we talked, well, I got over the whole race divide between us, and I think I'm in love."

"Really?" Clythe exclaimed. "You fell in love with a Ghar prisoner?"

"No!" Rhona beamed. "Made up the entire story, just now! How are you so gullible? I'm talking absolute nonsense because it's none of your business and you already know loads about me. This... this one I'll keep to myself, I think."

The familiar hum of a reactor drifted across the warm breeze from one of the Dukes down below. The second in line fired up its systems and then the third. Seconds later, the low thrum of the anti-gravity engines beginning their initiation cycle also started, quickly winding up to a high pitch squeal before it continued up and out of the panhuman audio spectrum.

"They're playing our song," Jemmel said, "time to go back to work."

Sessetti felt a mixture of emotions as he walked down toward the beach with his squad and was left wondering what out of the fear, nausea, excitement, and resentment was actually his mind, and what was feedback from the others through the squad's shard. Perhaps a little bit of all of it was his. Up ahead, Squad Jai filed into the first transport drone, harried along by the perpetually angry Rall. Sessetti did not miss having him run the squad.

"*Even though the night has to end, don't wear a frown baby, 'cause we rocked the house! We rocked the house!*" Rhona sang softly; not a chorister's voice, but not bad.

Sessetti smiled at the gesture as he recognized the lyrics he had written.

"*Same time, different place,*" he joined in with Rhona, as they approached their transport and Qan clambered up through the open door into the cramped interior. "*The faces change but the songs are the same! We'll rock the house! We'll rock the house!*"

One by one, the rest of the squad joined in the song as the doors closed behind them and the column of green and white transport drones took Beta Company back to war.

***

Humming idly to himself, Owenne dusted off the sand from the tails of his coat as the lead transport drone sped toward the frontlines. Tahl, Van Noor, and Cane were the only other occupants of the drone – as with the rest of Beta Company, their feedback through the shard was refreshingly calm compared to their state prior to a few days' leave. Owenne was glad to have a more efficient fighting force at his disposal, even if it had cost him three days. News from the 12th Assault Force had been positive; the Ghar had seemingly been stopped dead in their tracks and had even dug in defensively in some places. Still, this was a major inconvenience which Owenne did not need or appreciate; without the Ghar's appearance – and now Freeborn mercenaries to add to his woes – he would already have ascertained whether Markov's Prize was indeed Embryo, or just another backwater planet teeming with billions of panhumans begging for the chance to join the Concord. Even if they did not realize it.

"Mandarin Owenne," Narik's words were suddenly projected across to him through the shard, "you are not heading toward the Nienne Desert as planned."

"I changed the plan, old boy," Owenne replied, "what of it?"

"The bulk of the Ghar forces on Markov's Prize are in the Nienne Desert. One would expect you to close with them and eliminate them. As planned."

"Then perhaps one should re-visit the strategy guides," Owenne replied, "as I'd much rather bypass a straight fight against a foe renowned for their armor and guns, and clip them from behind."

"And yet here I find you heading directly for Pariton, their capital city. Coincidentally the location of the planet's central archives."

Owenne tutted and rolled his eyes, attracting the attention of the other passengers.

" If affording myself the opportunity to check the planetary archives is a happy byproduct of eliminating the enemy, then so be it."

"Let us speak directly, Owenne." A hint of anger entered Narik's voice. "This is no byproduct. You have found no evidence of this planet being Embryo, so now you are diverting the course of the entire campaign to suit your vague hypothesis. You are gambling with the lives of our soldiers, and the odds are astronomically against you. What do you think you will find?"

"If we take the capital, the final remnants of the planetary resistance will crumble," Owenne delivered his answer in a deliberately patronizing tone. "And if the resistance crumbles, the Freeborn will leave, as there won't be anybody left to pay them. With both the resistance and the Freeborn gone, we have the advantage over the Ghar. Then we win."

"The resistance and the Freeborn are both openly opposed to the Ghar," Narik countered. "There is no logical reason to remove them at this juncture. They are attacking your enemy."

"They are also attacking me!" Owenne snapped. "And if I defeat the resistance, then they will join us as soon as they are under Concord control. As for the Freeborn, they can bugger off. I don't want their help."

"Your words lack integrity," Narik persisted, "you are heading to the capital for your own reasons and..."

Owenne severed the shard communication connection and pressed his fingers against his aching brow. Van Noor glanced across.

"You having problems with HQ?"

"Nothing you need concern yourself with," Owenne replied, "but I do intend to go and have a wander around tonight. I'd like to get a better appreciation of the capital city and what we are up against. Make sure I've got a couple of your people to bring some guns along with us."

"I'll keep you company," Tahl offered, "I know that under that cold exterior, you're just a big softy who wants companionship."

"Then I'll come along, too," Van Noor cut off Owenne's reply, "if only to stop the two of you getting your heads blown off."

***

Pariton
Capital City
Markov's Prize

L-Day plus 58

Van Noor exhaled in disgust as he cast his eyes slowly across the horizon. On some of the views available through his visor, it was actually possible to see the clouds of pollution wafting through the city's moonlit, empty streets from its centuries of archaic industrial output.

The ugly, angular buildings jutted out from the flat ground in clinical rows, as if deliberately contrasting the flowing, curved lines found in most Concord cities. The buildings were relatively intact as the Concord Assault Forces had not attacked Pariton during the initial landing; the only combat which had taken place in the city was between the Ghar and a few isolated bands of resistance and, judging by the surroundings, that fight had been brief and one-sided.

Allowing himself a smile, Van Noor glanced down at the small model soldier in his hand. One package had made it across the galaxy to him from his children to wish him a happy birthday. His daughter Alora's artistic skills continued to amaze him; the package contained a beautifully painted soldier wearing the flamboyant dress uniform of a bygone era. His son's drawings of spaceships touched him just as deeply. Van Noor used a small compression box to carefully shrink the soldier down to the size of a thumbnail before safely stowing it in one of his utility pouches. He mentally chastised himself – if he caught any of his troopers carrying personal possessions which could be used against them in the event of capture, he would have torn them to pieces.

"Looks clear," Tahl said from where he crouched at the street corner. "Let's keep going."

Tahl, Van Noor, and Owenne moved silently across the broad street and down a narrow alleyway between two buildings that reached up perhaps fifty stories to touch at the dark sky above. Van Noor patched in to check the scanner sweeps from the trio of spotter drones they had positioned ahead of them. Still nothing.

"How close do you want to get?" Van Noor asked the pale mandarin.

"Close enough to see what we're up against," Owenne replied crisply.

"Judging by the strength of what we've already sneaked past to get this far, I'd say we could use some help here," Tahl offered.

"The 12th Assault Force is holding the line at the Nienne Desert," Owenne responded. "We wont be getting any help here. It's just us."

"Is there any reason we're not with the 12th, amassing our assets to give the Ghar one almighty kick in the nuts, instead of scattering ourselves thinly across the planet?" Van Noor asked as the trio stopped again at the edge of a road intersection.

"Leave the strategy to me, Senior Strike Leader," Owenne grumbled. "You just worry about making sure your troopers are clean shaven and have shiny boots or whatever it is a senior strike leader does."

An alert flashed across Van Noor's viewscreen from one of the spotter drones. He immediately patched in to the drone's optical sensor array. Four spindly Ghar stood in a loose group at a road junction, their faces hidden beneath thick helmets. Bulky packs were strapped to their backs with small scanner dishes revolving slowly above their heads. Each Ghar held a long rod with a control box at one end.

"Tectorists," Owenne identified the group.

"Why have they got a scanner unit on patrol in the dead of night a good hundred yan behind their first line of defense?" Tahl queried. "We're near something."

"Whatever we're near, they're not expecting us," Van Noor added, "so they're looking for MAA resistance."

"My interest is piqued," Owenne remarked dryly. "Let us go take a closer look."

Van Noor held up a cautionary hand to stop the mandarin.

"Tectorists do one thing – scan for the enemy. You remember the intelligence briefing on Ghar forces? The one the two of us delivered to the company? There's no point in us blundering any closer, they'll detect us and raise the alarm."

"Fine," Owenne smiled tersely. "Ryen, go do your nin-kwan-fu or whatever it's called, sneak up to them and break their necks."

"Contrary to what movies will tell you, martial artists can't actually turn themselves into smoke and sneak around undetected," Tahl replied. "I suggest we skirt around and find a gap in their defenses to sneak through."

"Bloody hell!" Owenne snapped. "That'll take an age! Why can't our drones jam them?"

"Good question, well presented," Van Noor said as he checked the feed from the drones to find an alternative route. "For some reason, all of our kit struggles to deal with Ghar equipment because it is too primitive, so we can't jam them. You would have thought older stuff is easier to bugger about with, but that's a question for you to take up with C3 Design and Procurement. Which, if memory serves, has a lot more NuHu working in its ranks than strike troopers."

"There's a route," Tahl said, drawing a yellow line along the shared map on the trio's shard display. "We double back for a couple of minutes, head north, and then dive through this gap toward this open area."

The three made their way back along the alleyway and diverted their track to the left of the tectorists and their detectors. The spotter drones continued to slowly move forward to paint the way ahead, finding another unit of tectorists a little way to the north. Slowly, painfully, over the course of the next thirty minutes, the three Concord soldiers crept through the Ghar line toward the open square to the east. Tahl ordered one of the spotter drones to move to the square and give them an idea of what lay up ahead. The visual feed which was projected back to them made Van Noor feel sick with fear and rage.

"What are those bastards up to?" He hissed.

A group of a dozen Ghar Outcasts, their skinny bodies clad in black armor, herded a group of perhaps fifty women and children into Pariton's city square. Mothers carried crying infants, older children clung to each other's hands, as the hunchbacked soldiers shoved and pushed them toward the tall wall of the old city hall.

"Bry, move up to the left and take down the pair at the front of the column," Tahl ordered curtly through gritted teeth. "I'll take center. Owenne, go right and..."

"No," the mandarin said firmly.

"You've got a better plan? We need to hear it quickly," Tahl replied.

"We skirt around and push on," Owenne said evenly.

"We push on, they die!" Van Noor growled. "Can't you see what's going on here? The Ghar have taken all of the able-bodied men into slavery and this is what's left! The women and children who don't have the strength to last long as slaves, they just put them against a wall and shoot them!"

"I know precisely what is going on," Owenne held up a hand to stop Van Noor, "and it's all very sad. But it's a handful of lives compared to far bigger stakes. It's sad, but I'm not willing to give away our position and jeopardize the safety of our own forces back at our hold up position. We move on."

"Then I'll do it without you," Tahl replied assertively. "Bry, go left, I'll go right."

"You realize that I could use my superior shard connection to activate the drugs dispensers in both of your battlesuits to effectively sedate you and follow my orders?" Owenne threatened.

"Use your superior shard connection to check how powerfully I feel about saving the lives of those women and children," Tahl stared back at Owenne. "All the drugs in the world won't override that. We're going in, now."

"And your plan to extricate the survivors if you succeed?" Owenne snapped.

"Through the sewers," Van Noor tapped his foot against a metal grate in the cracked pavement beneath him.

"It'll still alert the Ghar to our presence at this city!" The mandarin clenched his fists in rage. "It still risks our position and the lives of the men and women under your command, Tahl!"

"We're Concord soldiers," Tahl retorted, "our job, our oath, is to protect the lives of our citizens. This is a Concord planet, and even if it came to it, I would extend that oath to any woman and child. I am prepared to give up my life, and the lives of soldiers under my command, to protect women and children. And yours, Mandarin. I'll gladly sacrifice you to save them. Now I'm done debating, Bry and I are going in. So either help us, or try to gun me down. If you opt for the latter, I guarantee you that I'm faster and you'll come out of this far worse."

Owenne swore and checked his pistol.

"You pair of overly sentimental pricks! Come on, let's go and be heroes!"

***

Even with the Ghar's grotesque face hidden beneath its helmet, Tahl could see the surprise and alarm in the little humanoid's body language as it span to face him. Still a good dozen paces away and now caught out in the open, Tahl raised his carbine neatly to his shoulder and fired a pair of aimed shots into the Ghar, puncturing holes in its torso and sending it crumpling down into the rubble. Screams echoed from the crowd of civilians as Van Noor opened fire to the left, lancing bursts of plasma through two of the Ghar soldiers before they had a chance to react. To the right, a single shot issued from Owenne's pistol, decapitating one of the hunchbacked soldiers.

Reacting faster than Tahl would have given them credit for, an order was barked out from one of the diminutive creatures and the nearest three Ghar span to face Tahl and fired their lugger guns, the primitive weapons held low at their hips as they sprayed long bursts of fire in his direction; panicked women and children scattering amid the firefight. A handful of the hastily aimed shots impacted with the hyperlight shields projected from Tahl's armor as he sprinted towards the Ghar, flaring up purple tinted hexagons of light around him. One or two of the shots managed to penetrate the protective energy shield but deflected from the physical plates of his armor.

Hurdling the remains of a brick wall and closing the final few paces, Tahl reached the closest Ghar and swung his carbine around, connecting with his adversary's chin and lifting it off its feet with a sickening crunch of broken bone. The second Ghar let out a yell and leapt toward him; Tahl spun on his back leg and brought an armored foot sweeping around into a hook kick to connect with the Ghar's face, sending the shrieking monster twirling around to land in a twisted heap in the dusty rubble. The Ghar was already clambering back to its feet when a third creature ran at Tahl, swinging its lugger gun around its head like a club. Tahl effortlessly blocked the first attack with his forearm before snapping a clenched fist out into his opponent's neck, crushing its windpipe and sending it choking to its knees. The second Ghar rejoined the fight instantly; Tahl beat the shorter creature to the initiative and knocked it back to the dirt with a front kick before rushing over to drop a knee into its chest, pinning it in place as he beat it to death with his carbine.

The four Ghar who had occupied the center of the column of prisoners now eliminated, Tahl quickly glanced to his left and right to check on Van Noor and Owenne. Van Noor was dispatching his final assailant whilst Owenne backed away from a trio of Ghar, his stave flailing around viciously infront of him whilst he fired off a salvo of ineffectual shots from his pistol. A Ghar raised his lugger gun and unloaded the remainder of a magazine into Owenne from close range – the mandarin span around with the force of the blast and fell back to the ground. He fired his pistol as he fell back, stitching a line of plasma across the gut of one of the Ghar and killing it where it stood. Tahl raised his carbine and took careful aim before blowing a hole through the back of another of Owenne's adversaries. The final Ghar panicked and ran, scrambling off into the nearest alley as Tahl ran over to Owenne.

The mandarin staggered to his feet, swearing viciously and looking down distastefully at the spreading red smear that marred the sleeve of his jacket.

"Well, I hope you're happy," he sneered through gritted teeth.

Tahl checked the mandarin's vitals through the shard and, content that he was stable, figured that sarcasm would probably be more comforting to the NuHu than compassion.

"Just honored to fight by your side, sir," Tahl smirked. "The way you backed away from those terrifying midgets whilst trying to swipe at them with your little stick. Inspiring."

"When you've finished with the crap banter, I could do with a hand over here," Van Noor called over the shard. "I've stopped a couple of rounds."

"Anything serious?"

"No, not really. But it bloody hurts."

"And what's your plan with these?" Owenne cut in, gesturing to a ragged group of four children who cowered in the one remaining corner of a bombed out building.

Tahl's smile faded. He took off his helmet and walked slowly over to the children, his hands outstretched passively as he crouched down next to them.

"You're coming with us now," he said softly, "we need to get you somewhere safe."

***

"What the hell happened here?" Strike Leader Rall exclaimed as he walked out to meet the ragged column of people.

One arm looped around Tahl's shoulders for support, Van Noor continued to limp at the head of the line of refugees, pain flaring in his hip with every step, despite the medication. He looked over his shoulder at where the fifty women and children were silhouetted against the amber glow of the horizon as the twin suns neared their morning ascent. The rest of Rall's squad was in position behind the feint blue glow of their kinetic barriers, although the spotter drones on sentry duty had alerted the company about the return of the mandarin's patrol – and their addition.

"We figured we needed a few more recruits to bolster the line, so these would do," Van Noor grimaced. "Now stop asking stupid questions and get these people food, shelter, and medical checks."

Rall turned and began barking orders to his troopers as a second squad emerged from their accommodation dugout to assist in organizing the disheveled refugees. Owenne walked briskly over to Tahl and Van Noor, his stave tucked neatly under one arm and two bloodstained holes in the sleeve of his other.

"Happy now?" He sneered.

"Yes, as a matter of fact," Tahl shrugged. "We've just rescued fifty people without so much as a mishap. Sure, you took a couple in the arm and Bry got shot in the bum, but I didn't even get a scratch, so I'm feeling quite smug."

"It's not in the arse, it's in the hip!" Van Noor protested.

"Keep telling yourself that, cupcake, sounds a lot braver," Tahl smiled.

Van Noor's response was cut off as a young woman tentatively approached the trio. A grimy, blonde girl of perhaps five years of age clung to the woman's neck, half asleep in her arms.

"Are you the one in charge?" She asked Owenne.

The mandarin glanced across at Tahl with a thin smile before facing her.

"That would be me," he confirmed coolly.

"I just wanted to say thank you," the woman said. "I don't agree with what you are doing here, I don't see what gives you people the right to just invade planets and force them to adopt your way of life. But those monsters would have killed all of us, including my daughter. I would rather we both lived out our lives partially lobotomized and duped by your IMTel, than be gunned down by those animals. For that, thank you."

"Yes, yes, you're welcome," Owenne looked uncomfortably down at the ground and waved a hand dismissively.

He turned back to Tahl and Van Noor once she had gone.

"Right. Back to work. The Ghar will either have found the bodies of those we killed by now, or at the very least will be looking for missing soldiers. Assemble the company, we're attacking. I'm not giving them a single minute more than I have to to be prepared for us."

"You want to smash headlong against a Ghar force who is dug in defensively and we know very little about?" Van Noor exclaimed.

"This city must fall!" Owenne snapped. "It is the key to everything! Now, I've danced to your sentimental tune tonight, I've done what you wanted. It's time you two remembered the heirachy around here. I don't hold military rank, but I do carry the authority of my status, and that means you are subordinate to me. Assemble your troopers, I want to be on the move in thirty minutes."

Van Noor watched the mandarin pace away, his hands clasped at the small of his back.

"He's not telling us everything," Van Noor warned, "there's something more to this."

"The thought crossed my mind," Tahl agreed. "Come on, let's get that slug out of your arse and a patch on you, so you can join in the next exciting episode."

"Well, I'm glad to see you're having fun," Van Noor gritted his teeth as he leaned on Tahl and limped toward the holding area's medical dugout. "You've been happier than I've seen you in ages for a couple of days now."

Tahl smiled and nodded. He looked up at the dawn sky silently for a few paces before answering.

"What we just did," he explained, "that's the best thing I've ever done. It's the most I've ever achieved in my life. I don't like killing people. I hate it. Sure, I feel no remorse for the Ghar and perhaps I should, but when it comes to these planets we invade, the Isorians, Freeborn, any of them, I often wonder why we're killing each other in a nearly infinite universe where there's room for everybody. But tonight, we did something good. Something really special. If we hadn't done what we did, fifty innocent mothers and their children would have been murdered in cold blood. Jumping out into that, gunning those monsters down, for the first time I can remember, it really felt... exhilarating. I was happy to risk my life tonight because we were protecting the innocent and killing creatures whose motivation is so evil, that to me, they're no better than two dimensional monsters from kids' stories. If I have to fight and kill, well, tonight was worthwhile. It's the first time I really felt I did something good."

"You finished?" Van Noor frowned. "You know your problem? You think too much. And you think with your heart instead of your head. Remember where your brain is, mate. Yeah, we did the right thing tonight, but I think we do the right thing more often that you give us credit for. We're not some evil empire expanding across the universe to drag every planet we meet into our dark clutches. And beyond that? I don't give it much more thought. And you shouldn't, too."

The two soldiers stopped by the entrance to the medical dugout. Three medical drones were already busy checking over the first of the refugees who had arrived. Van Noor turned to Tahl.

"I'll get patched up. Don't leave without me."

***

Markov's Prize's first sun was now peering over the horizon, casting long shadows across the grey ground as Beta Company advanced toward the outskirts of the city. On the left flank, Owenne patched into one of the spotter drones which had swept ahead and updated his appraisal of the enemy defenses. The ground leading up to the capital was sharply contoured, with the connecting roads taking advantage of the few natural breaks in the razor-edged ridgelines and steep slopes around the plateau topped city. A handful of defensive turrets had been built at various points around the city, with subterranean power supplies safely hidden from attack. Primitive scanners were also built atop tall towers, most of them a hangover from the city's previous defenders.

Owenne had selected a defensive line which was dead center between two of the large gun turrets, far enough away from them that fire support would be indirect and inaccurate. Owenne watched as Beta Company's seven T7 transport drones rushed toward the city, flanked on the left by a pair of M4 combat drones, and on the right by an assorted collection of smaller weapon drones. He glanced, almost nervously, at an isolated spot height which jutted up midway along the defensive ridgeline. The slope was too steep for a drone to tackle without entering into atmospheric flight and exposing itself to anti-aircraft fire. If the Ghar realized the tactical importance of that spot height, the attack would stall and possibly even fail. And Owenne would not stand for that. Not when he was this close to his objective. He watched in silence as the first explosions began blossoming up from the ground around the transport drones. To the left and right, Alpha and Cian Companies carried out their own advances. But Beta Company had front and center and would take the brunt of the enemy fire.

***

A volley of fire smashed into the dark rocks in front of Tahl, sending chips and stones twirling through the air. Behind him, the Duke's plasma light support turret swiveled in place and fired over the top of the three troopers of the company command squad, raking lines of blue projectiles against the advancing squad of Ghar Outcasts. Cane and Van Noor stood up to lean over the natural rock barricade and raised their carbines, adding their own fire against the enemy soldiers.

"Squad Jai, from Command," Tahl transmitted from his crouched position behind the rocky barricade. "Move to marker indigo and provide fire support to Alpha Company's advance to marker sierra. I'm moving an M4 across for further support."

"Command, Jai, copied!" Strike Leader Rall replied as his squad instantly reacted to the order, moving across the three dimensional battlefield projection which appeared in the corner of Tahl's visor.

He winced as he read a casualty update from Alpha Company on his left flank, advancing into the teeth of the Ghar defenses.

"Bry, I've sent Rall's boys across to the left," he called to Van Noor. "I'm giving them both of our M4s as well. Alpha Company is getting murdered."

Van Noor ducked back down beneath the edge of the rocks as shots continued to blast away against the far side.

"What's up?" He called across as he checked his carbine.

"It's those turrets," Tahl returned his attention to the battlefield projection. "They've got more range and more accuracy than Owenne predicted. They're tearing Alpha Company apart."

Before Van Noor could respond, the three troopers of the command squad were lifted up and flung into the air by a deafening explosion. Tahl's world faded to black before he even hit the ground.

***

Whilst his vision still swirled from the concussive impact of the blast, Van Noor's hearing had been completely preserved by his helmet's automatic audio filters. Trying to focus on the blurred images of his armored hands pressed against the scorched earth underneath him, Van Noor slowly pushed himself up to his knees as the shrill scream of another shell whistled somewhere to the right before a detonation sounded and the ground shook again.

Van Noor quickly checked the bio readouts from the command squad shard. Cane was dead, Tahl was critically injured but stable. His vision focusing, Van Noor saw the top half of Cane's body a few paces to the left. Tahl lay face down at the edge of a small gully a few yan further on. On the left flank, Squads Jai and Denne were attempting to hack down a quartet of Ghar battlesuits atop a shallow ridgeline; to the right, Squad Teal was advancing against a small horde of Outcasts, their carbines cutting swathes through the ranks as a pair of D1 drones added their own firepower to the mix. Another shell landed in the dead ground in between Van Noor and Squad Teal, throwing up clods of earth and a shower of stones.

Forcing himself to his feet, Van Noor staggered over to Tahl and dropped down next to him. He slid back the company commander's visor; blood was trickling from Tahl's mouth, nostrils, and ears. His eyes stared blankly up at the sky, yet his vital signs were stable.

"Come on, mate," Van Noor gasped, hauling the wounded soldier up over his shoulders, "let's get you out of here."

Another shell impacted the ground close by, throwing Van Noor back down. He cycled through the visual feeds from the company's spotter drones until he found the source of the bombardment. Nearly halfway between the gun turrets to their left and right, an isolated spot height atop a steep slope gave a commanding view of the battlefield. A Ghar battlesuit with a deadly disruptor bomber was raining down shells into the advancing Concord troopers, covered by the natural rock around it and defended by a conventionally armed Ghar suit and a multitude of Outcasts. A torrent of plasma fire spat down from the position and tore into one of the company's Dukes, blasting the transport drone apart and sending its flaming wreck sinking to the ground. If the firing position atop the steep hill was left alone, Beta Company's advance would stall, leaving them isolated in the open. The hill had to fall, or the company was doomed, and with it the entire attack. But attacking the well-defended hill across open ground and up a steep slope was as good as suicide.

Van Noor shook his head. He despised sending troopers to their deaths, but the hill had to be attacked and distracted at the very least. He quickly checked the battlefield projection to ascertain which squads were closest before sending out his orders.

***

Qan leaned against the hull of the destroyed Duke, raised his carbine to his shoulder, and fired an aimed shot up at the Ghar defenders at the top of the ridgeline before ducking back down into cover as a hail of return fire rattled against the remains of the drone transporter. Hunkered down by her squad, Rhona glanced across to where Althern and Squad Xath were similarly pinned down by the ferocity of the Ghar defensive fire. The seven strike troopers were squeezed into the minimal cover presented by a tiny gulley in the rock, to the left and a little way behind Rhona's squad.

"We need to get over to the right!" Gant shouted, his raised voice standing out as an indicator of his stress levels as the active noise reduction in the troopers' helmets made it unnecessary. "If we stay here, we won't last long!"

"Yeah, I see that," Rhona agreed, sending an order through the squad shard to drive her spotter drone around to the right of the raised ground and look for more cover. "We'll need covering fire from Squad

Xath and whatever command can give us."

Before she could pass her intentions on to Althern, she heard Van Noor's voice through her helmet.

"Squad Wen, Squad Xath, from Command – advance and take position at marker delta."

Although not impossible, it was uncommon for advance orders to come from the senior strike leader rather than the strike captain.

"Confirm the boss is okay?" Rhona found herself blurting out.

"The boss is wounded but stable," Van Noor replied. "Look, this entire attack is getting mauled. The key position is right in front of you. I need the two of you to take your squads and go straight up that hill. I'll give you everything I can to support you, but you need to get their attention away from the rest of the company so we can regroup."

It was only then that Rhona realized marker delta was the top of the plateau which was home to the Ghar units pouring fire down into the Concord forces below. Three battlesuits – one with a heavy weapon – at least a dozen Outcasts, a couple of heavy weapons mounted on mobile tripods, and a heavily fortified turret to either side. All dug in and nearly impossible to see, let alone shoot.

"Wen copies," Rhona replied to Van Noor and Althern. "We'll take lead, Xath follow us up to the left."

Rhona saw Althern give her a thumbs up from where his squad waited in the cover of the gulley to the left. She checked her immediate vicinity and found a pair of C3D1 combat drones to her right, supporting Squad Teal. Rhona's need was greater – she activated a command override and connected with their shard, diverting the two drones and sending them speeding toward her position as shells began to rain down on the Ghar above them.

"We've been ordered to take that hill," she said to her squad, noting the immediate sensation of fear ripple back from them through the shard. "That position is giving hell to everybody else, and we're closest. We ain't got time to go around, so we're going straight up and gunning them down. I'll take point with Jem and the lance, the rest of you fan out and keep a good distance apart. Althern's boys are right behind us. Let's go."

The feeling of terror was not just from her squad. Rhona understood her orders, but a voice at the back of her mind told her that this was as good as suicide, and that this simply was not worth dying for. One hill by one city on a single planet on the fringes of nowhere was not worth dying to take, especially when it would be forgotten by this time tomorrow. And even though Rhona knew that was her real voice telling her, and that it was the C3 shard overriding her own natural survival instinct, there was nothing she could do about it. The fear was overridden by a need to carry out her orders.

Rhona nodded to her troopers and ran out from behind the cover of the wrecked transporter and up the hill. The first few paces were surprisingly easy as she planted her feet down on the hard rock, propelling herself up the steep slope as her squad followed her up. Althern led his squad not far behind, sprinting up toward the Ghar above. Then the enemy noticed them.

Sparks danced sporadically from the ridge above as the Outcasts' muzzle flashes lit it up, spewing fire down into the advancing strike troopers. Rhona heard a familiar, dull hum as her hyperlight shields glowed purple around her, fending off projectiles from the primitive weapons above. The sun eased above the horizon directly ahead, painting the dull rock in a warm glow and silhouetting the Outcasts as they scrambled for better firing positions. Rhona heard her own breathing and her racing pulse as she continued to lead the attack, the destination never seeming to draw any closer.

A line of explosions erupted along the ridgeline as the support Van Noor had promised finally arrived, sending plumes of grey smoke wafting up into the windless sky and blocking out a little of the fierce sunlight.

"Come on, buddy, get up!" Rhona heard Gant's voice as he supported one of the other troopers. "Keep going!"

Rhona concentrated on the two weapon drones she had added to the assault, sending them shooting up the right flank and opening fire with their plasma light supports. The relentless fire continued from the Ghar defensive positions above, and Rhona felt a momentary surge of pain and fear through the squad shard, followed by an empty void as one of her troopers was killed. She did not check to see who – it did not matter right now.

One of the Ghar battlesuits lumbered up to the rocky parapet above and leaned forward, bringing its weapon arm to bear. The huge gun thudded and the ground shook as an explosive projectile slammed into the earth in the middle of Squad Xath, picking three of the strike troopers up and flinging them across the hillside. Plasma bolts swept up in return as some of the troopers began firing from the hip as they ran. A second Ghar battlesuit appeared up ahead and plasma fire swept down the slope, one of the bolts slamming into Rhona and knocking her to the ground. Her left shoulder smoking from a jagged tear in her armor, Rhona recovered her carbine, crawled groggily back to her feet, and continued the charge up the hill, ignoring the pain which flared up from the wound.

A large outcrop of rock just below the crest of the ridge loomed into view, presenting respite from the hail of fire. Rhona dived into cover, feeling a thud next to her as Jemmel pressed against her a moment later. The short woman leaned around the edge of the rock and fired a rapid burst from her plasma lance. Rhona ordered the two drones up over the ridgeline and opened fire with their weapons, sending the Outcasts scurrying for cover as a trio of their number were torn apart by the plasma. Rhona grabbed a plasma grenade from her utility pouch and lobbed it over the outcrop, waiting for sound of the detonation before rushing out again to climb the last few yan and hurl herself onto the top of the hill.

"Squad Wen," she commanded, "engage the battlesuits! Take down that bomber!"

Five or six Outcasts lay dead at her feet, the remainder of the squad were edging back as the fire from the two drones cut them down. A Ghar battlesuit remained at the crest of the peak, firing down relentlessly into Althern's squad. A second suit pivoted on the spot and fired a long burst into the two Concord drones, blasting one apart spectacularly. The third suit – a bomber armed with a heavy weapon – turned in place and lined up with Rhona, aiming the collosal weapon directly at her. The voice at the back of her mind came back again as she sprinted forward, asking her why she was here and why she would die this way.

The Ghar did not fire. Its weapon arm shifted back and forth rapidly as it tried to clear a jam. Rhona did not have time to appreciate her immense good fortune; another of the lumbering suits turned to face her and Jemmel, and it fired a rapid burst into them, cutting them both down. Rhona let out a cry as pain flashed up in her right hip. She looked around frantically for her carbine and saw it a few paces away, smoking and bent out of shape. With a cry, she staggered back up to her feet again as her shields continuously flared purple around her. Her vision swimming from the automatically injected medication which flowed through her bloodstream, she staggered forward toward the Ghar bomber. Another shot struck her dead in the face, snapping her head back painfully and cracking her visor. She tore her helmet off and threw it aside, wincing as the fierce sunlight met her eyes and the acrid smoke burned her lungs. She raised her right hand and fired a small bomb from her wrist-mounted x-sling, impacting the bomber suit harmlessly.

The huge suit cleared its jam and fired, sending a huge shell whizzing past Rhona and impacting the ground behind her, causing her to stagger down to her knees with the force of the blast. Blinking blood out of one of her eyes and gritting her teeth to ignore the pain in her left shoulder and right hip, Rhona staggered forward again and skidded past the Ghar bomber's legs. Sessetti suddenly appeared next to her beneath the Ghar suit, dodging a lightning strike aimed at his head from the machine's crude claw. The two troopers wordlessly packed plasma grenades into the Ghar's legs before quickly running away, expecting a deadly shot to the back at any moment. The grenades detonated, blowing one of the Ghar war machine's legs off at the knee and sending it toppling over and then rolling down the hill where it smashed and ricocheted off the rocks on the long fall.

Rhona looked around to assess the situation. A second Ghar suit had been blasted apart by the second D1 drone, although that too now lay in a smoldering heap at the crest of the hill. The three surviving troopers of Squad Xath had taken cover behind the Ghar suit and were pelting the final surviving Ghar war machine with plasma fire as it clumsily retreated in the wake of the handful of surviving Outcasts. They had taken the hill. But it was not enough – the two turrets at the top of the ridgeline were still raining shells down on Alpha and Cian companies.

"Troopers! On me!" Rhona shouted.

The handful of survivors from both squads moved over to take position by Rhona. Althern was not among them.

"We've got to take that turret," Rhona gasped, clutching on to her hip, "if we take that turret, Alpha Company can get up the hill and we can all swing around to help out Cian. No time to spare. Let's go."

Rhona limped over to the body of one of her troopers.

"I'm sorry, pal, I need this," she whispered to Jemmel, patting the dead trooper gently on the shoulder before taking her plasma lance and turning to lead the next attack.

FOURTEEN

Outskirts of Pariton
Capital City
Markov's Prize

L-Day plus 59

Van Noor felt another wave of energy course through his body as his battlesuit injected another shot of synthetic adrenaline into his bloodstream. He walked along the rocky ridgeline that connected the two gun turrets which had caused so many problems to the assault. After the guns had been silenced, Alpha Company was able to break through on the left flank before curving around to alleviate the pressure from Beta Company in the center. With the Ghar reshuffling their defenses to deal with the breakthrough, Cian Company then surged forward on the right and punched through the entire defensive line. The rumble of guns and artillery was still audible to the east as Ghar patrols tested Cian Company's defensive positions but, judging from the reports which were filtering through the shard, Cian's position was strong.

Sliding his visor back, Van Noor took in a lungful of the midmorning air. His wound to the hip from the previous night was still troubling him, but it faded to insignificance as he watched the troopers of Squad Denne carefully remove the ten dead strike troopers who had fallen to take the critical spot height which centerd the Ghar defense. Up ahead, stood by one of the still smoking bunkers, was one of the survivors of the bloody assault. Van Noor checked the trooper's details via his shard connection so as to remember his name.

"You okay, Lian?" He asked as he approached the young soldier.

The shorter man turned and regarded him with red ringed eyes, his hands still clutched tightly onto his carbine.

"Yes, Senior," Sessetti answered quietly.

"We all saw what you did, son," Van Noor stopped next to Sessetti. "Without that push, a lot more men and women would have

194 *Beyond the Gates of Antares*

died. I'm sorry about your squad. But it wasn't for nothing."

"Yes, Senior," the trooper repeated.

"Who'd you lose?" Van Noor asked hesitantly.

"We lost Qan on the initial push up the hill," Sessetti replied slowly, "along with Strike Leader Althern and half of his troopers. Jem died at the top of the hill. We lost the rest of Squad Xath and Gant whilst we were attacking those two turrets. It's just me, Clythe, and Strike Leader Rhona left. Everybody else is dead."

"I'm sorry," Van Noor said genuinely, resting a hand on the man's shoulder. "If you hadn't had the guts to do what you did, we'd all be dead. Go get yourself checked out by the medics. Where's your squad leader?"

Sessetti nodded to the smoking gun turret before slumping off back down the hill. Van Noor walked over to the turret, noting with interest the evidence of impact damage where plasma grenades had been used to blow the access doors off. He leaned over to enter through the narrow door, nodding as he saw the armored walls stained with the distinctive shade of Ghar blood. Rhona sat on the breach of one of the guns, her armor removed from the waist up, and her body glove sliced open from her left wrist to her shoulder as a medical drone set about closing a vicious wound which ran the entire length of the limb. Her face was stained black from smoke and a crop of messy hair fell down to obscure most of her features. Her dark eyes wearily looked up at Van Noor as he approached.

Van Noor opened his mouth to speak, but the words escaped him.

"We took your hill," Rhona slurred.

"I know," Van Noor nodded, "I know. You did a great job, all of you. Taking the hill was enough, Rhona, why did you push on to the two turrets?"

"The opportunity was there and I didn't know how long the window would be open," the exhausted soldier replied. "C3 Junior Commander's handbook goes on and on about..."

"Flexibility and adaptability, I know," Van Noor interjected carefully. "I'm not criticizing what you did. I expected you to buy a little time, not crack open the heart of their defenses. Look, Rhona, I know we don't get on. But what you did here... it's frustrating. To do what you did took equal measures of skill and bravery, mixed in with a lot of luck. That skill and bravery you demonstrated is the frustrating part, because it's clear you're far more capable than you like to let on. But the luck part? You can never rely on that, so please take my advice when I say don't ever do that again. I'm not questioning your ability, not after what you just proved to everyone, but I am questioning your luck. Don't test it again like you just did."

"Yeah," Rhona nodded, wincing as the drone finished sealing the wound on her arm and set about repairing the scar tissue. "When we got to the top of the hill, one of those suits was pointing a gun the size of a starship right at my face. The thing jammed. I've sat here wondering... well, I think you're right about luck, Senior. But three of us had enough of it on this hill this morning, and ten didn't."

The medical drone completed its work on her arm, leaving it clean and unmarked in stark contrast to her blackened, bloodstained face. Rhona stood up and hauled a plasma lance over her shoulder before dragging her beret on over her disheveled hair.

"I owe you an apology," Van Noor found himself admitting. "The caliber of person I thought you were wouldn't have been able to do what you did. I didn't order you up here because..."

"I know. You ordered me because I was the closest to the hill. I never thought it was personal, not for a second. My squad was in the right place. Or wrong place, depending on how you look at it. But I owe you an apology, too, Senior. I've been an absolute bitch. I know that."

Van Noor walked back out into the morning sunlight with Rhona as the drone flew off to find its next patient.

"I was angry with you because of the way you spoke about Strike Captain Tahl," Van Noor admitted after checking no one else was within earshot. "I don't think you fully appreciate what sort of man he is. To put it in context, he was ordered to take a few days leave to get his breath back, which is why he was away when I pulled you to pieces in my office. Instead of taking care of himself, he dropped everything to travel halfway across infinity and back to spend his entire leave getting to my family to check on them for me. That's the sort of man he is."

Rhona closed her eyes and nodded.

"I didn't know he did that," she said, "but it doesn't surprise me. I'm kinda sick of hearing the sound of my own voice whining on about my sad life, but I ain't met many good people. He's one of them. The best, I think. I wouldn't want to be fighting for anybody else."

"Glad we agree," Van Noor said. "Another thing – Mandarin Owenne wants to talk to you. About those two drones you took control of."

"Say what?" Rhona exhaled angrily. "Seriously? We get ordered up Hell's mountain, and he's upset because I took control of a couple of assets we needed..."

"He's not upset," Van Noor held his hands up. "He seemed more curious about how you did it rather than why. Go see him when you've got your breath back."

"Sure," Rhona narrowed her eyes and nodded hesitantly before limping away.

She stopped after a few paces and turned to face Van Noor again.

"I've got a couple of questions."

"Go on."

"How many will we get back? How many of those ten dead men and women d'you reckon we'll see again?"

Van Noor felt suddenly deflated and weary at the thought of even answering the question.

"I don't know, Katya. Three? Maybe four if we're lucky? We won't know for a while. It's not what you want to hear, but from my experience, I've found it best to assume they're all gone. Anything we get back is a bonus. I'd let them all go."

"Yeah," Rhona said, "I ain't looking forward to facing that once the shard assistance in my head backs off."

"What was the other question?"

"How's the boss?"

"He's good. Conscious again, all okay, just under observation by the medics at the bottom of the hill. One of those advantages of being on our team. If he wasn't Concord and didn't have the medical support we've got, he'd be spending a couple of months in hospital. At best."

"And he really did that for you?" Rhona furrowed her brow as her tone dropped to a near whisper. "Just dropped everything to look out for you on that one chance he had at some leave?"

"Yeah, he did."

Rhona nodded slowly. Van Noor watched her as her eyes focused on the horizon, the barely perceptible winces, nods, and shrugs she gave over the next few moments being indicators of the conversation she was clearly playing out in her head.

"I'm gonna go say hello. With your permission, Senior."

"Sure," Van Noor replied, "but check in with Mandarin Owenne first. Probably not best to keep him waiting."

***

The palatial country house and its grounds stood impeccably in the glow of the evening suns, the hedgerows of the ornamental gardens casting long, double shadows across the perfectly mown blue grass. The house itself was perhaps five centuries old, its archaic clinical edges and straight walls marking it out as of a bygone era but still possessing a vintage beauty of sorts. Until the Ghar invasion, it had served as a curious mixture of a country retreat for one of the planet's most prominent politicians, and a local tourist attraction.

Rhona was, for the first time, glad of her rank, as it entitled her to a room within the grand house itself; what was left of her squad – Sessetti and Clythe – were billeted in what had once been the servants' quarters. After the mauling at the hands of the Ghar that morning, the

44th Strike Formation had been pulled back further west away from the city outskirts, leaving the rest of the 17th Assault Force to take their place at the frontline. Modern warfare – in the space of a few hours, Rhona had gone from leading a suicidal charge in the face of a murderous enemy, to taking a long bath in her private suite in a stately home in the countryside.

As ordered, she returned to the ornamental gardens at the back of the huge house and found Mandarin Owenne where she had left him an hour ago. The NuHu had ordered her to 'rethink her attire' after she had reported directly to him in her cracked and burned battlesuit, her face still blackened from the smoke of the engagement. She now wore the green trousers and collared shirt of her barrack uniform, complete with her now battered black beret.

"You took your time," the mandarin sneered as he swilled the contents of a crystal glass thoughtfully with one pale hand, ignoring her salute.

"I put a lot of thought into my attire, sir," Rhona replied.

"Very funny. Now let's get to business. How did you order those two drones to help you this morning?"

Rhona paused. It occurred to her that she had already escaped with one flippant answer and pushing her luck further was ill advised. She realized how intimidated she felt, despite her façade. This was her first ever one-to-one talk with a mandarin, and whilst Owenne's reputation was that of an individual who did not take himself particularly seriously, the entire race of NuHu still held a high place in society. And a certain reputation.

"In accordance with the instructions laid down in C3P512 – the Junior Commander's Field Guide, sir," she answered after a pause, "chapter five, paragraph four states that…"

"I know what the bloody book says," Owenne sank the potent smelling contents of the crystal glass before grabbing a decanter from the garden table next to him and recharging his glass. "What I want to know is how you, whilst running up a hill under fire, leading a squad of strike troopers, and retaining the mental capacity to plan and coordinate a rather brutal assault, still managed to mentally activate a command override on a pair of drones and give them a detailed plan of action, including waypoints and target prioritization. To put it bluntly, that isn't easy to pull off."

"Dunno, sir," Rhona replied truthfully, "I just did it."

"Would you consider yourself clever? By normal panhuman standards, I mean."

"Not really. I've had two occupations in my life. Take my clothes off for drunk guys, and kill people. Neither are what I'd call academic vocations."

"I'm aware of that," Owenne stared intently at a spot just in front of her booted feet, "but putting aside the fact that you deliberately exaggerate your regional accent in an obvious attempt to hide your academic childhood and near genius level of intellect in certain areas, would you consider yourself a clever individual?"

Rhona paused. NuHu were certainly not known for their ability to interact with people, let alone pick up on behavior and character. She had been imitating her father's accent for so many years that it now felt natural, even though the need to mask her academic leanings and put on a show of bravado and confidence were now long gone.

"Yes," Rhona said, "I would consider myself intelligent. I spent my entire childhood prioritizing academic pursuits wherever possible. I haven't had the chance to continue that for nearly a decade now, but assuming I survive my stay in the military, I would hope the Concord would make better use of me once I return to civilian life."

"We could make better use of you right now," Owenne stated, one hand resting awkwardly at the small of his back.

"What do you mean?"

"You've done your bit with a carbine. I think you'd be better employed at force intelligence. Strike Captain Tahl promoted you early, which looks good for you. Senior Strike Leader Van Noor not only told me that he thinks you have the best data recall he has ever seen, but he also recommended you for a medal after this morning."

Rhona paused. She had honestly appreciated Van Noor being the bigger person and reaching out to her after what was the most terrifying ordeal of her life, and she was glad that she at least tried to meet him halfway. But a medal? That, she had not expected.

"But you don't approve medals, sir," Rhona replied, using the opportunity to mask her shock. "You wouldn't let Strike Captain Tahl have a medal for smashing a dozen of those monsters up with his bare hands. Why would you give me a medal for running up a hill?"

"You know how the system works," Owenne looked up distastefully as a large, purple-feathered bird landed on the roof of the house and cawed noisily. "Medals are awarded for individuals who give service in excess of what C3 expects of them. Strike Captain Tahl was the undefeated champion of the most violent and competitive unarmed combat competition in the known universe. I expect him to defeat adversaries in close assault. Given his background, I believe he is achieving mediocrity, perhaps a touch above, but nothing more. You, on the other hand – I wouldn't expect an individual of your background to lead an assault against a well defended enemy position and then continue an advance to disable two enemy gun turrets on her own initiative, without orders."

"We're not defined by our past," Rhona argued, "I thought that was the entire reason you'd brought me here to talk."

Owenne smirked slightly.

"Quite so. But the fact remains, I am approving the recommendation that you are decorated. And I recommended you take the opportunity to leave all the mud and blood behind for the Tahls and Van Noors of this universe, and go do something more useful. Come and work with me at force level. My favor will get you far, if you have the ambition."

Rhona took a step back and narrowed her eyes. Owenne recoiled in confusion before his pale blue eyes opened wide.

"You misinterpret my intentions," he said, his tone possessing some urgency. "I appreciate that you are well used to men making you offers based on your obvious aesthetic appeal. I am not one of them. The thought of... exchanging bodily fluids with anybody makes me want to be sick, quite frankly. No, I appreciate you are about as close to physical perfection as a panhuman will ever get, and I'd quite happily put you on a shelf as one would with an attractive ornament or vase. But nothing more."

"Right," Rhona placed her hands on her hips and continued to eye him suspiciously, wondering if his complete inability to look her, or anybody else for that matter, in the eye was something to read into.

"You have nothing I want," the mandarin waved one hand dismissively in the air as he turned to face away from her, "but in your current role, you are a wasted asset. I want what is best for the Concord, so I want you to change jobs. Give it some thought."

"Not really interested, sir," Rhona shrugged.

"Oh, but I think you are," Owenne looked up and made eye contact for the first time. "Your current role is to kill people and have them try to kill you. It is patently obvious, even to me, that both of these things are abhorrent to you. The system chose you for military service and the system doesn't drop the ball. There are no mistakes. How you choose to spend your time in the military is largely out of your hands; but right now, you have a choice, and this won't happen very often. Go on, you're dismissed. Think about it."

Rhona was thinking of everything but changing roles as she walked back toward the house. Thoughts of her brother often forced their way forward, but right now she mainly dwelled on Gant, Qan, and Jemmel. Still lost in thought, she nearly walked straight into Tahl at the foot of the staircase leading up to the accommodation rooms.

"Sorry," she managed, taking a step back.

"I've been looking for you for a long time," Tahl said. "I heard what happened. How are you... holding up?"

Rhona looked around at the rows of paintings along the walls, their ornate brass frames working well with the gaudy, floral wallpaper.

The lack of technology made her feel a little homesick for the times before the Concord.

"I'm alright," she forced a smile, "but what about you? I heard you took a few hits. I was meaning to check in but, well, I had to report to Mandarin Owenne and I lost track of time."

She realized that she had stepped in and pressed a hand against his elbow, and she immediately regretted crossing the line of formality. However, she felt a warm glow when he allowed it, not even mentioning it.

"Are you really okay?" He asked quietly. "When thirteen soldiers run up a hill and only three walk down, it's pretty normal to be... affected."

"How can I be affected?" She sighed. "I've got drugs running through my veins and C3 controlling my thoughts and emotions. I want to grieve for my friends, but I can't because I'm really not that bothered. I want to care, but the system won't allow me to. So yeah, I'm fine, but I don't want to be. I want to feel something. I owe them that."

"I'm sorry you all went through that. As soon as there is any opportunity to get some rest, I'll make sure that the three of you are the first to leave this place."

"I'm not looking for favoritism," Rhona said, careful that her tone did not sound argumentative.

"I wish I could promise you that it isn't," Tahl admitted, "but if I'm being honest, it's beyond that now."

Rhona stepped up to lay her hands on his chest and look up at him. As she leaned in, a door to her right was flung open and three strike leaders from Cian Company walked into the corridor, engaged noisily in conversation. Rhona rapidly took a step back and failed to suppress a smirk.

"I'll have that after-action report to you by tomorrow morning, sir," she said formally as the three troopers passed by them.

"Erm... good, see that you do... no rush..." Tahl stammered.

Rhona walked past him to climb the wide staircase leading to her room, appreciative of the momentary distraction from the melancholy thoughts racing around her head.

***

The buzz of half a dozen polite conversations drifted across the hot, night air as Van Noor stood alone at the edge of the courtyard, staring up at the stars. He searched the dark purple sky until he found a familiar constellation, and then counted his way across the flecks of light to find home. That morose sensation of homesickness had been kickstarted a few hours before when, whilst wandering the grounds which surrounded the impressive old house, Van Noor had chanced upon a child's treehouse tucked away in the corner of a vast field. At that moment, he had made the decision that as soon as he was given any leave, he was going straight home and getting his family back. He was adamant. Nothing would change his mind. Now, four or five hours later, his confidence in the plan was already faltering.

"You don't have a drink," a familiar voice grumbled from behind him.

Van Noor turned from his position by the small fence which separated the courtyard from the ornamental gardens and saw Owenne striding boldly over from the dining hall, carrying three crystal glasses, with a potent looking bottle under one armpit.

"Man of your caliber, this far from the frontlines, momentary respite from responsibility, you should be drinking."

Owenne slammed the three glasses down on a white garden table next to them and set about filling them from the bottle. Behind him, the leaders and captains of the formation's other companies sat on benches and chair in small groups, enjoying the mild evening with drinks and smokes. Owenne returned a respectful nod from Strike Commander Orless, the formation commanding officer, who sat with a quartet of strike leaders from Alpha Company.

"Where's that soft bugger, Tahl?" Owenne enquired as he thrust the filled glass into Van Noor's hand. "He should be down here and drinking, too."

"I don't think he drinks much these days," Van Noor said, taking a tentative sip from the glass and then exchanging an approving look with the NuHu mandarin. "This stuff's good. Did you find it here at the house?"

"Yes, as a matter of fact."

"So what's the plan now?" Van Noor enquired. "You've dragged us off here to the other side of the world, we've cracked a hole in the Ghar defenses and surged through, now what?"

"Good gosh, man, take a break!" Owenne beamed without making eye contact. "All is going to plan and another formation is keeping the pressure on whilst we get our breath back. Enjoy the view. Enjoy the silence."

"How do we get our breath back?" Van Noor folded his powerful arms. "We need replacements. At full strength, our company should be up at eighty-one troopers. We entered this campaign with substantially less than that. Now we're down at twenty-five. Twenty-five soldiers in the entire company. So what's your plan for getting our breath back?"

"A reinforcement ship was on the way to the Sen System to bolster the defenses. I've... diverted it here. It's due to enter the system in two days. Then you'll get more soldiers."

"How many?" Van Noor demanded. "You're talking about one

ship and we've got two entire assault forces down here, with every company in every formation hanging out. How many reinforcements?"

"Once the troopers have been proportionally divided in between the two forces, you can expect to receive, say, twenty replacements in your company."

"Twenty?" Van Noor exclaimed with enough volume to bring attention from the troopers spread across the courtyard. "I lost thirteen men and women this morning!"

"Then rejoice!" Owenne slapped a hand lightly against Van Noor's shoulder. "For your company will be stronger in two days than it was this time yesterday, even if all of the replacements are straight out of training. Ah... here he is!"

The mandarin stepped across to force the third glass of spirits into Tahl's hand as the company commander walked out to meet them. Van Noor had known the younger man long enough to pick up on his body language and detect when something was not quite right. But it would have to wait; if it was personal, it was not worth bringing up in front of Owenne.

"The mandarin was just telling me about the legions of new troopers he's arranged for us," Van Noor greeted. "We get twenty boys and girls fresh from training."

"Gets us to half strength again," Tahl shrugged, "better than nothing, I guess. God help them."

Owenne shrugged before grabbing his bottle and wandering off to talk to some soldiers from another company. Van Noor flashed a smile at Tahl.

The two men stood silently at the edge of the garden for a few moments, looking across the neat beds of flowers under the stars.

"You tried to contact your wife?" Tahl finally spoke.

"No," Van Noor said, "I've lost count of how many letters I've sent to the kids. But nothing to Becca. Comes back to that courage you were talking about. I haven't got enough of it. But it's better than it was, I've got contact with my children and that's turned my entire world around. It's not all I wanted, but it's enough for me. More than enough, to have them back. Gotta keep looking for the positives."

"Glad to hear it," Tahl flashed a smile. "I'm glad you turned your world around. I'm off for some sleep. Look... thanks for saying what you said to that pompous prick. I wasn't in the mood for that tonight."

"Any time," Van Noor shrugged. "Catch you in the morning."

Van Noor looked out across the gardens and to the fields beyond as Tahl walked away, his eyes just about making out the little tree house at the edge of the field.

***

Surrounded by invisible night insects which chirped and rattled softly, Sessetti sat at the edge of the first field behind the enormous house's servants' quarters, looking glumly up at the night sky. It was near midnight and after writing the now standard letter to his parents, full of lies about how well he was and how well it was all going, he was now at a loss.

"Shall we write a song?" Clythe offered from where he lay in the long grass next to him.

"Not really in the mood," Sessetti admitted.

"You haven't really been in the mood for about a month," Clythe replied.

"Yeah, funny that, isn't it?"

"Well, you need to get your head back into it, because when we go home, Dane is going to expect us to have come up with something. We can't expect him to just sit there waiting for a couple of years without having something to show for it."

"Oh, grow up, would you?" Sessetti snarled, turning to face his old friend. "Dane's already in another band. It doesn't matter! Our school band doesn't mean anything! None of it is important anymore! When you go home, you can get another band together."

Clythe sat up but remained silent. Sessetti could imagine his expression in the darkness. He did not regret what he had said, but he instantly regretted the way he had said it. Clythe needed a reality check, needed to understand that life had moved on from the adolescent days of band practices, parties, and gigs.

"How're my two pals?" A happy voiced chirped as Rhona flopped down to sit between them, wrapping an arm around each of their shoulders.

In each hand she clutched two large bottles of pungent smelling spirits. Detecting that Sessetti had noticed the bottles, she continued.

"That big house had some sort of booze cellar, so I swiped these for us before all the important people could get to them. I guess technically it's looting, but I figured you guys are worth it."

Sessetti was suddenly aware of a fourth figure in the darkness behind him. He turned and recognized Varlton, a seasoned trooper from Squad Teal.

"Varl's just been transferred across to us," Rhona explained, "so we're up to a staggering four troopers next time we're in a fight."

"Hello, guys," Varlton said as he sat down opposite the trio. "I know you had the worst day possible. I'm not here to try to replace any of your friends, I'm just here to do my best."

"You can start by drinking," Rhona said as she threw a bottle over to him, "because back where I'm from, you spend a proper amount of time thinking about friends when you lose them. Now I know we're

204 *Beyond the Gates of Antares*

not supposed to grieve right now, but nothing says we can't drink and talk about them all night, to show to each other that we care and we'll miss them."

"They could come back," Clythe offered as he pulled the top of his bottle, "you never know. They could have had successful regens. Rae did. She's back home and all fine now."

"I think we're kidding ourselves if..."

"Maybe they will!" Rhona cut off Sessetti's response. "But for now, I'm gonna start by taking a swig for Qan. I knew Jem and Gant a little better because at times they both hated me, and so we argued a lot, but I never knew Qan so well. He didn't really talk about himself much, but when he did speak up, it was either to be the diplomat in an argument, or to make us all laugh. I'm sorry I didn't get to know him better. He deserved it."

Rhona raised her bottle and drained the equivalent of two glasses in one prolonged swig.

"He was a good guy," Varlton added. "I knew him when he first arrived straight out of training. Like you said, kept himself to himself, but his heart was always in the right place."

"See you around, pal," Clythe said quietly, "I hope the system brings you back. I want them all back, but if I really had to choose, it would be you."

"I want them all back too," Sessetti exhaled, "but if just one could come back, even for an hour, I'd want to see Jem again. She wasn't the nicest, she seemed to love winding us all up and watching the arguments, and I never understood that. But I think we all knew it was a front, and beneath it, she was hurting from something and just didn't know how to deal with it. I think she was a good person underneath it all. And... when we were on leave, I woke up next to her and we never had a chance to speak about that and work it out. And now I never will."

Clythe burst out laughing. Sessetti felt rage burning inside him as he turned to glare at him.

"I'm not laughing at you," Clythe managed, "I'm laughing with you! Because if Jem was still here, then we'd all be laughing as she tried to squirm her way out of this! I wish she was still here so I could point right at her face and laugh!"

Rhona began laughing, too.

"Aw Jem... I wish you'd have told me, so I could make your life hell. Just like you would have done with me if the situation was reversed."

Sessetti unclenched his fists and took a breath. After a while, he laughed a little, too.

"It is pretty funny," he admitted, "I can still remember her face now when we both woke up, stinking of booze, and realized what had happened. I think her words were simply… 'oh, crap,' or something like that."

He took a long drink from his bottle and lay back in the grass.

"Wherever Gant is now," Varlton said, "I hope he's got good hair. I never knew him that well, but it always struck me that his curly hair was pretty important to him."

"He was pretty vain," Rhona admitted.

"We all thought you and him would become an item," Clythe said, "when you were arguing right at the start."

"Nah," Rhona shrugged, "he's not my type. I say that to a lot of guys, but I actually mean it with him. Good guy, great soldier. That's how I'll remember him. Cheers, dude."

Rhona drained another quarter of her bottle. Sessetti followed her example and took a long drink of the fiery liquid.

"Remember that time Qan found the picture of Gant's mother?" Clythe began laughing again. "Man, some things in this life should be sacred…"

FIFTEEN

Firebase Ghia
Outskirts of Pariton
Capital City
Markov's Prize

L-Day plus 62

The Duke slowed smoothly as it neared Firebase Ghia, the latest Concord stronghold built on Markov's Prize. Strike Trooper Tannen Rechter looked nervously around the transport drone at the other occupants, all of whom – like him – were freshly qualified and had never seen a day's combat. A trio of Dukes were carrying out shuttle runs from the landing site where the replacement soldiers had been delivered to, and Rechter found himself in the last transport bound for the 44th Strike Formation.

He pressed his hand against his armored chestplate in an unsuccessful attempt to feel the wedding band which hung on a chain around his neck. His wedding day had not been what he had expected, although he appreciated Rila's romantic gesture in proposing to him within minutes of C3 calling him up for military service. They had known each other since they were five years old; their mothers were best friends and they had been to school together. All his life, grown ups had told him that he would marry Rila one day and he had resented it, but as a young adult, he realized that resisting his love for her was only to prove everybody wrong, and that was no reason at all. Now, at nineteen years of age, he could spend the next two centuries of his life with her. He just needed to survive military service.

The Duke stopped and the doors sprang open. Rechter felt another wave of calming thoughts brush gently through his mind from the shard as an automatic reaction to the fear he felt. It did not seem to be doing much, which made him wonder just how awful a state he would be in if his armor did not provide chemical assistance to stabilize his emotions. Rechter stood and followed the other nine troopers out of

Duke and into the sunlight.

The terrain surrounding Firebase Ghia was very different from the barren wasteland of the landing site. Lush blues and greens painted the surrounding fields and jungles under a clear sky lit with the system's twin suns. The ground was churned up in places by muddy craters which could be nothing other than the evidence of shelling. An age old manor house stood a few dozen yan away, surrounded by smaller, similarly archaic buildings. Lines of machines, ranging from the smallest spotter drones up to the hulking C3M4 combat drones, lay under kinetic shelters whilst maintenance drones carried out checks and repairs. Only a handful of troopers were actually visible – Rechter assumed most would be safely underground in the firebase itself. To the east, pillars of grey smoke rose ominously from the far horizon.

A soldier wearing hyperlight armor and a black beret was the only one waiting for them as they quickly filed off the Duke. The stern looking soldier regarded the new strike troopers as they ambled uncomfortably across to him. One of the new soldiers took the initiative and barked out a short series of commands.

"Squad! Form two ranks!" The woman yelled, unnecessarily loudly considering that the command came through the troopers' helmet sound interface.

Not wishing to waste any time with arguing over what right the woman had to give commands to fellow replacement soldiers, Rechter took his place in the second rank of five soldiers and stood smartly to attention with his plasma carbine resting against his left shoulder. As the stern trooper walked over to them, Rechter's shard connection commenced a re-integration program as it coupled with a new system. Lines of text scrolled across the left hand side of his visor display as he connected with his new unit, both administratively and personally. He felt just a little more confident and at ease with his situation, but inexplicably tired and a little resentful. That was the overwhelming emotion which was filtering through the shard he, and the other replacement troopers, had just become a part of.

"Ladies, gentlemen," the trooper said as he came to a halt in front of them, "I've just integrated you within our company shard. Welcome to you new home. You are now a part of Beta Company, 44th Strike Formation. Currently a part of the 17th Assault Force under Commander-in-Chief Diette. I am Senior Strike Leader Van Noor, second in command of Beta Company. You will, no doubt, be apprehensive about arriving. Make no mistake, this is no peacekeeping duty you've joined – we are at war with a formidable opponent. But we will win. This is the first time any of you have ever been outside the Concord, and certainly the closest you've ever been to war. I can feel through the shard that you are nervous, and that is a perfectly normal reaction which will pass, in time. For now, I want you to report to your strike leaders which I will be assigning to you directly. The company commander, Strike Captain Tahl, will no doubt be around to meet you all individually. That's all, dismissed."

At the command, the new troopers all turned to the right in unison and took one pace forward. A command and waypoint was transmitted to Rechter's display; he and two other replacements were now a part of Squad Wen. The trooper who had ordered them into ranks, a woman named Meibal, according to the shard connection, was also joining the same squad along with Losse, a tall man he had a nodding acquaintance with from basic training.

"Rechter, Losse, follow me," Meibal ordered, turning to jog toward the waypoint off on the other side of the vehicle hangars and toward the old mansion which lay serenely in the late morning sun.

The three troopers arrived to find four soldiers sat informally on a wooden fence which ran around one of the fields adjacent to the mansion. At least Rechter knew they were Concord soldiers based on the information displayed from the company shard; to look at, he saw a quartet of figures with the vague outline of strike troopers, each covered from head to toe in a thick layer of something dark brown and viscous. All were mid-conversation, and laughing. Meibal removed her helmet as she approached, revealing her dark skin and delicate features. Rechter and Losse followed her lead. The first trooper sat on the fence looked up as they approached, a soldier who the shard identified as Varlton.

"You must be the new guys we were promised," Rechter could just detect a smile on Varlton's face under the thick coat of mud which covered him. "How was your trip?"

There was an uncomfortable silence until Meibal responded.

"Strike Trooper Meibal, reporting for assignment to Squad Wen. This is Rechter and Losse."

"Yeah, I can see that," Varlton answered. "As you're new here, let's learn something about you. One interesting fact about yourselves, from each of you. Go. Starting with you."

Varlton pointed at Rechter. He said the first thing which was always on his mind and, to him at least, was interesting.

"I just got married the day before I started my training as a strike trooper."

All four mud-covered soldiers looked at each other and let out the same 'aww' simulteanously.

"That's a good start," said a trooper who the shard identified as his strike leader, Rhona. "I like a romantic story."

Rechter was unsure whether he had been met with sarcasm, but the response did not feel welcoming.

"I graduated top of my class in every stage of training," Meibal added her own interesting fact.

"Boring," chimed the third trooper, a soldier displayed by the shard as Clythe.

"I can burp the entire alphabet," Losse offered.

"Way better!" Clythe grinned. "I like that! The wedding story was sweet, but alphabet burp gets my vote."

"Enough of the ritual humiliation," Meibal placed her hands on her hips, squaring up to Rhona and looking up at the taller woman. "You're in command here?"

"Yeah, I am." Rhona hopped off the fence, chunks of mud falling from her limbs as she did so, "I'm Kat. This guy here covered in mud is Varl, he's the squad second–in–command. The guy over there covered in mud is Bo, he's our lance gunner. The quiet one is Lian, he's like a super martial artist and the boss's favorite little trooper. Don't worry if you get Lian and Bo confused, they came as a package deal, and even without all the mud, I still can't really tell them apart."

"I've had four lessons," Sessetti offered quietly. "I'm not really a super martial artist."

"I've got to ask," Losse grimaced, "what happened to you guys?"

"We're just back from a little recon patrol in the city," Varlton explained, "we ran into some of the MAA types – they're the guys who used to be the planet's army and are now a sort of resistance force – and we had a bit of a shoot out. Anyway, team genius Clythe decided we needed to fall back and led us across what we thought was solid ground. It wasn't."

"Turns out that one of us hit a main subterranean water pipe," Clythe said, "so it got a bit... swampy. Anyway, could be worse. Some of the guys from Squad Jai took cover from an attack a few days ago, they dived into something the locals call a sewage treatment plant. Turns out the natives actually produce waste from their food and drink, like animals, and all that waste has got to go somewhere. So the Squad Jai guys decided to swim in it. So all of a sudden, my decision today doesn't seem so bad."

"Look," Rhona explained, "here's the deal. Forget everything you've seen on war movies, forget all the tough talk and crap from basic training. You guys know how to shoot and you know tactics, so we're not here to give you a hard time. You're in our shard now, or at least you will be when I upload you in a moment, so we're your family out here. I'm your pretend big sister, so if you've got any problems, then you come talk to me. Don't bother with rank unless somebody important is around, it's first names and nicknames. You've already met the senior – don't piss him off, his bark is colossal, let alone his bite. The company commander is 'sir', until you've been here for a while, and then he's 'boss'. You've lucked in with him, he's..."

"Is he the Ryen Tahl who..." Losse began before trailing off.

"Yeah, that's him," Rhona replied, arousing Rechter's curiosity over what his new commander was famous for. "He's a good guy, he's got our backs. A few of us here have seen that personally. For now, just go drop your stuff off in your rooms and then come back here. I'll give you a tour of the place once I've showered all this mud off. Y'all cool, or any problems so far?"

"Are we defending this place, or are we straight up against the Ghar?" Rechter asked, ignoring an admonishing look from Meibal. "They haven't really told us much of what's going on out here."

"The Ghar had two main landings," Rhona explained, "one here at the capital, another in the Nienne Desert. We're facing them at both and it's a bit of a stalemate. Here in the city, we've also got the MAA in the fight, so it's like a big threesome, just nowhere near as sexy. The MAA have some artillery and they've bombed this firebase twice now; if the alarm goes off, then just head underground to your room and get a good movie. The bombing lasts a few hours and does nothing. Odds are we'll be in the city again in the next couple of days, but don't let that worry you. We're here to help and we'll take you by the hand until you're used to things. Just... try your best to relax and enjoy the weather. Last planet we were on had acid rain every day which would melt your face off. There's always something to be happy about, right? Get going, I'll catch you in a few minutes."

***

Van Noor suppressed a yawn as he leaned over the holographic display of the city which was projected in the center of the briefing room. Stood around the flickering, cyan image was Tahl, the other five company commanders of the 44th Strike Formation along with their own senior strike leaders, and two soldiers from the 3rd Drop Formation. Briefing them all was Owenne, who had taken charge of the planning in the absence of Strike Commander Orless, who had been summoned to the Assault Force HQ.

The normally crowded briefing room seemed all the more sterile with only fifteen occupants; the standard white walls of every C3 Firebase seemed less homely to Van Noor now than ever before.

"The Ghar have moved a number of units across to Pariton from the Nienne Desert," Owenne continued, highlighting a series of animated arrows on the three-dimensional map projection, "so it's looking more and more that this will be the site of the decisive battle. Reports coming through indicate that MAA presence is on the increase, so whether that is a pro or a con at this stage is still to be confirmed. Thanks to the shipments of Freeborn weapons which have slipped through, the MAA are now a threat to our forces but are also a threat to the Ghar. One way or another, both have to be dealt with to successfully conclude this campaign and confirm the planet as being completely in Concord hands."

Van Noor's attention drifted off a little. He was well aware of the strategic situation, although Owenne's push to Pariton still confused him. C3 had established a solid perimeter in the Nienne Desert and the campaign was turning in their favor until Owenne suddenly upped sticks and dragged half the assault force across to the city. An unknown area with potential for civilian casualties. It made no sense.

"...so I'll be leading a reconnaissance patrol into the center of the city this evening," Owenne continued. "I'll take a Squad from Beta Company with me. You up for an evening stroll, Ryen?"

"Yes, I'll be glad to tag along," Tahl replied.

"Probably worth watching your back, then, Mandarin," remarked Davi, the senior drop leader from the 3rd Drop Formation, bitterly.

Van Noor felt his temper spike and he was speaking before he had even thought of the words.

"What d'you mean by that?"

"Wouldn't worry about it," Davi folded his arms. "If you haven't worked it out by now, you're probably not going to."

"If you've got something to say, just spit it out instead of talking in dumb little riddles!" Van Noor snapped. "If you ever..."

"Okay, Bry, okay," Tahl rested a hand firmly on his shoulder. "Come on, let's take a walk."

Van Noor saw the disapproving looks which followed him from the other assembled soldiers as Tahl led him to the back of the briefing room. Simultaneously, Drop Captain Mosse led her deputy to the other side of the room for a similar talk.

"What's up?" Tahl asked quietly. "That's not you. Kicking off in a formation level brief? Come on, Bry, what's going on?"

"I know you've got a history with those clowns, and I know you made some enemies, but I'll be damned if I'm gonna just stand by and keep my mouth shut while some insubordinate asshole with a superiority complex, based on the fact that his hat is red, decides it's okay for him to serve you neat crap in front of the rest of the command staff. Not on, mate, not acceptable."

"You're tired," Tahl said, his hands held out passively. "We're overdue some proper time at home. I know there's a lot going on for you, but from what you've told me, it sounds like things are looking better on the home front. Don't lose the plot now, not whilst we're this close to wrapping things up here and going home."

"Are we?" Van Noor demanded. "First off, it's been time to go home for the last three planetary assaults, and I don't believe for a minute that this is the last one. When we're done here, that bastard Owenne will just send us to the next planet, and then the next one after that. Second, something's wrong here. Owenne wants this city too badly. Things were looking up in the desert, and then he moved us here. This will be the third time he's wanted a personal look in the city center in as many days, and he hasn't given us a single solid reason why. Something's up, Ryen."

"I know, I know," Tahl muttered under his breath, "I've noticed. But what do you want to do? Just call him out on it and ask why we changed our approach?"

Before Van Noor could reply, the assembled soldiers finished the brief and filed toward the exit. Owenne stopped momentarily by Tahl and Van Noor.

"I'll let you children sort out your differences. Be ready to go tonight. Without any adolescent emotional baggage."

The mandarin left, leaving only Mosse and Davi. Van Noor felt a surge of anger rise again, and he stomped over to the two drop troopers.

"Now everybody else has gone, you can say what you want to say before I take your precious red tiara and shove it up your ass!"

"Piss off, you second rate prick!" Davi snapped. "If you've spent your entire career slumming it in the strike corps with all the other losers who aren't good enough to specialize outside of basic infantry training, that's your problem and not mine!"

"Senior Drop Leader, that's enough!" Mosse thundered. "Wait for me outside!"

The short drop trooper exchanged one last look of contempt with Van Noor before dragging his red beret on and barging his way past to the door. Mosse turned her glare to Tahl.

"A word, please, Strike Captain," she seethed before walking out of the briefing room.

Tahl looked at Van Noor and raised his brow expectantly.

"I'm sorry, Ryen," Van Noor said, "but I'm not taking this from them. You shouldn't, either."

Tahl followed Mosse, his shoulders slumped.

***

"Do you even bother trying to reign in your own troopers, or is that sort of behavior encouraged under your command?" Mosse began angrily, a finger of reprimand pointed squarely at Tahl as the two stood in the relative privacy of the walkway between the towering manor house and the entrance to the subterranean firebase. The suns were setting, painting the whole world in shades of orange. The not unpleasant scent of a plant used for flavoring drinks wafted across the air in the evening breeze.

"Senior Strike Leader Van Noor was speaking up in defense of me," Tahl said gently. "He thought he was doing the right thing. It was a show of loyalty, that's all."

"Lunging at one of my troopers in front of the entire formation command – and a mandarin, no less – and then insulting the entire drop corps?" Mosse snapped.

"He's been on continuous operations for a long time, and he's got a lot going on in his personal life," Tahl said, again keeping his tone passive. "He's..."

Tahl paused. Van Noor had leapt to his defense after being provoked. It should not have been Tahl who needed to explain anything.

"Davi was acting like an idiot," Tahl decided, "his behavior was wholly inappropriate and Senior Strike Leader Van Noor was simply the first to point it out. I don't need to explain my man's behavior. I support it."

"You support it?" Mosse spat. "Who the hell do you think you are, Trooper? You treated Davi like crap back in the day, and he has every right to feel the way he does!"

"Back in the day was over ten years ago, Abbi. I'm sorry about how he feels, but if he, or you, for that matter, think that is an excuse for blurting out personal grievances in a high level brief, you are mistaken. And as for who I am? You haven't got your promotion yet, so right now I'm an officer of equal rank, and I'll talk to you in any way I feel appropriate. And I'll certainly defend the actions of men and women under my command if I feel it is appropriate."

Mosse took a step back as if she had been struck. Her shock gave way to anger a moment later.

"You can't change," she sneered, "you can pretend all you want to, but you can't change. You're still the same bastard you were when we were kids, no matter how much you pretend you've found God or have become spiritual or whatever other lies you want to hide behind. I was wrong to think anything else of you. It's a good thing the drop corps kicked you out when it did, because you're not one of us. It's a good thing I dumped you when I did, too."

Mosse turned her back and walked away. Tahl watched her go, reeling at the words and their effect on him, but keeping his mouth shut. A few moments passed before Van Noor appeared next to him.

"I owe you an apology, Boss," he said quietly.

Tahl turned and forced a smile.

"Don't worry about it, Bry, just try to keep a lid on the temper next time, for both of our sakes."

"Things not too good with your ex?" Van Noor asked hesitantly.

"Nothing I want to get into right now, not when we're about to face another night of fool's errands at the beck and call of Owenne. It's funny though, isn't it? How different people see moral high grounds in such different ways. Two people can have an argument – one person calls the other every name under the suns and then storms off, knowing that they have the moral high ground because they got all the insults in and got the last word. The other person keeps their mouth shut and thinks they have the moral high ground because they tried to keep things civil and let the other person vent their feelings without lowering themselves to insults."

"I reckon I know which one you were," Van Noor said. "D'you think you'll ever get back with her?"

"No," Tahl replied without hesitating, "I don't see her that way anymore. I want her to be happy, I want things amicable between us, but I could never see her that way again. And then there's her side of things. Even if she saw me that way, it wouldn't matter. She's fully committed to C3 now, no room for personal baggage. You can't start thinking about marriage and kids when you want to be commander-in-chief of your own expeditionary force."

"And you?" Van Noor ventured, looking up at the setting suns. "Is that what you want?"

Tahl laughed, a little louder than he was expecting even himself.

"What I want? I want you, me, Rall, Vias, Rhona, Yavn, all of us to survive this mess and go home. I just want all of us to get through this last push, kick the Ghar of this planet, and finally get some leave. Not a couple of days locally, not a quick trip back home. Months. Months of garrison duty, retraining, and recuperation. I want to wake up knowing that I'm going in to work, and all I have to worry about is the weekly training schedule and getting the guys through periodic assessments and progress tests. All that admin crap that's waiting for us back home. I can't wait for it, because nobody dies. I'm sick to death of being shot at. I'm sick to death of writing letters to parents and loved ones. I want us all to go home."

"You've set your sights low, my friend," Van Noor grinned, "and I like it. Come on, let's go take the mandarin on another sightseeing tour of the touristic city center, and we can get ourselves one step closer to that dream of yours. I'm off to get my kit, I'll catch you in a couple of minutes."

Tahl waited until Van Noor had departed and then headed out to the fields to take a few moments to calm himself. The suns lingered on, still casting long shadows across the waist-high crop fields he wandered through, refusing to dip underneath the horizon and allow night to come. By the time Tahl walked back to the firebase, he saw Owenne and Van Noor stood with Squad Wen, armored and ready to go.

"What's going on?" Tahl demanded as he approached.

"We're taking Squad Wen with us on the patrol," Owenne replied as he checked his pistol, "what does it look like?"

"If we're taking anybody, it's Squad Teal," Tahl said, "it's their turn on the rota and they're in good shape. Wen is seven troopers, half of which arrived from training about six hours ago. Two of the remaining four have limited experience. They're not ready."

"I want Strike Leader Rhona to come," Owenne smiled at the dark haired woman, who looked uneasily at Tahl. "This will be a good education for her in her next role. I've assessed her skills and offered her a position in force intelligence."

Tahl was speechless. He fought down the rising anger and spent a moment to compose himself before replying.

"It's my company, Mandarin Owenne, I run it. I'm not sending three troopers who've never fired a shot in anger straight into the heart of a Ghar controlled city."

Owenne paused and nodded before staring at Tahl's feet with a grim smile.

"It's your company, as you say," he admitted, "but as a mandarin, I do have the authority to tell you how to run it. But I'm not like that. We go back a little way, you and I. So I'll meet you halfway."

Owenne turned to the assembled troopers who had been silently witnessing the exchange with interest and concern.

"Squad Wen, you're dismissed," Owenne said. "Go get some sleep. Except for you, Rhona, you can come with us."

Tahl watched as the remaining troopers walked away. One of the young soldiers, Sessetti, stopped and then walked back. He opened his mouth to speak, but Tahl held up a hand to stop him.

"I appreciate the gesture, Lian, but the answer is no. Go get some sleep, like the mandarin says. I need you in top shape."

"Yes, sir," Sessetti replied quietly before leaving again.

"Sir?"

Tahl turned to look at Rhona.

"Yes, what is it?"

"I know this isn't a great time, sir, but I really need to talk to you about an issue with one of the troopers in my squad. It really can't wait. I need to get this cleared up before we go out on this patrol."

Tahl turned to Owenne.

"Make it quick," the mandarin said.

Tahl walked in an uneasy silence with Rhona, back to the crop field he had just returned from. He worried with every step, knowing his mind was not on the job. He was about to go out on patrol with a NuHu he did not fully trust, an old friend who was coming apart at the seams, and a subordinate he had inappropriate feelings for which he could not shake, no matter how hard he tried.

"What is it?" He asked Rhona as soon as the two were out of view of everybody else. "Which one of your people has got the problem?"

"Me," she said softly, "I'm the one with the issue."

"You're off to intelligence after this?" Tahl tried to keep his tone from sounding hurt. She did not owe him any explanation.

"No, I'm not," Rhona shook her head, keeping her dark eyes locked on his. "He offered me the job, and I said no. He wouldn't accept my answer, told me I had to think about it. The answer is still no."

"You should take the job," Tahl said. "You'd be safe. You'd be away from all this. You could do your time and then go home."

"Go home where?" Rhona exclaimed. "What home? I'm not like the others, I've got nothing waiting for me if I ever leave this. I don't want some dumb job looking at surveillance footage and collating information which will send some poor dudes off to their deaths. I want to stay here. I want to be a soldier in your company. That's why I needed to talk to you before we go hit the city tonight. I... whatever is going on between us, it's incomplete. Don't go getting shot tonight. Or ever. Don't leave this incomplete."

Tahl took a step closer, close enough to be in her personal space. "So what completes it?"

Rhona slipped her arms around his neck and kissed him for what seemed like an age, a long perfect moment which took all of his problems away. She then rested her forehead against his, her eyes still closed as she clung to him with the last rays of the system's second sun shining through the small space between them.

"I don't know what completes it," she whispered, "I just need you to know that I'm not screwing around with you. I know we're from different places and I know what people from your part of the universe think of people from my part. I'm not here to mess around with your feelings. I'm really confused about what the hell is happening between us, what happens next, how we hide it from everybody; hell, I'm confused about everything. But right now, it's the best thing in my life and it's all that's keeping me going and giving me the strength to pretend to my guys that all is cool and I'm okay."

Tahl held her, truly at a loss for words. He finally spoke, more out of necessity to tell her something after she had been so honest, rather than because he had thought his reply through.

"This isn't right," he whispered. "I've forced this on you, you told me what you thought of me and I can't..."

She kissed him again.

"Seriously, sir, shut up with that," she laughed. "Don't hit me with the chivalry so late in the evening. I'm not sixteen, I know what I'm doing, so give me some credit. Just tell me you feel the same way and stop leaving me hanging here and making me feel like an idiot."

"I feel the same way," Tahl said truthfully.

"Good," Rhona took a step back and unslung her carbine from her shoulder, "then don't get shot. Don't leave this incomplete. Let's go, Boss. I've got your back."

SIXTEEN

Pariton City Center
Capital City
Markov's Prize

L-Day plus 62

Every footstep which crunched down on the rubble seemed as loud as bombs to Rhona as she crept forward through the skeletal remains of the blackened buildings. Days of bitter fighting had taken their toll on the planet's capital; the once beautiful business and administrative center of the city was now reduced to smouldering grey, with the stars scattered across the indigo blue night sky above clearly visible through the holes in walls and missing roofs.

Rhona was on point, at the very front of the reconnaissance patrol. Several yan ahead of Owenne, Tahl, and Van Noor, she was only just visible to them. Her utility pouches were all but empty to stop any extra noise from their contents rattling around; all the technology in the world would not stop a Ghar hearing an unruly racket, and the four soldiers were reduced to employing the same noise cancelling methods as their forefathers from centuries before.

Stopping at the remains of the corner of a skyscraper, Rhona sank slowly to one knee and raised her carbine to her shoulder. The wind whistled through the remnants of the tall buildings. The marker which Owenne had set for them was still a good half hour away, appearing as a steady white cross on the central display unit on her visor. To the left, lines of text scrolled periodically to inform her of her vital statistics, chemical enhancement usage, geographical position, and nearest escape routes in case of ambush.

The route ahead seemed clear. Rhona slowly raised herself back to her feet and took another few crunching steps forward. She thought of Tahl, half a street behind her. This was not going as she had planned. Once she had forgiven him for his earlier transgressions, it was simple enough to add up her attraction to him with all evidence pointing to him being a genuinely good person, and the result was an opportunity for harmless flirting, possibly leading to a meaningless physical encounter or two with no commitments and no repercussions. Instead, she found her mind wandering to how she could prove that, even given her background, she was capable of providing something meaningful. Tahl had spent his leave travelling back to Concord space to try to help Van Noor in some way in which she was not privy to the details. Perhaps that was it. Next time she had leave, she could travel back to the Concord, find this martial arts woman who had given Tahl such a hard time in his youth, and tell the old bitch what she thought of her.

It occurred to Rhona only a moment too late that her concentration had drifted away from her job at a critical and dangerous moment. Without warning, the ground suddenly gave way beneath her and she was falling through darkness amid rubble and stone which dropped down all around her. She let out a cry, more of surprise rather than pain, as she landed face down on a hard and uneven surface, stones and debris falling all around her.

"Katya?" A familiar voice called across her shard connection as she struggled up to her hands and knees. "Are you okay?"

She swore viciously, fumbling around for her carbine as her viewscreen automatically increased its output to take advantage of the little ambient light available. She checked her suit readouts – she was fine, completely unhurt, but the gauntlets, torso, and knees of her armor had been cracked by the fall. Her surrounding swarm of microscopic nanobots had already set about repairing the damage. She appeared to be inside a tunnel, manmade judging by its precise, smooth lines, with extinguished lamps lining the curved walls.

"Katya?" Tahl called again. "Your readouts say you're okay, can you hear me?"

"Yeah," Rhona replied groggily, "yeah, I'm good, Boss. Sorry, didn't see that coming. I've fallen down into what looks like an old subterranean transport hub."

"Can you see a way back up?" Van Noor asked as her three comrades appeared on the lip of the crater above, silhouetted against the starry night sky.

Suddenly, to her left, a shadowy figure emerged from the darkness and began sprinting down the tunnel away from her.

"I've got movement!" Rhona reported, running after the figure into the near darkness.

"Katya, wait!" Tahl ordered.

The figure was hunched over and running almost with a limp, but the head start put Rhona at a distinct disadvantage. Sprinting around a long corner in the tunnel, Rhona continued toward a well-lit area up ahead. As she closed the distance on the figure ahead, she scanned the runner and saw that they were struggling not due to a limp, but from carrying a large, bulky package. Rhona's first thought was that the interloper was carrying an explosive device – she carried out a quick system check on her carbine to ensure it was ready to fire.

The figure and its package disappeared around another corner up ahead. Rhona followed and then came to an abrupt stop. She was at the edge of a transport network station, where crowds of perhaps a hundred disheveled and ragged refugees were sitting or lying on the platforms, huddled together for warmth. The runner who she had been following, a young woman with pale skin and red hair, gently placed down her package – a boy of five or six years of age – and protectively nurtured the child behind her, staring at Rhona defiantly. A panicked cry was emitted by a woman somewhere in the crowd on the platform, and perhaps a dozen or so of the refugees leapt to their feet and ran for another tunnel at the far end of the station. A boy, no older than ten years of age, ran out to face Rhona and threw a large stone at her. Her hyperlight shields flared purple and deflected the projectile harmlessly to one side. This resulted in more screams and cries of panic from the crowd as more men and women jumped to their feet. The boy fearlessly scrabbled on his knees for another rock until a thin man from the crowd ran forward and dragged him away.

It occurred to her then what she must look like to the thinning crowds of people who backed away from her on the platforms, or sat still and stared at her silently with a mixture of contempt and resignation. A futuristic killer from the stars, clad in bulky armor which changed color to blend in to its surroundings. Right now her armor was as black as the shadows she stood in, the ominous glow of blue from her plasma carbine was all that lit her and silhouetted her dangerous and threatening form, her face masked behind the inhuman visor of her helmet. Rhona quickly clipped her carbine to her back and deactivated her armor's reactive coloring to leave it in its default white and green colors. She took off her helmet and dropped down to one knee, looking at the small boy who was being dragged away from her and holding her hands out passively.

"It's alright," she said softly, "I'm just lost. I'm not here to hurt anybody."

A few confused murmurs rippled through the remaining refugees.

"Is she an angel?" One girl of no older than four asked.

"No, she's anything but that," a parent replied angrily.

Rhona slowly stood and took a step back.

"I'm going," she started, "I'll leave..."

Five figures suddenly ran out from the tunnel behind her to quickly form a loose semi-circle around her, aiming weapons at her head. The soldiers wore the primitive black body armor that she had encountered in opposition when she first landed on the planet, but they were armed with far more modern magnetic guns, weapons which were well capable of piercing her armor.

"Drop your weapon you Concord bastard, or I'll give the order to gun you down where you stand," an authoritative voice called from beside her.

Rhona obliged, slowly and carefully placing her carbine at her feet. Another squad of five soldiers moved past her and quickly ushered the remaining refugees along through the tunnels and out of sight. As they did, a second voice called out from an elevated platform somewhere to the right.

"She's a squad leader, she's armed with a wrist-mounted x-sling. Similar to a grenade launcher. Tell her to unload it."

"You heard," the first voice said, "unload that thing on your wrist."

Rhona held up her left wrist and cupped her right hand beneath it, jettisoning the x-sling's magazine and then placing the small explosive projectiles at her feet.

"Y'all gonna gun me down now, 'cause I'm getting bored just standing here," Rhona said, tossing her head to flick a rogue lock of hair from her face.

Even without her suit's readings, she could feel her racing pulse and felt a shot of stimulant enter her bloodstream to attempt to control the terror which was rising within her. She tried to activate a distress call through the company shard, but found something was blocking her. A soldier moved across and kicked her in the back of the knee, buckling her legs and forcing her down to her knees. The first speaker moved around to stand in front of her. A tall, slender man with greying hair, his aging face would have placed him at perhaps 150 years of age in the Concord; here on Markov's Prize, he was probably barely over 40. Rhona risked a look to either side. There were perhaps fifteen soldiers she could see, but the voice from the right came from a shadowy area above one of the platforms. She felt suddenly very alone; not just physically, but emotionally. Her connection to her shard was being suppressed somehow.

"Give me your name, rank, and unit," the greying soldier ordered.

She saw a badge of rank on the front of his armor and recalled it from an intelligence brief a few weeks before. The man was a captain in the Markov Alliance Army, formerly the planetary self-defense force.

"Katya Rhona, Strike Leader, Concord Combined Command," Rhona replied. "You ain't getting my unit, Captain."

"What the hell's a strike leader?" The officer spat. "Give me a proper rank, none of this 'space commando' crap."

"A strike leader is a junior commander in the Concord basic infantry," the voice from the right said. "She's the equivalent to one of your corporals."

The greying soldier crouched down and leaned in to look Rhona in the eyes.

"You bastards have invaded my planet," he began slowly, "killed our women and children, and destroyed everything dear to us. A corporal isn't worth much to me. So I'm going to give you one more chance to prove your worth before I start cutting that pretty face of yours to pieces. Give me your unit strength and location. Now, Corporal."

"Go to hell, you piece of crap," Rhona forced a dismissive smile, fond memories of time with her family and a string of regrets from her life suddenly forcing their way to the front of her mind out of nowhere as the tall captain stood, grabbed her by her hair, and unsheathed a black bladed knife from his belt.

"I wouldn't do that, if I were you, old chap."

Owenne's voice echoed from the shadows as the pale faced NuHu jumped down from a platform to the left, his coat billowing out around him as he slowly sank to the ground with inhumanly slow speed and control. A squad of five MAA soldiers instantly aimed their mag guns at him. Owenne issued a deep, booming laugh which succeeded in unnerving even Rhona.

"Good gosh!" He smiled. "I thought your captain was stupid enough in threatening one of my troopers, but now you imbeciles have actually threatened me! I hate to be a cliché, but do you know who I am? What I am? What I am capable of doing?"

"He's a New Human Mandarin," the voice from the shadows said. "He's..."

"Come out from there, Freeborn," Owenne interrupted, "we're not at the bloody theater, so we can all do without the amateur theatrics. You know who I am, I know who you are. So be a good fellow and come out into the light. You and your band of pirates."

Rhona looked up and saw six figures, wearing long cloaks and overcoats of dark brown, step out into the light above the nearest platform. They carried plasma carbines, signalling that they were elite Freeborn mercenaries. The leader, a dark skinned man with a short beard and shaved head, looked down at Owenne. Rhona tried to send a mental message through to Owenne, but again found her connection to the shard blocked. No doubt it was some machinery operated by the Freeborn. Freeborn mercenaries were notorious for their cutting edge technology, derived from travelling the length and breadth of known space whilst trading their martial skills for science and technology.

"They're Vardanari," Rhona shouted across to Owenne, her eyes still flitting around as she looked for escape avenues for when the stand off would inevitably result in gunfire. "They're the inner guard force for a Doma, kind of like a clan leader."

"Yes, thank you, Strike Leader, I'm well aware of the social make up of these reprobates," the mandarin remarked dryly.

"How does she know that?" The MAA captain insisted. "You said your machine would suppress their knowledge!"

"I know because I used to be Freeborn," Rhona said, momentarily enjoying the look of surprise which registered on the faces of all six men on the gantry above, "but I wised up and joined the A Team instead of slumming it on a filthy pirate ship floating across space."

"Never mind her, it's the NuHu who's in charge here," the Freeborn Vardanari leader said, "and I've met your sort before. You're very capable. But not really capable enough to take on twenty men single handed."

"True," Owenne conceded with a smile and a wave of one hand.

"You've come here to rescue your girl with just a pistol?" The MAA captain nodded to Owenne's holster.

"What, this?" Owenne grimaced. "Come, come! That's my secondary back up! My primary back up is this stick. You see, my kind have a rather curious ability to manipulate nanobots to an extent which is simply impossible for any other species. This stick is my amplifier, and I can use to form a blade of nanospheres whose acceleration would create such a force that it could cut through a Ghar battlesuit like freshly fallen snow. But as I said, that's my primary back up. I don't really like to get my own hands dirty. That's why I brought a Tahl."

"What's a Tahl?" The captain asked.

"Glad you asked, old boy," Owenne replied, nodding to the shadows to his left.

Rhona saw Tahl move out of the shadows like a blur, driving straight into the nearest squad of five MAA soldiers. It was over within perhaps three of four seconds. Tahl drove an elbow into the gut of the first man with enough force to bend him over double, then slammed a fist into his face to send him flying back to slam motionless into the tunnel wall behind him. Before the first man had landed, Tahl whipped a leg around to smash a foot into the face of a second soldier, dropping him down to the ground before dispatching a third man with a side kick to the abdomen and a reverse punch to the face. He swept the legs from beneath the fourth soldier and slammed an armored boot down onto the side of his head to pin him in place, whilst he grabbed the last man and span him around helplessly to hold his neck and one arm in a vice-like lock.

Three men lay unconscious; a fourth soldier cried out in pain with Tahl's boot pressed against his head, whilst the last man gurgled and fought for breath in Tahl's grip.

"Well, that's a quarter of your boys down," Owenne said nonchalantly, "and I've got two prisoners now, whilst you only have one. And I'm barely warming up. Shall we do that again?"

Van Noor stepped out by a second group of MAA soldiers. Having seen the fate of their comrades at Tahl's hands, the five men raised their hands and stepped quickly away from Van Noor.

"Stand your ground!" The MAA captain barked, dragging Rhona up to her feet by her hair and holding his knife to her throat.

Both men who were suffering at Tahl's hands suddenly cried out in pain as he increased his force on them in response.

"It's three Concord soldiers!" The Freeborn leader shouted. "They're not supermen! They're just soldiers! Shoot the bastards!"

"No!" The captain held his hand up. "Let my men go."

"Send my 'space commando' *corporal* back over, and I'll stop my monster here from ripping your men apart," Owenne said seriously.

The captain opened his mouth to speak, but without warning, the earth shook violently as explosions sounded from the planet's surface somewhere up above. Half of the assembled men fell to the ground whilst those who remained upright struggled to do so. A moment later, a large clump of tunnel roof smashed down from above, causing Rhona and the MAA soldiers near to her to jump back instinctively. A second and then a third pile of debris fell down from the roof to form a barrier across the tunnel mouth. Rhona looked over her shoulder, saw the opportunity to run, and took it. She had barely moved two paces before two MAA soldiers tackled her to the ground whilst a second pair trained their weapons on her. She let out a sigh of resignation as she was dragged back to her feet.

"Concord?" The captain shouted out from where he stood by the barrier of masonry and debris. "You still there?"

"Afraid so," Owenne's muffled voice could just be heard from the other side of the rubble, "and I've still got five of your men. Now tell your pirate friends to drop that shard suppression device right now, or your soldiers may see my unpleasant side."

"Do it," the captain nodded to the Freeborn leader.

"But…"

"Just do it!" The officer yelled.

Rhona let out a sigh of relief as she felt the connection to Tahl, Van Noor, and Owenne renewed.

"Hang on," Tahl transmitted, "we'll get you back. We're not leaving without you."

"I know," Rhona replied. "Don't worry, I'm fine. This guy clearly has loyalty to his men, he won't sacrifice them."

"Neither will we," Tahl replied.

"I'm sending coordinates to my trooper now," Owenne shouted

from the other side of the rubble barrier. "You get her there. Safe and sound. One hour. If you're late, I shall start experimenting with my magic nano stick. You wouldn't want that for your soldiers."

"One hour," the captain agreed, picking up Rhona's carbine and slinging it over his shoulder, "but if you hurt my men…"

"Yes, yes," Owenne shouted back, "threats, posturing, alpha male, all that nonsense. Be there in an hour."

Rhona raised her hands as she was marched down the tunnels at gunpoint.

***

It would only be a short time before the questions started, Rhona figured, as she was marched along the subterranean transport tunnel with the dozen MAA soldiers. The Freeborn moved at the head of the column with the captain, whilst Rhona was pushed along at the back, three mag guns levelled at her as she walked. The shard suppression device had been activated again, and she had no means of communicating with her comrades. Doubts began to nib away at her, leaving her wondering whether she would ever see them again or even survive the night.

"If you're Freeborn," a grizzled looking soldier with a scar on his chin suddenly asked, "why are you with the Concord and not with those guys up at the front?"

"It's not that simple," Rhona answered after considering her words for a moment. "All of known space is split into factions, empires, territories, just like your planet was in ages gone by. The Concord is the largest territory in known space. We're like your evil empire, I guess you've already jumped to that conclusion. The Freeborn are more a collection of thousands of different smaller factions, most of them based around trading fleets wandering through the stars like nomads. I was born within a Freeborn house, but I became Concord."

"Why?" A second soldier asked, much younger than the first and nervous looking.

"I didn't have a choice," Rhona said, "and neither do you. You'll lose. Everybody does, eventually. Planets with far greater technology than yours have fallen. Half of your planet has already fallen. You can put me up against a wall and shoot me, but in a matter of days, you'll all be Concord citizens. Some of you might even get enlisted in the military. In a few days, some of you will be learning to use this same armor I'm wearing now so you can invade other planets. That's how it works."

"Don't talk to her!" A broad soldier snapped. "Don't listen to her crap!"

"You think I'm the bad guy here?" Rhona asked. "The real world ain't black and white. There's no clear right and wrong. You guys held a knife to my face and threatened to cut me up, and now y'all claiming the moral high ground?"

"That was the captain," the first soldier said, "and he's got every right to feel the way he does. He found his wife and children up against a wall alongside fifty other dead civilians. So yeah, you're the bad guys."

"That wasn't us, that was the Ghar," Rhona replied as the column of soldiers rounded another corner. "You want a true evil to vilify? There you go, take them. They're monsters, through and through. Nothing more. We don't kill civilians. Hell, we even offered you a peaceful entry into the Concord, no strings, no conditions, but you turned it down. Oh, y'all didn't know about that? That's because you're puppets to politicians. We don't even have politics in the Concord. Our system is robust enough that people can just do what they want. That's how our system works."

"We've heard all about your IMTel," the soldier with the scar spat. "Some invisible computer which gets into your head and controls your thoughts. Controls your every action. That's why our politicians said no to your offer. We want our freedom. And we'll fight and die for it."

"Yeah, that you will," Rhona risked a smile, "but you're dying for nothing. Do I look like I'm having my thoughts and actions controlled to you? The shard can suppress negative emotions. It has the ability to curb sadness, anger, all the things which make you feel bad. That's how it's pretty much eradicated crime. The only crime we've got comes from those who aren't IMTel compatible, and that's a tiny minority. So, do I think I'm the bad guy for invading your planet? Yeah, a little. I never wanted to kill anybody. Except the Ghar, I've got no moral dilemma there. But the Concord is a wise parent, and you guys are the child. You think you know what you want, you think you know what's best, but you don't. We need to show you, by force if we have to. This war? This is us putting you guys in the naughty corner until you wise up, grow up, and listen to us. I lost my mom because my Freeborn house's medicine wasn't cutting edge, and I lost my pa to crime. If my family had been born in the Concord, I'd still have both my parents. So you fight and die for your cause all you want, your cause is nothing but crap and you are fighting and dying to stop your children from having longer, safer, and happier lives. And you let me fight and die for my cause."

A little natural light from the night sky was visible ahead as the tunnel inclined up a little to move toward the surface.

"So all of this," began a short soldier who had remained silent up to this point, "all of this is your soulless, computer IMTel reaching machine omnipotence and deciding the best thing it can do is try to make everybody in the universe happy? You realize how crazy that sounds?"

"Yeah, you got it," Rhona sighed. "It ain't perfect, but it's the closest to perfect we're ever gonna see. And all that's stopping this planet, all of your friends and family, from getting to be on the inside of the club? You guys. You're all that's standing in the way. But that's cool, I'd be doing exactly the same if I didn't know better."

"What, you think you're the same as us?" The soldier with the scar grimaced. "You come down form the stars with your perfect face and clean armor, telling stories about how back home everything is perfect, and you think you can relate to us?"

"Across all of time," Rhona replied as they moved closer to the moonlight ahead, "for the entire history of panhumanity, some things have never changed. Any planet, any age, from the days of spears and shields right up to now, soldiers will always get treated like crap by the people above, and they'll always feel better about it after whining like a baby to their pals. So yeah, I can relate to you 'cause it's exactly the same in my army."

Rhona's response triggered a few sniggers from the surrounding soldiers. The MAA captain whipped around and stomped back to the rear of the line.

"What the hell is going on here?" He growled.

"I'm establishing a rapport with your boys so that it's difficult for them when you order them to shoot me," Rhona smiled with a wink.

"Why would I shoot you?" The tall captain scowled. "I gave my word to your... commissar or whatever the hell that thing was, that I would get you to the exchange point, Corporal."

"Yeah, well that's all cool, but there's half a legion of Ghar out there who might not like that plan. So could you be a sweety and give me my shooting stick back?"

The grey haired soldier slammed a fist into Rhona's cheek with enough force to knock her to the ground. Rhona winced and shook her head as she staggered back to her knees.

"Keep your mouth shut," the captain said, "or I'll take your gun and shoot off your kneecaps. I've already watched that animal hanging around your boss beat the crap out of five of my men, so I'm not averse to handing you back in worse condition that you arrived."

Two soldiers helped Rhona to her feet as the column continued to move. The group emerged from the subterranean tunnels back to the city center. The wind had died away and a layer of smoke and dust hung eerily at waist height, punctuated only by the skeletal remains of buildings punching up into the air like despairing hands reached up for the heavens.

***

Somewhere to the north, another series of staccato crackles snapped as yellow flashes lit the night horizon. Seconds later came the now familiar deep thuds as heavy shells landed somewhere amid the ruins of the sprawling city. Van Noor quickly checked the Company Intelligence Shard, but there was no news of Concord units in combat, meaning that whoever was shooting and being shot, it was an exchange between the Ghar and the MAA.

Van Noor looked around the site Owenne had chosen to meet the MAA and exchange prisoners. The multistory building was composed of floors of thick, grey concrete, open to the elements, and used as a vehicle park before the invasion. The exchange was taking place on the top floor, allowing clear shots from the x-launcher crew Owenne had located on the roof of the next building. That, combined with the eight strike troopers of Squad Jai, plus the lowest two floors of the vehicle park being rigged with explosives, meant that the initiative was firmly in the hands of the Concord delegation.

"What's taking so long?" Tahl growled, pacing up and down in the open area on the top floor of the building.

"We're the ones who are early," Van Noor said, "we're not expecting them for another ten minutes or so."

"What's the plan after the prisoner exchange?" Strike Leader Rall asked from the rubble where his squad hid in the corner of the floor. "Are we letting them go or taking them out?"

"We let them go!" Owenne snapped. "What else do you think we would do? We're the heroes in this, remember? Not the villains!"

"You're all heart, mandarin," Van Noor smiled beneath his helmet.

"Don't talk drivel, man!" Owenne scoffed. "I couldn't give two buggers about shooting some backward cavemen from a planet which is about to fall. But if news of that gets around? That would be cataclysmically bad. We need the moral high ground. Always."

Van Noor could feel the anger, fear, and desperation surging through the shard from Tahl even before he spoke again.

"This shouldn't be taking so long," the strike captain seethed. "They should be here by now!"

"A word, sir?" Van Noor gestured to Tahl.

Letting out a suppressed grunt of anguish, Tahl stomped over, his armored fists clenched tightly.

"What's going on, Ryen?" Van Noor muttered quietly, communicating conventionally rather than via the shard. "I know you get attached to your people, but this? Is this because it's Rhona? You told me that you'd explained the score to her and this was all put to bed. Have you still got feelings for her?"

"Well it's not up to me, is it?" Tahl hissed through gritted teeth.

"I didn't choose to feel like this! I know it's not ideal…"

"Not ideal!" Van Noor interjected. "Within the entire spectrum of leading a military unit on combat operations, falling for one of your subordinates is significantly worse than 'not ideal', Ryen! Now look, I hope this goes down the way we want it to tonight, but either way, you and me are having a talk about this when we get back to the firebase. Now go sit this one out with Rall's boys, me and Owenne will do the talking."

Tahl threw up his hands in resignation. A message was transmitted through from Squad Jai's lookout – the MAA troopers were approaching.

"See?" Van Noor grinned. "They're here. Now go back off and let me handle this."

Owenne walked over to Van Noor, hands clasped at the small of his back, as Tahl walked away and the MAA troops arrived at the ground floor of the building.

"Having problems, Senior Strike Leader?"

"No, nothing to worry about. You know Ryen. He's always been soft when it comes to the welfare of his men and women."

"Yes," Owenne uttered the single syllable with distaste. "Well, we need people like him to keep soldiers happy. We need people like you and I to get the job done."

"Yeah," Van Noor suppressed a laugh, "I often stay up late at night wondering, 'why am I so similar to Owenne?'"

"Funny," Owenne rolled his pale eyes. "Now look sharp, here they come."

The black armored MAA soldiers and their Freeborn allies filed up through the doorway from the stairwell and took position at the far end of the rooftop. Rhona was led out to the front by two soldiers who stood with her alongside their captain.

"Where's my men?" The captain demanded.

Owenne nodded to where Squad Jai was hidden in the rubble-strewn corner. The eight strike troopers stood up, revealing not only themselves as a show of force, but also the two prisoners they held.

"Where are the other three?"

"Unconscious, where they fell," Owenne replied evenly. "I didn't have the manpower to carry them. If you hurry up with this exchange, you can go and pick them up before the Ghar eat them alive."

"That wasn't our deal!" The captain yelled, pointing a finger at Owenne. "You said you would bring my men here!"

"I never said anything of the sort, you merely assumed it," Owenne said calmly. "Now, last time we met you had five more soldiers and we still bested you. Now you're five men down and I've got eight guns here and an x-launcher a few yan away which is zeroed in on you right now. You're not in any position to bargain. Send my soldier back. Now."

"You first," the captain insisted.

Owenne nodded, and Rall's troopers released the two MAA soldiers. The pair walked quickly across to their commanding officer, who nodded to the soldiers holding Rhona. She walked across the rooftop toward Owenne and Van Noor. Van Noor noticed that she had a painful looking cut at her temple and significant swelling over one eye.

"You alright?"

She nodded.

"Next time your strike captain tells you to wait, you bloody well wait, woman!" Owenne snapped. "Time is marching on and I have things to achieve tonight! That does not include babysitting you! Clear?"

Rhona nodded again.

"We're done here," the captain called out. "Pray we don't cross paths again."

"Yes, yes, last word, alpha male, well done," Owenne replied dismissively.

Tahl jumped down from the rubble and walked purposefully over to Rhona. He leaned in to inspect the wound on her face.

"Who did this?"

"It doesn't matter, Boss," Rhona shrugged. "You know me. Always shooting my mouth off. The guy only did what the senior here has been wanting to do for the last few months, right?"

Van Noor did not smile at the joke. Tahl tore off his helmet and threw it aside before striding out across the moonlit roof after the MAA soldiers.

"Ryen, wait!" Van Noor called after him. "Ryen!"

"Who assaulted my soldier?" Tahl yelled as he walked across. "Which one of you attacked a prisoner in your custody?"

A few murmurs rippled through the ranks of the soldiers. Van Noor sent a warning order to Squad Jai, readying them to open fire.

"I did," the MAA captain snarled, walking back out to face Tahl, "and I…"

Tahl's fist flew up into the soldier's gut, connecting with a sickeningly audible thump and lifting him off his feet. The man seemed to hang on Tahl's fist for a moment as he gasped and wheezed before slipping down to his knees. With a crunch of bone, Tahl lashed his elbow out into the captain's jaw, sending him unconscious to the floor.

Rall's troopers moved forward, their carbines at the ready and aimed at the crowd of MAA soldiers. A few men put their hands up, others at the back were already leaving via the stairwell. Tahl reached over and reclaimed Rhona's plasma carbine from the prone MAA officer, before walking back to Owenne and Van Noor.

"Go on," Owenne said to the remaining soldiers, "disappear."

The MAA soldiers left the rooftop, leaving the Concord troopers alone. Rhona walked over to Owenne again, her expression fearful.

"I'm sorry for all of this, sir, I..."

"Shut up and go home," Owenne sighed. "Squad Jai will get you back."

"We're not all going?" Van Noor asked.

"Of course not! We've still got a job to do! And perhaps we'll do better with smaller numbers and less chance of being detected."

Van Noor waited until Rhona was out of earshot, leaving him with only Owenne and Tahl.

"Okay, enough of the shit, Owenne," he said in a half whisper. "What's going on here? You've been using naval assets to scan this planet for weeks. You abandoned a perfectly good defensive position at the Nienne Desert to bring us here. We're out on these seemingly random reconnaissance patrols, taking big risks to go nosing around parts of a map which aren't Concord. Something's going on."

Owenne narrowed his eyes and raised a pensive finger to his chin.

"Did I miss some big change where troopers are permitted to question higher level strategy, or am I right in believing your job is to do whatever I bloody well tell you to because I'm the mandarin here, and you are not?"

"Jyn," Van Noor had never heard Owenne's first name before Tahl used it. "We've known each other a long time. I know you well enough to know that whatever you're doing, you're doing it because you think it's best for the Concord. Now if you tell us, we might be able to help you more than we are at the moment."

Owenne turned his back and watched as Rall's troopers departed, leaving the mandarin with only Tahl and Van Noor. As the footsteps receded down the concrete stairwell, the silence of the night was broken only by the crackle of small arms fire somewhere in the city. Owenne turned back to face them.

"Have either of you ever heard of Embryo, in the context of Builder technology?"

Both men shook their heads.

"It will take too long to explain now," Owenne said, "but when we get back to the firebase, I shall tell you what I know. Something to look forward to. A rare session of openness from me whilst we watch the suns rise over a good bottle of something strong from that large house. But for now, just trust that I actually do know my arse form my elbow, and do as I say."

"Understood," Van Noor nodded, "let's get back to it."

SEVENTEEN

Firebase Ghia
Pariton District
Markov's Prize

L-Day plus 63

A small group of cattle resided some three or four fields down from the mansion outside the firebase entrance, and they were particularly vocal as the second sun peered over the horizon. Owenne stood on the balcony outside his suite on the second floor, swilling a glass of a pungeant, viscous amber liquid that he had found in the cellar a few days previously. His cap was discarded, but he still wore his long coat, covered in a liberal coating of grey dust from the night in the city ruins. Tahl leaned back on the shallow wall which ran around the balcony, made up of smooth pillars of white stone topped with immaculately cut slabs. He still wore his hyperlight armor but had jettisoned the top half, leaving his torso and arms clothed only in the black body glove which was worn beneath the armored plates. Van Noor had insisted on cleaning up after the night in the city and wore his immaculate barrack uniform, despite the close proximity to the city and the likelihood of the firebase suffering another, albeit largely ineffectual, bombardment from MAA or Ghar guns.

"So was it worth it?" Tahl asked, running a hand across his grimy face. "Are we any closer to achieving whatever it is you want to achieve?"

"We're a little closer," the mandarin replied pensively, "but not much."

"Come on then," Van Noor grunted, "time for the big reveal. What's the deal?"

"The deal," Owenne replied quietly, "is that you two will probably be very angry with me because there is a distinct chance that I am killing your men and women and putting everybody in danger for absolutely nothing."

Another of the curious, bulky animals in the fields to the east let out a hollow warble. Tahl winced and shook his head a little, a sign Van Noor had come to recognize as one of increasing fatigue.

"Enough of the false theatrics," Van Noor suppressed a yawn, "we get it. Owenne gone done something bad. We're forewarned. Go on, why are we here."

"Embryo," Owenne replied, "it's the archeological term for one of the first Builder remnant sites, possibly one of the most important. Scattered clues have been found over the last few decades, but nothing tangeable. Nothing definate. But if we could find the Embryo site, it might unlock so much of what we don't know about the Antarean gates. Why they shut down, maybe even how to delay or stop that. Maybe… some even think Embryo might hold the secrets behind how they were built in the first place."

Owenne grabbed the bottle of the fiery drink from the little table on the balcony and refilled his glass. He wordlessly offered it to Van Noor and Tahl. Van Noor shook his head. Tahl shoved his glass unceremoniously forward for a top up. After seeing Tahl uncharacteristically sink half his glass in one go, Van Noor changed his mind and filled his own again.

"So the upshot," Tahl said, "is that you think Markov's Prize is Embryo?"

"Yes."

"Why?"

"IMTel records only have fragments of the complete picture. Hundreds of wars over thousands of years of panhuman history have resulted in any clear, complete description of Embryo being completely lost or distorted. All we can hope to do is fit the pieces of the jigsaw together as best we can and try to work out what the picture is, based on with what we have. It's almost easier to work out where Embryo isn't rather than where it is, and that eliminates about ninety quantum of Antarean space. So really that only leaves a few thousand planets and a several centuries of searching. Easy, really."

"Without some crap lesson in astronavigation," Van Noor interjected, "what evidence do you have and why do you think it's Markov's Prize?"

"It's not as simple as narrowing it down to one sector of Antares," Owenne explained. "The clues point more to clusters of stars rather than actual coordinates. We know Embryo was on a planet with a breathable atmosphere and in a system with two suns."

"If Embryo dates back several millenia," Tahl said, "the last few thousands of years could have changed that atmosphere. That clue may well be out of date."

"It might, but given the stability of planetary atmospheres, the laws of probability are overwhelmingly in favor of nil significant change.

Other clues point to an isolated system with only one neighboring system. Like this one. Embryo was relatively close to its twin suns, giving it a hot atmosphere. Like this one. I could keep going, but the upshot is Markov's Prize ticks off every clue we have. But so have the last three planets I have investigated over the last twenty years. This could be it. It probably isn't. But I have to try. Any surviving records will be in the city center archives, and that's why we were patrolling there all night. I need to know what opposition we're facing around the archive library. Whatever is in there, it'll be on paper, or digitized if we're very lucky. Either way, I need to get in that building."

"Why push it now?" Van Noor grumbled. "We had a perfectly good position at Nienne. We could have defeated the Ghar. We could have taken over the planet and then you could have strolled right in there and read books to your heart's content, or whatever processor or generator you have that passes for a heart."

"I was more than content to wait, until the Freeborn turned up. The Ghar? Those war hungry idiots are only here to use Markov's Prize as a stepping stone to the next Antarean Gate so they can enslave and kill more people. Our crossing paths is an unhappy coincidence. But the Freeborn? No, not a chance. They know why I'm here. They have ambitions of their own. I can't let them beat me to that building. And now that the Ghar have it, I can't let some stray bomb or missile destroy it. Now I know the MAA are using subterranean tunnels to travel under the city, I'm even more concerned. Time is not my ally."

"That's all well and good," Tahl spoke again, "but some things still confuse me. First off, why all the secrecy? Why not tell us the plan? Second – why one building? This planet was advanced enough to network its information."

"Look, I wouldn't expect a pair of gun toting thugs like you to understand the intricacies of what is at stake here!" Owenne snapped. "It might not be this building, I don't know! But if this planet's scientists had no idea of the importance of Embryo – and judging by what I've researched so far, they most certainly did not – then networking and backing up some ancient paper archives hidden in a draw somewhere wouldn't be top of their priority list! They did't even know what was right under their noses! It should be obvious, even to the two of you, why this is so important and why there is a real need for secrecy! If this site is here, right under our noses, it could unlock secrets which the Concord could use to alter billions of lives for the better!"

"Could it," Tahl folded his arms, "or is that speculation?"

"It's an educated guess," Owenne admitted, "but a highly, highly educated one. One I am willing to bet on."

"But you're betting the lives of Concord soldiers," Van Noor said.

"Yes. Yes, I am. And I don't do it lightly. I don't care for your troopers, but I do value them. I value them greatly. And I don't want to waste them. So why the secrecy? Because I'm rolling a die, gentlemen. I'm taking a gamble with no concrete evidence. But if it pays off? The conflict of the Seventh Age is all but over. The PanHuman Concord wins. If the Freeborn find Embryo? The technology goes to the highest bidder, eventually to both us and the Isorians, and the conflict continues. Worse still, if the Isorians find it? The Concord is finished."

Color began to seep into the world as the suns rose higher. A gentle morning breeze brought a wave of warm air across the balcony, rustling the leaves of the trees surrounding the huge house.

"This is crap," Van Noor spat. "Do you realize just how many 'what ifs' and 'maybes' and 'potentiallys' you're basing your assumptions on? We should be taking the war to the Isorians with proven facts, not hoping for a miracle by throwing the ball to the far end of the field and hoping somebody is there to catch it! This is nuts! Lunacy!"

"And that's why I didn't tell you," Owenne replied, his tone defensive, "and that's why I'm giving you a clear and direct order not to tell anybody else. Go on, Killer, you say your piece, too."

Tahl stood up straight and looked across at the other two men.

"Tell me there is a significant chance this would actually mean something," he finally said. "Give me your word, Owenne."

"What?" Van Noor spat. "Come on, Ryen! Use your head! We deal in facts, not mad schemes!"

"I give you my word," Owenne said seriously, "I've spent my entire life following this trail. All of the joking aside, I trust you to fight and kill because you are better at it than I am. Please, trust me to do the thinking and the calculations. If this is Embryo – and I think it is – and one of the research facilities which was instrumental in creating the very gates themselves is here, on this planet, this will add more to the stability and security of the Concord than anything we've ever seen, in our generation."

"Then I'm in," Tahl nodded. "Bry and I won't say anything. To anybody. We'll support you as best we can."

***

Feeling weariness sinking in after a full night on patrol, Tahl clambered slowly through the access door of the Duke transport drone and sank down into the nearest seat. Owenne had ordered him to the Assault Force HQ, to report directly to Commander-in-Chief Diette. The reason was twofold; mainly to pass on the details they had learned during the night regarding the MAA and Freeborn forces they had encountered, but also to finalize the details of the Commander-in-Chief's visit to the 44th Strike Formation for the presentation of medals.

Two soldiers had been selected for award, and one of them was in his own company. Following Owenne's recommendation, Rhona was to be awarded the Concord Silver Cross for leading the assault on the Ghar defensive positions outside Pariton.

Tahl winked the sleep out of his eyes as he fastened his seat restraint before taking his beret off and tucking it into one of the epaulettes of his shirt. It was good to be out of armor, even momentarily, as with all of the ergonomics and temperature control in the world it was still bulky and unnatural to wear. The doors to the Duke began to slide shut until a hurried shout to stop was issued and a hand bolted through the doorway to stop them. Rhona vaulted through the door and offered Tahl a quick smile before sitting down opposite him. The doors locked shut and the Duke raised itself to a hover with a barely detectable tremor before yawing around and setting off toward Assault Force HQ.

"You lost?" Tahl asked.

He noticed that her facial wound had been treated and was now fully healed. As petty as it seemed, he was glad he had taken down the perpetrator.

"Mandarin Owenne said I should visit HQ," Rhona replied, tipping her beret stylishly to the back of her head in flagrant disregard of C3 regulations on standards and military bearing. "I figured now was as good a time as any. He still wants me to leave the strike corps and go join Intelligence."

"You going to?"

"Nah. Sir."

"You sure? It's infinitely safer and it's a quicker path to promotion," Tahl offered.

He tried his best to sound sincere, as it was the best course of action open to Rhona, even if he did not want her to take it.

"I'm sure, Boss," Rhona replied, "it's not for me. Look... I'm real sorry about last night. About ignoring you and running off and getting into trouble. I honestly didn't mean to ignore you, it wasn't a conscious decision. I just got caught up in the moment and gave chase. I'm sorry, sir, I didn't mean to be disrespectful or anything."

Tahl rubbed his eyes and stopped himself from blurting out the first response that leapt to mind. The response that she should drop the formalities. Van Noor was right – this was a disaster. When did 'sir' stop? Should it? This was a subordinate who he might have to order to her death. Would working in intelligence change that? Would it make a personal relationship viable and not break any regulations? But then again, a personal relationship was a ridiculous idea, C3 aside. Tahl grew up in a system where a man and a woman married and stayed together for the two or three centuries of their life, perhaps another two or three if they chose to renew their vows after jumping into their clone bodies. But Rhona was from a place where personal relationships and sex were two entirely different things, where a dozen partners was no sign of infidelity and certainly would have no impact on a marriage. That could never work. Rhona was the sort of girl who Tahl's mother had told him to have something casual with, to get it out of his system before he found the right one. That was, of course, back when Tahl's mother spoke to him more than two or three times per year.

"Boss?" Rhona leaned forward, fixing her dark eyes on his. "You okay?"

"You don't need to apologize," Tahl said quietly, frantically searching for the right things to say and a way to extricate himself from the mess he had created and was solely responsible for. "You made a mistake, that's all. It was unintentional and it was justifiable in the situation. I wouldn't be much of a boss if I punished you for that. Just learn from it. I make mistakes all the time, you know that better than anybody."

Rhona's look of concern for him turned to something more defensive.

"What d'you mean by that, exactly?"

"You know what I mean. This, us... I screwed up. My job is to get you through campaigns, alive and in one piece, same as every other soldier in this company. My job isn't to put pressure on you and mess around with your feelings. I've got to stop it."

"Nah, you don't, sir," Rhona shook her head.

"This isn't about work, this is about us. Drop the 'sir.'"

"I kinda like the rank gradient," Rhona flashed a smile. "It turns me on."

"Could you be serious for just a second?"

"I'm sorry, Ryen," Rhona shrugged. "Go on, I'm listening."

"I... I don't know what I was saying now, I've lost where I was."

Rhona slipped off her seat harness and took the single step across the cramped passenger hold to sit on Tahl's lap, her legs straddling his and her arms around his neck.

"You were saying something about me being a mistake, right?"

"Right," Tahl said weakly, his resolve failing.

"That's guilt," Rhona said, "what you're saying right now is because you feel guilty about doing morally the wrong thing, and you're scared about being found out and breaking regulations an' all that crap. You've done nothing wrong, I told you that before. Believe me, I know what I'm doing, and I don't need you to protect my feelings or make my mind up for me. I'm kinda good at doing that myself. So that's that done. And as for breaking regs? Yeah. If we get found out, we're screwed. But I really like that. How far is it to HQ?"

"What? Another half hour, I guess?" Tahl stumbled on his words.

"Cool," Rhona said, unbuttoning her shirt, "because I've got a great idea about how we can kill some time and how I can prove that I'm worth the risk."

***

Firebase Ghia Accomodation
Pariton District
Markov's Prize

L-Day plus 63

The room shook again, a little more violently this time, still not much, but enough to shake a few small piles of dust from the top of the light fittings. Rechter glanced up at the lights from where he lay on his bunk. He was glad of the shard connection, the feeling of indifference which flowed over him from the more experienced soldiers in the squad accommodation area. Without that connection, he had little doubt that his niggling sensation of fear would be full blown terror. He looked back down at his datapad and continued to compose a message to his wife, his thoughts appearing as words on the screen as soon as he had mentally confirmed them.

"It's not so bad now," Clythe continued his conversation from where he sat in the center of the squad's communal area. "When the Ghar first arrived, they had those horrific, great battlesuits everywhere. That was bad enough. On top of that, they also had..."

"Plasma amplifiers," Meibal folded her arms from her position stood bolt upright in the center of the room. "Yes, I know. I studied the intelligence reports."

"It's rude to interrupt," Clythe said with great deliberation. "Where was I? Yes, the Ghar had loads more suits, and plasma amplifiers, which made life a lot harder. I'm not saying they're easy now, but the job certainly seems a lot more achievable than it did when they first arrived."

"How do you find the Ghar compared to other armies you've faced?" Losse asked from where he sat on a wide sofa on the other side of the communal area as the room shook again from another shell exploding somewhere above their heads.

"Dunno, really," Clythe admitted, "I've only faced the planetary defenders and the Ghar. This is my first planetary assault."

"Your first!" Meibal spat. "And here you are, holding court like some sort of veteran! I thought you'd seen more action than that, the way you carry yourself! How long have you been on the frontline?"

"About two months," Clythe shrugged indifferently.

"Two months!" Meibal repeated. "Why, we'll be just as experienced as you in…"

"Approximately two months, I should imagine," Sessetti remarked dryly from where he lay on his bunk, idly flicking through the articles of a music holozine which was displayed in the space above him.

"Given how many people we've lost, I reckon a couple of months facing the Ghar is worth multiple time," Clythe said. "What d'you reckon, Varl?"

Varlton looked up from where he was preparing snacks in the small kitchenette in the corner of the room.

"Yeah, I reckon. I've been qualified for a year or so and the Ghar are certainly the toughest thing I've faced. But like you said, more so at the start of a campaign. They seem to lose momentum as soon as their logistics dry up, although racing their scutters is good fun if you ever get the chance. The Isorians, on the other hand, they're a bunch of real bastards. They don't let up. They don't play fair either with all their stealth and cloaking and sniper rifles. Still, I'd rather take my chances against them than the Ghar. At least the Isorians treat their prisoners well, by all accounts."

A deep thump sounded from directly above and the lights extinguished for a brief moment, replaced by the dull blue of the emergency lighting system until the primary lighting restored.

"That was a close one," Varlton remarked as he sat back down on the sofa. "Good thing we've had time to get a subterranean vehicle park built now, or I reckon that would have been the end of a drone or two."

Rechter finished his message and posted it in the shard's pending bin, ready to be transmitted across the cosmos to his wife, light years away, as soon as external communications were restored. He thought of her, carrying on with life and preparing for a vocation as a school teacher. The closest they had been to real disruption to their plans had been when a trial run had been carried out at some of the local schools whereby children were taught by educator drones alone, without any panhuman interaction whatsoever. Fortunately the trial's results were less than impressive and, as many had theorized, the benefits of receiving education via traditional panhuman interaction were, in many parts of the syllabus for many subjects, irreplaceable. This allowed Rila to continue to pursue her long-term ambition of working with children. That had been the closest to real disruption, the closest until C3 selected Rechter for military service. Even with all of the positivity toward his current predicament provided the company shard, Rechter hoped that this was temporary. Very temporary.

"It's a shame that the strike captain was not happy for us to accompany him and the mandarin on that patrol last night," Meibal said, "I'd imagine that would have been quite an experience."

"You desperate to get your head blown off?" Varlton exclaimed. "Just chill out. You'll be spoiled for opportunities to get shot at sooner than you think."

"I want to make an early impression," Meibal declared confidently. "I've never settled for second place in anything I've done, and I don't intend to start now. The intelligence briefs on this planet's military say that their higher ranks – their officers – are selected based on education and are given rank from the outset. It makes me wonder if we should be adopting a similar system, rather than forcing us all to start our careers at the very bottom as mere troopers."

"If you knew your history," Sessetti intervened from his cubicle again, "which clearly you don't, you'd be aware of the fact that in ages past, that system was the norm rather than the exception. C3 is aware of it, but we do things this way for a reason. It works better. Rank is given out solely on merit and experience. If you're as good as you keep saying you are, you needn't worry. You'll be a strike commander this time next week."

Varlton and Clythe burst out laughing. Meibal's face reddened and Rechter felt her anger and humiliation through the shard, alongside the mirth from everybody else. He wondered if his sympathy for her would filter through to the others as he watched her storm off to her cubicle and shut the door behind her.

***

17ᵗʰ Assault Force Headquarters
Approximately one hundred kiloyan west of Pariton
Markov's Prize

L-Day plus 64

The ranks of strike troopers stood smartly to attention in the midmorning sunshine. All six companies of the 44ᵗʰ Strike Formation had been moved to the Assault Force HQ, giving them a brief two days out of the frontline whilst other units held the defensive positions around Firebase Ghia. The six companies of the 44ᵗʰ – each at approximately half strength – stood in their green barrack uniforms in blocks of three ranks, each block made up of the forty to fifty troopers in each of the six companies. The HQ itself had been set up in another town hall – the norm, it appeared, during this campaign. The old town hall consisted of two wings extending out from a central clock tower, each wing being three floors high. The town square which sprawled out in front of the grand building was dominated by a tall column in the center, atop of which was a statue of a military hero atop a riding animal of some description from an age gone by. At each end of the square was an ornamental sculpture, surrounded by neatly cut yellow flowers.

Van Noor stood at ease next to Tahl at the front and center of Beta Company, facing the east wing of the town hall. A small command group stood in front of each company; Ghia Company was the most well-placed with a strike captain, senior strike leader, and two troopers. Alpha Company had only their senior strike leader; everybody else from the command team was dead.

The main doors to the town hall swung open and Commander-in-Chief Diette, along with four officers of his entourage, paced to the center of the wide stairs leading down to the square. Primary Strike Leader Jayne, the 44th's highest ranking strike leader, bellowed out a command, traditionally via a loud shout rather than through the shard. Van Noor could not make out the wording from this range, but he, like every other trooper, knew the meaning of the command and stood smartly to attention.

Diette stood at the top of the stairs, his hands clasped behind his back as he looked down on the men and women of the 44th.

"This campaign," he began, his voice clear through the shard as if he were stood only a few paces in front of Van Noor, "is all but over. Whilst you have been taking the brunt of the Ghar assault on the frontlines, the enemy supply lines have been cut by our comrades in the 12th Assault Force. Whilst the fight against the Ghar has swung in our favor, the local defenders who continue to oppose us have been reduced to a handful of isolated, combat ineffective units. They are surrendering in increasing numbers with each passing day. The Freeborn mercenaries who have attempted to capitalize on this fight for their own ends are badly outnumbered and have backed the wrong side. We anticipate victory in the next few days.

"This victory is due to the combined efforts of every element of both the 17th and the 12th Assault Forces, working seamlessly in unity. Every element of the two assault forces has been vital, but you, the men and women of the 44th Strike Formation, have been front and center for the entire campaign. You have gained the most ground, neutralized the largest number of enemy forces and, sadly, you have suffered the greatest number of Concord casualties in this campaign."

The senior officer paused for effect, his hands clasped behind his back as his grey eyes scanned across the assembled soldiers.

"But this has not been in vain. Another planet enters Concord care and with it, millions of people will see an exponential increase in quality of life. This would not have been possible without your sacrifice. When this campaign is over, the 17th Assault Force will be dissolved and the 44th Strike Formation will be assigned to a new force, along with every other formation. I may be moving on, but should the 44th ever find its way under the command of a force I am leading in the future, I'll always know that the 44th is a unit which never gives in, always stands firm, and have proven its members to be the pride of the strike corps."

Diette took a step back and nodded to Jayne. The silence was only broken by the planet's flag which rippled in the wind atop the clock tower. Van Noor had always found the silence following formal addresses to the troops to be rather uncomfortable. Sometimes a lot of heart and soul seemed to go into these speeches, and a round of applause felt appropriate. However, that was thoroughly unmilitary, and so the three hundred men and women remained rigidly and silently stood to attention.

"What do you think of that?" Van Noor asked Tahl through the company command shard, hoping the network was not being monitored at formation level.

"Pretty good. I've heard better, but I've certainly heard a lot worse."

"Yeah, I'd give that speech a seven out of ten," Van Noor remarked as Diette's entourage waked down to the foot of the stairs.

The strike captain commanding Ghia Company marched out to meet the staff officers, stamping to attention before them and snapping up a smart salute. Diette returned the salute and a brief, inaudible conversation took place before Jayne addressed the entire strike formation through the shard.

"Presentation of award. Strike Trooper Dian Vortez. On L-Day plus 39, whilst operating in the Nienne Desert, Squad Jai of Ghia Company advanced to engage a Ghar assault force. In the ensuing combat, Squad Jai was eliminated by heavy enemy fire, save Strike Trooper Vortez, who lost a hand. Cauterizing his wound, Vortez proceeded to recover the dead and wounded of his squad, running into heavy fire on six occasions with no support, despite being heavily wounded. Vortez's actions resulted in three strike troopers being evacuated to a medical facility quickly enough to save their lives. For his selfless actions in the face of a determined enemy, Strike Trooper Vortez is awarded the C3 Service Medal, Second Class. Strike Trooper Vortez!"

Vortez marched out from his squad at the call of his name, both his original arm and his newly cloned hand swinging smartly. He came to a stop in front of the commander-in-chief and saluted. The two exchanged words for several moments until Diette pinned the medal on Vortez's uniform. The two again exchanged salutes before the trooper marched back to his place in line. Jayne continued with the award announcements.

"Strike Leader Katya Rhona. On L-Day plus 58, Beta Company

was ordered to assault a heavily fortified enemy position on the outskirts of Pariton. Strike Leader Rhona led a two squad assault across open ground in the center of the enemy defenses. With one squad falling as casualties, Rhona continued the advance and destroyed a Ghar battlesuit with heavy weapon which had halted the advance. Having already been wounded and with half of her squad having fallen to enemy fire, Rhona took her squad's plasma lance and led a second attack on an enemy gun position. She was again wounded, but led her squad on a third assault where she neutralized a second gun, allowing the Concord assault to continue and ultimately succeed. For demonstrating leadership and courage in the face of enemy fire, Strike Leader Rhona is awarded the Concord Silver Cross. Strike Leader Rhona!"

Van Noor watched as Rhona marched out to meet the commander-in-chief. Her uniform immaculate, her movements smart and soldierly, Van Noor felt proud to have her in his company for the first time. He felt that same pride replicated many times over through the company shard. The same procedure of saluting, small talk, pinning on the medal and marching back in line was repeated until Jayne yelled for the company to dismiss. The troopers turned to the right as one and marched a pace forward before then filtering off into small groups as the buzz of conversation swept across the town square. Van Noor watched as Rhona and Vortez were ushered back to Diette, whilst a drone recorded the event in video capture and stills for the formation archives, as well as the media back home, no doubt.

Strike Commander Orless, the 44th's commanding officer, made his way over to Tahl and Van Noor.

"Morning gents," he greeted crisply. "Strike Captain – good to see you looking smart and presentable. If you turn up to HQ again looking like you did yesterday, you'll be sorry you did."

"Yes, sir," Tahl replied.

"I expect the highest standards of dress and military bearing from my company commanders, Ryen, not turning up to brief the commander-in-chief looking like they've been dragged through a hedge backward. Don't let it happen again."

"Sir," Tahl nodded as Orless walked away.

Van Noor turned to face the younger man. It was completely unheard of for Tahl to let his standards fall, even when he had been broken, shot, and stabbed. Even more confusing, Van Noor could sense no remorse or embarrassment through the company command shard, only a sort of smug amusement.

"What the hell was that about?" Van Noor demanded as the soldiers on the square fragmented into small groups and departed in different directions.

"Long story," Tahl shrugged. "Just had a surprisingly interesting journey to HQ yesterday. Shall we go find somewhere to get a drink?"

"Yeah, alright," Van Noor nodded.

He looked across at where Diette stood in front of the town hall, flanked by the two medal recipients as the drone hovered in front of them to take pictures. Rhona glanced across at Tahl. There was a look between them. Van Noor took a sharp intake of breath. It all made sense. Tahl was not over her at all. And what was worse, judging by the look he had just seen, Rhona completely reciprocated. Van Noor turned to Tahl and opened his mouth to speak, but then he stopped.

His first thoughts were that he felt betrayed that Tahl had hidden everything from him. But the momentary feelings of hurt were quickly replaced by disappointment, wondering why Tahl had not trusted him and what he could have done to have been more approachable, to be a better friend.

"You alright?" Tahl asked.

Van Noor nodded. His job was not to reprimand his friend. His job was to pretend he knew nothing about what was going on, and do everything in his power to cover up and stop anybody else finding out.

***

Owenne grumbled a few curses under his breath as he followed Diette across the town square. The suns were high, and despite the ultraviolet radiation blocker which was programmed into his nanosphere, the dry, prickly heat still irked him. Most of the troopers had dispersed now to take advantage of a few hours away from the frontline; only the squads of the two medal recipients had been held back at Diette's insistence.

"They seemed like a good bunch," the commander-in-chief remarked to Owenne as they walked across from Vortez's squad to Rhona's. "Morale seems high. Perhaps there's enough fight left in these men and women for one more planetary assault."

"I wouldn't, if I were you," Owenne warned. "Probably better to end on a high rather than to have to explain why you lost an entire assault force when you pushed them past breaking point."

"You stick to your technology and nanospheres," Diette gave a warning smile. "I'll do the people management."

Diette and Owenne arrived at where Rhona stood by her squad of six troopers. She turned and called them to attention, but Diette held up a hand to stop the formalities.

"Never mind that, never mind," he smiled. "Come on, don't stand to attention, gather round."

The seven troopers formed a loose semi circle around Diette and Owenne. Owenne took the opportunity to quickly read the service records of the other soldiers and learn their names for the tediously inevitable conversation which would follow.

"So you're the lot who charged up a hill and knocked the Ghar off the top," Diette nodded in approval. "Good, good. They can wrap themselves up in their tin suits as much as they want to, they're still no match for old fashioned panhuman courage and ingenuity."

"Strike Troopers Sessetti and Clythe were with me on the day, sir," Rhona said quietly. "Strike Trooper Varlton was brought across to bolster the squad after our casualties. Strike Troopers Rechter, Meibal, and Losse have just joined us from training."

"Strike Trooper Meibal, sir," a youthful, dark skinned woman stepped forward to introduce herself before Diette could speak again. "I graduated top of my class in all elements of training."

Owenne suppressed a smile as he connected with the squad shard and felt a wave of resentment surge forward from at least half of the troopers. He could not help himself and turned to the woman to address her.

"Well, with the best training available, it's still no substitute for the real thing. So probably best you stay quiet and try to hang on the pearls of wisdom from the soldiers who actually have seen combat, eh?" Owenne leaned forward and flashed a smile at her.

"No, no!" Diette held a hand up again. "You can only assess a soldier on the opportunities they have been presented with, and it's not fair to discount Strike Trooper Meibal just because she hasn't had the opportunities of some of the more experienced here. I too came top of my class in training, so perhaps there's a budding commander-in-chief in you yet!"

"Yes, sir!" Meibal beamed.

"It was Sessetti and Clythe who were with me on the day, sir," Rhona repeated.

"Good, good effort all round," Diette said, standing in front of Clythe. "You did a grand job supporting your leader. Won't be long before you've got a squad of your own."

"Thanks, sir, but not for me," Clythe said politely. "I'm just in for as long as C3 wants me, I'm not a lifer or anything. Glad to be a part of this, sir, but I've got a life waiting for me back home."

"Fair enough," the commander-in-chief nodded, "takes all sorts. Same for you, Strike Trooper?"

Sessetti paused before replying to the question which had been aimed his way.

"No, sir," Sessetti said firmly. "I'll stay with the strike corps for as long as it'll have me."

"Good!" Diette beamed.

"What?" Clythe turned to face Sessetti. "What about the band?"

"This is a discussion for a bit later on, guys," Rhona dashed across to stand in between Diette and her soldiers. "May I escort you and Mandarin Owenne to the town hall for a drink, sirs?"

"Probably best," Owenne grinned. "Looks like this one might kick off a bit! After you, Strike Leader!"

EIGHTEEN

Firebase Ghia
Pariton District
Markov's Prize

L-Day plus 66

Tahl lay back on his bunk and stared up at the ceiling of his room, taking in every detail of the sterile, white syncast plates as his mind raced over the last few weeks. He had badly wanted to believe the commander-in-chief's speech at the town hall, that the Ghar were on their last legs and that this would soon be over. Tahl had not seen a shred of evidence to support any hypothesis other than that of the Ghar being dug in and set for the long haul, prepared to fight long and hard to take Markov's Prize and then leap to the next world for plunder. But even if and when the Concord were successful, then what? Onto the next planet, and the next after that. Assuming he survived, the day would come when he could go home, but there was no home to go to. A father who had disowned him and a mother who barely tolerated him.

"You're looking thoughtful," Rhona said from where she lay with her head on his shoulder. "D'you ever just declutch that brain and coast, instead of thinking all the time?"

Tahl looked across at her and shrugged in apology. Only the bed sheet which lay across them clothed them both, and it was nearly dawn up in the world above.

"Just glad the ceiling isn't shaking with enemy artillery for once," Tahl said as he looked up again. "You know, because of our overreliance on technology, they can find our bases and bombard us easier than..."

Rhona lay back and ran her hands over her body.

"Oh, tell me more about artillery strike coordination, sir, it gets me so hot!"

"I'm sorry," Tahl smiled, "I shouldn't be talking about anything related to work."

"It's not for me, it's for you," Rhona propped her head up on one hand next to him. "I just think you need to chill out more. I guess I just wonder what you'll do when this is all over."

"I was just wondering the same thing," Tahl admitted.

He momentarily considered asking her about what their future was but pushed the thought away almost instantly. He knew what this was – a casual, physical fling between two single people to act as a distraction from the terrible situations they faced every day. He needed to be grateful for what he had, no matter how fleeting it was.

"What'll you do when you can go home?"

"I only think one day ahead!" Rhona smiled slyly.

"Why?"

Her smile faded away.

"It gets me down," she admitted. "I don't wanna get all serious, but I haven't really planned surviving my military service."

"Why not?" Tahl sat up.

"Just... people like you make it to the end of movies. Not people like me."

"Real life is very different, though," Tahl said, confused at the analogy. "You've got to go into this all with some optimism."

"It's not pessimism, it's just... acceptance," Rhona shrugged, "and I'm cool with it. I've made my peace."

"What about your brother back home?" Tahl said.

"He's only just talking to me again. We kinda fell out. It was my fault. Yeah, definitely my fault."

"What happened?" Tahl asked.

"Doesn't matter," Rhona winced, "you wouldn't wanna hear. Jeez... I can't win this. If I don't tell you then it seems like I don't want to talk to you, but if I do tell you..."

"You don't have to tell me," Tahl smiled, "I know what this is between us. You don't owe me anything, you don't have to talk to me about personal things. I'm not putting pressure on you."

"You see, that's exactly the problem. You think you know me, but you don't. You think you know what goes on inside my head because you judge me based on the persona I project, but that projection is a lie. A front. I never told you that what's going on between us is meaningless to me, you just assumed it. You just assumed I'll finish with you and move on to the next guy."

"Okay," Tahl conceded, "tell me what happened between you and your brother."

Rhona's face dropped.

"Aw... crap," she sighed, "this is literally the worst personal anecdote I have to prove my point. Okay, I'd just qualified as a strike trooper and I had a couple of weeks leave before shipping out. I went to spend my time with my brother at his college. I spent two weeks drinking and partying, and I slept with two of his best friends. They both found out, they had a big fight over me, and it all got very messy."

"And here was me thinking you were a nun," Tahl risked a smile.

"You're not making this easy for me. Look, I made a big mistake and I learned from it. I learned that what was acceptable behavior back where I'm from is not acceptable here. That was, like, a year ago, and you're my first guy since. The point is, you've assumed this means nothing to me."

"Isn't that better for you?" Tahl lay back down again and looked back at the ceiling. "Doesn't it put less pressure on..."

"Stop with the pressure!" Rhona interrupted, her voice sounding hurt and serious for the first time. "Let me decide what I want to do! You're trying to be open minded and accepting of my culture's customs when you really don't have to. Yeah, people are a lot more open about sex where I'm from but that hardly means I can't control myself! Where you're from, a physical relationship is something special between two people that means something. I get that. I respect it. It's something I'm pretty sure I'm capable of doing."

"I don't get what you're saying," Tahl sat up again. "You're saying that this isn't just a casual fling and this means something to you?"

"Yes!" Rhona exclaimed. "Jeez, you're as bad as that mandarin sometimes! Look, I've never done the whole relationship deal before, but you're the first person I've ever met that makes me want to try."

"Why?"

"Because! You're just looking for compliments now," Rhona sat up on the edge of the bunk and turned her back on him, folding her arms. "Because... you got dragged away from the life you were supposed to have, and now you're all alone. You never complain about it, you just get on and do it. You're the only person I've ever met who I think can really understand what it's like to feel straight out of luck and that every road you take ends up further from the life you were supposed to have. You're the only guy I've met who I can relate to."

Tahl sat behind her and embraced her for a few moments until she pried herself away and recovered her clothes from the floor.

"We're out of time," Rhona said as she pulled her uniform on, her back still to him. "I gotta go get my squad together. We're moving out in less than an hour."

"Right," Tahl nodded, at a loss for words.

Rhona finished dressing herself by pulling on her boots and tying her hair back into a ponytail before turning to face him. He could see that she had been crying.

"I've got to go get suited up," she said coolly, her even voice in direct contrast to her tear glistening eyes. "Just... stop second guessing me, okay? I know your customs, I'm not going to go upsetting you by screwing around with other guys. Just show some trust in me. Maybe forever will work out, I don't know. The odds are stacked against us. But let's at least try."

By the time Tahl had mentally worded his apology and how to tell her that he felt the same, she had already gone.

***

"One of the other guys," Sessetti told Rechter and Losse as he ran his diagnostic tool over the armored plates of his suit, "told me to always go for the most obvious parts to look for damage. The maintenance drones are programmed to spend longer searching out the cracks and internals, not the surfaces."

Eager to learn, Rechter ran his own diagnostics tool over the plates of his armor as Sessetti showed him. The three sat down in the center of the communal area, clad in their body gloves as they carried out last minute checks on their arms and armor.

"If you're not ready by now, you never will be," Clythe said dismissively from where he lay on his bunk. "You'd be wiser spending your time chilling out rather than getting worked up over nothing."

"You'd be wiser spending your time getting the latest updates from the Formation Intelligence Cell," Meibal added from where she sat on the edge of her bunk with a datapad. "There are updates coming in all of the time."

"Let me guess," Varlton offered from where he stood in the corner of the room by the food dispenser, "capital city full of Ghar, MAA, and Freeborn? One of them has attacked the other and exchanged marginal territorial gains for a few casualties? Same thing we're about to go do?"

"You heard the commander-in-chief," Meibal replied, "this is the last big push. We're right at the end."

Varlton laughed and let out a low groan.

"Oh, jeez! Every commander in every army, since the first poor sods fixed bayonets to the end of their guns in some mudhole thousands of years ago have been spinning that ridiculous lie!"

"Diette also said you could be a commander-in-chief someday, so we know he's a liar," Clythe offered.

"Ignore him, Mabe," Sessetti smiled to Meibal, "you do whatever you think is best to prepare yourself. Reading intelligence reports sounds as good an idea as any to me."

The door to the communal area opened and Rhona rushed through, still clad in her barrack uniform.

"Morning, dudes," she smiled, "ready to go win the war?"

"Where've you been?" Varlton asked. "We're supposed to be at five minutes' notice!"

"I'm a bit behind schedule because I spent I spent a night of passion with my secret lover," Rhona winked as she pulled off her shirt.

"Yeah, funny," Varlton grimaced. "Come on and get ready. We'll get the call to saddle up any second now."

"Preferably within the confines of your own cubicle," Meibal added. "I don't want to see you prancing around in your underwear, again."

"I kind of have to," Rhona shrugged, "as part of my duties as squad leader, morale is top of the agenda. These guys are about to go into combat, so showing them some leg is the least I can do."

"What's the most?" Varlton asked.

"Yeah," Losse piped up, "jokes about your secret lover aside, are you single?"

Rechter looked across at Losse.

"That's pretty direct," he commented.

Rhona smirked as she took her body glove from its stowage and quickly inspected it for damage.

"No, I've got a guy," she said after a pause.

"What?" Clythe sat up on his bunk. "You've never mentioned that before! Why'd you never say anything?"

"It's personal," Rhona said as she pulled on her body glove and fitted her breastplate over her torso, "I like to keep some things to myself."

"Says the woman who spends ninety quantum of her time in her underwear surrounded by hormonal men," Meibal muttered.

"Jeez, what is it with women in this squad?" Rhona shook her head as she fitted her leg plates. "First Rae, then Jem, now you. I ain't apologizing for being this hot, girl. None of the guys ever complain. Just get over it and move on."

"Stop changing the subject," Varlton said. "Who's this guy of yours?"

Rhona looked down and paused, tapping one of her shoulder plates absentmindedly against one hand before smiling softly and fitting it.

"He's about my age," she answered, "he's taller than me, he's tough when he needs to be, and soft the rest of the time. And we nearly understand each other. Nearly. We're getting there."

The room fell silent for a few moments.

"I'm glad for you, Kat," Varlton smiled, tapping her on the shoulder.

"Maybe tell us what's going on next time," Clythe suggested. "There's enough secrecy going on around here as it is."

Sessetti stood up and let out a sigh.

"Oh, change the track, would you? I'm sick of hearing this same

254 Beyond the Gates of Antares

song now."

Clythe leapt off his bunk and paced out to stand in front of Sessetti.

"At least the song from me is consistent," he growled. "You just lead people on and then drop them with no warning! Out of the blue!"

"I don't have to answer to you!" Sessetti snapped. "I'll do what the hell I want!"

"That's you through and through, isn't it? You selfish prick!" Clythe shouted, shoving Sessetti in the chest.

Sessetti's fist lashed out and connected with Clythe's jaw, snapping his head and sending him reeling. With a chorus of shouts, Varlton and Rhona leapt forward and stood in between the two.

"You two, pack that in!" Rhona yelled, shoving both soldiers apart. "What the hell is this all about?"

"It's about that dumb bastard insisting on clinging on my coat tails for the rest of his life!" Sessetti shouted.

Clythe sank back on his bunk and hung his head, blood dripping from his split lip.

"Lian, sit down and shut up!" Rhona bellowed. "You wait right there! Don't go anywhere!"

Rhona walked into Clythe's cubicle and shut the door behind them.

***

Clythe had never looked so pathetic to Rhona. She folded her arms and looked down at where he sat silently, unable to look up and meet her piercing stare.

"Go on. Explain that crap away."

Clythe let out a long sigh.

"All my life," he began, "I've been in his shadow. His parents were more popular than mine, he did better at school, he did better at sports, everything. He was the cool one who the girls liked, I was the loud mouthed, lippy friend. He's right, I've spent my whole life clinging to his coat tails. This band was everything to me. I'm not dumb, I know we're never going to be famous. But it made me happy. Playing music made me happy, and he's like a brother to me. The whole point in us invading other poor bastards' planets is to get them onboard with the IMTel so they can do what they want. What about me? All I want to do is be in a band and play music. I'm not asking much! I want to tour places with my friends, see different worlds, give strangers a great night out when they come to see us. But instead I'm stuck here in the military in a war against some huge bastard metal suits, fighting for a planet whose people hate us. And I've got a bad feeling about this next one. I've lucked in so far, but you know, I think it's my turn now. And... this wasn't what was supposed to happen."

Rhona exhaled slowly before sitting down next to him. She put an arm around his shoulders and pulled his head against her neck, like she used to do with her little brother.

"You'll be okay, dude," she said gently. "I don't think you've run out of luck. You know what I think? I think we're owed some good luck after the last few weeks. I think that poor old Gant, Jem, and Qan used up our bad luck for us, and now we'll be okay. I also think that if we were back home, all sat together with drinks and looking up at the stars, this wouldn't be so bad. We're about to go into combat again and the whole world seems bad. I feel the same way too. I feel sick, I'm so scared, despite what the suit is pumping into me to stop it. But dude, you don't need Lian as a crutch. You're your own guy. You're not his shadow. Let him chase his plan here, and you go home and chase your dream. If he isn't the right guy to share it with, you go find the right people and make your own band. You've got two hundred years to get it right. So see your part in this dumb war through, and then leave it behind."

Clythe remained silent, dabbing at his lip from time to time.

"You okay?" Rhona asked after a long silence.

"Yeah, I'm good, big sis," Clythe stood up slowly. "Thanks. I mean it. I'm not going to fix anything now, so I might as well just face what's ahead of me. I'll come up with a plan when we get back, I guess."

Rhona stood up and forced a smile for him, despite the fear and hollowness inside. There was so much left unresolved in her mind and at best, the next few days would force her to leave it all remaining unresolved. At worst, she would be killed. Rhona opened the door back to the communal area and gestured for Clythe to go out first.

"Get out of here, you bonehead," she sighed, clipping him around the back of his head as he walked past, before she then pointed to Sessetti.

"C'mon, you idiot, get in here. You're next."

Before Sessetti could move, Van Noor's voice came through the shard.

"Beta Company, assemble in the embarkation area."

"Guess it'll have to wait," Rhona said, slinging her carbine over her shoulder and taking her helmet from the shelf next to her cubicle. "Let's go do this."

***

Pariton City Center
Capital City
Markov's Prize

L-Day plus 67

The entrance to the enemy complex lay only a few dozen yan ahead, partially hidden amid the rubble. A subterranean transport tube – a clear favorite method of travel for the MAA – emerged from the ground, half-buried in grey bricks and twisted metal support rods from felled buildings. The entrance had been detected by a spotter drone which had stealthily followed an MAA patrol in the early evening; the soldiers were tired from days of continuous fighting, no doubt, which explained their lax approach to security. Owenne had already planned on waiting until nightfall to advance, so as to take advantage of the enemy's inferior night vision devices; however, the discovery of a way into an MAA defensive complex was now an opportunity which could not be missed.

The four Dukes – all that was required to transport what was left of Beta Company – moved rapidly over the uneven ground, flanked by a pair of escorting C3M4 combat drones. The big M4s swept their searchlights across the ground ahead to search for any enemy troops who remained undetected by scanners, the drones' searchlights set to a visual spectrum which could only be detected by Concord forces who were tuned into it so they remained invisible to the enemy.

"Ten seconds," Tahl said, unstrapping from his seat and moving to stand by the door.

Even with his facemask down, Tahl could tell that Van Noor was frowning at him. The procedure was to remain safely and securely seated until the vehicle came to a stop, as the final few yan was when an enemy attack was most likely to occur. Tahl ignored the procedure – he wanted to be first out of the door. The seven troopers of Strike Leader Rall's Squad Jai were ready behind him. Tahl connected to the Duke's external sensors and checked around the vehicles as they covered the final few yan – still no sign of the enemy. The lead transport drone came to a stop by the tunnel entrance, quickly sank down to the ground with a jolt and opened its doors.

"On me," Tahl commanded, jumping down to the ground and dashing through the tunnel entrance with his carbine raised, Van Noor and Squad Jai following behind. Tahl sent a mental command to Squad Jai's spotter drone and ordered the machine to scout ahead through the tunnel as he set up waypoints for his other three squads. Within seconds, the spotter drone was reporting enemy activity ahead. Tahl relayed the information to his strike leaders and began a jog down

the tunnel at the head of Squad Jai. Around a bend was another of
the transport stations, similar to the one he had confronted the MAA
patrol in during Owenne's last nocturnal jaunt. Tahl stopped at a gentle
corner in the tunnel. The spotter drone had detected a squad of ten
enemy soldiers taking cover in the ruined station ahead. There was no
need to speak to his soldiers – a simple string of mental commands via
the shard gave them all the instructions they required.

Tahl and Van Noor sprinted around the corner and broke off to
the left as Rall and half of his squad dashed off to the right, his remaining
troopers dropping to the ground where the tunnel opened out into the
station. The boom and hiss of mag gun fire met the Concord troopers
as they moved, echoing around the cavernous station. Immediately, the
strike troopers still in the tunnel returned fire, sending lines of boiling
blue plasma back at the MAA soldiers who hid in piles of rubble or
behind the square, brick buildings on top of the station's platforms.

Tahl took cover behind the burnt out remains of an archaic
monorail train which sat in a twisted heap in the corner of the station.
Van Noor was close behind him, jumping for cover as projectiles slammed
into the metal around them. The spotter drone reported another force of
MAA soldiers moving to bolster the defending squad – another twenty
men, signifying the rest of their unit.

"Command, Squad Denne," Vias transmitted from where Tahl
had positioned his squad by the transport drones. "We've got a unit of
soldiers heading toward us from the northeast, about thirty guys."

"Got it," Tahl replied. "Squad Wen, double back and dig in next
to Denne to defend the disembarkation site."

"Copied, Boss," Rhona replied.

Tahl brought his attention back to the firefight in the station.
Rall had advanced with three of his troopers along the right hand
side, gunning down two of the MAA soldiers as they tried to fall back.
Tahl would normally be content to exploit his force's superior armor
and firepower by digging in for a prolonged exchange of fire, but the
MAA reinforcements were only moments away; and now that they had
been equipped with far more potent mag guns by their Freeborn allies,
he needed to execute a rapid and aggressive attack to wipe out the
first enemy squad before the next arrived. With Rall on the right and
supporting fire from the tunnel entrance, he set two new waypoints for
flanking attacks.

"Let's go, mate," he breathed to Van Noor, jumping back to his
feet and sprinting along the left of the station as a torrent of plasma fire
swept through the air from behind him in an attempt to suppress the
MAA defenders.

The spotter drone had highlighted three enemy soldiers taking
cover inside one of the platform waiting rooms up ahead; plasma fire

from the tunnel entrance smashed through the building, punching holes in the brick walls and creating a cloud of dust from the shattered masonry. With clinical precision, the supporting fire ceased as soon as Tahl and Van Noor were within a few paces of the building. Tahl was first through the doorway; he found one man dead at his feet and the remaining two staggering up to face him in the cloud of dust. With his carbine still set to single fire, Tahl raised the weapon and shot both men in the chest. With the room clear and some cover secured for his men, Tahl sent another waypoint through the shard to order Squad Teal to catch up with him and take up a firing position in the small building.

"Get down!" Van Noor snapped.

Tahl dived to the floor as Van Noor took cover by the doorway, leaning against it and firing a steady stream of plasma into the far end of the station as a squad of MAA reinforcements swept out of another tunnel, firing at the Concord troopers as they advanced. Projectiles buzzed through the air above Tahl's head, and he saw Van Noor's hyperlight shields flash in response to accurate fire, forcing the senior strike leader to fall back from the doorway and take cover. Moments later, Yavn and his six troopers from Squad Teal arrived next to them, taking up positions by the doorway and windows to return fire.

Tahl quickly patched in to the shards of Squad Wen and Denne. They were aggressively exchanging fire with the second MAA unit which was approaching the disembarkation point, but the combined fire of the Duke drones and the two squads had already accounted for over ten enemy soldiers. It was not a completely one sided exchange – both Vias and Rhona had each lost one of their troopers to enemy fire. A burst of mag fire caught one of the strike troopers by the doorway, puncturing his armor in the legs and gut and sending him clattering to the ground with a scream of pain. Tahl ran across and dragged the bleeding soldier away from the doorway before quickly setting about administering first aid.

"I've got him sorted, Boss!" Van Noor shouted as he knelt down next to Tahl and the wounded man. "You lead the company, I'll sort Weyne out!"

Tahl patched back into Jai's spotter drone to update his tactical picture. Twenty MAA soldiers had pushed through the tunnel, and one squad had taken position in the station whilst the second was providing covering fire from behind. Tahl assigned the spotter drone back to Squad Jai and sent a targeting feed to Rall's plasma lance gunner, ordering him to fire at the tunnel entrance whilst Squad Teal's lance did the same. Both weapons fired a continuous beam of superheated plasma at the tunnel, cutting into the roof and ripping the structure apart. Rocks ploughed down from the already unstable tunnel, crushing several of the MAA soldiers and cutting off the remainder of the squad, leaving only the ten in the station to deal with.

"Squad Teal," Tahl commanded the surrounding soldiers, "enemy soldiers at my marker! Rapid fire!"

Tahl took position by one of the shattered windows and fired short but rapid bursts from his carbine into the concentration of MAA soldiers which had taken cover by the next platform along. Plasma fire and mag fire were exchanged between the two squads as Rall continued his charge up the right hand side of the station, outflanking the last MAA soldiers and setting up to catch them in a withering crossfire. Caught between the two squads of strike troopers, half a dozen of the enemy soldiers were killed before the handful of survivors broke and fled down another of the transport tunnels.

The subterranean battlefield fell silent. Tahl quickly patched back into Wen and Denne, and thankfully found that the firefight outside the tunnels had been a similar success. Tahl slowly stood and dragged off his helmet to take in a lungful of air. Behind him, Van Noor had stabilized the wounded trooper.

"Tahl, you've stopped," Owenne's voice spoke through the shard. "Have you taken the station?"

"Affirm, we've beaten back two groups of MAA infantry. Estimate we eliminated about half of each unit before they ran. Station is secure, we've punched a hole through their lines."

"Good," Owenne said. "Good. How many casualties have you taken?"

Tahl quickly checked his soldiers' readouts via the company shard.

"Four dead, five wounded. Two seriously."

"Good," Owenne said again, "that won't slow you down at all. Keep going, Killer. I need you to punch a hole straight through to the archive building."

"And the Ghar?" Tahl countered, expending more than a little effort to ignore Owenne's disregard for the impact of his dead soldiers. "We've done the easy bit, smashing through the MAA line. What about when the Ghar move in from the east?"

"I've got five companies from the 61st Strike Formation already engaged with the Ghar," Owenne responded. "I'm keeping them off you. You've got the soft underbelly of the city so you can clear a path to that building. You let me worry about the rest."

"Copied."

"Boss!" a trooper from Squad Teal called. "One of these guys is still alive! Just about!"

"Go sort him out," Tahl nodded to Rall, who turned to jog quickly over to the wounded enemy soldier.

"By 'sort him out', I mean that you are to provide medical aid and stabilize him for evacuation," Tahl called after Rall to dispel any potential for confusion.

"I know, Boss!" Rall replied. "What did you think I was going to do?"

Tahl turned to look across at his other strike leaders. Van Noor and Yavn stood waiting for his orders.

"Get the dead and wounded into the Dukes as quickly as you can. We're moving again the instant the wounded are on their way out of here."

***

Jumping involuntarily with every blast from the x-howitzer battery behind him, Owenne clasped his hands at the small of his back and stared out to the east. The horizon was broken with the skeletal remains of buildings, terrain which his strike troopers were fighting their way through even as he waited. He was so close to his prize now, he felt as if he could practically walk right up to the building and peruse the archives as if inside an old fashioned library. The guns spoke again, sending another salvo of shells toward the Ghar reinforcements which were moving up to attack the 48th Strike Formation on the right flank of the Concord advance.

"Mandarin Owenne," Mandarin Luffe's voice chimed in his head, "news from the second of the Ghar reinforcement battlefleets. The Ghar invasion force at Banaab was annihilated by naval bombardment. Banaab is now secure. There was a naval encounter of significant size in high orbit and we sustained some losses. Mandarin Narik was amongst them."

"Good," Owenne replied. "Good that Bannab is secure and good that Narik has finally got his hands dirty. One assumes they recovered his body and he will successfully regen?"

"That is correct."

"Then assuming the surgical procedure is a success, I shall look forward to ridiculing him for not taking better care of himself," Owenne smiled. "And the other Ghar battlefleet? What news?"

"It will be entering the Zolus System imminently, I estimate it will be at Markov's Prize in three days."

"Three days? Why the devil are you wasting time and resources in Banaab when I need help here! I'm practically within walking distance of the best lead I have ever found for Embryo, and you're telling me that even if I am successful in punching through the Ghar, MAA, and sodding Freeborn lines, there's another entire army of little monster bastards in tin cans on their way here? Send me a couple of dreadnaughts and a carrier or two! Stop arseing around in backwater systems and come and help here!"

"Your lack of emotional control does you no credit, you must..."

"Are you sending reinforcements, woman? Yes or no?" Owenne demanded.

"Negative."

"Then sod off and stop wasting my time!"

Owenne severed the connection and swore in his rage. He needed Tahl and Van Noor to open up a path to the archives. And he was running out of time.

NINETEEN

Pariton City Center
Capital City
Markov's Prize

L-Day plus 68

Rechter hunkered down lower behind the narrow lip of rubble as the mag light support weapon chattered into life again, a stream of invisible projectiles sweeping over his head as he lay motionless between Sessetti and Meibal. The advance had faltered in front of an enemy position dug in beneath an enormous, collapsed road bridge which had once spanned a valley leading to the city's old industrial region. The spotter drones were slowly filtering information back from the enemy positions ahead; hastily dug trenches snaked their way through the rubble underneath the massive bridge, punctuated by six weapons dugouts protected by kinetic barriers. Mag light supports and kinetic barriers – further evidence of the Freeborn's assistance to the MAA defenders.

"Orders are through," Rhona announced from the end of the line of prone soldiers. "We're to advance and take marker delta. That's that gun position up ahead. Once we've punched through the line, the other boys and girls will overtake us and clear out the trenches."

Rechter shivered. He thought of his wife. He thought of Strike Trooper Losse, a man he had only known for a few days, who had been shot through the head in their first firefight. Rila, back home, deserved better than that. He could not allow himself to go home to her in a box.

"Varl; take Meibal to the right and draw their fire," Rhona ordered, sending a series of waypoints to her troopers' visual displays. "Lian, you go with Rechter to the left. Bo, you're with me. Wait for my go, I'll get us some covering fire."

Rechter glanced across at Sessetti. Despite what Meibal said, Rechter saw Sessetti as an experienced soldier – practically a veteran in his eyes – and was a little more comfortable to be following him in. From somewhere behind them, a series of dull thunks announced x-launcher fire, and the arc of their projectiles was highlighted on Rechter's visual display. Scoot shells – cruel, specialist munitions which transmitted a sub-harmonic pulse which incapacitated the nervous system – erupted in quick succession just in front of the gunpit, the angle of the bombardment only just being able to reach the target due to the overhang of the battered bridge above the gun.

"That's us!" Rhona called. "Go!"

Sessetti was up and dashing across the rubble to the left, his armored feet slipping on the broken bricks and stones as he ran. Rechter was close on his heels, his carbine swinging in his arms as he struggled to keep pace. After only a few seconds, the mag light support in the gun pit burst into life again – the scoot bombardment had not been close enough. Rechter looked over his shoulder and saw the ground around Varlton and Meibal obliterated in a hail of fire, dust kicking up around the two troopers as purple hyperlight shields flared up to try to ward off the torrent of fire.

"Don't stop!" Sessetti warned. "Keep going!"

Rechter looked ahead and tried to pick up his pace again to catch up. A second gun pit, off to the left and on the fringe of the defensive position, turned to face them and fired. Rechter dove to the ground and clamped his hands over his head. Blind panic seized him for a moment before an automatically administered cocktail of drugs coarsed through his veins, taking the edge off the terror. Sessetti was above him, hauling him up to his feet.

"Pick up your weapon and follow me! That fire isn't even effective yet! Keep moving before they zero in on us!"

Rechter followed Sessetti as they closed with the enemy defenses. Sparkles of fire from the trench line announced small arms now adding to the line of weapons trying to gun them down. Behind them, Squads Denne and Teal were already catching up to puncture a hole in the line.

Opaque patches of purple flared out in front of Rechter. It took him a second to realize that he was being hit by enemy fire, but the clouds of dust which spat up from the ground as the mag light support blasted away at them soon galvanized him into diving back to the ground for cover. Up ahead, highlighted as blue diamonds on his visual display, Rechter saw Rhona and Clythe advance to within only a couple of yan of the target marker. The gun was still firing away at Varlton and Meibal, who valiantly dashed from cover to cover, somehow still alive and running.

"Blasting, heads down!" Clythe's voice came through the shard.

A succession of staccato crumps announced the eruption of grenades, and the first gun pit fell silent. Still pinned in place, Rechter could only watch as Varlton and Meibal caught up with Rhona and

Clythe, and the four troopers stormed into the smoking gun pit. Squad Teal, meanwhile, sent streams of suppressing fire into the gun on the left, diverting its attention away from Sessetti and Rechter.

"Come on, now's our chance!" Sessetti said as he leapt to his feet.

The two soldiers covered the distance to the gun pit quickly, their hyperlight armor still flaring from isolated shots from the trench line. Arriving at the gunpit, they found the four strike troopers stood over five bodies, all of them dressed in long coats woven out of camo-reactive material. Freeborn.

One of the men, still alive, moved a hand for a pistol holster at his side.

"Don't be a prick!" Rhona yelled, stepping over to point her carbine down at him. "Don't do it! Don't you..."

The mercenary unholstered his pistol and Rhona shot him twice in the chest.

"Dammit!" She yelled, sinking to one knee and tearing off her helmet to issue a string of harsh expletives.

"C'mon, Lead," Varlton rested a hand on her shoulder. "Vias's boys are in the trench. We've got to help them clear it out."

Rhona pulled her helmet back on and hauled herself back up to her feet. Rechter still had not killed anybody. He did not relish the thought, but given Rhona's background, he imagined it was even harder to kill one of her own, close enough to look them in the eye.

"Lian, get on point," she commanded, "follow my marker. Let's go."

***

Owenne watched with a fascination he found uncharacteristically morbid as a trio of strike troopers dragged three Freeborn mercenaries out of the trench to dump them unceremoniously in a shell crater a few paces away. He also noted with interest that, whilst there was no time for ceremony, some effort had been put into disposing of the bodies of the MAA defenders, who had been laid neatly in rows with their helmets placed over their faces. Why the strike troopers had chosen to deal with the bodies of their enemies differently, Owenne had no idea. He did not care, either.

"Where's your strike captain?" Owenne asked one of the troopers as he levitated gently down into the trench.

"Straight down the trench, first bunker you get to, sir," the trooper replied.

His hands clasped at the small of his back, Owenne opted to levitate along the ground, utilizing his superior connection with his field of nanobots to support his own body weight rather than trudge through the mud and dust. He arrived at the bunker and found Tahl and Van Noor briefing their four remaining strike leaders. Old-fashioned paper maps had been pinned to the walls of the bunker by the previous occupants. The assembled troopers formed a circle around a simple wooden table, their helmets removed and their carbines slung on their backs.

"Morning, all," Owenne greeted. "Good job, advance is going well so far. I see you've only lost four troopers this morning. Good, good. Keep that up, we'll need every man and woman we've got to face the Ghar again."

Tahl exchanged a look with Van Noor. Owenne had never been good at interpreting panhuman non-verbal communication, but it was apparent that he had said something offensive. It irked him how easy panhumans were to offend.

"Four dead, six wounded," Tahl said. "We've also lost half a dozen drones, including an M4. I've got less than thirty soldiers left who are fit to fight."

"It's enough," Owenne said, glancing around at Tahl's strike leaders.

He connected to the company shard and quickly re-familiarised himself with their names and career histories. Yavn – the most experienced soldier in the company after Van Noor, overdue for promotion to senior strike leader. Vias – dependable, but morale was flagging. Rall – impestuos, hot headed, had just applied to transfer to the drop corps for the third time. Rhona – the least experienced, least battle hardened, showing the worst symptoms of fatigue. Better suited to Intelligence.

"With the 48th moving up on the left flank, we're in a good position to sweep south and cut off the rest of the MAA from the city center," Van Noor proposed. "That way we'll..."

"You're going straight to the city center," Owenne said, "you know the objective. I want Beta Company, 44th Strike Formation, front and center. I'll give you all the support you need, all of the drones and artillery you could ever wish for. But it's down to you to smash through the Ghar line and get me to the objective."

"What's the objective, sir?" Rall asked.

"Your strike captain and senior strike leader know the objective. You just follow their orders and we'll have this planet under Concord care by this time tomorrow."

Silence greeted Owenne's words. He assumed that meant his instructions were clear, no questions required.

"Understood," Tahl nodded slowly, exchanging a glance with Van Noor, "we'll hold position here and wait for instructions from Strike Commander Orless. He's currently briefing Delta Company."

"You don't need to wait for him," Owenne said.

"So when do you want us to move, sir?" Van Noor asked.

"No time like the present," Owenne replied. "Off you go. Forward march, and all that."

***

"Targets visual, twenty yan left of marker beta!" Sesssetti called from his position by the window on what was left of the first floor above.

"Squad Wen, single shots, pick your targets and open fire," Rhona ordered.

The squad had taken cover behind a line of hastily positioned kinectic barricades in the ruins of a decimated industrial building, half a day's advance to the east of the breakthrough at the bridge. Beta Company were part of a small, thinly spread defensive line along with the rest of the 44th, save Alpha Company who had sent three squads ahead to scout the Ghar positions.

Rechter mentally chastised himself as he peered through the sights of his carbine and saw a fuzzy, ill-focused mess. He had changed his visor to night vision as the darkness of early evening crept in, but had forgotten to do the same with his weapon. He jumped slightly as Meibal fired her carbine next to him, sending a bolt of blue energy flying off across the near flat sea of desolation which lay between them and the government buildings ahead. Rechter changed his sight setting and raised his weapon again.

Zooming in, he saw four strike troopers frantically running back across the dead ground, one of them limping and struggling to keep up with the others as all of them slipped and stumbled across the treacherous rubble beneath their feet. Then, behind them, Rechter saw a Ghar for the first time in his life; a monstrous machine of dull, metallic silver, its reactor exhaust glowing a feint green atop if bulbous back. The three-legged war machine tottered after the fleeing strike troopers, its squat legs struggling even more on the uneven surface than the soldiers it was chasing down. Rechter fired a shot from his carbine but saw the bolt of blue fly well wide of the mark. He corrected and fired again, a little closer this time.

"Alpha Squad Cian, this is Beta Wen," Rhona called across the formation shard. "You got three Ghar right behind you and transports inbound to pick you up. You boys are better hitting the deck and getting out of their arcs of fire, the Duke'll have you outta there in a few seconds."

Rechter glanced across and saw a Duke transport drone escorted by a C3M4 hopping over hill-shaped mounds created by felled buildings. One of the three pursuing Ghar, the one Rechter had been shooting at, held its position and fired the brutal, multi-barrelled weapon on its left arm. Plasma fire spat out in a terrifying display of green energy, blasting through the back of the wounded strike trooper and decapitating a second soldier who had turned to help his comrade. Sessetti swore angrily and increased his rate of fire, sending off two or three hastily aimed shots per second.

"Aimed shots, Lian!" Varlton snapped. "Aim 'em!"

The now familiar screeching hiss of Clythe's plasma lance sounded from the right and a continuous line of blue plasma energy shot out and smashed into the building behind the right-most Ghar. Clythe brought his weapon left, bringing the line of destructive energy with it. Rechter saw the plasma lance tear a ragged line through the building before it connected with the battlesuit; the Ghar jolted with the impact and fell back a step, its crude armor dented by the blast but otherwise unharmed as the lance's safety valve fired off and the shot was extinguished.

The Ghar held position now, tucked in amid the dull, grey buildings - no doubt in an attempt to hide themselves from the rapidly advancing M4 combat drone and its lethal plasma cannon, one of the few weapons which was capable of blasting through a battlesuit with relative ease. The two Concord drones accelerated, sweeping in from the left in a desperate attempt to reach the last two strike troopers fleeing from the Ghar. It was in vain. The Ghar machines on the left and right opened fire simultaneously, sending a cascade of green bolts down to converge on the two troopers. The ground kicked up in a storm of dust and splinters of rubble around them, both men crumpled and fell down, dead as the carbine fire from Squad Wen continued to ping ineffectually off their killers.

"Command from Squad Wen," Rhona reported in. "Alpha Squad Cian's gone. We couldn't help them. They're all dead."

Before a reply came, another line of energy swept out from Clythe's plasma lance with a high-pitched screech. It connected directly with the Ghar in the center, and the suit was torn apart in a spectacular display which lit up the evening sky. Limbs shot off in every direction as the main torso was replaced with a rapidly expanding ball of green plasma. The plasma cloud expanded outward and washed over the two remaining Ghar. Rechter's jaw dropped as both suits exploded simultaneously, their own putrid clouds adding to the original results of the reactor explosion. A line of green hung errily in place where the three ferocious fighting machines had been only seconds before.

Clythe let out a whoop of victory.

"I've seen their reactors go up before, but never like that!" Varlton exclaimed.

"Chain reactor explosions," Rhona said, "it's detailed in the intelligence reports. Very rare, even rarer for multiple occurences, but it happens."

"Damn right it does!" Clythe leapt to his feet and held his plasma lance over his head. "In the hands of a skilled operator..."

"Luck," Rhona corrected, "don't get cocky. Your shot was skillful, the results were pure luck. The chances of three reactors going up like that? 'Bout one in a thousand. Enjoy the moment, because I doubt we'll ever see that again."

Rechter looked out at the four dead bodies which lay motionless in between him and the already dissipating green cloud.

"Command from Squad Wen," Rhona transmitted, "we got a hit on a Ghar and just saw a chain reaction explosion..."

"Ultra-skilled operator, requesting a medal," Clythe cut in before Rhona held up a hand to silence him.

"Lucky shot, but we've got an opening," Rhona continued. "No other enemy units in sight, and we've already got a Duke and an M4 with us for support. If we're looking for a crack in their defensive perimeter to exploit, this might be it."

"The bodies," Sessetti said, "we need to recover our dead."

Rhona glanced across at him and nodded as she listened to a reply over the command shard which the rest of the squad could not hear.

"Wen copied," she said before turning to face the squad.

"Varl, on point, advance to my marker. We're at the tip of the push into the government sector. The rest of the boys and girls are moving in behind us. We need to get up to that grey building and hold our position until the rest of the gang's here. We've got that M4 lookin' out for us, so we'll be cool. I've marked the postion of those guys who didn't make it; Command has assured me that there are measures in place to get them home. C'mon, let's make a move."

***

Van Noor paused at the entrance to the alleyway, warily eyeing the visual feed from the spotter drone which hovered at head height in the street ahead of him. The din of battle intensified as shells fell with a riotous crash to the left, and a pair of C3M4 combat drones burst through a brick building to the right, advancing through the ruined city center with some twenty strike troopers from Cian Company close behind. The two Ghar troopers at the end of the street, collapsed in a pile of rubble, were only detectable on standard visual spectrums: no energy, no heat; no sign of life. But that was no guarantee.

"Wait here, Boss," Van Noor nodded to Tahl. "I'll go take a look."

Not giving Tahl a chance to object, Van Noor sprinted across the wide street toward the adjacent alleyway on the other side. His breath labored, his eyes half shut, and his shoulders hunched, Van Noor waited for the flurry of shots from the Ghar troopers. Nothing came. He clattered into the cover of the alleyway on the other side of the street and turned to face Tahl. On the rooftops above the company commander, the six surviving troopers of Squad Jai kept their weapons trained on the seemingly destroyed Ghar battlesuits. Perhaps they really were dead. Van Noor peered around the corner of the alleyway and gave a nod to Tahl.

As soon as Tahl was in the open, both suits powered up and opened fire. A barrage of plasma fire swept down the street, blasting into the walls to either side, and kicking up rocks and rubble from the ground. Tahl's shields flared purple as his hyperlight shields defelcted the relentless storm of plasma, Squad Jai's own fire impacting harmlessly into the Ghar duo as Tahl continued to sprint for cover. Van Noor watched helplessly as their spotter drone was gunned out of the sky from the hail of fire. Just two or three paces from the relative safety of the alleyway, Tahl was span around and blasted to the ground as the torrent of fire finally penetrated his shields. Van Noor did not hesitate for a second – he leapt out and grabbed Tahl by the wrist before dragging him back into cover.

Van Noor looked down at the battered and smoking armor of his friend. Tahl immediately sat up, his body convulsing. Van Noor realized after a few moments that it was from laughter.

"What's so bloody funny?" He demanded.

"That!" Tahl managed. "That's the most scared I've been in a long time! It's one of those laugh or cry moments, and with the amount of chemical crap this suit is pumping into my veins to stop me from crying, I guess we're laughing!"

Another wave of fire swept up from the far end of the street, blasting into the rooftop where Rall and his troopers were attempting to gun down the first pair of Ghar troopers. Caught in a deadly crossfire, Rall's squad dived to cower beneath the edge of the roof. Van Noor risked a glance around the corner of the alleyway: another three Ghar troopers had burst through the walls of one of the government buildings further down the street. One of the battlesuits was armed with a long and ominous disruptor bomber.

"Dammit!" Van Noor gasped as he ducked back into cover. "Another three of the bastards, and we're caught in the middle!"

"Beta Battery from Beta Command," Tahl called, his momentarily explosion of humor now cut short. "Immediate fire support on my marker."

No answer came.

Van Noor swore again. "Comms are either interrupted or dead. Let's get Squad Teal up behind those three and keep them busy so we can fall back."

"No time," Tahl shook his head, "we need to push on to that archive building. We'll double back along the adjoining alley and take down those two at the other end. Then we can keep the advance going."

"With what?" Van Noor demanded.

"You and Rall's lot will shoot them, I'm going to punch them."

Tahl sprinted off down the alleyway and took a left turn to move parallel to the main road, Van Noor close behind him. The ground shook as another barrage of shells fell close by; whether they came from Concord, MAA, Freeborn, or Ghar guns was impossible to tell. Up in the skies above them, Van Noor saw three full squads of drop troopers leap purposefully through the smoke stained skies, lines of fire sweeping up after them and cutting one of the airborne troopers down before they disappeared from view.

Van Noor saw a series of orders relayed to the company appear on the map in the bottom corner of his visual display as Tahl ordered the remnents of the company to new positions. Denne and Teal moved up on the left flank; Wen took the right whilst Rall's squad Jai on the nearby rooftop were ordered to shift left to concentrate their fire on the pair of Ghar troopers which Tahl and Van Noor advanced toward. The company's x-launchers were ordered to target the three Ghar on the right flank, keeping them as occupied as possible with their specialist ammunition, although Van Noor had his doubts how much of it would land within effective range within the tight confines of the battered streets.

Tahl and Van Noor rounded another tight corner and saw the two Ghar troopers at the end of the alleyway, their scourer cannons pointed up at the rooftops above them as Rall's troopers poured down fire from above.

"Wait 'til I'm close enough and then give 'em everything you've got!" Tahl patted Van Noor on the shoulder before sprinting off down the alleyway toward the open street ahead.

Van Noor brought his carbine up to his shoulder and aimed to the left of Tahl, waiting until the strike captain was only a yan or so away from the enemy. Van Noor fired, sending a series of carefully aimed shots into the flank of the nearest Ghar. The fire from the rooftops had done its job – Tahl closed into contact without having to face the ferocious firepower of the enemy. Van Noor watched as the strike captain planted a foot on the Ghar trooper's knee and propelled himself up to slam a fist into the fighting machine's head, tearing it off the neck joint, and sending it crashing to the ground in a cloud of electrical sparks. Blinded, the Ghar trooper thrashed around frenziedly until a series of powerful kicks from Tahl crumpled one of the machine's kneejoints. Seeing the second trooper moving in toward Tahl, Van Noor shouted out a warning and sprinted along the alleyway, firing as he ran.

At that moment, a Duke transport drone crested a mound of rubble behind the undamaged Ghar and ploughed into it, crumpling against the armored bulk and tearing two of its three legs off. The one legged Ghar lay helplessly on its back, its limbs thrashing pathetically like an upturned beast as it attempted to roll over. Rall and his troopers dropped down from the rooftop, quickly and efficiently planting plasma grenades on both damaged Ghar to dispatch them as the Duke's doors opened, allowing Vias and Squad Denne to jump out.

"Well timed," Van Noor nodded to Vias, "although I doubt the damage to the front of that Duke will polish out."

"It did the job, Senior," Vias nodded.

"Quickly, get back in the alleyway!" Tahl ordered the two squads. "The three Ghar at the far end of the street will shrug off those x-launchers before long! This is the only opening we're likely to get. Follow my marker."

***

Owenne watched the battlespace evolve through numerous real time feeds from drones scattered across the city. The Concord forces continued to advance eastward, with the 44th Strike Formation punching through at the center, whilst the remainder of the 17th Assault Force closed in around the north and south. Ghar resistance was fierce, and frustratingly, the MAA and their Freeborn mercenaries continued to harry the attack from the rear.

The battery of x-howitzers behind Owenne boomed again, lobbing huge projectiles up to arc through the smoke filled sky and rain down on the Ghar forces ahead. Owenne allowed himself a smile as he saw a small mass of blue emblems on his mini-map advancing to within visual range of the archive building. Tahl's company was front and center, leading the way to Owenne's objective.

He glanced up at the sky, expecting the Ghar relief force to arrive at any moment. The latest intelligence reports had the Ghar still nearly two days away, putting the Concord forces ahead of schedule for seizing the vital building. However, the advance had come at great cost, and those companies which were still intact were made up of only a handful of men and women each. But it would be worth it. It had to be, after all this.

Returning his attention to battlespace management, Owenne directed a trio of C3M4 combat drones from his reserves to fill a gap in his line to the northwest of the city where Ghar resistance was at its fiercest, whilst simultaneously shifting the aim of his x-howitzer barrage to follow the retreat of enemy forces to the south of the center. From that direction, a company from the 201st Strike Formation advanced steadily behind a line made up of four T7s, flanked by a pair of M4s, shrugging off streams of fire from lugger guns and scourer cannons as they moved forward. Satisfied that the objective was well within his grasp, Owenne ordered a C3T7 transport drone to divert to his location so that he could relocate to the frontline. Given the casualties his force had suffered, any Ghar reinforcements would make holding the planet untenable. The archives were only minutes away, but even being so close, Owenne knew that time was running out.

TWENTY

Pariton City Center
Capital City
Markov's Prize

L-Day plus 68

Plasma fire from Squad Denne and Squad Jai swept across the square in front of the archive building, blasting an old statue of a city councilor in half at the waist before pelting against the four Ghar battlesuits which stood at the corner of the building. The twenty or so Outcasts scattered as the fire came, two or three being gunned down before they could react, whilst the others ran for cover. The return fire from the four armored troopers was swift, and Tahl felt the now familiar feedback of fear and the void of death as one of Rall's troopers was cut down.

"Bry!" Tahl called across to Van Noor as he ducked back down below the burnt out roadcar at the edge of the square. "Get me fire support, anything you can – zero it in on those battlesuits and the main entrance."

"Understood," Van Noor nodded before setting up two markers to form a firing line for whatever fire support he could muster.

"Command from Teal!" Strike Leader Yavn called in. "We've got five battlesuits and one of those command crawlers moving in on our position, south of you at marker delta!"

Tahl's eyes widened at the report of the enemy strength.

"Teal from Command, fall back, do not engage directly. If you can lead them away from my position then do so, but your prioirity is to protect your squad – how copied?"

Tahl waited desperately for a response as another wave of fire punched a line of holes in the metal of the vehicle he lay behind.

"Teal copied," a breathless reply finally came, "we'll lead them away from you."

A line of explosions rippled along Van Noor's markers, ploughing across the top of the Ghar battlesuits by the corner of the target building. Tahl nodded in approval as he saw the lumbering war machines slow to a near stop, pivoting in place in confusion as the suspensor net shells suppressed their mobility.

"Bry, get Squad Wen up here for more firepower," Tahl ordered Van Noor. "Keep these bastards occupied, I'll be back as quick as I can."

"Where the hell are you going?" Van Noor demanded from where he laid a few paces to the right.

"I'm moving around the back of the building to find another way in. I'm going to go and get Owenne's files so we can fall back again."

"Not on your own you're not," Van Noor ducked down as a salvo of solid projectiles rattled across the top of the car from the lugger guns of the Outcasts by the main entrance to the archive building. "I'm coming with you."

"I need you to control this firefight," Tahl argued. "I need you in command. Wait here!"

Tahl seized the opportunity to run to the right and vault over Van Noor as soon as he saw a gap in the firing, sprinting headlong for a narrow road which curved around the right hand side of the building and away from the four Ghar fighting machines. He cursed under his breath as Van Noor leapt up and ran after him.

"Vias, you're in command here!" Van Noor transmitted. "Get Rhona's squad set up to your left and keep 'em busy until we're back!"

"Understood, Senior."

The two troopers narrowly evaded the sporadic fire which followed them to the edge of the building. Tahl led Van Noor along the sandy colored wall, stopping by a smaller, more subtle entrance. He waited by the right hand side of the door and nodded to Van Noor to take position and prepare for entry. As soon as Van Noor stopped by the door, a hail of gunfire smashed against both strike troopers. Tahl felt the impact of solid projectiles slamming against his armor. He dropped to one knee and brought his carbine up to his shoulder, centering his sights on half a dozen twinkling muzzle flashes in the entrance to an alleyway opposite them. He fired a long burst on scatter, sending streams of plasma fire through the Outcasts crowded by the entrance, dropping two and blasting apart the brickwork around them before the survivors fled out of sight.

He turned to look at Van Noor. His friend sat crumpled and motionless against the wall, spatters of blood on the sandy stonework behind him and the pavement below. Tahl let out a cry of panic and dashed over.

"Cover," Van Noor wheezed, "get... cover..."

Clipping his carbine to his back, Tahl grabbed Van Noor underneath both arms and dragged him up to the door, leaving a smeared trail of blood behind. He scanned his friend's suit readouts and suppressed a howl of anguish – one lung collapsed, massive internal trauma. Even with his suit's attempts to stabilize, Van Noor would be dead within the hour.

"I'm going to lift you, mate," Tahl said. "This'll hurt, but I've got to get you out of here. We've got to fall back."

"Cover," Van Noor whispered, "get...inside..."

To amplify his point, a wave of plasma fire carved chunks out of the stonework around him as a trio of Ghar battlesuits appeared at the east end of the building. Tahl wasted no time in dragging Van Noor inside, praying that there was nothing waiting for him in the corridor as he helplessly backed into the uncleared building. Van Noor tensed up and tried unsuccessfully to suppress cries of pain as Tahl continued to drag him, moving quickly away from the doorway as the relentless enemy fire continued to blast the building's entrance apart.

"I'll get you to the front door!" Tahl said as he frantically looked around to orientate himself and work out which way he needed to go to get back to his company. "Our guys will have suppressed those suits by now. I'll get you straight out of the front door and we'll get you patched up."

As if in response, Tahl backed through a wooden door and saw a rabble of Outcasts at the far end of the corridor. He quickly fired a pair of explosive projectiles from his wrist-mounted x-sling, one into the enemy soldiers and another into the roof to collapse the ceiling and block off the corridor.

"Running... out of... options..." Van Noor slurred.

"You're stable, pal!" Tahl lied as he tried another corridor. "We've got a little time, just keep it together!"

***

The nozzle of his carbine hissed and steamed as Sessetti fired another three aimed shots at one of the Ghar suits by the main entrance to the archive building. Another wave of the seemingly suicidal Outcasts was pouring down a street from the north, ignoring the lines of fire which cut into their ranks from Squad Jai as they ran. Swearing under his breath, Sessetti fired another shot, and then another – finally he was rewarded for his persistence as the armor of the hulking machine gave way and a neat hole was punctured dead center over the operator's position; the suit locked up rigidly and toppled over.

"Have that, you bastard," Sessetti exhaled, instantly taking aim on another Ghar trooper and ignoring the heavy volume of fire which came his way in return.

"Squad Wen! Targets left of marker beta! Fire!" Rhona ordered from where she lay prone in the center of the squad, shifting the squad's focus to the rapidly approaching wave of Outcasts.

The combined fire of the three squads of strike troopers tore into the advancing rabble of Ghar soldiers, knocking down Outcast after Outcast. Their numbers thinning and their bulk now seeming almost harmless in comparison to what it was only seconds before, the last few Outcasts continued to charge across the open ground until they were shot dead only paces from the Concord line.

"Dammit!" Varlton growled. "They're going into the archive building! Those battlesuits are going inside!"

"Shoot them! Shoot the bastards!" Rhona yelled.

***

Only minutes away from the archives, Owenne allowed himself a slight grin from where he sat alone in the passenger hold of the T7 transport drone. He watched the battle unfold intently from his web of spotter drones as his flanks held and the central push stood firm at the very steps of the archive building. It had worked. They had reached the target before the Ghar reinforcements had even reached high orbit. Finally, after years of chasing countless dead ends across so many light years of space, Owenne had found something. He was going to make a contribution which would be remembered for centuries.

"Owenne, it's Tahl," Tahl's voice sounded urgent, nearly panicked, certainly not the tone he had come to expect from the veteran soldier. "I'm in the archives with Bry. He's wounded, I need help. I need you to get me out of here."

"Where abouts in the archives are you?" Owenne demanded.

"The...I'm in the archives themselves. We're surrounded. Both exits are blocked and we've got enemy units closing in on us."

"Can you see the archives themselves?" Owenne said. "The files? Can you see the actual files?"

"Yes! There's thousands of them! But Bry hasn't got much longer, and if you don't clear a path to me, I'm gone as well!"

"Get the file, Ryen," Owenne demanded.

"There isn't time! We've got minutes at best! Get a medical drone up here now and punch a path open to us!"

Owenne sank forward in his chair, closed his eyes, and rested his face in his hands. Ignoring Tahl's repeated demands for help, he reviewed his options. He could get a medical drone across easily enough, but given the reports he was receiving regarding the strength of enemy forces in the area, he did not favor his odds. A lightning punch through, seize the objective, and get out; that was the only way this would work. He was losing the initiative, and every minute that his forces were bogged down exchanging fire with superior Ghar forces would see his casualties increase and Ghar reserves pour into the area, now that they knew what he was after.

He would lose. This close, after all this, and Owenne would lose. Worse still, the information could fall into Ghar hands, or even to the Freeborn. That would be a disaster he could not allow to happen. A dozen outcomes, each with different probabilities to calculate and what the effect would be if they materialized, passed through Owenne's brain in a fraction of a second. His choice was clear. He swore viciously in a cry of rage and slammed a fist into the side of the transport drone.

"Cian Battery, from Mandarin," Owenne opened a channel to the nearest artillery battery. "Sending you coordinates now, concentrated fire. Make it accurate."

***

"Get...out of here," Van Noor looked up at Tahl, his voice barely audible, "go."

"Shut up, you idiot, I'm thinking!" Tahl snapped.

The central archive storage was a cavernous room with graceful arches, their angles lit up by sunlight which poured through tall windows and a green tinted, domed skylight. Row after row of grey, metal shelving units formed ugly, clinical lines across all three floors of the archive room. The main entrance to the room had already been destroyed by a brief exchange of gunfire between Tahl and two battlesuits which had somehow squeezed through the corridors, and another volley of explosives from his x-sling had ensured that that route would not be used again any time soon, in or out.

"Finish the bloody...mission," Van Noor said as blood flowed from one side of his mouth. "Get out of here."

"If you don't stop that valorous sacrifice crap, I'll shoot you myself," Tahl snarled, looking up at the skylight.

***

Her fists clenched in frustration, Rhona watched as her squad's fire only succeeded in slowing the two Ghar battlesuits which had just arrived from the east. With four dead troopers and their firepower reduced, the three squads of strike troopers had formed three sides of a square by the collapsed main entrance to the archive building and were fighting off a growing number of Ghar who arrived from the east. Four battlesuits to the left, another wave of Outcasts from the south, and nobody knew now many of the enemy had managed to get inside the building.

280 Beyond the Gates of Antares

"We've got to go in!" Rhona transmitted to the other two strike leaders. "The boss and the senior are in there! We've got to get them out!"

"How?" Rall demanded. "We're pinned in place! We're fighting for our own survivial here! We're doing all we can for them by digging in and holding out instead of running!"

Another barrage of plasma fire cut across Squad Wen's position and Meibal was thrown back, smoking holes cut across her torso. Varlton dived across to her and dragged her away from the firing line before checking her injuries.

"She's good, she's alright," he reported, "just superficial!"

"We need to storm that building!" Rhona urged the other two squad leaders again, a sickening clawing at her gut as she thought of Tahl surrounded on all sides by a remorseless enemy.

"Feon's right," Vias said. "We're barely holding on ourselves here, we're not in any position to mount an attack!"

At that moment, Rhona felt the sickening sensation amplify a thousand times as a series of artillery cooridinates were transmitted to a nearby battery, ordering fire directly down onto the archive building.

"Cian Battery, Cian Battery!" Rhona yelled. "This is Beta Company Wen Leader! Check your fire! Check your fire! You've been given targeting coordinates of a friendly unit! Do not fire!"

"Cian Battery from Mandarin," Owenne's voice came across the shard. "Your target is correct. Open fire as ordered."

"No!" Rhona screamed. "Do not fire! That's friendlies! Don't fire!"

"Stand down, Strike Leader!" Owenne growled. "I'm in..."

"Don't you fire, you murdering bastard!" Rhona yelled. "Don't..."

She felt her connection to the company shard suddenly severed. The mandarin had actually cut her off. He was going to kill his own men. For whatever this was all about, whatever was in that building, he was going to kill his own people. Ignoring the cries of alarm from her troopers, willing the enemy fire not to hit her, Rhona sprinted across the open ground toward the archive building.

***

"Come on, mate," Tahl said as he carefully dragged Van Noor up the open, spiral staircase leading to the top of the archives, "nearly there now."

The din of battle had intensified, and the building regularly shook as heavier munitions detonated nearby. Two of the three corridors leading to the central archive room had collapsed, and Tahl nervously eyed the last entrance as he climbed toward the skylight, wishing he had taken measures to deny the enemy this last route in.

Van Noor had stopped talking. Tahl had removed both of their helmets so Van Noor could at least see his friend face to face; hopefully that would offer some encouragement. But the older man's eyes drifted in and out of focus and his head lolled down sleepily with every few paces he was dragged. A burst of gunfire swept up into the skylight, shattering the grimy dome on one side and sending showers of broken glass crashing down on the marble floor not far from the top of the staircase.

"Ryen?" A familiar voice called from down below somewhere. "Ryen!"

Tahl peered over the bannister of the winding metal staircase and looked back down to the ground. Below him, Rhona sprinted into the room from the last open corridor.

"Katya!" Tahl shouted down. "What the hell are you doing here?"

Rhona looked up, her face hidden behind the cold, robotic exterioir of her helmet's visor.

"Ryen, we've got to leave! Now!" She called up in desperation.

"Up here!" Tahl called down. "I think I can get us out through the skylight..."

"There isn't time!" Rhona shouted. "That bastard Owenne has called an artillery strike in on this building! It's due any second! We've got to get out, now! There's a whole rabble of Outcasts right behind me!"

"Okay," Tahl nodded, "we're on our way down."

"Quickly!" Rhona urged as Tahl turned around to drag Van Noor back down the staircase. "I've mined the entire corridor and if any of those Outcasts..."

As if in reply, the entire corridor behind her detonated with an earsplitting thunderclap of explosions as several plasma grenades erupted as one. The explosion lifted Rhona up off her feet and catapulted her across the room as billows of smoke and chips of stone blossomed out behind her. Tahl shouted out to her and set Van Noor down before sprinting down the staircase. Rhona was quickly up and on her feet, dragging her helmet off to reveal her tired but beautiful face, sweat soaked strands of black hair falling down over her purple bandana. She held a hand up as he approached.

"I'm fine, I'm okay – where's the senior?"

"Up at the top, he's in a bad way. We need to get him out of here before it's too late."

The entire building rocked to its very core, the shock of the blast knocking Tahl and Rhona aside and sending them clawing out for balance. A second blast erupted, and then a third. Tahl looked across at Rhona. The look in her eyes reflected his own feelings. It was already too late. The artillery had arrived. Tahl stumbled over to Rhona, taking her shoulders in his hands.

"You shouldn't have come!" He shook his head. "You should have stayed put!"

"I couldn't leave you," Rhona met his gaze sorrowfully, wincing as another artillery shell caused an entire section of the building to collapse somewhere behind her. "I knew the risk. I... dammit, it's over now so it doesn't matter how stupid this sounds. I'd rather die next to you than carry on on my own."

Another explosion shook what was left of the building again, and a row of archived records to the left were knocked noisily to the floor. Tahl pulled Rhona in and rested his forehead against hers.

***

His vision blurred, and pain now replaced with only a dull ache, Van Noor moved a shaking hand to his utility belt and flipped one of the pouches open with great difficulty. Above him, the smoke had parted a little, and a few narrow pillars of light shone through the shattered skylight, picking out details in the masonry around him which his eyes could not focus on. He had heard the conversation below him. He knew they were being bombed into oblivion and again, for a second time, this would be the death of him.

Another shell landed and the southern wall of the room collapsed entirely, obliterating the ground floor in a cloud of dust. Van Noor slowly and carefully recovered the contents from his utility pouch, feeling the item expand as it was freed from the compression pocket. Taking in a long, painful breath, he forced himself to concentrate for one last moment, focusing his eyes on the carefully painted model soldier and the two pictures on his viewscreen. One was Van Noor's favorite picture drawn by his son – a fast spaceship zooming through the stars. The other was a family picture, the four of them together in the afternoon sun in their back garden, faces all smiles from happier times. His eyes lingered on Jabe, Alora, and Becca, taking in every detail he could of their features and imagining himself back in that moment from years before, enjoying the sunshine and the company of his family.

Another shell impacted the building as his vision faded.

***

Tahl could not see Rhona now, even if he was able to open his eyes. The explosions were deafening and the air was filled with acrid, stinging smoke. His head pressed against hers, the two held onto each other as they waited for the end. A shell detonated to the right, picking up heavy archive shelving units and tossing them through the air like discarded child's toys.

"I'm ready for death, I guess," Rhona said to him softly through the shard, her voice able to reach his mind directly and bypass the onslaught of violent noise around them. "But I can't get one thing out of my mind. Look... if, if your God protects you and you successfully regen, and you remember all of this, and... if by some miracle I come out of this, in one form or another... promise me you'll do all of this again. Win me over again, promise me that. I'm not a bad person, and if I get another shot at life, and I don't remember all this... Promise me you'll do this all over again. Promise you'll come get me."

Tahl nodded.

TWENTY ONE

The silence was jarring but fitted seamlessly with the sunlit, turquoise skies. Clouds slowly parted as rays of sunlight came down in golden pillars. Tahl opened his eyes. He assumed he was Tahl at least; he had no idea where he was or if this was what it felt like to be reactivated as a clone. He realized that he was still clinging on to Rhona. She looked up at him.

"Well, well, well!" Owenne's voice boomed out as the mandarin wafted one hand in front of him, stumbling over the rubble and through the rapidly dissipating clouds of dust. "Looks like the plan worked!"

Rhona's eyes widened and she jumped back from Tahl.

"Looks like you're all good, Boss," she nodded, smacking a fist into his shoulder. "Let's get you and the senior out of here."

"Bry?" Tahl looked up toward where the domed skylight once was, his mind still numb with confusion.

The staircase still stood, and with it, a pair of supporting pillars and a few fragments of each floor of the archive room. The rest of the building was entirely destroyed and clear, unobstructed views of the sky and the surrounding buildings were visible in every direction. A pair of medi-drones hovered up to Van Noor's prone form and quickly went to work as a squad of strike troopers advanced through the dust.

"Will he be alright?" Tahl asked as he looked up at Van Noor.

"I don't know, I'm not a bloody doctor," Owenne grumbled.

"What happened?"

"Artillery Procedure 151 Beta," the mandarin replied, "as planned."

"151?" Rhona asked.

"151 Beta," Owenne corrected, "a Beta Strike. You thought I'd called in an Alpha Strike when you started babbling and whinning at me, but it was a Beta Strike. I called in a precision artillery bombardment to destroy everything at my markers, not the entire area. I could see you quite clearly, and I was being very careful to obliterate everything around you. But not you. So this whole area has been pacified by every gun in the 17th Assault Force. Everything. I called support away from every other friendly unit in the city to protect you. I destroyed my objective and everything I've worked for to protect you. So remember that, next time you call me a bastard."

"Yes, sir," Rhona said quietly.

Tahl looked around, still dazed by the barrage.

"They're all dead, Ryen," Owenne explained, "that was the one positive which came out of all of this. The Ghar knew I wanted something here and poured everything they had into this area. One assumes the strategic genius leading their little rabble was willing to gamble on me being unwilling to sacrifice this building and what was in it, hence them bunching up their forces nicely. Unfortunately for them, their gamble was a poor choice. I was willing to sacrifice it all. For my friends. You're still a bunch of complete pricks for ruining everything, but it was the correct decision."

Tahl opened his mouth to speak, but found no words. He looked across at Rhona for assistance, but the dust covered strike leader only flashed a white-toothed smile in amusement at the entire situation before the mandarin continued.

"Now get yourself together because we need to fall back. The next wave of these little bastards isn't far away, and with reinforcements in the system, it's time we admitted that we've lost this one. The MAA and the Ghar can fight it out for Markov's Prize. We lost."

Forcing an unconvincing smile which did little to hide his disappointment, Owenne turned to stride off with a flourish of the tails of his coat. Tahl felt a wave of relief as he saw Van Noor limping slowly down the battered staircase, supported on both sides by the hovering medi-drones. The two men exchanged relieved smiles. Tahl turned back to the mandarin.

"Owenne!"

The NuHu stopped and turned slowly back around.

"Yes?" His tone was sarcastic as he spoke.

Tahl walked over to him, reaching into his utility pouch. He pulled out an ancient, dull brown folder made of thick paper and offered it to Owenne.

"Project Embryo," Tahl explained, "this is everything that was here. I swiped it all before it was too late."

Owenne stared impassively at Tahl in silence. His face broke into an ecstatic smile, and a deep, loud belly laugh echoed across the ruins.

***

Firebase Alpha
Equatorial Region
Markov's Prize

L-Day Plus 73

The gentle waves lapped over Rhona's ankles, soaking the material of her green barrack trousers up to the knees. Her bare feet waded through the crystal clear waters, finding another series of ridges in the sand. Staring out to where the sea met the horizon, Rhona stepped down on the ridges and broke them underfoot, feeling the sand waft up through the water around her. Several yan off to the right, she heard laughter and music from some of the troopers from her company, but it did little to disturb the peace she found in being alone in the midmorning sun. She had moved down the beach from where the others had set up next to the firebase itself to a stretch next to a narrow stream, trickling down to join the sea.

"You okay?"

Rhona did not turn to face the voice behind her on the beach. She suppressed a yawn and pushed her hands into her trouser pockets.

"Yeah," she finally replied.

"Would you rather be alone?" Sessetti asked.

"Nah, I'm easy either way."

She heard Sessetti walk out to sit by the edge of the water, near where she had left her boots. A few colorful sea birds circled overhead, their cawing adding some color to the gentle lapping of the waves. She glanced across at Sessetti and saw he was wearing his martial arts clothing, leaving her wondering if he had been training alone or whether Tahl had found time to get away from his work after all.

"You sure you're okay?" Sessetti asked. "I don't mean to pry, but you don't seem to be yourself."

"Why's that?" Rhona asked.

"I've spent nearly three standard months on this planet as part of your squad," Sessetti replied, "in all that time you've found a thousand excuses to strip down to your underwear in front of people. Now we're here, the war is over, we're perfectly safe, off-duty, on a sun drenched beach, and you're fully clothed."

Rhona failed to suppress a short laugh and turned to face him, shrugging.

"I suppose it says something of the duality of my persona," she said.

"Now I know something's wrong," Sessetti looked up from where he sat, "because the Rhona I know doesn't even know what the words 'duality' and 'persona' even mean."

Rhona had found herself at a loss ever since the retreat from Pariton. A wave of confused and conflicting feelings combined with weariness and a sense of loss were heightened when the Ghar fleet arrived and, to everyone's surprise, revealed itself to be an evacuation fleet rather than reinforcements. Within a day, every surviving Ghar was recovered and left the planet, and neither the Concord nor the MAA felt inclined to stop them. With no Ghar to distract the Concord invaders and the fear of Concord reinforcements arriving at any time, the MAA had called a ceasefire and negotiations had commenced.

"How're things with you and Bo?" Rhona asked, only half interested in the answer but keen to divert the conversation away from herself.

"Ah... he's still upset because I want to see this through for longer than he does," Sessetti sighed, "and I do see his point, but we're not joined at the hip, and I do resent him expecting me to run life decisions by him. He can do his own thing and I should be allowed to do mine."

"You wanna do your own thing so you think staying in the military is the best way to achieve that?" Rhona raised one eyebrow.

"Not when you put it like that. But I do want to try and make this work. It just feels more important than going to clubs and parties and singing. Singing about meaningless crap. I want to be out here and be a part of this. I hate to sound like one of those awful adverts back home, but I do actually feel like I belong here. I'm not ready to turn my back on that."

"I wouldn't worry. You and Bo'll both be around for a while yet. Three months' frontline time? Ol' Uncle C3 ain't gonna let you go home just yet. Not without giving a bit more first."

"So what are you going to do with your leave?" Sessetti asked. "You going to go see your brother? Or you seeing this guy of yours?"

Rhona shuddered at the thought of either and both.

"I'll worry about that if it ever happens."

"There's no 'if' about it," Sessetti said, "we're leaving in two days. That's what I meant before when I said the war was over. I figured you would have read the bulletin on the company shard."

Rhona folded her arms and blinked in surprise.

"The MAA surrendered this morning. The entire planet is now part of the Concord. The 17th Assault Force is being disbanded and we've all been given a month's leave before the 44th is sent to Lothen Major for training and reserve duties. We're going home."

Rhona swore.

"I thought you'd be happy." Sessetti stood slowly.

"Happy?" Rhona repeated. "About what? I've been on the frontline without a proper break for I don't know how long now. I don't have a house to go home to. I can't go see my brother because last time I saw him, it didn't go so well. And I'm terrified of seeing that guy I told you about, because I know that as soon as I go home and all the romance and excitement of me being a frontline soldier fades away, he'll see me for what I really am and realize there's nothing behind the pretty face. No substance. He'll get bored of me and I don't think I can take that. I don't want to go home! This is home! You said it yourself, you feel like you belong here! I..."

Sessetti held out both hands passively to silence her.

"Kat, you'll be fine," he said gently. "I'm sure your brother loves you and whatever happened, he'll get over it if he hasn't already. You don't have a house? Just go get one built. You're still thinking like a Freeborn. When we go back to the Concord, there's no money and no responsibility over a home. Just pick a site, pick a design, and get some drones to build it for you. Go and make whatever home you want, wherever you want. That's why we were fighting here, right? To give people that life, what we've got back home. And as for your guy? C'mon. You could pick any guy you wanted, anybody, and if you picked him, then he must be alright. Girls who look like you don't settle for somebody, they cherry pick the best. And if his head is screwed on the right way, he will see you for who you really are and everything will be fine."

Rhona sank down and sat in the shallow water, her legs stretched out in front of her as the waves washed over her waist.

"All this training is supposed to keep us stable, clear headed, calm. None of it is working. Lian, I'm petrified. I don't want to go back."

Sessetti walked out to sit in the sea next to her, a few paces away, which Rhona saw as an attempt to show that his intentions were purely platonic. It was a gesture she appreciated.

"I'm glad you made it through, Lian," she said without looking across at him, "you're alright."

The two stared out to sea in silence as Rhona wrestled with her thoughts.

***

The engineering drones backed away at the mouth of the neat tunnel they had spent the last four hours digging into the hillside. Owenne sent a mental command to one of them, forcing it to turn back around and illuminate its torch, filling the tunnel with light as he walked slowly down. He glanced down at the map in his hand, the ancient brown paper taken from the file Tahl had retrieved for him. If he had interpreted it right...

The politics of the whole affair were now of no interest to Owenne. At this very moment, on the other side of Markov's Prize, delegates from the Concord and the MAA would be sitting down to discuss terms for the future of the planet. The meeting was pointless, of course; it was purely there to smooth the transition and give the MAA fighters a feeling of ownership and worth. Once they were part of the Concord, whatever demands they had made could be slowly eroded and ignored.

Owenne reached the end of the tunnel and smiled broadly. The engineering drones had dug down to an ancient double door, its advanced synthetic construction speaking of a lost civilization, more advanced than the recently defeated people of Markov's Prize. This was something from a bygone age, buried and long forgotten. This was it. This was Embryo. Owenne sent an order to the drone, and the small machine hovered forward to pry open the door. Owenne closed his eyes and smiled again as a cloud of ancient, stale air wafted through the door and into the tunnel. He stepped through, his eyes following the beam of the drone's lights as it illuminated the interior. The research laboratory – for that was all it could logically be – consisted of a large, open plan main room with several smaller adjoining areas. Tables, chairs, computers, machines of a dozen different functions, all lay where they had been abandoned for whatever reason thousands of years before, covered in dust and earth from where the walls and ceiling of the subterranean facilitiy had parted after centuries of neglect.

Owenne let out a long, deep laugh.

***

Passenger Liner, Star Julienn
Low Atmosphere, Planet Gethsem
Concord Core

Lines of soldiers filled the upper deck of the passenger liner, each company of the two assault forces turned out resplendently in dress uniform, motionless as they stood three ranks deep. It was early evening as the liner ploughed slowly through the clouds, the ship's invisible deep space shielding protecting the soldiers from the cold of the atmosphere and the damp from the clouds. As the passenger ship continued its slow descent toward the docking bay, the clouds thinned to reveal glimpses of the two Concord Navy frigates which escorted her, one on each side.

Standing at ease front and center before the survivors of Beta Company, Tahl looked up through the gaps in the clouds at the stars which dotted the purple sky. He gripped his hands tighter together at the small of his back to stop them from trembling, hoping that his troopers would not notice the show of emotion. His collar felt tight against his throat, the green, single-breasted jacket of his dress uniform felt similarly constrictive over his chest. Over a year on campaign, when the regulations stated that a third of that was the maximum a soldier should spend on frontline service, unless operational reasons demanded an extension in extremis. He doubted that a series of planetary invasions to expand the borders of the Concord could be considered 'in extremis', yet here he was.

Here he was, back in the Concord and light years away from hostile forces, only minutes away from a docking bay which would be packed with the families of the homecoming soldiers. Every time he came home, he wondered if this would be the one, the homecoming when he would finally step off the gangway and see his parents waiting for him. Perhaps, given how long he had been away, this time would be different. Perhaps they would be there, for the first time since he joined the Concord Combined Command.

"44th Strike Formation... attention!" Primary Strike Leader Jayne bellowed, the command taken up along the decks by all of the assembled Formation Primaries. Tahl raised his left knee to waist height and slammed it down on the faux wooden deck, bringing his arms to his sides with his fists clenched to attention as the men and women of his company carried out the same, well drilled action simultaneously. The first skyscrapers of the city were visible below now as the passenger liner drifted down in its docking pattern, the thrum of its reactor growing a little louder as the engines worked harder to support the deceleration of the ship and decaying lift from its stubby wings.

"I still can't believe you buggered off and left me."

"Seriously?" Tahl answered mentally through the company command shard. "This? Again? Now, of all times?"

"I was literally dying," Van Noor replied mentally from where he stood a few paces to Tahl's right, "having bravely sacrificed myself for you, C3, and the 44th; and you dumped me on top of a staircase to bleed out all by myself."

"As I recall, you were looking for a posthumous medal, you idiot!" Tahl replied as the ship turned lazily to the right. "'Leave me, sir! You go on ahead! Tell them how bravely I died! The mission always comes first, sir! Don't you worry about old Senior Strike Leader Van Noor, the hero! Just make sure they tell tales of my bravery and build a statue or two! Don't tell anybody that I got gunned down by a midget with a gun from the First Age!'"

Tahl sensed Van Noor's mirth at his response and struggled to keep a straight face as he stood rigidly to attention. He heard the older man snigger from where he stood to the right. Mandarin Owenne, his staff tucked under one arm and clad in his signature coat and cap, walked along the deck and came to a stop by Tahl.

"Fall yourself out, Strike Captain, and come with me," he said curtly.

Tahl pivoted to face to the right and took one pace forward before pausing to signify he was leaving the parade. He followed the NuHu as he walked along the edge of the deck, past another three companies of men and women who stood to attention in file before he reached the ship's fo'c's'le', the open area of the upper deck at the fore end of the ship which led to the bow. Owenne stood at the very prow of the ship, well away from the assembled soldiers, and looked down at the city below as dozens of lights began to flicker on in the darkened sky.

"This is all very romantic," Tahl said, "but if you're going to try to kiss me, then clearly I've been sending out the wrong signals to you."

"Funny," Owenne grimanced, "I think I preferred you when you were panicking about getting your head blown off."

"So what's up?"

Owenne turned away for a few moments before looking up. Tahl found himself surprised that Owenne was actually making eye contact.

"That folder you nabbed for me," he said, "it meant a lot. Not just the information, but the gesture. I know that you know this was all a gamble. I gambled the lives of a lot of men and women for what could have turned out to be nothing. You didn't complain, you didn't whine at me for following my own whims, you just did your job. I wanted to say thank you."

"Quite alright, it was a whole bunch of us, not just..."

Owenne held a hand up to stop him.

"That information you found. If Embryo is a puzzle made up of a thousand pieces, the folder you gave to me had about twenty of them and leads to find perhaps another hundred."

"How many pieces of the puzzle did you have before this?" Tahl asked.

"Four or five. The analogy doesn't translate perfectly, but suffice to say, this is the biggest jump forward I've been able to make, and it's down to you. Now, both you and I know that I'm bloody hopeless with... people. I don't understand any of you and don't feel the need to. But I do feel the need to express my gratitude when necessary. So I've had a think and I've come up with three ways to say thank you. Here's the first."

Owenne reached a pale hand into the pocket of his coat and produced a small, red, rectangular box. He threw it over to Tahl, who caught it and opened it. The contents of the box came as a genuine shock.

"It's the Concord Gold Star," Owenne said. "I know I've stopped you from getting a medal for all of the Ghar you beat to death, and I stand by that decision because I'd expect nothing less from one of the most dangerous men in the known universe. But whilst C3 expects you to kill, it never expected much of you in terms of leadership. You've led the men and women under your command for over a year across half a dozen planets and in the face of high casualties, exhaustion, and some of the most dangerous enemies and environments in the universe. You exceeded everything C3 expected of you as a combat leader, so that medal is for your enduring leadership, not your battlefield prowess. I don't really know what makes your mind tick, but I know you well enough to figure out that a ceremony and fuss would just embarrass you, so just pin the bloody thing on your uniform and we're done."

Tahl removed the gold cross from the box and held it up by its green and white ribbon. He looked at Owenne.

"I genuinely don't know what to say. I know we all pretend that we're too cool to want medals, but... well... thank you."

"Just pin it on," Owenne waved a hand, "besides, it wouldn't do for your junior ranking girlfriend to have a better medal than you, would it?"

Tahl froze.

"Don't look so shocked. I may be clueless in the ways of normal people, but I'm still a bloody mandarin. I know what's going on right in front of my own eyes, particularly when I see and feel all through the IMTel. I know about you and Rhona."

"Right," Tahl exhaled, the gesture of the medal now seeming pointless when he considered how much trouble he was in, "so what now?"

"Now I reveal my second gift to you," Owenne smiled slightly, "which is that I keep my mouth shut. That information you risked your life to get for me, not knowing even half the picture of what I wanted and why, well, if your vice is a pretty girl under your command then so be it. There's worse vices. If you ever do get found out, and you need that problem to go away, get in touch with me and I'll do what I can to help you both."

"Again, thank you," Tahl stammered. "If I'm being honest, I really am surprised by this sudden show of heart."

"If you knew what was in that folder and the significance it holds, you probably wouldn't be surprised. It's worth a lot more to me that a bit of dress uniform jewelry and pretending I haven't noticed a minor indiscretion. We shouldn't expect anything less, really. We put men and women together in high pressure situations and remove the inhibitions and control which the IMTel has placed on them all their lives. Then we act surprised when relationships occur in frontline units, again and again and again. It's panhuman nature, or so I'm told. Fortunately I'm one rung up on the evolutionary ladder so it doesn't concern me."

"And the third gift?" Tahl asked.

Owenne smiled broadly.

"Glad you asked."

The remainder of the mandarin's response was cut short as the passenger liner's manoeuvring horn sounded – a long, deep tone which resonated along the ship and up through the deck. It was answered by the frigate to the left with a series of shrill, high pitched blasts from its own horn before the escort to the right joined in, filling the evening sky with sound. A ripple of sparks erupted along the rear decks of both frigates simultaneously as they fired a series of countermeasure devices up to arc through the sky, leaving colorful trails. Seconds later, a collosal sequence of fireworks fired up from the docking station ahead, painting the sky with reds, blues, greens, and yellows as stars and spirals banged and fizzled above the three starships.

"I couldn't have you all come back to just a normal homecoming," Owenne explained as the deck of the liner flashed through a sequence of colors, reflected from the vibrant skies above. "Not after how long you've all been away. I sent a message back and demanded something special. I don't know what's been organized, but it had better be bloody good."

Tahl turned around to see that the ranks of troopers had been dismissed and now crammed themselves against the guardrails, shouting, screaming, and waving to the crowds of people who had gathered on the rooftops below to greet the homecoming soldiers. Owenne walked around to stand in front of Tahl and offered his hand. Tahl shook it.

"Until next time, old chap," Owenne said before turning and walking away.

***

His eyes frantically scanning face after face in the bustling crowd on the platform below, Van Noor impatiently nudged his way along the forward gangway from the docked passenger liner. All along the platform, families were reunited with troopers in emotional displays as fireworks continued to bang and burst in the skies above. Van Noor reached the platform and threaded his way through gaps as they opened in the crowd, standing up on his tiptoes periodically to peer above the heads of the clustered groups around him. He saw Rechter, one of the new troopers from the last wave of replacements, tightly embracing his wife. But still no sign of his own family.

"Senior," a voice shouted. "Senior! Over here!"

Van Noor turned and saw Sessetti and Clythe standing in the center of a line of people, a familiar young woman stood between them with one arm around each soldier.

"It's Rae," the young woman announced. "Ila Rae. I was in your company until a month or so ago."

"I remember who you are, Ila!" Van Noor smiled, initially holding out a hand to her, but then thinking better of it, putting one arm around her to pull her into a slightly awkward embrace. "Glad to see you in one piece. You've come all this way out here to see these two losers?"

"Yeah!" Rae nodded proudly. "Yeah, I have! I kept an eye on the news and saw when you were all coming home and thought it would be nice to catch up."

"They're good lads, the pair of them," Van Noor said, turning to the other four in the semi-circle who he assumed were Sessetti and Clythe's parents. "They've done the 44th proud, and they've done me proud."

His words seemed to have a positive response, but Van Noor still found himself eagerly looking around for his own family.

"Can I have a word, Senior?" One of the parents asked, a tall man with grey eyes and a thin face.

Van Noor flashed an encouraging smile to the others as he walked away with the tall man, bustling his way back toward the gangway to find a small space by the passenger liner's hull.

"Hayne Sessetti, Senior," the man nodded respectfully, "formerly of the 461st Strike Formation. My son doesn't know I served; I've never told him. I only did five years, which wasn't much back then. I...I don't remember much, hardly any of it, really."

"It's good to meet you, sir..." Van Noor started.

"I was never promoted," the older man stammered, "I'm certainly not 'sir', not to you, Senior. I'm not what you'd call academic, not very bright at all, really. But I am bright enough to know that C3 took away nearly all of my memories from five years of service because I must have seen and been involved in some truly terrible things. I know my son owes his life to those who command him in the field, and from what I do remember, I know the job of a senior strike leader is relentless and nearly always goes without the recognition it deserves. For those two things, I wanted to say thank you. Thank you for keeping my son alive."

Van Noor stared at the man wordlessly, at a complete loss as to what to say to what was one of the biggest compliments he had ever received in his life. He nodded slowly.

"Thank you, sir. Thank you for taking the time to say that, it means more to me than you can know. Lian is a good guy, he really is. He got himself through this, not me. But for what it's worth, that last planet was tough. Really tough. As and when we go back out again, if Lian can survive what we just saw, well, he can..."

Sessetti's father held one hand up.

"Thank you, but let's not tempt fate," he forced an uncomfortable smile. "Besides, I think there's somebody more important you need to see."

The tall man nodded and looked over Van Noor's shoulder. Van Noor turned and saw his son and daughter sprinting toward him from the edge of the crowd, screaming gleefully as they did so.

"Daddy!"

Van Noor dropped to one knee and was nearly knocked to the ground as his children ploughed into him, one into each shoulder. He wrapped his arms around them both, kissed them, and shut his eyes tightly. He remembered the feeling of bleeding out in the archive building, of revisiting some of the perfect moments of his life when he thought it would soon all be over, and realized that there, at that very moment with the fireworks above and his children in his arms, he was living through a perfect moment there and then. After what seemed like an age, he looked up over Jabe and Alora's heads and saw Becca, his estranged wife, looking down on them with her arms folded.

"You can see them whenever you want to," she said cooly. "You're their father and they need you. But as for us... let's just see how things go. I'm not promising you anything. But we'll see."

Van Noor nodded, smiled, mouthed a 'thank you' and returned to holding his children.

***

Now that the crowds had all dispersed from the platform at the docking station, Tahl could see the funfair at the bottom of the hill which had been set up for the families of the homecoming soldiers. The fireworks had stopped but the illuminated rides lit up the night sky in their absence. Tahl sat alone on a bench at the platform, watching as the very last soldiers and their families headed down to the funfair or toward the city center. A few of the passenger liner's ship's company were now walking down the gangway, their working clothing exchanged for civilian attire for a night on the town.

Tahl loosened his stiff collar and looked down at the long kitbag which lay at his feet. His parents had not come. Every last man and woman he had seen who had walked down that gangway, even including the senior officers, had been met by somebody. Everybody except Tahl. It was another laugh or cry moment, but he had neither the energy nor the inclination for either. He stared silently down at his polished toecaps and wondered what to do with his life now that he had some time to himself. But that was the problem; he had too much time to himself. There was nobody else. He wondered if it was fate, or sins of the past coming around to repay him for his attitude earlier in life.

He thought of his father's words and Master Janshea's words

when he had finally come back to the Concord after years of competition fighting. He did not remember the exact words, but paraphrasing was enough to make him feel bad about himself. The words of Zhen Davi and Abbi Mosse were still fresh in mind; he remembered those very clearly. The words ran around his head again and again as he ruminated over what his responses could and should have been, until he realized that another phrase had actually been spoken to him in the here and now, and that he was no longer alone.

"Buy me a drink, soldier boy?"

Tahl looked up to see Rhona, stunningly beautiful in an elegant dress of yellow, stood in front of him.

"Don't look so surprised," she smiled. "I can do feminine and respectable if the situation calls for it."

"What's the situation?" Tahl asked.

Rhona's smile faded and she sat down next to him before taking one of his hands in hers.

"I'm here to take you out for the night. Hell, I'd spend my whole leave with you if you'd have me, but for tonight, I just wanna take you somewhere nice. We could go get a meal and talk, then go catch a movie, or find somewhere nice for a slow dance and a walk. A night where we can get away from everything and get to know each other better. We'll get away from the city, go somewhere quiet out of town where none of the others will be, and we don't need to be afraid of being seen together."

"What about your brother?" Tahl asked.

"From what little you told me," she said, "I knew your folks were never gonna show. I don't mean to criticize, and your family business is none of mine, but I couldn't have you come home to nothing. I couldn't have you be alone. So I told my brother that we'd been delayed in theater by a couple of months and so he shouldn't come out here."

The enormity of the sacrifice she had made for him was not lost on Tahl. He looked across at her but felt too humbled to match her soft smile. He opened his mouth to say the three words which would change everything between them, the three words he knew he now felt, but decided she did not need that pressure in her life.

"You look beautiful," Tahl said, "truly beautiful. You always do anyway, but never as much as you do right now."

"Then we're well matched," she said as she stood again and offered her hand to him. "And thank you, the effort is all for you."

As Tahl took her hand, linked his arm through hers, and walked away from the platform, the whole world very quickly seemed fine again, perfect even.

EPILOGUE

44ᵗʰ Strike Formation HQ
Lothar Major
Concord Core

6 weeks later

"Get off the grass!" Strike Leader Jemmel roared, her booming order making the two offenders jump and quickly dash off the shortcut and back to the long, winding path which snaked across from the accommodation area toward the gym.

"Glad to see the new promotion and the miniscule authority which comes with it hasn't gone to your head," Rhona remarked dryly as she walked alongside Jemmel. "I think I preferred you when you were dead."

"I was about to say the same thing about you," the shorter woman retorted, "but at least I had the common courtesy of getting everybody's hopes up for far longer by staying dead for more than five minutes."

The two walked along the impeccably maintained path, cutting through the short grass which enveloped the garrison as the early morning sun shone down from a cloudless sky. Tall trees of greens, yellows, and reds punctuated the gently undulating grounds. The 44ᵗʰ Strike Formation had been based at Lothar Major for two weeks, following a month of leave. Rhona still felt a gnawing guilt for only seeing her brother for a quarter of that; aside from the first week's decompression therapy sessions and combat drug weening, the rest of it she had spent with Tahl.

"Turn that crap down!" Jemmel bellowed up at an open window in the troopers' accomodation block as a tirade of offensive language washed out over a percussive beat accompanied by a simple rhythm. "There're people trying to sleep after night duties!"

"You've got a lot of pent up anger," Rhona remarked dryly. "If you want, I can have a word with the senior and see if we can transfer Lian Sessetti into your squad. So you two can..."

"How did you know about that?" Jemmel yelped. "He told you? That bastard!"

"To be fair, you'd just died and he was very tasteful about it," Rhona said, "but yeah, I know. That must be really embarrassing for you. How will you cope?"

"Do you have an 'off' button? Seriously?"

Rhona's attention was diverted by an archaic looking road vehicle which crawled slowly into the vehicle park by the company HQ, a steady stream of thin, white smoke wafting up from underneath its yellow bonnet. The vehicle came to a stop and Van Noor opened the door to step down onto one of the huge, black tires before vaulting down to the ground.

"I don't know what time you're running to, Senior, but 'round here we start work at oh-eight-hundred," Rhona called out, tapping two fingers on the back of her wrist in the universal gesture of warning somebody about being late – the origins of the gesture were long forgotten.

"Piss off, Kat!" Van Noor shouted back. "One of the big end bearings has gone and it'll take me a bloody age to repair."

"Where the hell did you find this, Senior?" Jemmel asked, quickening her pace to head over to the powerful looking yellow vehicle. "I've only seen these things in museums."

"They're an oddity for eccentrics or guys with really small genitals who feel the need to overcompensate," Van Noor explained as he dragged his kit bag up onto one shoulder. "I used to build these for about twenty years. Now you ladies know what I did before I joined up."

"Did Kat ever tell you what she did before the military?" Jemmel smiled slyly. "She used to get paid money to take her clothes off and have weird aliens fondle her boobs with their slimy tentacles. She doesn't like to talk about it, though."

"Alright, Jem, don't be a bitch about it," Van Noor sighed, "besides, Kat's got a bit of ribbon on her shirt there which says she's actually significantly, and I'll use that word again – significantly – braver than you. Top of the morning to you both, anyway, carry on."

Van Noor walked off to the HQ, whilstling cheerily to himself.

"Well, that's not fair," Jemmel planted her fists on her hips. "You got the medal for a battle in which I died! I gave my bloody life and I got nothing!"

"And I would gladly sacrifice your life again and again if it meant collecting more of these little accessories," Rhona smiled. "And if you think that bringing up my body in conversation is the way to embarrass me, clearly you don't know me at all. It's actually one of my favorite topics of conversation – even more so now that I get to decorate it with medals you don't have."

Jemmel span around to growl another angry retort but snapped quickly to attention as Tahl walked toward them on the path.

"Good morning, sir!" Jemmel brought her hand sharply up into a smart salute.

"Hey, Boss!" Rhona saluted, throwing a suggestive wink in for good measure.

"Good morning Jem, Kat," Tahl returned the salute with a smile before carrying on toward the Garrison HQ building.

Jemmel watched him go until he was out of earshot and then turned back to Rhona.

"What the hell was that?"

"Say what now?"

"That wink! I saw that wink!" Jemmel looked away and half closed her eyes as if carrying out a series of complex mental calculations, before her eyes widened. "No!"

"What?" Rhona demanded.

"You're nailing the boss! You've let slip three things about your new boyfriend – incredibly good looking, lives locally, will destroy anybody in the universe in a bar fight. You're nailing the boss!"

Rhona rapidly composed herself and considered one of many pre-prepared lines of defense before selecting a plan of action.

"Jem," she smirked dismissively, "do you have any idea, any idea, how ridiculous that sounds?"

Jemmel paused.

"Yeah, you're right," she agreed, "that guy's a class act. He'd never risk catching anything off you."

Rhona breathed a sigh of relief and mentally chastised herself for her lack of tact as the two reached the company HQ building.

***

The reactive window field struggled to cope with the ferocity of the midday sun as it shone down into Tahl's office at company HQ. He leaned back in his chair and stared at the holographic projections which hovered over his desk, giving him statistics, readouts, and a dozen different graphical representations of the monthly and biannual training returns of the men and women under his command. The morning brief at the garrison HQ had been filled with the same issues, gripes, and arguments – too many superfluous training requirements to stay on top of, distraction from core roles, taking up too much of the day with inane and pointless drivel which detracted from the entire aim of resting and recuperating a badly mauled unit, fresh from the frontline. Tahl agreed with it all. However, the counter argument was always the same – C3 demanded that those training exercises and evolutions were carried out, and the IMTel didn't make mistakes, so therefore the training was important.

Tahl looked across the various titles of the training modules which his troopers needed to undertake and seriously questioned just how much C3 understood in terms of the requirements for training for war. Disaster relief awareness training, health and safety considerations in setting up an office workstation, correct seating posture for office work, organizational physchology in the workplace, reporting and investigation processes for safety related occurences in the workplace... the list was nearly endless. All, well, some of these were important in the right context and as a periodic reminder, but the sheer length of each training evolution and the regularity with which every soldier needed to undertake them was absolutely crippling.

Tahl stood and walked over to the window. He deactivated the field and allowed sunlight and fresh air to pour into his office. He smiled. Life was good. He would be cramming in several hours of overtime every night this week just to try to solve the burden of training requirements, but life was still good because nobody was trying to kill him, he was not responsible for life or death decisions on a minute by minute basis, and he was going home to his own house every night, with three days off work for every five he attended. Turning back to his desk, he noticed a flashing red light on his communicator, signifying that he had missed some attempts to contact him.

"Three missed calls; two military shard, one personal shard."

Tahl opened a channel to the office refreshment cabinet and ordered a cool drink of something horrifically childish and sugery which he knew he would pay for later when having to exercise it out of his system. A panel slid open in the wall and presented him with the fizzing, black liquid as he activated his missed calls.

"Military shard, today, 1124, Brytlen Van Noor, Senior Strike Leader, 44th Strike Formation. – Hello mate, it's me. I'll cut to the chase – I need a big favor. I'm duty senior for two nights next week and... Becca has agreed to go out on a date. I can't afford to mess her around, I really need to do this. Could you take one of my duties for me? It just means staying on the base for the night and shouting at any of the youngsters who turn up drunk in the early hours. I promise I'll pay you back, I know you know how important this is. So much so that I've already told the primary that you agreed to do the duty for me and he's confirmed it in the roster. Sorry for being such a cheeky bastard, but I know you find that endearing. Cheers, bye!"

Tahl could not help but laugh. He was genuinely ecstatic that Van Noor had his children back and that it was not beyond the realms of possibility that his marriage might also be saved. A night staying on the base would give him a chance to catch up on the growing pile of staff work clogging his information suite.

"Military shard, today, 1131, Katya Rhona, Strike Leader, 44th Strike Formation. – Good moring sir, sorry for bothering you. I'm afraid I've had some bad news regarding the night training exercise planned for this week. The ranges have been double booked so I can't get my squad in. Rall's lot are still planning to achieve their night firing currencies tonight, but regrettably I've had to reschedule for next week. I'm really disappointed that we won't be able to take advantage of this valuable training opportunity, but it won't set us back in the long run. Apologies again, if it's a problem, then I'll report to you this afternoon as soon as we've finished our biannual training on food hygiene awareness."

"Civilian shard, today, 1133, Katya. – Hey babe, it's me! Great news! That dumb waste of time exercise this evening has been double booked, so I've done the heroic thing and backed down so some other moron can spend the whole night sleeping in a ditch. So that means I can invite myself around and stay over at your place! I'll choose the wine, you fire up the hot tub, and I'll be over for about eight."

Tahl choked with laughter at the last message and spat out a mouthful of the vilely addictive sugar drink. He sat on the open windowsill and looked out across the canopy of trees which surrounded the southern approach to the garrison. Life was definitely good. A few minutes of pleasant daydreaming passed by as he contemplated a second drink, when his communicator beeped into life.

"Strike Captain Tahl," he greeted.

"Hello, old chap, we meet again," Owenne's voice came through the shard.

"Hello! How're things wherever you are?"

"Interesting," Owenne replied after a pause, "some interesting developments. Which is why I'm contacting you. Look, don't get overexcited and start packing your bags or anything, but there's an even to fairly good chance that I'll need your help. Soon. Possibly within the next month or two. Armed and ready for a bit of a fight. I know you're due a proper break, but this is important. You see, it's about that folder you found..."

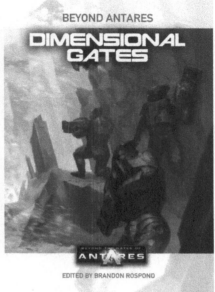

Look for more books from Winged Hussar Publishing, LLC
– E-books, paperbacks and Limited Edition hardcovers.

The best in history, science fiction and fantasy at:
www.wingedhussarpublishing.com

or follow us on Facebook at:
Winged Hussar Publishing LLC

Or on twitter at:
WingHusPubLLC

For information and upcoming publications